Sphere's Divide: I
Pilgrim of Element

J.C. Norman

Clink
Street

Published by Clink Street Publishing 2015

Copyright © J.C. Norman 2015

First edition.

ISBN: 978-1-910782-33-0
Ebook: 978-1-910782-34-7

For Granddad

INTRODUCTION

The night was old, dark and damp but the hour was early. The sun wouldn't rise for another couple hours and the forest lay quiet and still as silence echoed throughout, only followed by the wind sweeping the trees gently, their leaves dancing to the song of silence. A cold breeze swept through the forest and onto an open field behind it. The sky opened waiting for the sunrise whilst the ground was damp from the morning dew. At the edge of the forest but not too far out into the open field, a man in a soldier's uniform and body armour sat, but judging from his rugged unshaven look and the scruffy way he wore his armour he was no military man. A hex burner sat in front of him with a small fire keeping him warm while cooking a small pot he filled with water on top of it. Every now and then he added to the fire with small bits of leaves, sticks and a cube of wax, listening to the fire crackling the sticks and watching the water boil. His only companion and partner lay asleep near him turning and kicking, slowly waking to the soothing heat and sound of the welcoming fire to a cold morning.

After a few moments he added to the boiling water a mixture of vegetables he and his companion gathered the night before and a packet of dried vegetable powder to thicken and flavour the water. After pouring the powder into the pot he threw the packet onto the fire and with a small knife he cut the vegetables and let them all cook together in the small pot, stirring occasionally with his knife. After a moment of sitting quietly staring at the fire as if in a trance, in the corner of his eye he noticed his companion start to fidget more frequently and decided it was his time to wake up. He turned to him giving him a push with his leg rolling his partner over with enough force to wake him.

"Get up, ya bastard," he croaked quietly. He'd not spoken since he woke up and without clearing his throat barely a whisper came out. His partner was a little younger than him with a lot less experience in his eyes. Not a very stocky guy but with enough youth and strength to pull his weight in an unforgiving world.

He woke up with a groan, sat up rubbing his face wrapped tightly in the uniform and armour he wore.

"It's nearly ready," the first man said referring to the pot of cooked vegetables now beginning to look like a stew. "If ya want some, you better get your cup out."

In his bag, his partner found two big plastic cups with metal wire attached to the side as a handle. These sorts of cups were made this way for armies to use one cup to have soups and coffees to keep them going, as well as drinking or using to brush their teeth or shaving, needing only to wash and carry around one all-purpose cup. He handed them to his friend and stood up.

"I'm going to go around the bushes. I'll be back in a second Mark."

"I wouldn't if I were you Scott. You'll be pissing out all that hot water in you. You'll be freezing. Wait until you get breakfast and a hot drink in you, then go," Mark told his companion. Scott listening to his smart, wiser companion now sat back down. Scott looked up to Mark a lot as they had travelled around Sphere for some years now, as mercenaries of opportunity, petty thieves. They have been guarding each other's backs for some years now. After endless mishaps, close shaves and lucky escapes they had grown fond of each other and learned to live as brothers. It was Scott who learned the most, always listening and looking up to Mark as a companion, a mentor and loving him like an older brother. Mark, now stirring the pot one final time then poured half of it in Scott's cup then in his own and sat sipping the watery sludge with vegetable chunks in silence. It tasted horrible, too watery for his tastes but was hot, he only cared for that. Scott took out a clean spoon he kept in a small plastic baggy in his bag and started eating the chunks of vegetables before getting to the watery soup after.

"It tastes good," he implied but Mark did not answer. They both knew very well that it was horrible and his small attempt to complement his companion's cooking failed. But no matter how bad it tasted it was breakfast and it would keep them going.

After they finished Mark poured some more bottled water into the pot and put it back on the fire to boil again while Scott with some bottled water of his own rinsed out their cups. After the water boiled again Mark pulled out another packet, this time containing some ground up coffee beans and shared them out evenly into the two cups again, disposing of the packet in the fire and pouring the water into the cups. The drink was far worse than breakfast, with no milk nor sugar they were left with hot, black coffee with small bits left in the cups from the meal floating on the top.

"Ughh," Scott said at the taste of the horrible coffee, sucking in through his teeth, tasting it at the back of his throat. This time Mark noticed Scott's reaction to the drink, smiling and letting out a small laugh at the screwed up face Scott made in disgust, "Yeah, it is pretty bad. Just drink it quickly and get it down ya, we leave soon."

When they finished they packed up in a routine they had done many times before, with Mark extinguishing the fire and packing the hex burner in his bag, rinsing the pot and quickly scrubbing the bottom of it on the grass, ridding it of the carbon stain the naked flame had given it. Scott rinsed and cleaned the cups and his spoon then packing it back in its baggy. After everything was packed up Mark waited for Scott to relieve himself behind a bush. When he returned Mark looked at his companion, "Are you ready?" he asked.

"Run through it with me one last time, last night when you told me I was tired and missed some of it," Scott replied.

"Ok," said Mark. "Through this forest is the village of the small island of Walton. They mainly only trade with spices, food and knowledge and they only have guards that work on shifts through the night. They're basically farmers themselves. They do have some trained soldiers, but they mainly work throughout the day, which is good for us. So, if we sneak in there nice and early in the morning when the night shift guards will be tired and before the soldiers have a chance to wake, we'll be able to take as much spice or anything else of value as we can carry out no problem. Once we're out we'll make for the port on the other side of the island riding a lizzier where a pirate ship will meet us. Pay them and be off the island before anyone knows what's missing. We'll sell what we have at the pirate trading base in North Angland and then decide what we'll do after we get our money, got it?"

"Got it, let's go," Scott said, then finished packing and without looking back they headed into the forest, bags empty apart from their cooking utensils ready to fill with all that Walton Village had to offer.

The two companions walked quickly through the cold and damp forest so they could reach their destination before the sun had a chance to rise and dry and heat everything it saw. The trees were tall and exotic in the hot continent they were walking in, but there were also many smaller, greener trees and endless bushes, vines and weeds, climbing up the trees and consuming them, turning the forest into a portrait of life, with all sorts of different plant life all living in a harmonic society with one another. They avoided the paths that ran through the forest deciding to stick to where they couldn't be detected from possible scouts or guards.

"So, what's your plan once we finished with this job?" Scott asked his mentor.

"What do you mean?" replied Mark.

"I mean what are you going to do when this is over? You must have a plan? How are you going to retire?"

Mark stopped, looking confused at his companion, thinking for a second what to say. He finished his silence with, "I honestly don't know", he paused again. "I never really thought about it. When I was younger I always thought I would die doing what I do. I had a dream once. About owning land and farming, making it into a business. Maybe even write some books, telling the stories I've encountered. That we've encountered. I could change the names and places to protect us. I think a lot of people in the rich cities, even in Alpha the metropolis would enjoy hearing some of our mishaps and predicaments."

"That's not a bad idea."

"Maybe not..." he paused again considering this proposal. "...Perhaps I will. After we finish this heist and I have time to rest. I'll use my share and buy some land near Alpha in Septura. Very rich land there. I will do well.

"I'm getting tired and a little old of this lifestyle now. Soon I'll only be slowing you down. What about you my friend? Will you work for me once this is over?"

"Sorry Mark, that does sound a good idea and one day I might take you up on it, but for now I'm happy with the life I lead, stealing and fighting. The women love adventurers and I love the women. No boring working life for me."

Mark smiled at his naïve protégé. He couldn't help but see himself as he was many years ago in Scott's eyes. The fire of youth burned in his eyes, eager to make life as memorable as possible without regret. Enthusiasm for this next adventure ran clearly through him and the idea of drawing his blade, fighting the towns' folk single handed and escaping gallantly excited him. While Mark, with all the excitement ran out and only getting the job done quickly and quietly remained. But he was right. He was getting too old for the lifestyle he was living, far too dangerous and it was pretty good luck that he was here even now to tell his tales. Now would be a good time to quit while he was ahead and still young enough to live the rest of his life in peace.

"One day you'll learn," he told him. "But until then let's concentrate on what we're doing."

They carried on their journey through the forest, climbing over bushes and jumping over small ditches they encountered. After walking a short while they heard the sound of a twig snapping a few yards behind them. This made Mark stop in his tracks, crouching low. Scott followed, looking back to where they were moments ago, seeing nothing but trees and bushes. He looked back at Mark who was doing the same, trying to see if they were being followed.

"There's no one ther–" Scott tried to say but was silenced by Mark instantly holding his hand up. His eyes fixed on the forest behind them. They waited, not moving a muscle, waiting for some movement to come from the bushes. A tense silence filled the forest. The only sound heard was the heavy breathing Scott couldn't help but make. The silence was ended by another snap of a foot meeting the ground filled with twigs and crisp leaves crunching on the ground this time louder, heavier and more noticeable than a human foot. In the corner of his vision Mark saw movement and stood up in shock.

"Show yourself!" he called out to the stalker. Scott followed again, rising to his feet and standing beside his companion. They both thought along the same lines; there was only one of him and two of them. They could kill him silently and escape before anybody else knew.

A third step was made and out of the bushes came their stalker. A few yards away stood a beast. Its skin covered in a creamy fur, staring at them wildly with cat-like features. Its posture was like that of a human. The paws it stood on had ankles and its front paws had thumbs, all with long, sharp claws ready for combat. Although the beast looked as wild as a wolf, it wore clothing. A pair of torn old shorts covered it and its tailless behind and it left its top half open to the elements, showing them both its broad chest and pulsed biceps intimidatingly. It had a shaggy red mane that reached up from its chest and circled around its head and matched the ruby red eyes it had, staring at them with two long, horizontal, black pupils in the centre, narrowing at them. Mark noticed this and he thought maybe he could reason with it some- how. He had heard of these creatures before, a 'Leo' someone once said. A highly evolved lion, but what else he never knew. He thought quickly for a second, wondering what he could say to it, fear running through him, putting him off his line of thought. All the time the beast stared, waiting for one of them to make a move. Mark could see Scott almost paralysed with fear, with all colour gone from his face leaving it pale and white. He took a big breath sucking up all his courage against this beast, about to say something when Scott broke from his silence, drawing a short sword from its sheaf and diving toward the beast.

"No! Don't!" Mark called out in vain as the beast, its scare tactic complete, simply stretched out at the small, stupid man running toward it. Stopping Scott in his tracks, grabbing him by his face and the arm he held the small weapon in. Snarling at the now terrified young man. It twisted his arm, throwing him to the floor and with an almighty roar ripping his arm out from his shoulder. Scott let out a blood curdling scream as his bloody arm was thrown down like a useless broken toy. The beast then bit deep into Scott's throat, silencing him as its teeth sank into flesh, and with its mighty jaw whipped upwards, tearing away his throat. Scott, now unable to scream, gurgling from his own blood for only a couple of seconds, unable to take his last breath as his lungs began to fill, suddenly stopped moving. Mark could only stand in shock, watching his protégé and beloved companion, now nothing but a rag doll for the beast to discard as it done with his arm. Scott hit the floor in a bloody heap with a thump against the leaves and sticks on the ground. He would soon be consumed by the nature around him and forever a part of the forest. The beast's eyes now fixed on Mark. Its jaw soaked in blood showing its teeth. They wanted him now.

There was now no more thought in Mark's mind of persuading the beast. Only the instinct of survival, and his instinct told him to run. He turned and ran as quickly as he could, stumbling, but getting back to his feet as quickly as he fell, but he couldn't help but hear the beast snort, with either disappointment that he didn't fight or as a laugh realising he was now doing exactly what the beast wanted him to do. He ran toward the village.

They didn't know he was a thief, maybe they would help him but he only got about thirty yards away when he heard the beast give chase. He could hear every loud step the beast made getting closer. This made him try to run even faster but before long he could hear its heavy breathing and its steps now echoed in his ears like a charging bull. The beast leapt and landed on him, pushing him hard into the ground. He knew what this meant. Just about half an hour ago he was talking about his life after this next steal and now his life would end. No one would even bury him. With his only companion dead. No one would know they have died out here and would be left to rot if not consumed by this ravenous beast. Without any further thought he felt the sharp pain as the beast bit on the back of his head. He felt its teeth sink in and heard the grinding of its teeth against the bone of his skull. The beast then turned him over and pinned him to the floor. He looked it in its ruby red eyes. Every thought of survival came instantly to him. He could strike the beast quickly and try to run but fear and pain paralysed him. He could beg but how would beasts have any remorse and it was too late to play dead since he was looking it straight in its eyes. He lay for a few seconds in silence staring death in the face. The warm smell of blood from the beast's breath filled his nose and the thundering sound of his own heartbeat echoed in his ears knowing that would be the last time he could hear it. Finally he closed his eyes in defeat, accepting his fate as the beast opened its jaw and sprang down, covering his vision.

All was black.

1

The morning air was fresh and the remains of a small skyship was left in tattered ruins across an open field with a cliff looking north over the calm ocean and the forest to the south. Only the metal girders of the skyship remains lay broken and smouldering on the field like a burning skeleton. All the materials had burned away, turned from fire to ash and scattered in the night air. Cloth, plastic, wood, plaster and flesh had all sung the song of fire the night previously and no one heard. No one except the leo. The leo stood staring out at the seemingly ancient crash site wearing a dark green waistcoat with a brown underlay for insulation. A simple brown leather buckled belt sat around his waist which he tied the end of the belt in a knot. The belt held two small packs he used as pockets and for his legs he wore a pair of dark shorts and finally a light brown, sleeveless cloak made from thick wool, tying from his chest and hanging down to his knees. He was hunting deep in the forest when he first heard the ship flying over and crashing in the distance. He stood so far away but could hear the thumping of the propellers as they cut through the air and the droning sound of the ship's thrusters and the fading call from the engines as the ship flew from his hearing. The forest was so quiet in the night, every singing cricket and owl could be heard and so the distant echo of the crash alerted the whole forest like an alarm. He knew however that as small as this island was the humans of the village south of the forest and their small ears would not be able to hear the frightening crash. He knew it was his responsibility to travel to the wreckage. Three hours and two kills later and he had reached it as the sun rose. The air was moist through the forest but here was dry. He could still smell the stench of burning flesh as he walked past the corpses, ashes and rubble. The humans would be waking soon and would notice what was left of the smoke. The fire had subsided by itself long before the walking lion had reached it. He walked proudly through the remains of the wreckage and deceased and stood like a symbol of life itself whilst surrounded by so much death. He couldn't identify the bodies, since most were nothing but ashes the true number would always be unclear. He knelt down and touched some of the ashes, rubbed his furry, golden fingers together and watched as the ashes blew into the wind. This person would never be known. Not even the ship would be recorded nor recognised. This island was so much more primitive than the rest of the world. The leo sighed, stood up and sniffed the sky. There was nothing here, no survivors, no remains that could be recognised and the bodies barely even needing burying. That was all until he smelt a faint odour a few hundred yards away from the ship. He looked out to where his nose pointed and saw a distant tree overlooking the ocean.

The tree stood on the edge of a small cliff overlooking the ocean. A beautiful sunrise opened up the sky turning it shades of orange and red spreading far across a blue sky. There he sat, up against the tree clothed only in a pair of shorts. A metal pole lay up against his right shoulder. It was more like a staff, or a weapon than a pole. At nearly two metres in length with two hand-sized strips of gritted texture on either side of it where hands would hold it for grip and support. He was unconscious but breathing steadily. Slowly his eyes opened and he saw the sunrise, overwhelmed by its brilliance, only matched by its reflection in the calm sea turning it into an almost symmetrical portrait of wonder to his eyes. The sound of the sea moving steadily, crashing into the cliff below rhythmically and neighbouring gulls calling and crying to each other as they aimlessly flew soothed him as he listened. For several minutes he sat there resting. The heat of the warm sun against his half naked structure, listening to the sounds of life and staring out across the burning sky. His mind was blank and unable to make any thoughts, only taking in what its senses were telling it, like a computer turning on. He slowly gained more consciousness, hearing more sounds and seeing more out into the horizon. He then heard the sound of heavy footsteps behind him getting closer and before he had time to think what it could be, the footsteps stopped and in front of him stood a beast. It towered over him looking down at him. Its bottom jaw soaked in dry blood from a creature it possibly killed the night previously. It looked him straight in the eyes seeing no sign of a threat. It saw him not as food or an enemy but looked at him like it was concerned about an injured traveller. Although he only just woke up and was now looking deep in the ruby red eyes of a beast he felt no fear or discomfort and the beast saw this. Lying there still staring straight at it, like he was trying to figure out just what it was and why was it in front of him, staring back at him. The beast looked up and down at him looking for injuries before finally asking, "Are you dead?" Its voice was deep and powerful but its words were comforting to this confused young man. He was still too confused to answer, only looking around now, getting more and more feeling and consciousness. The beast then reached out his arms, taking hold of his head gently, telling him to relax. He tilted his head forward and checked the back of his head for injuries, marks or scratches. Nothing, not a dent nor bump lay on his skull. When the beast was satisfied with what he saw he slowly and gently put his head back up against the tree.

"You don't seem to have any injuries but your presence here is still unclear to me, what's your name boy?"

Boy was really the wrong word to use here. For he wasn't a boy, rather a young man in the prime ages of his life. But still the young man was clueless as to what was going on.

"Name?" he replied answering his question with another.

"Yes, name. Everyone has a name," the beast told him then putting his hand to his chest, tapping his fiery red mane that reached up to his head that poked out from his green waistcoat. "My name is Raiden. It's what people call me if they want my attention or want to talk to me." His words were subtle, like he was talking only to a small child. "You don't have a name?"

Again the young man stared clueless at Raiden. He honestly

didn't know.

Raiden quickly glanced back at the smouldering remains of the skyship behind them and looked back down, "It can't be amnesia, for you have no injury." He paused thinking what to do. "How about I give you a name? Just until you get your old one back?" he suggested.

"Yes," the young man said. "Please."

"Ok. Well, I once had a brother. His name was Valadad. I would like to name you after him. I shall call you Val."

Val, whilst still sitting up against the tree smiled and nodded in approval to his suggestion. *Val*, he thought to himself, "Yes, I like it, thank you," he said to the beast and Raiden smiled down back at him. There were too many questions Raiden wanted to ask this strange young human but he was patient, Val looked to have many more questions to ask.

Val, now getting more movement in his body stretched out his arms looking at his hands. They were fur-less and much smaller than Raiden's big beast-like paws. The more Val looked, the more he noticed how much smaller he was to Raiden and the only fur noticeable was the short, light brown hair on his head.

"We are different," Val said pointing out the obvious but not understanding why.

Raiden looked a little sceptical for a moment but thought what anybody else would. The smell of the skyship reached his nose again and reminded him to be patient with this potential survivor.

"Yes we are. You are a Human and I am a Leo."

"A what?"

"A Leo. A creature that evolved from an ancient wild animal called a lion. You do know what a lion is don't you?"

Strangely enough Val did. He had a picture in his mind of a wild beast with cream fur and that walked on four legs and had a tail. As he pictured this animal more he noticed the similarities between it and Raiden in front of him. He had golden cream fur to match the lion's and they each shared the redness of the long mane on the back of his head and around his neck. The facial features too but Raiden's mouth was a little smaller than a lion's but still had large sharp teeth. The same cat-like eyes with wildness burning through them looked down at him like two red rubies with small dashes of brown, cut in half by a vertical pupil.

"Yes, somehow I do know what a lion is. As do I know what a human is but there are differences between you and a lion's—"

"That's good," Raiden interrupted. "You seem to be getting more and more back. Can you stand? I would like to take you back to the village near here. It's a long walk but they will help you. They are good people. Follow me," Raiden told him picking him up slowly. "I will tell you all about leos on the way."

Val tried to stand but his legs were still too weak to lift his weight. He stumbled back down to the floor but with this Raiden picked him up and threw him over his shoulder with ease, like he didn't weigh anything at all. He then picked up the staff lying on the floor and walked back toward the village.

"We must pass a forest on the way Val. It won't take long," he told him. His voice was still very strong and deep but now Val thought this normal since he never heard anybody else talk before. They turned and Val saw the field behind him, the skeletal girders reaching up from the ground like long bony fingers and littered with ashes and burned materials.

"What is that?" Val asked from Raiden's shoulder.

Raiden sighed and started walking towards it, "I was hoping you could tell me that. Like where this ship had come from, how many people were on board and where it was heading."

"Ship?" Val asked again.

Raiden shook his head in contempt, "Never mind."

With Val over Raiden's shoulder he could only see the back of his feet move across the dirt and leaves of the forest once they passed the crash site. He stared at them thinking of the lion again.

"So tell me about your kind then Raiden," he said wanting

to make conversation. Raiden walked in silence for a few metres carrying the confused Val. Something felt a little tense in that moment. He seemed like a closed shell all of a sudden and a little irritated at the question but Val thought maybe this was Raiden's character, quiet and reserved.

"Very well," he said finally. "We were once big wild beasts but just like you evolved from creatures called apes. We evolved from lions. Our bloodline and ancestry is lion, we are lions. Just like you we first lost our tails and started walking on two legs developing ankles and feet like yours. Using our front paws as hands then developed thumbs, again like yours and soon we even started to develop smaller mouths and tongues enabling us to communicate with the other creatures on Sphere."

"There are more?" Val asked, now interested in the answer.

Raiden grunted with this question. "Yes there are. You will learn about them soon enough. Let's stay on one topic at a time shall we?" he suggested. He then put Val down on his feet.

Val staggered a little before finding his balance like a new born fawn and thanked Raiden for the lift. Raiden simply nodded and carried on walking leaving Val to catch up behind him. They walked for an hour and a half when Val saw on the floor a bloody hand and beside it the body of its owner with a gaping hole in its throat. Raiden walked past this not caring for it or its terrible smell.

"Don't be afraid. He was a thief. He and his companion planned on stealing from the village I protect. I stayed out last night tracking them down. I heard them plan a robbery of the village, stalked them down and…" he stopped his sentence not really wanting to explain to Val what was obvious to him.

"Ok, I'm sorry… where is his companion?"

"Over there," Raiden pointed over to a second body a few yards away lying on the floor behind a shrub.

"Where's his head gone?" Val asked but again Raiden did not answer leaving Val to assume the worst.

Val trusted Raiden and even after learning that only a couple of hours ago he brutally murdered two full grown men. He then understood why Raiden's bottom jaw was soaked in dry blood. He bit that guy's head right off. But even though stacked up with this hideous fact, Val only trusted Raiden even more. He felt safe. He was walking with a highly evolved murderous lion with the strength to rip a man's arm off. What could be safer? Raiden then got to a path and quickly explained that the village was near and started walking a little faster toward it. Val had to jog a little to catch up with him. Even though his incredible size Raiden was quite fast but Val having more to his movement and balance had no difficulty catching up.

They followed the path out of the forest and into blissfully hot sunshine shining down upon a strong wooden bridge either side of two hills of stone. Trees, bushes and moss surrounded them, looking over a river running clear and falling from the hill into a small blue lake, then running its course further down the river through the forest before finally meeting its final destination in the sea on the other side of the island. Val couldn't help but stand and stare in wonder at the sight of this tropical haven, smelling the clean fresh water in the air and feeling the sun almost burn his face if it wasn't sprayed by the falling water as they passed it walking over the bridge. But Raiden wasn't as keen as Val was to stand and watch the water fall.

"Val! Come, I can't wait forever. I got to report back to the village. They have to know of the thieves trying to steal from them while they sleep, the crashed skyship and the strange, nameless, mindless, half naked young man who seems to be obsessed with water," Raiden called over in a sarcastic tone.

Val read this instantly knowing that Raiden meant nothing by this and took it as his cue.

"I'm coming Raiden, sorry, wait up!"

They walked over the hill and followed the path around across acres of green plains. In the distance Val could see hundreds of trees as far as he could see hiding a village within it.

He could see some huts and buildings of wood and stone that stood out more than others. They had reached the village on the island of Walton. But something else caught Val's attention. Now out of the forest Val had a good sight of the sky now bright blue but within the sky were two round, white things that sat perfectly still in the sky. One was much larger than the other, close enough to see huge crater sized holes in it.

He pointed to them asking, "What are they Raiden? That one is huge."

Raiden looked up and smiled replying, "They're Satellites Val, Moons. They circle sphere forever. The closest one keeps the tides in the ocean moving by gravity."

Val didn't really understand what that meant but decided not to ask any more on the topic thinking Raiden would soon be tired of his questions.

As they approached, a young man riding what looked like a big, two legged lizard approached them. The lizard had a big tail behind it that swung left and right as it ran giving it balance. With only having two small arms in front of it and a saddle on its back carrying the man. Val stopped when it arrived. The man giving a nod of recognition to Raiden, Raiden returning the nod and the man calling, "Good morning Raiden! Who is that with you? He looks cold."

"His name is Val. I'm taking him back to the village. He may need medical assistance."

"Very well Raiden. I shall ride back to the village and tell them to open the gates. I shall meet you there," and with that he and the lizard turned and sprinted back toward the village.

"What *was* that thing he was riding Raiden?" Val couldn't help but ask after their encounter with the strange creature.

"It is called a Lizzier. It's the best and fastest means of transport we have around these islands. They are a very ancient creature to Sphere. They are reptiles. There are lots of them here in many different sizes and shapes."

"Really?" Val asked.

"Yes. Most people actually have phobias of them because they look carnivorous when actually they're harmless. They are herbivores."

"Then why do they look carnivorous? I can understand why people are scared of them."

"Nobody knows for sure, that's just the way they are. Some people say they were once carnivores and soon adapted to eating leaves and herbs. I however believe that it is a defensive thing. They look like predators then no predator will go for them."

"That makes sense."

"Thanks. Most of the species live in foreign islands and some say that in a place called *The Forgotten Islands*, huge and carnivorous cousins of them live there. They are known as *Dinosaurs* or more commonly known simply as *giant lizards*. But no one can say for sure because no one ever goes over to that remote part of Sphere. Hence why it is called The Forgotten Islands."

There was that word again, Val thought, *Sphere?* He heard Raiden mention it before.

"What *is* Sphere, Raiden?" he asked.

Raiden turned to him and gave him a look as if he had asked a really stupid question but he was patient with him and answered.

"Sphere is everything and everywhere. It is the air you breathe, the ground you walk on and the people you talk to. It is the planet that is home to every being on it."

Val understood clearly now what Sphere was and now understood what a dumb question that was but he thought it had to be asked sooner or later. Better sooner than later though to save him from looking like a fool but then again there were going to be lots of things he would look foolish for not knowing. This made him glad again he was in the company of Raiden. He scratched his head and bit his lip thinking too hard about it before finally catching up with Raiden again who had moved on ahead again.

"Damn he moves fast," he said under his breath to himself.

They reached the village gates soon after. A huge wooden wall, countless logs and tree stumps far too tall for humans to climb over stretched as far as Val could see protecting the village from anything that may threaten it from outside. The gate was also tall and heavy, operated by a mechanical device on the inside turning cogs and lifting the gate door high enough for the two to enter. Waiting for them was the lizard and the rider who dismounted and welcomed Val and Raiden then ordered for the gate to be closed again. Val looked around him at the village. Many huts everywhere were all made from wood and stone with moss over every roof to blend in with the green grass underneath and farming land for what looked like miles spread out into the horizon. Many farmers who had woken early and began their daily work. Children helped as well while the younger children ran around loudly and wildly with glee. There was a very welcoming smell of food cooking, bread and possibly soups of vegetables, meat and spices in the air. In the distance Val could see a tall building almost like a castle, with great stone pillars reaching up supporting the roof made of metal, wood and stone. A courtyard in front of it with many of what looked like soldiers standing in a big square spaced apart from each other evenly by a couple of steps. In perfect timing the soldiers stepped forward and punched in front of them again and again, turning in a pattern simultaneously throwing punches and kicks. They all looked professional and well-disciplined in their training.

"This way boy," Raiden said nudging him out of his concentration and the rider led them down towards the practising soldiers. When they were spotted, the soldiers were stopped by their superior. A huge man in size who stood a foot taller than Val and the rider (still only a dwarf to the leo though). The man smiled at the sight of Raiden and walked over to them.

"Good morning Raiden," he said in a loud and confident voice. "How did your night in the sticks go? What's your report?" Then looking at Val and adding, "Why is there a half-naked man in my courtyard and in this fine village? You know how we disapprove of outsiders."

Whether this was supposed to scare Val or not he never knew

but Raiden showed no sign of fear. He stood straight adding another couple more inches to his height putting his chin up until it was just above the man's head.

"Sergeant, this boy I found lying up against a tree on the coast of the island wearing what you see now. He seems to have no memory of anything. He didn't even have a name sergeant. Last night in the dead of night I heard the sound of a skyship hitting the ground, it almost landed in the ocean but instead crashed in a field on the cliff-side. The number of deceased is unconfirmed sir but I suggest you send a team out to investigate properly."

"This sounds serious Raiden. Do you have any idea of where the ship was from?"

"No sir. I got to the site too late. It sits on the north edge of the island. I found nothing but this man sitting uninjured nearby. Also, this was also in his possession." He gave the staff to the sergeant who looked at it closely.

"It looks to be Septurian. I believe it was possibly made before the Leo Divide, very finely made. Where did you get this son?" The sergeant asked Val but it was Raiden who answered.

"Sergeant, I'm afraid the boy doesn't know where he got it from. I suggest some medical assistance for him while I give you my full report. There is news I must give you regarding the outsiders you predicted would come."

"Very well. I shall see to it that the boy gets checked out by the doc."

"One more thing sergeant…"

"What is it Raiden?"

"The boy. His name…is Val."

The sergeant nodded adding, "After you brother. Very well," then he looked over to Val again. "That's a big name to live up to Val. Raiden must have high expectations of you to name you after Valadad. Best not let him down. Now go with this man," he gestured to the man on the lizzier beside him, "he will take you to the village doctor. Once you have been cleared by him come back and meet me inside the building you see behind me. Raiden and I have some business to discuss."

The rider the sergeant referred to then took Val away and led him across the village where Val caught more sights of the working village once more. They walked for what must have been an hour across the fields and on the paths provided. Val soon became a little cold for the first time in the exotic heat. His feet began to hurt having no shoes to protect his feet from the pebbles and sticks and he started to feel hungry. The rider soon started to notice his aches and after a long time of telling him about the village, the farmers and his and Raiden's job of being a scout to the island he promised him that some food and clothes would be given to him by the doctor.

They reached the doctors at last. A building that looked incredibly clean and modern and it stood out from all the other buildings surrounding it.

"You'll find that even though this island and village is behind with the technology all the other cities around the world have, our clinic and hospital is the exception. We regularly get new supplies of medicine and parts to mend broken machinery so we never go without. Don't let the paths of stones and sticks make you think that we're a primitive society. After living in Alpha, the metropolis I personally think this is the best place on Sphere," the rider explained to Val as they walked in but Val was not really interested. He felt better after standing in an air conditioned room with a smooth clean floor to walk on and comfortable chairs he sat on.

As the rider went to find a doctor, Val sat in a chair waiting next to an older man looking at him. His skin was considerably darker than Val's and Val couldn't help but stare. The man sat with his arms crossed dressed in blue robes of cheap but reliable cottons and a bushy black beard around his face. His hair was short but thick like wire with small grey hairs growing through suggesting wisdom to his otherwise strong posture.

"What's the matter, never seen a black guy before?" the man

said in a harsh tone but Val never answered, just looked back at him worried that he offended him. The man saw that Val never meant anything by it and realised he had scared the poor, half naked boy.

"You really haven't have you? I'm sorry lad. I never meant to frighten you. To be honest I was a little nervous of some naked guy staring at me myself," he tried to joke making Val let out a small laugh.

"Yeah, I'm sorry about that. My name is Val."

"I'm Zahied, nice to meet you." He stuck out his hand and held firmly as Val shook it. "So why are you here Val, lost your clothes?"

"I don't know, I woke up like this and was brought here. I don't really know what's going on."

"You must have had a good night out," Zahied said jokingly but Val looked confused.

"Whenever I have a really good night out I end up lying naked somewhere with no memory of the night before, don't feel so bad kid," he tried to make Val feel better by getting him to laugh but it was no use.

"It's a little different than that, it's not that I don't remember last night, I don't remember anything—"

"Mister Val," then come the voice of a doctor, "I've just been told of your condition and you've been moved up to the top of the queue. Please come this way."

Val followed him hearing Zahied moaning behind him and calling, "How's that fair!" but took no notice and continued forward hoping the doctors here would be able to answer the question for him once and for all.

2

The small town of Eloma was more like a village than a town although it had all the requirements to be classed as a town like streets, a town centre; schools, hospital, town parks, many houses made of bricks and stone and concrete and roads connecting them all into the civil society.

Only because the size of this town was so small it made it look like a village and the miles of farmland and fields that surrounded it. This small place even though it wasn't a major city of Sphere had its own arena in the centre of it standing tall like a coliseum made of stone and marble. The stands were full of the whole town waiting patiently, the noise of every voice echoed around the stands like a football stadium before kick-off. Performers were welcoming the crowd with acrobatics the crowd clapped and cheered to. Dancers followed and performed their trained dance to loud music with the crowd clapping to the rhythm and cheering their applause once they finished as the main attraction would soon begin.

Below the stands, hidden in the stadium was a small dark room with the only light being from candles lit around the room, the small flames from the candles sitting comfortably and making the shadows dance around them.

There on the cold stone floor was a young woman, sitting on her ankles with her hands on her thighs silently. Her head bowed down and her eyes closed. Her long, dark black, silky, shoulder length hair hid her face while her head bowed. Her beauty was matched by no one in the land and even though she was only clothed in dark rags of a simple vest and black leggings her toned body made it look presentable and fashionable.

She sat there in a trance for several minutes in mediation until the door opened behind her. A female tigian walked in not saying a word at first but the young girl knew she would enter and didn't react. The female tigian then stood behind her, dressed in a white kimono decorated with black flowers and gently rubbed the girl's shoulders with her orange, furry hands and said, "It's time, are you ready?"

The young woman took one last breath and looked up to the wall facing her, opened her eyes, "Yes, as ready as I'm ever going to be."

She then stood up and faced the tigian. She only stood to the highly evolved tiger's breast and looked up to her as a sister and a mother. The tigian had the warmest, apple green eyes she knew, covered with a furry face with orange and black stripes circling around her face with a black nose. She had small patches of white fur around her eyes and above her lips that reached around to her wide, furry cheeks.

"I've been training for far too long now. Now has to be my time. What do you think? Do you think I am ready?"

The tigian smiled warmly and said, "You have always been ready, that is why I have been so supportive of you."

She reached over and rubbed the girl's soft white cheeks gently with the back of her furry hand. Her eyes were a dark brown with deep black pupils to match her silky hair. Her features were small, like her nose and pink lips, all apart from her eyes which shone with a youthful potential and intelligence.

"Yes you have, and I thank you for it."

"Now go out there and show them what you are made of," the tigian said then stood aside for the girl to exit. But just before she had a chance to walk out the room the tigian said, "One more thing…"

The girl turned around.

"… If you should succeed, allow me to be your Guide."

The girl smiled then, "Of course. Wish me luck."

Then without any more time to lose she walked down the hall and to a man standing up against a tall metal door; the screams and chants of the audience waiting the other side of it.

The man went to open the door, "Good luck, I'm rooting for you," he said.

"Thank you."

He opened the door revealing the centre of the stadium. The roar of the audience now shook the stands as she walked on to the dusty arena of dried, dead grass under a blue sky littered with white clouds.

There she stood with the screaming audience all around her, chanting her name over and over. An uneasy sense of nervousness came over her as she stood there on the dusty arena amongst the crowd of people who had come to see her fight. She knew she could not let them down. On the other side of the arena another door opened and a young man walked out. The audience in the stands screams now doubled with excitement and a whole new vibe filled the arena. They both knew each other and so walked over to one another. Her feet tingled in excitement as she slowly edged toward him. Every step she took she felt the excitement of the crowd like a vibration running through her body and her own sense of nervousness set in as she edged closer to who would be her first real opponent. She knew that soon they would be fighting in battle but believed in herself and controlled her feelings as she now stood before him, staring him in the eye. The young man was taller than her and bigger with strong shoulders. He had an excited look on his face as did she, with short, curly ginger hair. So the whole audience could see, they bowed to one another and shook hands.

"May the best man win," the ginger man said.

"Woman," she joked as she shook his hand. He laughed with her jest then they both turned around and took twenty steps back and turned again.

She stood there staring at him. He was staring back and knew he was just as nervous as she was and the crowd stayed completely silent now, eager for the battle to start but waiting for the announcer to arrive. Then like an invisible door was in the centre of the stadium a tall square beam of light came from nowhere exposing a blinding white light and out from the strange door stepped a familiar figure, the girl's master and mentor, the announcer of this fight. The hunched, wrinkly creature stood dressed in brown robes the colour of dust, with stringy grey hair and a large nose that all the elders possessed. He now stood in the centre of the stadium between the two fighters and waited as the crowd applauded his entrance. The elderly figure stood still and waited for the door to disappear again before lifting his hands high. As soon as he dropped them the stadium was suddenly quiet. This was like he commanded total silence from the crowd or that he somehow cut out all the noise. He did this so that he could shout loud so the people unfortunate enough to sit way at the back could hear what he was saying without amplifying his voice. The creature was an elder, a very spiritual, intelligent creature to Sphere that was often even accused of magic in a more ignorant world.

"My fellow companions, townspeople of Eloma, city men from Hiro and travellers from your distant homes! Today is a special day for this town for it is the day that my two star pupils would battle for the chance of their pilgrimage if they so choose to go!

"As we all know the pilgrimage is a sacred task that only few cities have the privilege to compete against and it has been far too long since an elementalist from our small town has succeeded in this pilgrimage to become the Elemental Lord! That is why with my latest pupils I have taught them a different way, a way that might benefit them on their journey!

"So without any more delay I would like you to put your hands together for on my left side, a young man I found to be a good fighter and has made an excellent pupil, Elementalist Barry!" He waited for the crowd to clap and whistle before he continued.

"And on my right, a girl I have hand picked out and trained since birth. Born and raised here in Eloma, Elementalist Acarlie!"

The ground then roared for them both. Acarlie looked up at them all clapping, whistling and waving. The hunched figure put his hand up again and silenced the crowd again, then opened a door out of thin air as he did before with only a gesture of his elder hand and said.

"When I walk through and the light door closes the battle begins!"

He then walked through the door and disappeared and reappeared high in the stadium in a special seat where he had the best view.

Acarlie watched as the door slowly disappeared and then looked at her opponent Barry.

She felt a cold chill of excitement and nervousness all at the same time as she realised the battle had begun.

At first they both stood still listening to the roar of the crowd but it was Barry to make the first move. He took a step forward and bent his knees lowering his stance, then circled his hands around from his left to right then waving his hands like the wind, and as he did this the dust around his feet began to rise and circle around him, centring him in the middle.

Acarlie stood still and relaxed herself and slowly lifted her right hand to her chest with her first two fingers pointing upwards. Just like Barry's combat stance the dust around her feet rose and spiralled around her. She took a breath then took a step back turning around in a circle and elegantly waved her arms in a spiral motion then pulled them to her chest and pushed out causing the spiral of dust to explode around her and send small dust clouds to fly all around the stadium like a miniature galaxy of dust sparkling in the air. This instantly pleased the crowd as they screamed in joy.

Barry made the first combat move and with his hands risen, controlling the wind and dust around him then all with gestures of his hand turned the dust circling him into a ball of moving dust particles. He pulled his hands to his chest and when he suddenly pushed them out the dust ball, as if fired from a gun started speeding toward Acarlie who only lifted her right hand again and swiftly swung it to her right side and the ball deflected off her and charged into a wall, exploding and again pleasing the crowd. But as she did this she looked over to Barry again to see that he was charging toward her. He jumped at a height and length that was unnatural for any normal person and stretched out his leg, kicking her in the chest and knocking her backward. As she fell to the floor she rolled on her back and flipped herself back on her feet, but Barry was already there swinging his fist toward her. She raised her arm, blocking his attacks again and again, trying to wear him out before attacking him herself but he was relentless and a very strong fighter.

They carried on fighting and the crowd roared and screamed constantly throughout and even the elder above them clapped and cheered, proud of his two star pupils. Acarlie often had to roll out of the way of Barry's attacks, which she was very good at because she was very agile and swift. He was slow and bulkier than her and because they had been training together for years now, she was very aware of how he fights.

Excitement swelled through the crowd constantly, because like a lot of people throughout Sphere, an Elemental Battle was a rarity and considered the most enjoyed sport because it only happened once in every couple years because of the elementalists' training. But it was because of their training together she was also holding back being fully aware of how strong Barry was. This was an important fight for her and she couldn't afford to lose.

The crowd then realised what the elder was saying about their new training technique. They had mastered the technique of hand to hand combat rather than just controlling the Element of Wind. It was a spectacular fight for anybody else to see considering it was between a boy and a girl, but of course they were no ordinary people, they were elementalists.

Every now and again Acarlie managed to knock Barry down to the floor but before she could execute any move from there, he always managed to kick at her and scramble to his feet. He thrust himself forward, shouldering her and forcing her back against the stone wall of the arena. She hit the wall hard, slamming her back against it and cracking the back of her head. She felt dazed for no longer than a few seconds and shook off the pain in her head to see Barry charging her again. She side stepped and grabbed Barry, pivoted and threw him to the ground over her hip and finished by punching him in his nose. She grew up knowing and training with him and loved him like a brother and so could not pull herself to use her full power but enough to make him feel it. He however thought differently and kicked from the floor and smashed his foot in the side of her face. As she stumbled back he jumped up and swung his leg around trying to catch the bottom of her legs. His foot swiped and tripped her and again she fell hard. He then jumped on top of her, trying to use his manly weight and strength to win this fight but as he jumped she threw her hand to the sky, a force of strong wind blew upwards from the ground. Dust and dirt picked up and threw him straight back against the wall.

The crowd screamed as soon as they saw the elemental power they both represented with joy and excitement. Acarlie rolled back and got to her feet while Barry slowly forced himself back up and caught his breath back before following her back away from the circular wall. She tried to kick him again but he dodged and punched. She parried and turned, bringing her elbow up to strike the back of his head and pushed him away. He jumped toward her and tried kicking her then blocking her counter attacks, before successfully kicking her back a step, then instead of attacking he only threw out an empty hand and suddenly Acarlie was flying backward to crash on the floor on her back yards away.

She groaned as she turned over to pick herself up and when she was on her feet she felt a terrible strong gust of wind blowing against her. A gale force wind throwing her black hair back and stepping her back and shielding her eyes. When she looked up she saw Barry standing, his arms stretched out with a look of extreme concentration on his face because he was controlling this wind trying to knock her back. She then pushed her own arms forward and the wind then changed direction and headed for Barry. They both fought trying to push the wind in each other's direction and Acarlie saw that in the middle of them both was a small cyclone made from both forces of wind in each direction spinning clockwise between them. Whilst holding both hands forward she kept one hand up, pushing the wind and with her free hand started waving it back and forward, spinning the cyclone between them faster and faster. Soon it started gaining size and she noticed Barry was starting to weaken from this force battle. She then pulled both hands to one side and wanting to throw the spinning cyclone and all the other wind energy toward Barry. It was like it weighed a ton as she tried to step forward and push it though, screaming as she did, forcing her hand forward like she took all the energy and forced it all back to Barry, falling to her knees in weakness as she did. Barry then took off and flew all the way across the arena, the audience gasped as he struck the wall with an almighty thud exploding all the dust around him to scatter slowly on the audience. He tried to stand and get to his feet but when he stood and looked over at Acarlie still kneeling on the floor catching her breath back he fell to his knees and then fell face down on the floor.

The stadium was deftly silent again still marvelling at all the dust falling over them. Acarlie stood up in this silence. She saw that Barry was not getting back up and turned over to the elder. The elder lifted his hand and shouted, "We have a winner!" and the crowd screamed and cheered, whistled and stamped their feet. The whole stadium shook while Acarlie stood smiling and waving at the crowd. The feeling she encountered then she knew she would never feel again. She had won and now had the chance of going on the Elementalists' Pilgrimage. A dream she had wanted for so long and now the roar of the satisfied crowd had confirmed that for her. She would leave this town where she had spent her whole life in endless training and now could see the world and represent her town and school in the League of Elementalists. A true dream unfolding around her and the excitement she felt was magnified with all her people around her screaming and shouting and cheering, calling her name and praising her.

Some medics then came into the stadium and started treating Barry, sitting him up, treating his cuts and bruises, giving him water and lifting him to his feet and helping him toward Acarlie. He shook her hand and held it high for the audience to see he wasn't sour for loosing and hugged her and said to her, "I should have known better not to challenge you against a battle of element. Physical wise, I think I could have had you, but not using our element, congratulations."

"Thank you Barry, I thought you had me there though, I honestly did."

The elder then silenced the crowd again and shouted.

"Congratulations Acarlie. You have defeated Barry and been declared the High Elementalist of Eloma and being High Elementalist you get the choice. Do you want to stay here and study the Element of Wind and fight off any other elementalist on their pilgrimage or do you want to go on your own pilgrimage knowing the dangers of it and leave Barry here to study and become our protector?"

Acarlie looked up and shouted, "Barry would make a fine protector and with more study would be more mastered in the Element of Wind than I. I wish to go on my journey as an Elementalist to face the other nations and to bring honour back to Eloma as the Elemental Lord!"

The crowd cheered again of this statement and started chanting, "Honour to Eloma! Honour to Eloma!"

"So who do you choose to be your Guide and Sacred Guardian on this journey Acarlie?"

"I wish my Guide to be my friend and physical training partner, Tigian Sheeria Katsan!"

"Very well, go back inside now I shall speak to you soon, both of you."

The crowd cheered them both out of the arena and when she got back into the candle light room, Sheeria, the tigian she spoke to before was waiting for her, embraced her in her arms and congratulated her.

Acarlie was in her room in an underground section for the students of the arena, which was actually the elemental school, packing some bags eagerly waiting to venture on her pilgrimage she had been training for so many years for, when Sheeria walked in. She had some bags packed of her own and was as excited as Acarlie. She however was much older and more mature than Acarlie and never showed it.

"Remember you still have your leaving party tonight Acarlie. The local townspeople won't have you leaving without seeing you away. You are an important member of this community now. You may even have more say than the mayor himself because of your title."

"I know, isn't it exciting Sheeria? Finally after twenty-two years of training I can finally leave this place and go and see the world."

"You mean you want to leave this place that much?"

"Sheeria, I have lived here all my life, brought up by Elder Argo to never leave this town and train, train and train. I have been dreaming of leaving this place for years now."

"I know but…"

"No, you don't know, you come from Angland and have seen the other cities around the world. I have not seen outside of this town. It has become a prison to me. I've heard so many stories about the world outside it but I can only imagine what it is really like."

"But you know the danger of going on this pilgrimage don't you? You may never return. No one who has returned from a pilgrimage in decades, don't you think that's putting a lot of pressure on you?"

"If the worst happens I would die happy knowing that I have had the chance to live the Elementalists' dream of journeying onto victory. I feel sorry for Barry; if he feels the same way I did

I'm sure he feels sorry that he will have to wait before he ever gets another chance to go."

"It may not even be that long though, that's what I'm trying to say child, decades of elementalists from Eloma and not one made history, not one made it to the end, not even to the E.L. Also do you know who you will be up against? Zane; the proclaimed greatest elementalist that ever lived. How do you think you will ever beat him?"

"You know, you're an Elementalist's Guide and Guardian now and are supposed to be more supportive Sheeria," Acarlie raised her eyebrow and cocked her head to a side.

Sheeria then bowed her head in shame, "I know Acarlie, I just care about you that's all. I have been training you for years."

Acarlie stepped forward and reached up for the tigian and wrapped her skinny arms around Sheeria's thick, furry neck and embraced her. "Then protect me on my journey. You look after me outside the arena."

Sheeria smiled warmly when the young human was in her arms. Acarlie was very dear to her and worried often while looking after her. She herself had seen Acarlie grow since she was first born and had been there like a mother herself watching her grow and prosper into becoming the High Elementalist of Eloma, "What about you?"

"I'll look after myself in the arena. Now help me pack please."

"Ok then, you know you're going on a pilgrimage not a holiday. You can't take so much, you'll never be able to pack it all. Look, what is this?" she said picking up a suitcase full of clothes and accessories. "You must have your whole wardrobe in here. No, take it all out."

"But what about when I speak to the kings, queens, presidents and prime ministers of nations? I can't see them while dressed in my combat gear. They will laugh me out of the city."

"That's why you will take one pair of presentable clothing, keep it separate from the others and wash and iron it when we have been given sanctuary by the city's leaders. Look, how about this one?"

"No, I don't like that one, it's too short. I find it hard to walk in."

"Ok then, how about this?" Sheeria held up another dress.

"That has a hole in it!"

"This?"

"This too much like your kimono."

"Ok, you can't argue with this though. Master Elder Argo bought you this on your last birthday."

"No, it's red."

"What's wrong with red?"

"It's just that red is more of a colour that represents fire. I feel elementalists who study the Element of Fire should wear that."

"Oh, so you want to wear a colour that represents your element? I'm sorry Acarlie but you're not standing in front of world leaders in a see-through dress."

Acarlie nearly screamed with the thought of that and burst out laughing. Sheeria then pulled out a number of other suits, dresses and outfits with Acarlie continuing to point out little things about them which she never liked about them for a full twenty minutes before finding the clothes she wanted to wear.

When they were all done packing Sheeria took the bags out to the stables across town while Acarlie waited in her room taking one last look at it. Acarlie would have been known as a sensible girl if she lived on Earth. Smart, beautiful and a model pupil for any tutoring she could have been taught but because of her upbringing in Eloma and being stuck in there all her life and being under the watchful eyes of tutors and elders she couldn't help but be a little naïve in some of her actions. The world outside enchanted her as it would for anybody else in her shoes but she never let her dream get in the way of her study and training. She would still keep her youthful innocence but slightly mischievous character when outside classes when with Barry or her younger elemental apprentices but when faced with it would always do her task before anything else and that is what the teachers loved about her the most.

Soon after Barry walked in. He looked upset like Acarlie thought he would, but he had a smile on his face.

"The celebrations are just starting now Acarlie so I might not be able to see you again for a while. I just wanted to come and see you while I still have the time and congratulate you again."

Acarlie moved over to him and gave him a hug.

"I don't know what to say Barry, I'm sorry. I had a feeling that you wanted to leave this place as much as I did."

"I'm not upset," Barry lied. "I'm happy for you, I'm still an elementalist and I will continue my training. I just want to wish you luck. We've grown up together and you're like a little sister to me so just promise me you will come back. Promise me you will come back and have that rematch," he smiled at her.

She then gave him a kiss on the cheek, "I promise I'll come back but you got to promise me that you will take care of Elder Argo and the town."

He laughed and said, "Ok, I promise. Now come with me, the celebrations have started."

3

Val walked out of the doctor's office feeling unsatisfied with the answers the doctor could not supply. With half an hour of scans and checks the doctor came up with nothing and could only present to Val that he was the picture of health, normally a welcoming outcome but now only brought forward more questions for Val.

The hospital did however manage to dress him a little more than before. He was now only dressed in a light blue surgical gown but even though he had a little more clothing on Val still couldn't help but feel a little cold as he followed the rider back through the village to meet Raiden and the sergeant back at the military headquarters. The sun, still high in the early sky now was reaching higher meaning noon would come soon. He couldn't stop thinking about how the doctor couldn't help him, and wondered why all this was happening.

If he was so well he wondered why he could not remember anything that happened before this morning. What happened at the ship wreck where Raiden found him? Who was he really? So many more questions flowed through his mind and stayed there repeating like an irritating record caught in a cycle, *who am I? Where am I from? Why don't I have any injuries? Why are these people helping me and why am I here?*

Soon he had to blank them out by making conversation with the rider again. He asked him about Alpha, the city where he said he came from and the rider began to tell him of his adventure after being exiled from the city and his family. How he and his friend searched for his sister around the great cities of Sphere before finally finding a home here and settling down on his own (but that's a story for another day readers).

They walked under the warm sun with only a slight brisk breeze to creep under his gown and make his skin crawl. He was happy that the air soon became warm and welcomed the light breeze eventually. The grass around him were all of now dry but fresh, sharp like daggers but softer than butter, sitting on the ground like the Sphere's green hair. Soon not even the path irritated his feet. He felt his soles harden and made it easier to walk up to the gates of the village entrance again, past the small huts of marble, wood and plaster, decorated with cotton curtains and some with only sheets to cover the doors.

Eventually they got back to the headquarters and the soldiers were now not in the courtyard practising but inside, resting and chatting to each other quietly. When one of them saw Val and the rider he escorted them in a small office, away from the chatting soldiers. He knocked on the door and poked his head in muttering something and Val heard the strong voice of the sergeant say, "Send him in," and the soldier pulled his head back through the door telling Val to enter and sending the rider away.

Val said a quick thank you and goodbye to the rider, who shook his hand replying, "That's ok pal, we'll meet again," before leaving and letting Val open the door to the office.

The office was big and neat, with two comfortable looking sofas against a wall and bookshelves full of books and magazines. The sergeant sat behind a desk with Raiden standing behind him with folded arms, both of them looked at Val.

"Take a seat please," the sergeant said with his hand out pointing to a chair in front of his desk.

Val sat reluctantly looking up to Raiden anxious as to what they summoned him in for. The staff that was beside him when he woke was lying on the desk in front of him. He then knew whatever they called him in for, this would be the main point of discussion.

Raiden uncrossed his arms and began talking softly, seeing the nervous Val, "Welcome back Val. Sergeant Theydon and I have done some research on the staff and we have found some information that might shed some light on your past."

Val smiled then, moving to the edge of his chair eager to know but Raiden and Theydon didn't seem so happy, they glanced at each other then Theydon said,

"The staff is from the continent Septura. Made by the finest weapon smiths in Alpha in a country called Feydon and considering how Alpha is much more advanced than the other cities around the world, I'd say this is probably one of the finest quality staffs ever made. The last time anybody saw one was last year when Feydon's army conquered a small country called Decrenia. The people from that country took a last stand in the Battle of Osiris…"

When Theydon said this Raiden looked down to the floor feeling discomfort to his words but Theydon then explained as Raiden stood silent, his head lowered, "You see we and everyone else on Sphere know of the Battle of Osiris. The people of Decrenia didn't have a chance. Some countries even sent some troops themselves to help them but it was all over in a single night. That was a terrible day for many families around the sphere. Feydon slaughtered the entire army as well as many soldiers from around the globe that lent their strength to Osiris's cause.

"So you see why everyone mourns that day. Especially Raiden, for you see that was the battle that took Raiden's brother's life away from him. Possibly even from a weapon similar to the one before you. This only leads us to the conclusion that you must have been in that battle and considering that you have one of the enemy's weapons, we think that you must be from Alpha… and therefore an enemy of the united nations of Sphere.…"

Val sat stunned by this news and a little scared as to what would happen to him.

"Because we don't know if you're from Alpha or not and the fact that you have no memory means that we won't treat you as a prisoner of war but you must understand that this is a very serious and delicate situation. You have shown up claiming that you have no memory, but since the results from the doctors have proved to us that there is nothing wrong with you physically nor mentally, it makes us think that maybe—"

"I'm not lying!"

"That's just it Mister Val or whatever your name is. We don't know that. Feydon has tried a lot of dirty tricks to win battles and it wouldn't surprise me that they would send a soldier to infiltrate our small island by acting as a mysterious traveller with memory loss."

"We have however thought of a way that might prove what country you came from," Raiden then said. "I have seen many fighting styles in my life and considering how you woke with a weapon means you must know how to fight. You may have no memory but you do know how to speak, walk, eat and so on. So I would like to see how you fight. I think fighting is instinct and for a soldier, the style you fight will be conditioned into your mind and might tell me where you have been trained."

This stunned Val even more, "You want me to fight?"

"Yes we do. It may be the only way to prove to us if you are friend or foe. My men have been informed and have been pre-paring for your fight while you have been away. Now if you would like to follow me Val. Oh, and here, you will need your staff back," Theydon said giving him his staff back.

A little arena was made out for him by the time they got out of the office and into a main hall of the complex. A circle of men surrounded the hall with a single soldier standing in the mid-dle awaiting his competitor. The crowd opened up to let in the increasingly nervous Val, while Raiden and sergeant Theydon walked up a small flight of stairs round the side of the hall and on to a corridor that overlooked the hall from above. Val's opponent was given a pair of Tonfa. A wooden martial arts weapon held in each hand, a wooden handle that attached to a long arm that reached from the holder's fist to behind their elbow.

"Rules of engagement!" Theydon called down to the two fighters. "This is no more than a sparring exercise to see Val's fighting skills. So I want to see no foul play, no attacks to the eyes, groin, back or throat. No one is to step in. No one is to throw in any weapons, nor pass back weapons that may be lost. No one is to cheer anyone on. There is no winner nor looser in this fight and most important of all... the fight is over when the opponent taps out or is given the chance to surrender or when I call for the fight to be over. I don't want any unconscious people to send to the medic or any broken bones to send to the doctors. Do I make myself clear!?" His words were sharp and harsh so the fighters would understand.

"Crystal clear, Sergeant!"

"What about you Mister Val, do you understand the rules I have given you?"

"Yes but I still don't see how this would settle—"

"Then we are ready. The fight begins now!"

At those words his opponent began walking around him slowly. Val was still confused and couldn't believe that he was now in this predicament and wasn't ready for when the fighter threw a punch into his stomach. The hard wooden end of the Tonfa struck hard on him and instantly sent him onto his knees and as he looked up he saw the fighter raising his arm across his ear ready to bring it down, chopping it onto his head. Val quickly rolled to his side narrowly avoiding the potentially painful attack. As he got up he looked into the eyes of his opponent, staring back at him with expert concentration. Not taking his eyes off him for a second. As his opponent circled around him again, Val began to think how he would beat such an opponent. This fighter was no amateur. He knew what he was doing and was professional enough not to take Val down quickly but to take his time and seek out Val's skill in combat. He came in for another attack but this time Val saw it coming and managed to slide to an open side. Again and again his opponent swung his pair of Tonfa and went to kick him occasionally but Val quickly learned to move aside and wait for another attack. He looked up briskly to see Theydon and Raiden watching him, waiting for him to finally make some attack but he didn't; he was too scared to make any offensive moves. He just kept moving and dodging but soon his opponent's attacks were coming more frequently and violently being aware of Val's quick movements and fear to strike. Val was caught with a kick to his side and began getting suddenly pummelled with attacks high and low of his body. He fell to the floor and his opponent quickly jumped on him but Val scrambled away, kicking him aside, giving him time to jump to his feet. Enough is enough Val thought and as he began to get his breath back he gripped onto his staff with both hands, adrenaline pulsing through him and pain thumping over his bruises. He never felt so alive then as pure energy flowed around his body giving him concentration. His opponent saw this and stood in a defensive stance. He gave Val a wink and a nod as if to say, '*Let's see what you got.*'

Val then was first to strike and again swinging his staff high and low, moving back and blocking when he needed to. He found it quite easy to block with his staff and found that his concentration on the fight was helping him manoeuvre around him. Now they looked like fighters training in combat, rather than the one-sided beating Val was on the receiving end of.

He swung the staff around gripping with both hands giving it support and precision and even managed to get a couple of kicks into his opponent's side. Ducking, blocking, back stepping; jumping, turning and striking whenever a chance arose. Val found he must have a skill in him all this time just like Raiden said he would, deep in his subconscious, buried in conditioning was the ability to fight in combat. But there was no mistake, his opponent was holding back and when he decided to make his move he did, then came in with quick attacks constantly.

This time Val was much more ready and didn't go down straight away, blocking successfully with his staff and even striking hard on his opponent's head leaving the crowd surrounding them to gasp.

His opponent fell to his knees holding his head but this fight wasn't over. Before Val had a chance to finish him off his opponent swung his leg around catching the back of Val's ankles making him fall hard on his back. He dropped his staff and heard it roll away and before he had a chance to look around and pick it up his opponent jumped on him punching him in his face twice. He tried to reach for his staff by putting his hand out looking for it with the other hand trying desperately to stop the fists of his attacker. Suddenly he felt the cold metal of his staff in his grasp. He swung it up quickly catching the fighter on top of him by surprise and rolled over on top of him. The tables were now turned and Val was on top of his opponent but this time Val had his weapon where his opponent dropped his when he pounced on Val. Val with his knees on his chest didn't punch him or strike him with his weapon, they both knew Val was the victor. Val raised his fist but instead of striking down he looked up to Theydon and Raiden who were both looking shocked.

"Fighters stop! The fight is over. To your feet soldiers!" he called down and Val stood up helping his opponent to his feet.

Theydon and Raiden appeared again from upstairs and walked into the circle of men.

Both eyes fixed on Val. Raiden with a look of puzzlement and Theydon just looked shocked. Theydon looked Val in the eyes, confusion overwhelming him then said, "How…did you do that?" he asked sounding too dumbstruck to speak.

"How did I do what?"

"You know damn well what it was Val!" Raiden shouted in who clearly sounded disinterested in games and got straight to the point. "Your staff! How did you pick it up like that?"

"I don't understand Raiden. I just reached out and found it on the floor and took it."

"Don't play dumb boy. You were lying right here and your staff was all the way over there," he said pointing to a spot on the floor where his staff had rolled away when he fell. Raiden was right. From where Val was lying and with someone on top of him it would have been impossible for any man or beast to reach where his staff was lying, far away from any man's reach. Val stood still trying to understand what had happened and tried to remember how he did it. One of the soldiers stepped up in Val's defence and said, "He reached out and the staff just appeared in his hand sir. It was like he was summoning it to his hand from the spot where it lay. It didn't even move from where it was. It just disappeared...right into his hand. I've never seen anything like it before."

Raiden listened to him and looked back at Val, staring into him trying to tell whether he was hiding something. But he trusted Val, walked over to him and took his staff away from him and took a couple of steps back.

"Let's see you do it again then Val. Take your staff away from me."

Val stepped forward and reached out to take it from him.

"You misunderstand me Val. Take the staff from where you stand, just like you did before."

"How can I? I don't even know how I did it in the first place."

"Just like the man said. Reach out your hand and call your staff. You done it once, we all saw you do it."

Val did as he was instructed and put his hand out. He held up his hand for a minute, staring at his hand, the staff, Raiden, and back down to his hand. He tried opening and closing his hand a couple of times before giving up on that idea.

He then heard Raiden giving him a little support, "Come on Val, I know you can do it, just like before. Focus and take the staff to your grip."

Then it happened, just like when it was lying on the floor his staff disappeared from Raiden's grip and instantly appeared in Val's. Not even a trace of dust was seen now in Raiden's fist but nothing but air. In only a split second it was like the staff vanished through a split in the illusionary sheet of reality and teleported straight into Val's hand again.

Everyone gasped at once in marvel at what they all had just seen. There was no such thing as magic on Sphere, even the great elementalists could soon explain how they could perform their tricks but this was new and unseen, only by the small few who just witnessed.

Val, looking the most shocked looked up to Raiden who was smiling, then crossed his arms in triumph and nodded. Theydon was the first to speak then, smiling at Val, "Wow. Whatever that was, that was amazing," he then walked over to Raiden and whispered something in his ear. Raiden nodded and whispered back. Theydon nodded and turned around standing beside Raiden and looked back at Val.

"I am pleased to inform everyone here that after the fighting technique Val had shown us. We are happy with what we have seen. Though Val does have some fight in him somewhere, there is definitely nothing from Alpha's or Feydon's teachings.

"However you do definitely have something from the continent Septura in you but we can confirm it is not from the enemy. And so Val, we would be pleased if you would join us and become a Walton Warrior. Protector of Walton under the service of his majesty King Kerry, ruler of the country Racoves."

Val nodded instantly and Theydon called one of his men to find a uniform for him.

Moments later the man returned saying, "Sorry sir, I could only find some light lizzier armour and a traveller's cloak."

"Very well, everyone I want you all to help Val into his armour while Raiden and I consult. The elders sent me a message today summoning me on important business and since seeing the marvels and mysteries of Mister Val. I think he should be the one to see them. So make him look presentable."

Val was then moved aside by all Theydon's men gathering around him taking off the gown and sandals the hospital had given him shortly before, firstly giving him a simple black T-shirt and measuring and fitting on some light armour made of lizzier skin. It was a dark green, scaled material which looked like it could withstand some melee attacks that covered the most of Val's chest and it had little shoulder pads made of metal which fitted him well. Then he was given a pair of dark trousers which he fitted over his shorts. They tucked his shirt in and pulled some of the straps on the back of his armour tight and tightened the buckles. They even brought in some pairs of socks which he put on and they gave him some more telling him to keep them clean and dry at all times and were telling him stories of theirs about not looking after their feet and the consequences they endured because of it, all while they were fitting on some steel toe-capped boots that came up just to his ankle, tying them and tucking in neatly while he sat on a table watching.

He stood up and walked around a couple of steps instantly liking the new outfit. Punching the padded bits in his armour and swinging his arms around. He found that he had much room for his agile physique. The armour wasn't constricting at all for him. Which he knew would become handy in the future. Then finally he was given the traveller's cloak. A well-crafted, hooded and sleeved long, thick cotton cloak that reached just past his knees. The clock was surprisingly mauve-purple, black and blue with an outline of finely woven yellow and red lines into the outline of the cloak and decorating the cloak with little diamond shapes and zigzag lines all over it; reaching from the bottom and all the way around the tip of the hood and back down the other side. This cloak wore like a Gi or a dressing gown but longer, and reaching down past his knees, the material was thick and looked waterproof with a hood and a lot more finely made. Val wondered how they got this type of cloak because it didn't suit the rest of the armour they gave him and he didn't see any of them wearing one.

When he asked they just told him that the cloak had been in the lost and found bin for ages and never thought to be thrown out.

A moment or so after he was geared up Theydon came back in and lined his men up.

"That's better Val, looking like a warrior now, how does it feel?"

"It feels good, thank you sir."

"No no Val. You don't call me sir yet. You look like one of us but you're not yet officially signed up and so before we do that I have a small assignment for you."

"Assignment?"

"Well really it's more like a request. You must travel to the end of the island to see the elders. Raiden will be your guide. You will see what it is they want from us and it's a perfect time for you to ask them any questions regarding yourself and your staff.

"The elders are the wisest beings on all of Sphere but I'm sure you already know that. I'm sure they can help. Raiden will fill you in along the way. Is everything clear Val?"

"Yes sir...I mean, yes Theydon. I'll go now, where is Raiden?"

"He is around the back preparing the lizziers and some rations. It will only be a day's journey there and back so you will need supplies. Go now Val and I will see you tomorrow as soon as you get back."

Val nodded as he walked to the back of the hall. Before he left he turned around and looked at Theydon and his men all standing at attention. Bowed his head and said clearly, "Thank you all. I shall see you soon," and with that he turned and headed for the back door.

Val found Raiden outside packing bags on to a saddle on each of the two lizziers' backs, one much bigger than the other and was clear that this would be Raiden's ride, the other being too small to hold his stature. Raiden looked around and saw Val approaching and nodded in agreement at Val's new uniform and look and rubbed his fingers down his read mane under his chin like a beard.

"Looking better kid, at least you don't look like an outsider anymore. We can make our journey now. It's not too far if we ride quickly. We can get there by sundown if there is nothing blocking our path. Now I'll give you a minute to acquaint yourself with your lizzier. Her name is Domieneo, she is only young and so if you want to ride her you have to let her know who you are first," he said bringing Val toward the young, horse sized lizard. She stood before him standing upright and strong, she had an elegance about her presence as well as looking fast and swift while Raiden's lizzier looked much older, stronger and wiser, like he had been close to Raiden for a while now. He held out his hand a little hesitant at first and stroked the top of her head and he could feel that she felt the same way pulling away at first but he kept his hand out and waited until she came back. She let him pet her head for a short while before standing upright again, stretching out her neck and letting out a small high pitched cry. Val couldn't help but think that if she were much smaller that cry would have been like a bird's tweet, short and sweet.

She then stood much closer to Val and rubbed her head against his shoulder.

"She likes you Val, lizziers are very loyal creatures but are picky about who they give their loyalty to. My Bluey here took a whole month of training and riding before he finally accepted me as his owner. He used to run away from me at first and then throw me off his back."

He said rubbing Bluey's head then adding, "So make sure you treat her well, keep her clean and fed and you'll find that she will have her own little bits about herself you will have to learn in order to keep her happy. If you mistreat her, she will leave you and if she does it in the middle of an open plain, or desert you're finished."

"I will Raiden, don't worry. So they can run through deserts as well then?" Val asked.

"Yes, because they're lizards they can survive a longer time without water than other creatures," Raiden said mounting on to the back of Bluey. "Now grab onto the saddle and pull yourself on."

Val tried to pull himself up but couldn't get the technique of swinging his leg around and fell. Raiden, whilst laughing didn't bother to help him. He thought to himself that the boy must learn to do this on his own. Val tried a couple more times unsuccessfully before Domieneo ran around the back of him, put her head between his legs and lifted him up on her back herself. This made Val nearly fall again but managed to control himself this time and sat triumphantly on the saddle. He then took the reins and followed Raiden.

The gates opened again and they were both out of the village and Val finally saw how fast the lizziers actually were. Raiden wasn't lying when he said they were the fastest means of transport. It took a while for Val to understand how to rock in timing with Domieneo and within the first couple of hours he mastered it, but thought it would take a while before the pain on the bottom of his back would pass. He still found the whole experience very strange and at certain times had to cling on tight but Domieneo was gentle with him and slowed down from time to time, only speeding up to catch up with Raiden and Bluey.

It was now nearing sun down and the lizziers were now marching along after resting for an hour. Val was still captivated by the sight of the island. Even when coming to the end of an evening with a cold wind starting to settle over the desolate land of endless trees and rocks as far as the eye could see, Val could still sense something enchanting about the land. Like even though there was not a single man-made object in sight, there was this ever going presence to it, like a valley that never sleeps. All he could hear was the sound of the land, as if the wind was passing messages from one rock to the next and the trees twisting and turning, longing to be with their distant family of trees so far away but unable to move from the spot where they lay. The sunlight now dying turning the scene into a shade of aqua blue and before long the setting sun changed the horizon orange then a fiery red before leaving it dark and one by one the stars lit up the sky. A stream flowed quietly beside them with deer and other small creatures breaking their journey for water, taking no notice of these great lizards walking past them. This place seemed so beautiful to Val and the silence soothed him while he wondered if the rest of Sphere was like this place as well.

Soon Val felt the urge to ask how much longer it would be before they arrived.

"The elders' village is not too far now, we are nearly there," Raiden answered him.

"Who are the elders anyway Raiden?" Val asked again.

"You don't know the elders Val? This is strange, you seem to know so much, even with ancient animals like lions but you have no knowledge of elders?"

Val shrugged and waited for Raiden to raise an eyebrow and continue, "Really the correct question should be *what* are the elders?"

"What do you mean?"

"You may think by the name of 'Elders' that they are elderly humans, when really they are not. They are actually their own species. They're known as *Elders* because they are the oldest intelligent beings on Sphere; even older than humans but their wisdom and intelligence is different from what humans would consider as intelligent."

"What do you mean?"

"You're a human Val, you wouldn't understand. Even I don't understand, but let me put in the way I was told as a cub. To survive, humans rely on science and mathematics, formulas and equations that engineer the universe while the elders rely on the forces of Sphere to help them survive. For instance, to live in a cold environment humans would build a big shelter, conserve their heat and wear protective clothing while the elders might heat their surroundings up or cool their body temperature down," Raiden tried explaining to him.

"How can they do that? That's impossible without the proper equipment. Do they use magic or something?" Val asked intrigued by these creatures.

"I told you, I don't know, the same as I don't know how humans ever built big mechanical machines; we leos were bred for battle."

As they continued talking, the village now came into sight. Only a few small wooded huts sat together at the bottom of a hill with small camp fires burning, lighting up in the darkness.

"You say they are their own species? What do you mean by that? You say that you evolved from lions. What did they evolve from?" Val asked again as they approached the village.

"No one really knows, they are older than humans and even they don't know. They are mammal though. Although if you asked me I would say they are most like a frog."

"How can you say that? That's not a mammal?"

Raiden just nodded then and dismounted his lizzier and Val followed, walking into the village and was greeted by the elders.

4

At first look the elders looked like Raiden suggested they would, but after seeing them closer Val understood why he thought that. Their head and nose was shaped similar to a frog's, with a big jaw and black dotted eyes. They had bushy white eyebrows and fair white hair on a flat head. They all walked slowly with a slight hunch, even the tallest could not stand taller than six feet and all clothed in old robes. Even though *Elders* were just the name for the species, they all looked very old; like what a human would if he reached the age of one hundred. They smelt of the planet, of fresh air, water and sand and all walked slowly but with a humble modesty to them. The closest one to them looked the oldest, her face covered in leathery wrinkles and carrying a long stick she was using as a walking cane. Val could see her hand carrying the cane and noticed that they all only had four stubby digits on each hand.

"Welcome back Raiden, it is nice to see you again. I see my message reached Theydon in time, and who is this boy with you? He looks new and I have never seen him in the village before." The elder spoke with such a soft female, elderly voice which made Val feel comforted and he knew he would have a better welcome than he did back at the village. Raiden stood forward then got down on one knee and bowed in front of the elder. This wasn't like when Raiden was reporting to Theydon and had to behave with such etiquette, rather this was like he wanted to bow down to her, like he had done all his life and did it without thinking. This was an unusual sight for him seeing a creature as magnificent and strong as a leo bowing down to a frail looking creature with such love and loyalty. He couldn't help but admire Raiden for this, normally in the animal kingdom a bigger creature would attack and eat such a smaller prey.

"Elder Amber Pulaguy," Raiden began with his head still bowed, "your message reached Sergeant Theydon well. He sent me and I left as soon as I could. I also brought this boy with me in the hopes that you could shed some light on him."

He then started telling her about Val's problem. How he had no memory, no name, yet he had known some other things and the mystery behind the staff that he could summon to his hand.

He then rose and stood beside Val while that elder thought for a minute.

"Hmm…some facts in your words are familiar to me, thank you for bringing them to my attention Master Raiden. I will have an answer for you shortly," she said then shuffled toward Val, looking at him with a nurse's concern and said to him in a comforting tone, "Don't worry Val, you are in good hands now, my name is Amber Pulaguy."

She reached out and put a soft hand on his shoulder and squeezed lovingly like she had known him for years. Val didn't know what to say or do so he just did as Raiden did and bowed on one knee and said as formally as he could so he couldn't offend her, "Thank you Elder Amber Pulaguy, I am humbled by your hospitality."

Her hand went from his shoulder to rub the top of his bowed head and gently ruffled his brown hair, "You're very welcome young Val, now rise and follow me, both of you. I have something urgent I have to show to you that you have to tell the village council. Come, your lizziers will be well rested and fed as will you. This way please."

They were both led into a magnificently large hut, there wasn't much inside spare the dirt under their feet and leather skins surrounding them from the night outside though. Val could tell that elders didn't have the need for belongings such as humans do. In the middle was a fireplace with unburned wood waiting to be lit. Val watched in amazement as the elder walked past it and raised her hand toward the fire and suddenly the fire was ablaze. She didn't rub sticks together nor use any flint or start it with matches. She simply lifted her hand and the fire started according to the level of her gesture. Val found this incredibly amazing but looked over to Raiden who had obviously seen this before didn't even flinch nor even look at the fire. The elder then sent away two more elders for refreshments for the two travellers and then turned toward them.

"I'm afraid I have some terrible, dire news, news that involves the whole of Sphere."

"What is this news?" Raiden then asked.

"I know that you won't understand it at first, but there is a terrible darkness in the depths of outer space that is slowly edging toward our planet. I first noticed it last night while I was communicating with the planet in prayer and meditation. The planet is deeply scared of such a threat, for this darkness is an unstoppable force of extreme gravity that would crush the whole planet if it got close enough."

Amber looked at them both and saw they were both riddled with confusion. The other elders returned with some bread for the two confused travellers.

"I don't understand Elder, what is this darkness you speak of? I have never heard of such a force. Also if you have seen this vision would not the High Elders of Chippenham have seen this too? Is this a problem to bring to our small island?" Raiden said wiping his mouth awaiting an answer.

Amber smiled, "Yes I know young Raiden. I'm afraid that my skills for seeing through the eyes of Sphere have not left me yet and I honestly cannot say if the new High Elders have witnessed this plague yet. That is why I sent for you immediately, we cannot afford to simply ignore this and assume the rest of the world will settle this problem for us. Since I cannot explain, I will show you instead. Stand where you are and together we elders will show you what is coming," Amber told them. The elders all stood in a perfect circle around the fire and started chanting and murmuring to themselves each with their hands raised.

"What's happening Raiden? Why are they all chanting? What are they trying to do?" Val whispered to Raiden, who just shushed him and said, "I don't know Val, just stand still and wait and see."

The fire began burning brighter and brighter and then even Raiden couldn't help but stare into it. It rose so high it nearly reached the roof of the hut and started burning an electric blue that warmed the hut. The colour tinted the inside the hut with a pale blue that was soothing to the eyes and pleasing to look at.

Within a couple of seconds all Val could see was the burning blue fire and was unable to even hear the chants of the elders as the most unusual sensation came over him. He suddenly felt like he was flying straight upwards in the sky at a great speed. His stomach dropped and he felt paralysed by the force of it. This felt like he was falling to the ground at an extremely high speed from high up and upside down. He felt scared and paralysed and wanted to open his eyes and be back comfortably on the floor. In a second it had stopped though and he found himself standing next to Raiden in what looked to be outer space. He could see the planet Sphere before him, sitting amazingly still in space. The two moons far away and even the sun was just a big star surrounded by millions among millions of smaller stars all around them. He almost had a heart attack at this experience and he saw that even Raiden was uncomfortable. Val suddenly got into a panic and started breathing heavily, "We're in space Raiden! What's going on?" he started shouting.

Out of nowhere like a god-like figure, the voice of Amber came echoing through the heavens.

"Don't be scared Val, you're not in space. You are still standing in our hut with your feet firmly to the ground. You should be able to feel the floor under your feet. In space you would be weightless and therefore floating, as well as being unable to breathe. We elders have simply put the image in your mind that you are in space so you can see what we are trying to show you."

Val then caught his breathing pattern back and looked around. Amber was right. He could breathe fine and realised that he wasn't in space at all and took the time to take in the most beautiful view.

It was like they were standing in a three-dimensional environment. Everywhere he looked he saw stars glistening in the darkness. Even below where his feet stood he looked down and saw into the abyss below of countless stars so small and close they looked like tiny diamonds floating motionless in an everlasting dark sky. There were some distant planets in their solar system but were so small Val could not tell if they were only neighbouring stars to blend in with the others, so small and many they seemed to sparkle like dust in the light.

"Now if you will stand still we will show you what is coming toward the sphere," the voice came again and once again the awkward sensation happened as the whole scenery shifted around and flew miles into the distance, like a strange roller coaster ride. Val jumped down to the floor as it turned and shot forward believing that he would fall down but Raiden just stood still with his arms crossed and his eyes closed understanding that it was only an illusion. All the stars turned into long thin streams of light as they flew past them before they stopped again and Val could rise to his feet again.

There it was standing before them. The darkness Amber was talking about. In the middle of their view this thing was so massive they couldn't see past it nor around it and they were less than microscopic particles standing before a planet compared to it. They were dwarfed so much by this thing that it was like heaven itself and everything in it could fit in this thing a million times over and still have far too much room. As far as they could see was the light of a neighbouring star swirling around, being slowly sucked into the centre where a perfect line was piercing out from the centre of it with so much light it was blinding to look at. This thing must have been the most unstoppable force in the whole universe. Not even light escaped from its gravitational force. That's how big this thing was. Even the sight of it made Val's stomach drop, his knees weak and his blood chill and shiver through his body at such a monstrous sight.

"This thing is what is known as a Black Hole and is on a collision course for Sphere," Amber's voice came again, "such a thing should never happen. If this thing were even close to the planet it would crush it down to the size of a pea in less than a second and Sphere and every living being would be perished. Let me show you what I mean," and with these words, they and the black hole started speeding toward the planet in the direction in which they came. When the sphere was in sight it was so small that it was only a small dot in the night sky.

"Firstly, the solar system's gravitational pull would collapse and Sphere would fly away from the sun, freezing instantly and killing everything," Amber began. "Then this would happen..."

They then watched as all the materials that made up the planet started breaking away and started flying toward the black hole. This process was very quick like Amber said it would be and before Val could blink, it was gone, so were the moons and soon the sun, leaving nothing left but the hole. Sitting silently and eerie, alone in the darkness.

"Such a devastating blow to existence. Surely nothing can stop such a disaster awaiting the planet," Raiden said, closing his eyes and lowering his head.

Then just like they were dreaming their eyes opened and they were standing back in the hut. Val felt sick with this sensation and nearly had to run out of the hut to vomit but managed to control himself. Amber started the conversation again, "Now you have seen what is coming you must warn the council of the village. You will be given a bed tonight and you will leave first thing in the morning."

"No, we will leave immediately. Such news should not be left while we sleep," Raiden said.

"But you only just got here. At least rest a while and eat. Your lizziers need rest too. If you go now they won't have the energy to get you home."

"Yes Elder Amber," Raiden then nodded, "we will rest for half an hour and then leave. If we leave then we can sleep in the village and call the council together first thing in the morning. Will you join us?"

"I will be there but no, I can't leave with you now. I will need some time to assess the situation properly. Also I should ask the planet about Val. So I'm sorry you want to leave such a short time after arriving and sending you back on your journey. But if that is what you must do then I won't hold you back Raiden. May your lizziers give you a swift journey home, and young Val, I am sorry I could not give you an answer as quickly as you liked but have patience and I shall tell you what I know tomorrow when I next see you. Now both of you, go and get some rest. There is a guest hut on the edge of the village. Raiden you know where it is. Please take Val there. Food will be brought to you shortly."

Raiden bowed as he did before and thanked the elder. Val copied him and followed him out of the hut. Raiden led Val round to a smaller hut.

The small hut was much like the elder's large hut but it had some beds in there, each with some sleeping bags packed away which they both decided to leave where they were. Raiden went and sat on the floor outside the hut, his legs crossed and staring out into the now starry sky. His face riddled with trouble of the news they both heard.

Val came and sat down behind him.

"The air is calm tonight. The world seems so much at peace when it is like this," Raiden said to him slowly.

"Maybe it's because the world is troubled."

"Maybe…" Raiden then stopped, closing his eyes. He was as troubled as the planet was and who could blame him? They both were the first people to find out that the whole planet is destined for doom other than the elders that discovered it.

"Who would have thought that after everything this planet has gone through, suddenly an unstoppable force comes along and…" he never finished his words, it wasn't necessary as Val knew what he was going to say.

After a while some elders came and brought food for them and gave them both a blanket to throw them over their shoulders. As they were eating their bowls of hot soup Val was thinking and finally asked, "You say, *after everything the planet has gone through* Raiden?"

"What's your point Val?"

"Well…that is the point. What else is has the planet been through?"

Raiden took a breath and looked back at the stars and said, "Have you any idea exactly how old Sphere is Val?"

"Well, no."

"Neither does anybody else on this planet. This planet is so old it is probably the oldest planet around. Now listen carefully Val, because I'm only going to tell you this once.

"Once long ago, millions of years ago, when the world was still young, when only humans and elders walked the Sphere. Before leos, tigians, kingnines; pardi, ursas, porci; aeomon… (Val didn't ask)…and many other creatures even existed. The sun that we are currently orbiting began to die.

"When a sun is near the end of its life it begins to use up all its energy, increase its mass millions of times over and swallow all the planets close to it. The news was first told to the human presidents and the oldest of elders by a stranger. It seemed that nothing could stop such a thing happening but the humans were smart and the elders were powerful and soon after, the humans built a ship capable of flying through space itself and sent up a machine.

"Legend says that this machine was as big as a city itself, orbiting close to the sun. This machine, made by the greatest human scientists and engineers had the power of the all the strongest elders put together, compressed so closely together that if this machine exploded it could destroy a planet. This machine was like a satellite and what it did was channel the energy from the closest star into the sun. Therefore the sun, now fuelled with another star's energy didn't expand and didn't destroy the planet."

"Wow, how could such a thing be done?"

"I don't know this is only what the legend says. Anyway, it's not finished yet. After this was done and the sun was burning the energy of another star. The sun began to give off a different radiation and this radiation began to burn the planet's atmosphere and slowly kill all forms of life. The humans and elders began to fight over this act and great wars between them took place before finally they both separated. This was called '*The Divide*' or '*The First Divide*'."

"Divide?" Val asked.

"Yes. It was known as a 'Divide' because both creatures split apart from each other and stopped living together. The elders went and lived in peace by themselves managing to find a cure for themselves by mixing such potions together while the humans only sheltered themselves from the radiation, cocooning themselves from the sunlight. For years the humans tried everything to get the cure from the elders and began every dirty trick in the book including bombing and terrorising the elders. But the elders were stubborn and never gave up the cure.

"The divide lasted about ten years but the legend goes there was a young man from the cocoon city by the name of Zane. The human government, now evil and corrupt banished Zane from the city and sent him to die in the dead land surrounding it. But Zane found the elders who took him in, cured him and taught him to fight against the humans.

"Years of training later Zane returned to the city as a terrorist. He and some others rebelled against the government and eventually defeated them, giving them a new government and soon after peace were made between the elders and humans again and ended the divide.

"Just like before the smartest of humans and wisest of the elders put their minds together and managed to heal the planet. Ever since then the sphere has constantly orbited an everlasting sun. That's why there are so many other intelligent creatures here on the planet."

"But doesn't that mean that humans and elders would have evolved too?"

"Possibly, maybe they did evolve. Maybe they didn't need to. Both humans and elders are evolutionary perfect. They adapt to their own surroundings, perfectly, like sharks or some kinds of insect, they don't really need to evolve," Raiden finished his food and stood up.

"Finish up Val, I've rested enough. We need to get back to the village quickly and rest before morning," Raiden went over to Bluey who saw him coming and started jumping around excitedly. Val got up and took the bowls back to the elders, thanked them and caught up with Raiden who was now mounting Bluey and was leaving the village.

Val quickly jumped on Domieneo and rushed to catch up with Raiden who was now sprinting back toward the village.

As he caught up he shouted to Raiden over the sound of galloping lizziers.

"Do you think the humans and elders will be able to help the planet? I mean, what happened last time seemed impossible but they managed to help it. Maybe they can help again."

"Let's hope so Val, otherwise the planet is doomed. The council will determine what will be the necessary action for this and we shall abide whatever they choose to do."

"What about the other cities around the world? Surely more elders have seen this and are taking actions of their own."

"I don't know about that. Elder Amber Pulaguy is one of the oldest and wisest elders on the planet. She used to be in the High Council of Elders in Anavrin before she retired and lived here ever since, finding tranquillity here in Walton."

"That's another thing I wanted to ask you about. What's the deal with you and Elder Amber? You work as a ranger of the Walton Warriors and Theydon is your superior but why do you bow to Elder Amber?"

"She is an Elder, that's why. Leos have always been loyal to Elders. I may work for the Walton Warriors but as a species I will always be loyal to the elders. It's in my upbringing."

"Does that mean that humans don't bow down to them?"

"That depends on how they are brought up. I am happy that you yourself took to follow me when bowing to them. Because as far as I'm concerned, as long as you're with me you will live by my upbringing and tradition."

"Ok, I'm fine with that Raiden. Why do leos bow to elders anyway then?"

"You are full of questions Val…" Raiden chucked lightly, "…but ok. The leo species have always been the protector and guardian of the elders, like dogs were to men. But once many lifetimes ago, we leos took the planet from the humans, discarded the elders as our masters and ruled the planet. The elders washed their hands of us and humans became our pets and prey. It was a dark time for Sphere and we leos have always been so ashamed of our ancestors because of that. We ruled for thousands of years, while humans lived in the shadows of our society. Because of this, it was considered a *'Divide'*, again since we leos lived and killed all that were smaller than us.

"It wasn't until a strong member of our clan, defeated the leaders of us leos and liberated the humans and ended the divide. Ever since then we have had a strong relationship with the elders who forgave us and a mutual understanding with the humans who knew that we would win if ever there was a war and left us alone. At least until the last hundred years anyway, when the humans got their numbers back and engineered new weapons which are now forbidden and the leos began being hunted by the humans for sport and pleasure. This monstrous act ended in another divide known as *'The Leo Divide'* and still known by most today as '*The Last Divide*'. This would still be a divide today if the elders hadn't stood up for us and demanded the humans to stop their attacks in trade of power, something no man could refuse. So that is why it is humans who rule this world at the moment.

"Elders stay back and let humans do as they please and because of this the humans respect the elders and consort with them whenever they need help and made amends with the leo species."

"Oh, I see. So you leos are ashamed of your history and won't attack the humans, while the humans with their own shame of what they done to you are too scared to do anything again; and the elders live by their own peaceful lives are loved by the leos for standing up for them after their history and they are in a peaceful understanding with the humans."

"You talk as if you are not human yourself Val, but yes. That sums up the relationship with the three species and how they have in turn ruled the planet," Raiden finished.

They rode their lizziers as swiftly as they could and reached the gates of the village a couple of hours later.

Raiden stopped his lizzier and called up for the gateman to open the gate.

This was the first time Val heard Raiden roar and was taken back how powerful it was. It even spooked Domieneo a little but Bluey, who was used to it only flinched. It felt to Val like a second voice for Raiden, like he had a different, deeper voice box he switched to instantly and naturally. A few moments later the large wooden gate lifted and they walked into the village again tired and desiring a warm and soft bed. Their lizziers now exhausted at the run their masters made them do were taken to the stables to sleep and Raiden took Val to his small home. His home was much like the huts that the elders had and Val could see that it was made especially for Raiden because the door frames were much bigger than normal human doors.

As Val walked in after him he took his boots off and walked on wooden flooring which felt good on his feet. He noticed an extra room to his left and saw a manikin standing in the corner with this great heavy armour over it. He guessed it was Raiden's and said nothing. Raiden walked into his bedroom and took out some blankets from a wardrobe and placed them down on the floor telling Val to take his armour off and said, "Sorry I don't have an extra bed. You will have to sleep on the floor. Fold up your traveller's cloak and make a pillow out of it and get to sleep as quickly as you can. I know you have had such a big day today but tomorrow will be bigger and we both will need our energy." He then lay on his own bed and Val lay on the floor with many sheets over him keeping him warm.

Val lay for only a minute before finally saying, "Raiden, I never thanked you for everything you have done for me…I thank you."

Raiden never answered and Val smiled at this because he knew that he heard. He then turned over and enjoyed the last few minutes of the day to settle the pain under his feet and felt his head buzzing with information. He didn't even think about his own questions anymore nor the black hole but instead felt happy. This was the first day of his life and was thankful that he shared it with Raiden and considered him a friend and he soon yawned, sighed in relief and fell asleep.

5

Morning came too quickly for Raiden who previously had put a mirror at an angle outside his window. This mirror would wait for the sunlight and would deflect off the mirror and on to where his head would lay on his pillow acting as a natural alarm clock. He woke with a small, quiet groan, being careful not to wake Val, rubbed the sleep from his eyes with the back of his wrist, stepped over him and walked into his kitchen. His kitchen was just like any other room in his little hut. In the centre sat a large oak table with a single chair tucked in and an empty glass waiting for him as always. He walked past the table, picking up his glass in his stride like a natural reaction and filled the glass with the cold and clear water from his tap and drank slowly, feeling the cold and fresh water fill his insides and wake him, ready for the day. Raiden didn't do much with his time when he wasn't working. He wasn't human and didn't care much for possessions as humans did. He actually loved his job and spent most of his time out of the village in the wilderness. It was something that came incredibly natural to him and he pitied the humans who had no choice but to work at a job they didn't want to do. Even though leos lived considerably longer than humans he still believed that life was too short to waste your life dreaming of what you could do with your life. He had only lived on this island for a year and felt lucky that the village took him in, gave him a home and a job that suited him perfectly and that made him love the people of the village even more and therefore made him perform better at his job of protector of the village. Also he loved the time alone when he was out in the wilderness, even male humans have a natural instinct to solitude and leos were no different. Maybe he had spent too much time alone that he felt comforted by it but solitude was his friend and natural companion. When he was out alone everything seemed perfect to him. In the village he answered to Theydon and the council or commanding officers higher in command than him. He answered to his king and all the elders who would walk into his path but in the wilderness he answered to neither man nor elder; free to run his own path and live how nature would have intended, as long as he protected his village from intruders and unwelcome guests which he was very good at. He sat down in his large chair and stared blankly at the sky outside his window for a moment, wondering how near that terrible black hole was to the planet and how long it would take for the world to be affected by it. He sighed deeply and breathed steadily trying to control himself from the horror that eventually would be a reality in a matter of time, stood up and quietly left his hut to gather the council and bring them the news that he was carrying with him all night.

It was a few hours later because Raiden let Val sleep as long as he could but soon when the council had already gathered and started the debate on the situation that he had to wake him up. He nudged Val out of a sleep and with his deep growl of a voice said to him, "Come Val, get up and get dressed back into your armour and cloak. The council is waiting for us to attend," then walking over to a table with a mug of water that he had left for Val and gave it to him. Val took the mug, sitting up and sipping it while he slowly woke up and before long was on his feet attaching his armour to his chest.

"Where are the council Raiden? How far is it away?" Val asked him as he was tying his second boot.

"Not far, it's held around the corner from the guard's station you were at yesterday. There will be some food prepared for you there so don't worry about eating now. If you would like to use the restroom there is one in the next room on the left," he said pointing to another room.

Val quickly went in there noticing the manikin with oversized armour in the empty room again. When he came out he decided to ask Raiden what the armour was. Raiden didn't say anything for a minute, just stood packing a bag of rations and throwing it over his shoulder before walking out and finally saying to him. "It was my brother's uniform. It is the only thing I have to remember him. Valadad left to protect the people of Osiris a year ago now and insisted I stayed here, only he never returned, just his armour…"

Val fell silent then and didn't want to say anything that would upset him and hurried on behind him, throwing on his cloak and facing the fresh cool morning air. Before Raiden left his home the armour caught his eye and a quick glimpse of his brother's face entered his mind and he felt his heart sink but smiled as he closed the door and brought his mood back up when he also remembered the reason for his brother's death and the honour it brought to his name. He always had known his brother was a hero in his eyes.

Shouting and arguing was heard from outside the room which the council were meeting in as Raiden and Val entered quietly moving unnoticed around the side of the great hall as the council of mostly old but wise and strong men argued as most humans did whenever a debate occurred. There was a huge round table in the middle of the great hall which Raiden considered to be a symbol of individuality to every member there, where there was no one higher to anyone else. There were two empty seats waiting for them, one being bigger than the other seats there. This was his chair. As he sat down he noticed Theydon sitting across from him who was silently listening to the others. Theydon looked over to Val and Raiden and gave a silent nod which was returned the same way. They were then noticed by the tall elderly man who was making his speech to the council. He looked like an experienced traveller more than a man of governing responsibilities. He stood tall over the other members who all were seated and now listening to him, wearing a garment of finely woven white linen which fitted him loosely and the colour of his robes matched the short but noticeable white beard that covered his wrinkly face. He then raised his hand toward Raiden, "Welcome back Leo Raiden. I see you have brought young Mister Val," he then looked over to Val adding, "Val, my name is Quade, it is good of you to join us."

Val just smiled and nervously gave him a wave. "Hi." He didn't know what else to say and let Quade carry on his speech. Raiden could tell then that Val felt very out of his comfort zone here and gave him a little nudge of encouragement, nodded and winked.

"Now you two are here maybe you can help in this situation. Now we all are fully aware of what is coming toward us and the problem is way out of our league to do anything about it—"

"But like I said before..." came the voice of a large bearded man sitting down interrupting him.

"...This problem should be passed on to the councils of the greater cities where they have better scientists who could think of a better solution than us. This problem *is* far too great for us to handle so I say we should just pass the burden on to them."

"You are a fool Sendal," came the shouts of another man. "This burden is as much ours as it is anybody's on this planet. We have been unfortunate enough to be the first to hear about it but can't just pass it on to others. We should gather all the great minds of the planet and devise a way to save us all. Even if that means cooperating with Feydon."

"I will not involve neither myself nor any of my people with those snakes and back stabbers. They don't care about the black hole. They will only kill us and take our land, and that queen of theirs is an evil sadistic bitch!"

"In a time like this it does not matter what they will do to us. We have no choice and will have to regardless of the consequences. If we do nothing we will all die. Feydon is the most advanced country on Sphere and—"

"I will *not* involve myself with Queen Angel!" Sendal shouted slamming his fists down onto the table so hard that Raiden had to quickly pick up the glass of water in front of him. He put the glass back down then stood up saying, "It is not the Queen we need sir, but the minds of the scientists from the city. If we could get a message to them we could perhaps bring them to a location with all the other scientists and elders of the other major cities."

"Sit down and hush yourself Leo. Humans are talking and need none of your kind's foolish interruptions!" Sendal snapped at him.

Quade immediately then stood, slamming both his hands down making the whole table shake and shouted louder than Sendal did previously in Raiden's defence. "Control your insolent tongue Sendal! If you wish to make such outrageous remarks to a fellow member of this council then you shall be banished. I'll have you know that Raiden is the best guardsman to this village and his contribution to this debate is as every much as equal as yours. If you do not agree with this, you know where the door is!"

These words silenced Sendal, who then backed down in his seat.

"Of course, my apologies to you Mister Raiden and to the rest of the council," he then remained silent for the rest of the discussion.

Quade then turned to Raiden, "There is a flaw in your idea though Raiden. There is no way we can get such a message to the scientists, especially by ourselves. If we do then we will need the permission of King Kerry to communicate with them and I don't think he will be persuaded on the idea so easily."

There was a brief silence before someone suggested, "Maybe we can send someone in to the city to speak to them personally and draw them out of the city. We will still need to gather all the other cities' scientists' minds anyway."

"No we can't do that; their security is too heavy. The only way to enter that place as a traveller without being escorted back out is being an Elementalist, but that's a good point though. We still need to gather all the other great minds from Sphere," Quade said.

"Perhaps I have a suggestion and some information that you would find have great use in this discussion," came the elderly, feminine voice of Amber the Elder as she entered the great hall and approached the table.

In a move of etiquette everybody then stood up honouring the elder to the table. Everybody of course except Val, who remained seated because he was unaware of such table manners. Raiden noticed this and grabbed the back of his collar and quickly yanked him to his feet, nearly choking him in doing so.

"Elder Amber, you are always welcome in this council. Please, tell us what news you bring," Quade said then signalling for somebody to bring her a chair.

After she sat down she began saying, "Far to the east there is a monastery situated on an island not much smaller than Walton itself. There it has been for millions of years run by elders who have passed down the secret from generation to generation. This temple has all the records of the entire world's history in countless scrolls and human computer memory."

"I have heard of such a temple, the Temple Aragorth. First made before the First Divide by humans and elders. This was to keep the world's records safe," Quade came in.

"That is correct Quade, and there is has stayed and every detail from wars and divides to the extinction of species and even to the dawn of others has been recorded and kept safe there. Because the elders have been looking after it, it has remained untouched by any human war that has ever waged. There you will find information about how the sun was recharged all those years ago and only there you may find suitable information on how to deal with the situation."

"She's right," came the voice of one of the councilmen. "The problem is out of this world and so sitting idly will not help any of us. We need the information our ancestors had to go into outer space ourselves and tackle the problem head on."

"Even if we did go into space there is still no way we can solve this problem," argued the voice of another.

"That is why you must go to Aragorth. For the only reason it seems hopeless at this very minute is because we are all blissfully unaware of what records of technology our ancestors used to save our sacred planet as they did before.

"I'm sure when the sun was dying it seemed hopeless as it is now but they found a way, as shall we," Amber explained gracefully.

"I would also like to take the time to speak about young Val," she continued turning and walking over to him and addressing the council. "I tried communicating with the planet in meditation about Val and the answer was unclear. The only answer was the explanation of the staff he carries. Val, could you please hold up this staff of yours so the council can observe it?"

Val lifted his empty hand realizing he had left his staff back at Raiden's hut and concentrated, in a split second the staff had appeared in his hand as it did before.

The council all gasped at this strange trick and someone even shouted out, "Black magic, voodoo!"

Amber couldn't help but chuckle at this statement, "It always tickles me when humans call something that isn't explained by science *magic*. There is no such thing as magic my dear human, only something you as a species could not ever understand. I have been on the planet for many, many years and I still don't know how you humans manage to take out a diseased heart and implant a healthy one whilst still keeping the body alive. Nor do I know how you manage to construct great ships that sail the water and sky but I don't call it magic.

"Now Val, I have learned that when you woke yesterday the planet had bonded this staff with you, giving it to you as a gift. To anybody else it is a simple staff but to you it is far greater. Now please follow my instructions. Now that you have your staff I want you to break it in half."

This made Raiden raise an eyebrow intriguingly and he looked down at Val beside him.

"Ok?" Val said and took the staff in both hands and tried snapping it like a stick. He tried as hard as he could but this thing was solid. Not even Raiden could break this he thought. He eventually gave up and turned back to the Elder.

"No Val, don't try and use your strength. Use your mind, just like when you call it."

Val tried again and this time it broke in two easily.

"Now I want you to mould it into a square."

Val looked at her astonished but trusted her and tried what she asked. He managed to bend the edges of the two pieces of metal and connected them together making a small metal square. Everybody in the room gasped again and even Val was amazed by what he had just done but Amber just stood and continued, "Good Val. Now I want you to place it down and call it to your hand again."

He held out his hand again and called the staff. As it returned it also turned back to its original shape.

"Do you see what you can do with it now? You can turn it into any tool or weapon you please. The mass of the object will never change, only the appearance of it. Also it means wherever you may go you will always have this tool with you. You don't even need to carry it but leave it where it is and summon it when you need."

In all the years Raiden had been on Sphere he had never seen anything like this. He had witnessed Elemental Battles before and was aware of the powers and tricks of Elders, but nothing like this. He felt slightly proud of Val however and watched in fondness as Val put his staff back down.

"This still doesn't explain as to why I am here and why I have it anyway?" Val pointed out.

Amber smiled as she looked down at him and said, "I knew you would say that my boy", then addressed the council again. "Which is why I suggest that whoever may go on this voyage would take young Val with them. This journey or even the scrolls might shed some light on him and give him the answers he may be looking for. I'm sorry I was not any help to you, young Val."

Val then bowed down to her, "No Amber, you have been a massive help. Thank you for all your help."

He never saw this but behind him Raiden watched and nodded, proud of him.

"Then it is settled then," Quade informed the council. "Val shall go to the temple and—"

This time it was Raiden to interrupt them, "Begging your pardon Quade but Val is far too inexperienced to travel this place anywhere on his own. If he does go anywhere he will need a guide with him at all times."

"And who do you suggest Leo Raiden?" Quade asked but it was very clear for him and everybody else at the table to know what was coming next.

"I would suggest myself Quade. I have only been Val's guide for a day now and believe that if anybody should take him across the world on such a long journey, it should be me. I have experience with travelling and have been to many places around the world."

"Very well then, Raiden. Val, I am appointing you two on this sacred task given by both human and elder alike to travel over to the Temple Aragorth and seek out the scrolls, which are of grave importance to the planet's survival."

Raiden bowed to both Quade and elder, "Thank you. We shall not let you down."

Theydon then broke his silence and stated to the council, "Hold on a minute. I agree with the idea that Val should go the monastery but I believe that it will be far too dangerous for Raiden to go and I know that every one of us here can think of a big reason of why he shouldn't go."

Raiden understood Theydon's concern and spoke up, "I thank you for your thought Theydon and I understand what reason you speak of but the survival of the planet comes first. If I should die for the life of the planet then both I and all leos would be proud of such an act. Now I have been given this sacred task I feel my life now has a purpose."

Theydon stared at him like he really wanted to say something but decided to bite his tongue and stay quiet. Raiden was at least grateful for his old friend's courtesy and sat back down giving Theydon the slightest of appreciative nods.

"But there is still a question of how you two shall reach your destination from where you stand. This monastery is a very long way away and you both have no means of transport. A journey like this would need a skyship to travel there. How do you propose you get that?" asked one of the councilmen.

"That is a good question," Quade answered. "You can try going across the channel to Isolies to the city Lachine. It is closer than Hiro. If you speak to their president maybe you can persuade him to transport you there. If that fails you will have to visit Hiro and speak to our king."

"If you need travel across the channel maybe I can be of some use," came a familiar voice. Raiden looked and only saw a dark stranger but when Val looked he saw Zahied, the man he saw the day previously in the hospital. He carried on, "I have been on my own pilgrimage as a Caster for some time now and I have travelled here by a spice trading ship that leaves later tonight. I have a favour from the captain I can call in for the passage of these two here."

"Excellent, does this mean that you will also help us?"

"Of course I will. I would gladly travel with these two if it meant saving the planet. The journey would also help in my pilgrimage."

"Ok then, if you can do that for us Zahied that would be greatly appreciated."

"If we three get ready to leave now we will reach the docks in time for departure."

The old, bearded Quade clapped his hands now the decision had been declared, "Ok then, Raiden, Val, go and pack now and meet us all at the gates shortly. None of us know how much time we are dealing with here but this mission is of the utmost importance. Travel to the monastery, find the scrolls and return with them as quickly as possible."

Raiden stood once more to address the council, "Thank you Quade. I understand fully of the magnitude of this mission and the importance of our journey." He bowed to the council and again yanked Val to his feet to follow his lead. "I also thank you council for trusting me on this dire mission. On my honour as a Leo, I will not let you down."

The council all nodded and bowed after him and allowed both Raiden and Val to make their way away from the table and back to his home.

Raiden found his way back home and made Val pack for their journey. While Val went to pack he walked past his brother's armour again and decided he would say his goodbyes first. He sat down in silence with his legs crossed and closed his eyes in meditation. He remembered he always used to do this with his father's armour before the Leo Divide begun and found himself doing the same once he found out of his brother's death. He pictured his brother standing where the manikin was, wearing the armour like he did, proud and neat. His brother's dark fur always matched his father's and looked the mirror image of him while Raiden took his mother's golden cream fur but their eyes were both the same, the ruby red eyes of their mother was something they shared as well as the fiery red mane of their father. He sat in silence for moments before he smelt a human in the air, without opening his eyes he spoke softly, "Before you ask Val I am speaking to my brother. I am letting him know that I am going away for some time and won't be able to see him for a while."

"Your brother's armour Raiden, why don't you bring it with you?" he heard Val ask.

"I cannot bring myself to use his armour. It was his armour and he never used to let me touch it. I will honour that wish."

"But if you're going on a long journey maybe he would want you to have it with you? To keep you safe. That way he will always be with you right?"

Raiden thought for a moment before opening his eyes to see the shining blue, armour made of a leo discovered steel called 'Leoium alloy' shining before him like a message from his deceased brother. It gleamed down on him from the broad chest piece to the gauntlets and down to the metal grieves and shin protectors like Valadad was offering it to him from the grave. A sincere and forgotten smile crept to his lips as his heart suddenly pumped his body warm of proud family honour when he realised Val was right and stood up, "You're right. I will honour him by keeping his spirit alive by using his armour. That way he will be protecting me on this mission. He would want that." He reached up with giddy hands and took down the armour to admire it. All his childhood he wished to wear leo armour like his father, but it was something he never had the chance to do. By the time the divide started the leos began to fall and so did the Leo steel and armour all crafted from this strong alloy. Valadad's became very rare by the time Raiden was of an age where he could wear it but he never found the courage to ask his brother to wear it. He slowly lifted the body piece over his head and felt proud when it dropped on his shoulders and felt the weight both his brother and father would have felt when they both fought in their battles. He always was smaller than his brother and didn't expect the armour to fit as well as it did. Val helped him strap the buckles on the side and fastened them tight. The gauntlets attached like fingerless gloves and protected the back of his forearms and showed off his claws the same as the grieves, making him still stand on his paw-like feet but protected his shins. He made his way to the only mirror in his home, hearing the clanking of the armour as he walked; a noise that used to scare the victims and assert the wearer in any room. He stood tall and proud before the mirror. His chest out and dominant and looked at the gleaming blue metal of the leoium alloy and smiled again when he saw both his father and his brother looking back at him from the mystifying world behind the mirror. He never felt so proud to be a leo and nodded to the phantoms before wishing himself luck, grabbing Val and leaving his home, turned and took the first step away on this journey. He remembered when he first came here only a year ago and did not expect himself to be leaving now like this, like a true proud leo warrior like his ancestors before him. With his family armour protecting him and a mission that Sphere's history would tell for the rest of eternity. He only wished his family could be here to witness it but smiled warmly as his young human companion with his brother's name was walking ahead of him carrying the supplies.

6

Zahied always was a peaceful man. Casters never needed to be fighters and he was no exception. His pilgrimage for knowledge had seen him through many different cities and elder villages but so far the tricks and techniques he learned had not satisfied his thirst for knowledge. Walton however was useful to him. His small stay had first seen him to the elder village where Amber gave him a hardback leather book. A gift to him for helping the elders with farming labours and teaching the elders how to fix some human carpentry like doors, tables and chairs. The second was in the local hospital where he first met Val and there managed to learn a few healing techniques from the doctors and nurses. The life of a Caster was a peaceful one and one that always brought wisdom with a cast of friendly faces and favours. The pigment of his dark skin always suggested that he originated from an exotic part of Sphere and was exactly that. He originally came from a small island, twice the size of Walton but still small enough to pass as insignificant to the rest of the world. He tucked the book in his sky-blue and silver cloak of thick cottons he wore over a buttoned white silk shirt with brown leather leggings and mounted his lizzier whilst saying his goodbyes to the village as the young man and armoured leo had finally arrived. Zahied checked all his pockets and bags while he looked down and saw Amber approach Val. "There is something I never mentioned in the discussion earlier Val, something I wanted to speak to you myself about."

"What is it Elder?" Val asked.

"When I spoke to the planet, it not only told me about your staff but it told me that I must send you on this quest to the monastery. But I was never told why which is why I kept it secret from the others but I think that the other elders in Aragorth may be able to help you. I'm sure the planet has something big planned for you which gives me hope. It has given you a guide, a tool and a mission and I believe in you Val."

"Thank you again Elder. I won't let you down. Whatever the planet has in store for me I shall overcome it."

The elder then gave him a warm hug and wished him luck then turned to Raiden.

Theydon then came to them holding the reigns of two lizziers and brought them to Val. "Take good care of Domieneo Val. She has taken a shine to you, and good luck on your mission. I'm sorry you never had the chance to go through the procedures to becoming a Walton Warrior. But between me and you; you already are one of us. When you make it back you will be installed as a guard of this village. Don't you worry about that."

"Thank you Theydon. I won't let you down," Val bowed.

Zahied watched the whole time from a side line as Val said his goodbyes and nodded. This man apparently didn't know who he was but he did however remember all his mannerisms. Young men like Val normally were egotistical, arrogant, selfish or spoilt but someone had taught this man respect in his previous life. If it were true that Val didn't know his identity then maybe he was royalty Zahied thought, or a soldier. After a long goodbye the three of them all mounted their lizziers then headed away from the village toward the dock to the west and finally set off the travel the world to gain the necessary information from the distant monastery. A Leo, a Caster and a nameless stranger.

A few hours passed. The sun was still up and they decided to take their time and rest and sat around a small camp fire Raiden made out of a small hex burner and some flammable wax cubes he said he salvaged from the two thieves who tried attacking the village earlier.

"You know you could have just captured them and brought them to the village to be dealt with accordingly," Zahied said, sat down with his legs crossed, warming to the fire. "How do you know they were bad people? They could have been family men, only trying to feed their young or noblemen, or even people like you only following orders from their masters."

"Their intentions were to steal from the village and make an escape on lizziers. Probably the ones we ride now. They were dealt with the way I was ordered to. If I hadn't then maybe I wouldn't have found Val here and none of this would have happened the way it did and I would either be travelling alone or not at all."

"Ah! Chaos theory."

"What's Chaos theory Zahied?" Val asked.

"The Chaos theory is the study and science of surprises and the unpredictable. Where most science can be measured or predicted like gravity, electricity or chemical reactions. Chaos theory looks at other, non predictable phenomena like weather, turbulence or even life itself. That everything happens for a reason but the cause or outcome will always elude us, even if we are given all the necessary information. Where every small or seemingly trivial thing actually is a kind of build up for something that ultimately happens in the end. It's also called the butterfly theory," Zahied explained to Val's blank face.

"Call it what you will. It still means I was following orders and they had to die. Think yourself lucky I did. Otherwise we wouldn't be sitting around a fire as we are now," Raiden said as he put a pot down on the fire and started boiling some water.

As they sat and ate their dinner Val turned and spoke to Zahied. "Earlier on you mentioned that you were on your own pilgrimage."

"That's right. I am a Caster and on my pilgrimage of wisdom."

"What's a Caster and what is your pilgrimage for?"

"A Caster is someone who practices in some of the smaller tricks that elders perform. Because humans have never understood what the elders do, they call it magic. A term that couldn't be more wrong. Hundreds of years ago we Casters and female Casters were known as witches or wizards and were hunted and mowed down by the humans too ignorant to understand."

"Too ignorant to understand what?"

"That we are only trying to understand how the elders work. Try to think of me as a scientist studying the elders' way of life. Every city has its own information and books that casters would borrow or copy and study for themselves."

"Is that why you were in the hospital yesterday?"

Zahied smiled. He liked Val. "Ha, you do ask a lot of questions, don't you? But yes, I asked the doctor to copy some of his notes and teachings so I would study them myself. I was also in the elders' village a few days ago. Such nice elders there. They gave me this book on some basic little things they teach younglings so I may study them."

He took out the hardback leather book from inside his blue cloak and showed it to Val. Val looked inside it and saw mostly pictures with some printed writing on the bottom of each picture.

"Do you understand any of this?" he asked.

"Not all of it, and as a species I never will because you see the elders perform some of their tricks with gestures of the hand and because their hand is different to ours we will never be able to perform all they do. Also the other way they do it is all in pure thought and needs no gestures. Once again because we cannot understand anything else that can't be mathematically or scientifically proved we can never understand how they do this. So I just travel from place to place and learn whatever I can."

"I see. So how far will you travel with us?"

"As far as I possibly can. My help may be needed on your journey and if you are going to a place where countless scrolls of information are, it sounds like the perfect place I need to go on my travels, right?"

Val nodded and finished his dinner then they all cleared up and rested for a few minutes all sipping water while Zahied sat reading his book. After a while they packed up their camp and carried on their way again.

It wasn't far until they reached the docks all built out of wood and amongst the houses and huts that sat blissfully next to the coast and pebble beach sat a single ship, made of wood and metal. Its sails down and a plank on the side connecting it to the pier with sailors running up and down carrying cargo from what looked to be a warehouse beside it. They approached it and Zahied told them to wait there while he spoke to the captain then ran on board leaving his lizzier with them.

"Do you think the captain will let us gain passage?" Val asked.

Raiden squinted his eyes and tried to see where Zahied had gone before saying, "Let's hope so. One way or another we will have to gain access to this ship and I don't want to start a fight so early on in our mission."

But soon Zahied was running back with the good news, "Captain is fine with it, as long as we work here which shouldn't be a problem. Bring the lizziers on board, the ship is about to set sail."

They did as instructed and gave the lizziers to a man who took them down to the lower deck. After being welcomed to the ship by his friend Zahied took the captain to greet his two new guests.

"Raiden, Val, I would like you to meet my fried and captain of this ship Andre. Andre, these are the travellers I told you about, Raiden the Leo and Val the naked guy I met yesterday at the hospital."

"Nice meeting you two boys. Me an my crew are happy to give you guidance across this sea that is blocking your path," the captain said shaking their hands then shouting over to his crew. The man had a twang in his accent that told Zahied that he had ventured far around the world and was an experienced traveller. He also was a notorious gambler which was how Zahied first came to meet him.

"Pull the anchor up boys! Set down the sails while we still got the wind on our backs!"

"Aye aye Capt'n!" they called back and started pulling up the anchor and pulling down the sails ready for the voyage and soon the ship was leaving shore and moving slowly toward a horizon of water as far as the eye could see.

The captain then turned back to them all, "So I 'ere you boys are off to Isolies ey? What's your business down there if you don't mind me asking? Are you off to see the Elemental Battle? I 'ear they got some strong contenders up there this year. Gonna be a fine fight, let's hope."

Val was about to step in and correct him but Raiden came in first, "That's right Captain. I thought we would see how strong they are this year and maybe place some bets on the strongest. I've been to the elemental school in Lachine once before. The school of metal is a strong one and was looking forward to seeing them. Thank you again for helping."

Val quickly understood that Raiden and Zahied wanted to keep their real intentions secret and safe and decided to say nothing.

"That's a mighty good idea Leo, I'm a gambling man myself. Maybe I'll see you there and don't mention the favour; anything for my dear friend Zahied," he said giving Zahied a friendly punch in the arm.

"Now the journey there will take about a day getting to shore and you got about another three days on foot before you reach the city so in the meanwhile just do as my men instruct. The jobs will mostly be cleaning and mopping the deck. Any problems you come see me."

They mopped the deck of the ship for what seemed like hours under the late afternoon sky, all with the ship rocking with the waves underneath it. The sound of the ship crashing down rhythmically on the water was soothing if only the constant rocking wasn't a little unsettling. While they were moping Val came up behind Zahied as he mopped.

"Ummm…"

He didn't know how to ask but Zahied saw this coming and replied, "An Elementalist is a person who from birth is brought up by elders and taught a certain power what humans call magic. There are only as few places around the world that do this and each place teaches a different element of power; these places are called 'Elemental Schools'. For instance; some teach magic controlling the ground. Hiro, the capital city of Racoves has a school that teaches to control water and so on. The elementalist would train until they have perfected the art of the element they have grown up studying then would go on a holy pilgrimage to each city that has an elemental school in it and fight their star pupil. If they win then their star pupil would teach them the secret of their individual power and let the traveller continue on their journey until they gain all the powers from all the different schools and become the 'Elemental Lord', the one who has mastered all the elements. This title can only be given to one man at a time and he is considered a king of kings since he would have mastered all the different elements. A hugely popular and most sacred title to have. It is also popularly seen as a sport where people from all over the world would come and place bets on the winner."

"Why is it so sacred?"

"Because it is the closest thing that a human or any other creature has to actually mastering what humans call magic. Not all of the schools are proper elements though for the city we are heading for called Lachine only controls metal and they are considered one of the weakest forms."

"So what is the weakest one then?"

Zahied had to think for a moment. He raised his head to the sky and rested his chin on the end of the mop before saying, "The Element of Wind I would say. An elementalist from there hasn't become the Elemental Lord for decades."

"So who is the current lord at the moment?" Val asked but suddenly he was confronted and swung around by a creature much like Raiden.

He picked Val up by the scruff of his neck and pinned him up against the wall. He had cat-like eyes similar to Raiden's but his head was a slightly different shape, with less hair and the colour of his fur was not a golden cream colour but orange with some black stripes reaching around the back of his head across to his eye line. He put Val down with his huge hand-like paws but still keeping hold of him. He stared down at little Val and thundered with a voice as deep as Raiden's, "When the capt'n asks you to work, you work! We don't take kindly to people taking a free passage on our beautiful ship. Maybe you would like to swim the rest of the way."

Val was speechless. Being held by this creature was frightening for him all of a sudden and he froze up completely unable to make neither move nor sentence. The creature grabbed Val's arm before he had any time to respond and went to throw him overboard. Only when it turned around he was stopped in his tracks like he ran into a brick wall. The creature didn't notice at first and kept on staring at Val.

He quickly turned around, "Hey watch where you're going ya..." He kept his eyes low expecting a small human there, but instead he found himself looking straight into a huge armoured chest.

For one of the only times in this creature's life he had to slowly look up; and there a clear foot taller than him stood the leo, growling quietly under his breath.

"Is there a problem here Tigian?" Raiden asked the creature.

"A leo!? That can't be..." he said.

"Yes, now let loose of my companion. We have been given passage by your captain and are working," Raiden said then moved closer to the tigian and said again this time with more threat in his tone, "Let...him...go."

The tigian then dropped Val knowing what would happen if he were to fight a creature such as Raiden was.

"Very well Leo," he looked at Val again and tried to sound convincing but couldn't help but sound shaken up by what had happened.

"Just don't let me catch you slacking again," then walked away trying to hold his composure in front of his other sea men.

"Wow, thanks for that Raiden. I really thought he was going

to throw me overboard then."

"Don't mention it Val. Oh, and in answer to your last question. The current Elemental Lord is a Tigian. Just like the creature we just encountered now. Tigians are creatures that evolved from ancient creatures called 'tigers'," he said picking up a mop and giving it to Val then mopping with his own.

"The current E.L is a tigian from Alpha in Feydon. Their school there teaches the strongest of all elements, Fire. His name is Zane and is a national treasure to their country."

"Zane, I've heard that name before. The legend that saved the world last during the First Divide."

"Yeah that's right, probably named after him. Zane is the greatest E.L that will ever live. Not only is he schooled from the strongest school but as a species he will never be outmatched by a man for he will always be stronger, bigger and faster than them. Also, because his life span is longer than humans he will always outlive even the strongest of them."

"He sounds like quite a guy," Val confessed and squeezed the mop in the mop bucket and slapped the mop down on the deck to continue with his contribution to the work.

"He is, especially to the tigians. He is an inspiration to them," Zahied said from behind.

"So why don't elders go on this pilgrimage? Surely they would be better than the others," Val asked again trying not to cross mops with Zahied and Raiden.

Raiden turned his back to mop the other side of himself and explained, "They have neither need nor desire to. Though sometimes an elder will learn the ways of a human from birth and will become doctors but will never be as smart. This is the same thing with elementalists only the other way around. Humans will never gain all the understanding of the elders but can either study their work as Casters," he gestured to Zahied with a nod, "or be chosen at birth to be trained their way as elementalists. It is the same as tigians for example who could train to be elementalists but will never be as smart as neither humans nor elders but their strength lies in their physical advantage."

"I see what you're saying. Every creature can learn the ways of others but never be as good as them but special in their own way," Val was beginning to understand now.

"That's right. So with us I can teach you the way of a Leo. Now you will never be as good as us but compared to the other humans you would be greater because of your teachings."

Val smiled at this thinking how lucky he was at the thought of being taught how to fight by a leo and carried on mopping.

When they finished a peculiar small humanoid with a tail came and took their mops away. He was a little smaller than Val and was smiling constantly with youth burning in his eyes.

He came and took Val's mop. "Thanks buddy. There will be food brought to you shortly." Again this creature had a different accent of Sphere. He looked like a human only with a long, brown monkeys' tail on the tip of his spine that swayed as he walked. Because of his tail the humanoid creature couldn't straighten his back and so had to lean forward slightly and bend his knees until his spine was straight giving him a strange, squatted posture that shortened his true height.

Zahied walked up behind him and gave his mop to the small creature.

"Thank you sirs," the young, tailed boy said politely.

When the young man walked away Zahied noticed Val was staring at his tail and saw the fascination in his eyes. *Maybe Val is telling the truth about his condition. He truly knows nothing about the other species around here*, he thought and explained to Val. "They're called Aeomon Val. They used to be apes such as ourselves. They're our distant cousins."

"Really? They don't look like us."

"That's only because they still have their tails and therefore can't walk upright as good as us but trust me. Other than that, they could easily be mistaken for a human. Look, here he comes again. Hey Catch!" he called over to the aeomon. "I'd like to introduce you to my friend Val."

The aeomon ran over to him like an over excited child.

"Wow, nice to meet you Val. My name is Catch. I'm the captain's first mate on this vessel. Now then, where you heading?"

Val knew he shouldn't tell him what was really going on and told the same lie Raiden did previously.

"We're going to watch the Elemental Battle in Isolies."

The aeomon jumped with joy at this statement, "Wow, I absolutely love the Elemental Battles. Zane is my all-time greatest E.L ever, ever!"

"Really? Maybe while we are resting you can tell me all about him. I'm very eager to know about him."

"Certainly Val. I'll tell you what I know. Come and sit with me. No need to work now, come."

Zahied left Val to go with his new friend and only hoped Catch would explain much more about the elementalists without Val looking too ignorant and a stranger and end up embarrassing himself.

He couldn't help but smile and shake his head and turn to Raiden.

"Where did you find him my leo friend?" he called over to Raiden.

He wasn't as introduced to Raiden as he was to Val yet and still felt he had a lot to learn about the walking lion. Raiden shared his small laugh, "I honestly don't know. He really just showed up, like a phantom. The only survivor to a crashed skyship and it's like he's not of this world. I just have been given the fortune of making sure he's safe. Who knows what he is actually capable of?"

"Well, we shall both have to make sure we don't lose him," Zahied suggested.

Raiden grinned and pointed to Val and the young aeomon who were now leaning over the ship's railings and spitting off the side of the ship. "I think that might be easier said than done. Val!" Raiden called and Val looked over.

"Be careful there!"

Zahied laughed as Val looked back overboard and Catch pretended to push him over and ran away with a red faced Val chasing him.

"How about we find my friend Andre and have a drink with him Raiden? I think Val is in safe enough hands. It will be a few days before we reach Lachine now. We should relax and let the journey unfold," Zahied suggested again and Raiden replied with a nod and a playful pat on his back.

"Lead the way then my friend. This will be a good time for us to get to know each other."

For the rest of the night Val sat and chatted for hours to his new friend whilst Raiden and Zahied spoke to his friend the captain in the captain's quarters and ate the finest food the ship had to offer with him. Chatting for hours and telling stories in turn of the places they had been and the memorable characters they had met. The sun now setting set an orangey glow and reflected over the water as the air began to cool and the sky darkened. The ship sailed smoothly across the calm sea and into a beautiful horizon as the sun set over the sea and spread the last of the day's light across the sky in one more attempt to brighten the sky before the stars began to emerge and the two moons ruled the sky once more. Their next destination yonder was a long voyage away and so the ship carried them all on the first step towards the rest of their venture.

7

After Acarlie had packed all her things and was ready to begin her pilgrimage Barry, her last opponent and old friend led her up through the underground school and up to the open air arena for the celebrations in her name for the beginning of her pilgrimage. The arena she stood in her battle only a few hours ago had now became whole new atmosphere filled with smiling people. The sun was now down and the light from the stadium and party lights lit up the night sky in neon blues, yellows and reds and all the people from the audience were now walking around the arena with their friends and family. Little stalls were set up selling food or playing small carnival like games for the children. Children screamed of joy and music swam through the night air bringing excitement and celebration to the people who gathered.

Barry led her through the crowd and everyone who managed to get sight of them came running up either merry on the festive drinks or overwhelmed with excitement and gave them hugs and wished Acarlie luck on her journey.

Elder Argo was standing amongst the crowd talking to a young man when Barry and Acarlie came up to him.

"Ah, Barry, thank you for bringing Acarlie here."

"You're welcome master," Barry bowed.

"Now run back downstairs to your dormitory and study the elemental book of wind chapter four through to nine."

"But Master Argo, may I stay and see Acarlie off?"

"No Barry, you must go back down and study like I have asked you to. I will be down after the celebrations to see how you are doing."

These words must have struck a chord with Barry because he just stared at the floor and Acarlie sensed that these words had upset him but he did as his master instructed him.

"Very well Master. Acarlie, I wish you all the best."

They gave each other a hug and Barry whispered in her ear, "Remember our promise."

He bowed to both her and Elder Argo then left to go back down to his dormitory away from all the festive cheer and fun to study like his master requested him to.

"Now Acarlie, first of all let me congratulate you for your victory," Argo said with open arms to embrace his star pupil.

"Thank you master," she bowed and welcomed herself into his arms. "I couldn't have done it without your training."

"And you have trained so very hard. No one has earned this more than you. I am pleased with this outcome. The right man has outcome victorious, or shall I say woman? Now please walk with me. There is one last thing I need to teach you."

Argo slowly led her back past the partying people and to the side of the arena where the gates opened and took her up to the stands where they sat and looked down at the many people that were all in celebration of their school. The music had died down from where they were and she could again hear the sound of the wind sweeping over the top of the open stadium and out into the open sky which now glowed as the paper lanterns gracefully floated high above the small town to reach the stars above them, decorating the sky and being seen for miles in the distance past the horizon of farmlands and green fields. The old elder first looked to see that no one else was around. Elementalists' training was always done in complete solitude where the public could not see. Even though the public loved and adored what the elementalist did the elders and trainers always kept it secret from them so they wouldn't be afraid, jealous or most importantly, so children wouldn't imitate them.

"Now Acarlie, your training is now finished but you still have many things to learn about your power but you will only learn this through experience and battle.

As you learn from other elementalists you will find it harder to learn your own because you will be learning others but you must remember–"

"I know Master; this is my home element and whatever I learn this will always be my strongest element." She had been taught this lesson many times before and was eager only to learn more.

"That's very good Acarlie. You have been studying this element for years and will always be your strongest ally. I have taught you well but what I wanted was to bring you here and ask do you know what is your element is?"

"Why, it's the Element of Wind. One of the schools that actually is an element."

"That answer is both right and wrong," the old elder smiled.

She now felt a little confused. "What do you mean Master?"

"The real name for this school and its element is the Element of Unseen Forces. Many people have forgotten this fact and only know it as the Element of Wind because the wind is the primary strength of our offence and what travelling elementalists learn when they defeat us."

"Master, what does that mean and why am I learning this now?"

"It is called the Element of Unseen Forces because it uses the forces in the world that the eye cannot see, like wind, gravity and so on. The more you practice the more you will realise the real strength of this power. We don't teach you that when you are young because you simply were not ready for it. But now you have been declared the High Elementalist of Eloma and will be on your journey you have the time and space to practice this. Promise me you will. You may learn many more interesting elements but you must keep on studying your home element."

"I will Master, I promise."

"Very good Acarlie. I have already been speaking to your Guide Sheeria about this and it is something she had promised you would also uphold. Now we should get back to the celebration."

He led her back to the celebration of merry people but this time brought her to the young man he was talking to previously and introduced her to him. Acarlie at first felt shy to stand before him. This man was a tall, young and handsome man with broad, square shoulders, a strong chin and a welcoming smile with deep blue, small eyes with narrowed eyebrows.

"Now I would like you to meet Miles. He will be your guide along with Sheeria. He will make sure you will make it far."

Miles was finely dressed with finely groomed dark brown hair cut short and neat with the slightest of stubble under his chin and lining perfectly across his jaw line to reach up to his hair. He stood strong and proud with a sword to his side wearing a cream silk shirt with the top buttons he left undone showing his chest, a buckled belt and black leggings with hard boots. She was taken back by his handsomeness and charm as he spoke to her. He looked the build of a soldier and spoke in confidence and formalities.

"Honour to meet you Miss Acarlie. I have been watching your performance in the stadium, you fight well. I think there is hope for you."

"Thank you Miles," she didn't know what else to say and held her hand out to shake his. His grip was warm and her small hand disappeared in his as he shook politely.

"I am a mercenary of an old tribe from a village far away. On my travels for work Elder Argo has given me the chance for a job as guardian for you Acarlie so don't worry, my blade here Razor will protect us both," he said pulling out the sword at his side and showing it to her.

"You mean us three," said Sheeria as she walked up to them. She rested a comforting hand on Acarlie's shoulder and winked when their eyes met.

"Of course, my apologies. So Acarlie, Sheeria if your bags are packed and ready maybe you would like to walk around the stadium with me? I'd like to get to know the people I will be working for."

Acarlie's eyes widened and smiled with excitement then looked at Argo for approval.

Agro gave her a nod then she took his arm and they walked around the stadium with Sheeria following them.

"So Acarlie…" Miles asked as they sat down high in the stadium to get away from the crowd below. Back where the air was calmer and the night sky was cold but peaceful, "what made you want to become an Elementalist anyway?"

"I never chose to be. My elder chose me from birth and has been teaching me ever since," she explained.

Miles sat back and put one of his large boots on the chair in front of him. "Chosen? Well what made him choose you then?"

"Humans can never know. It's an elder thing. They just know what sort of people will grow to be elementalists." Acarlie felt the chill from the air then and put her palms in her thighs and hunched forward looking nervous to be talking to the strong soldier who lazed back with his arms stretched out.

"So he chose you then? You must be special then?"

"Yes, that is what we have been taught. Only gifted children have the power to become elementalists."

"That sounds like what they used to do with the old Ultra Soldiers back in the day."

"What's that?" she asked.

Miles looked up to the stars above and let Acarlie quickly admire the handsome man, "Teach them when they are young. Teach them to fight and follow orders so when they grow that's all they know. Only thing was the soldiers had problems in the outside world when they weren't fighting. Like a dog that has been bred for fighting."

"Are you calling me a dog? Elementalists are sacred people and the elders who train them are considered kings among cities," she asked sarcastically.

Miles laughed, "No I'm not calling anyone anything. I just like to know who and what I'm working for. I've never even seen an elementalist in person before and I don't know how long this voyage will take. Where is our first destination anyway?"

"It's a city called Lachine east of here in Isolies. I hope you have your lizzier handy because we're not going on foot."

"Don't worry, I have my Kelly waiting at the stables. She has travelled far with me and can handle herself."

They sat and talked in the stadium, enjoying each other's company and watching more paper lanterns lift from the festivities and float above their heads and beyond. Acarlie found she liked Miles the more he spoke and often just sat and listened to him and he told her about the places he had been to until Sheeria caught up with them.

"It's time Acarlie. Elder Argo is waiting at the stables at the exit of the town," she called from across the stands.

"Ok Sheeria. Come on you," she said giving Miles as playful push then ran down the stadium.

Miles nearly fell back with her push and jumped to his feet, "Oh, you're gonna get it now!" he called down and chased after her. Sheeria sighed at the two young humans and their banter then followed them out of the stadium.

Argo was waiting for them with some important council men at the stables next to three lizziers with bags packed on the back of the saddles. The goodbye was long especially for Acarlie who wouldn't let go of Argo when they hugged. She was half excited and half scared that she would never see him again.

"Just remember all your training. Stick to the sacred rules and practice whenever you get the time Acarlie. This journey won't be easy and you will have to rest accordingly and not drift away from your pilgrimage. No matter what happens, keep on track and never give up."

"I won't, I won't Master. Look after Barry while I am gone."

"I will, he will be fine which reminds me I should go check up on him soon."

When she finally let go of him he walked over to Miles and wished him luck then over to Sheeria. Sheeria adjusted her kimono and bowed down to him and he gave her a hug and said, "Remember, you are the Sacred Guide and Guardian. I know you have been studying the rules of this position for many years now Sheeria but now you will face the challenges of being a travelling Guide."

"I know Master. I would take my own life if it meant it would save hers. She will be safe with me Master. I won't let you down."

"I know you won't. I have faith in you. Now go, journey safe. Take whatever refuge you are being offered and whatever happens keep the Elementalist safe."

"I will Master, goodbye," she bowed to her old friend and master one more time and took one last glance at the town. She had lived here too long, even longer than Acarlie and felt she was leaving a part of herself behind when she left. But this wasn't the first time she had felt this emotion and the quickest of thoughts of a previous life flashed in her mind. She blanked them instantly. This moment was not about her to dwell on the past. Acarlie was the only thing in the world that mattered to her now and she knew the consequences if she failed. She promised and vowed she would not.

"Goodbye Sheeria, good luck."

When she looked around she saw young Acarlie had already pressed on forward with Miles and calling Sheeria to catch up. She took one last look back at Argo who gave her a nod then went to catch up with the other two.

8

The three travellers journeyed all night and all day in the sticky hot heat and many times Miles had to wait for the other two to catch up because their lizziers were much slower than his. Hours on end they travelled, over countless horizons and every time they crossed over a field or wooded area to see yet more fields Acarlie had the same moan every time. She felt so excited to be on this journey and remembered all the faces of the previous elementalists who left her school when she was young and felt so privileged to finally be following her dreams and journeying in their footsteps. She tried to make games out of her journey by counting the wildlife but when a flock of birds flew overhead they both insisted she stopped after her excessive counting. She then attempted singing but again was silenced quicker than she started and soon she was out of ideas and starting to feel tired and run down. The sun was starting to go down again and at the bottom of a hill that led up to a small cliff overlooking the rest of the land they set up camp with two small tents around a fire. Miles gathered wood for the fire and started throwing sticks into it to keep them warm. Acarlie was eager to eat all the food that she was carrying but Sheeria took some of the food away telling her to ration her food supply better. Miles, with the fire now burning sat down and took out his own tins of food he had bought from the Eloma shops.

"I wouldn't eat that Miles. One day my friend ate some of that food and was sick for days." Acarlie said as she sat down beside him.

Miles smiled, took no notice and took out a spoon and scooped out a big mouthful of slop and ate it in front of her.

"When you're out here, you eat whatever you can, regardless of what it tastes like. I doubt that your friend ate this and became sick. Otherwise they wouldn't sell it. He must have been ill," he said and took out another spoon full and offered it to Acarlie.

She moved her head back in disgust, "No thank you, I have my own food," and took out some bread that Sheeria hadn't taken away and tried placing it near the fire to toast it.

"Bread! Is that all you're eating? How do you think you will survive on just bread?" he mocked.

"It's not only bread I'm eating. We have some soup we are about to heat up. Elder Argo made it for us," as she said this Sheeria opened a compartment in her bag and took out a pot sealed up with tin foil and tied together with string and placed it on the fire.

They ate happily around the fire until it had almost burned out. Acarlie crawled inside her tent and climbed into her sleeping bag which was cold and curled herself up but it took her a while to get used to the temperature. Sheeria followed and lay beside her in her own sleeping bag and turned to Acarlie.

"I see you are taking a shine to Miles Acarlie."

"Shut up, no I'm not," Acarlie insisted but her lie was not very convincing.

"You can't lie to me Acarlie. I can't say I don't approve. He is a nice boy and like you said before as your Guide whatever you shall choose to do I'll always be behind you on your decisions."

Acarlie stared for a minute trying to work out Sheeria's angle.

"You can't lie to me either. You don't like him do you?" she asked.

"I never said that. I just mean you have only known him for a day. You don't know him at all yet."

"Shh, he'll hear you. Talk quietly."

"So you do like him then." She then turned over and continued, "Humans are strange, you have a tendency to like someone you only just met before you have any real time connect with each other and if you do you hide yourselves from them. Why? Why do you do that?"

"Because it's embarrassing letting someone know how you feel sometimes...not that I do for him. I just think he's funny and a nice guy...and cute."

"Cute? What do you mean by that?" Sheeria asked suggesting the obvious.

"You know I'm done with this conversation Sheeria. I'm going to sleep, good night Sheeria," Acarlie finished and also turned to face away from her tigian companion.

Sheeria laughed at this, "There you go again, hiding. We tigians never worry about things like that. When we see someone we like we just walk up to them and–"

"I don't care what you do Sheeria. Leave me alone I'm going to sleep."

Sheeria laughed again and said, "Very well Elementalist. Sleep well. I will forget this conversation," then snuggled into her sleeping bag and closed her eyes.

Acarlie only slept for an hour before she was woken by the sound of Miles moving outside. When she looked outside she saw that he was further up the hill by the edge of the cliff swinging his sword around, practising his technique overlooking the valley; all perfectly still with the light of the two moons giving the land a silvery glow to the atmosphere. She decided to walk up to him and tensed in the cold but ignored it. She could only see the silhouette of his body moving as he danced with his sword before the moons. His kata was strong and quick and his slices were delicate as he slashed and stabbed the air in front of him. Once he noticed her there he stopped.

"Don't mind me, please carry on," she said.

"No. I'm done now anyway. It's getting a little windy, can you do something about that?"

"No. We're taught not to abuse our gift outside the arena. Only in our elemental katas are we allowed to use it when not in combat," she walked up closer to him looking at his blade.

From the hilt of his blade an oily residue ran and trickled down the edge of the blade when he tilted it down to the floor.

"Why do you call your blade Razor Miles?"

He smiled liking the question she asked him. He had a fondness of his weapon and lifted it admiringly so she could see it in the moonlight.

"It's called Razor because it is exactly that. It was my father's and made by elders that used to live with my tribe. They made it with this gel that would always sit at the hilt. Whenever Razor would dent from a blow or begin to rust the person wielding it would simply tip it down and let the gel run down the blade and this would close the dents and always keep it razor sharp. This is one of a kind and the sharpest blade in the land. Think yourself lucky you're on the friendly side to it."

She looked at the blade. On one side it was blunt like every other sword and was straight and narrow. Near the hilt of the blade was a symbol of a lion fighting with another lion over a black sun and he explained that it was the clan emblem representing fighters in the light or the darkness. He then showed her the gel and, like she saw before the oily gel ran all the way down the blade and dried instantly making it look extremely sharp.

She sat down on the edge of the cliff and looked up at the clear sky. She loved the night sky and tonight was clear enough to see all the bright stars like pin pricks in a velvet sheet that covered the planet, shielding it from the heavenly light the eye could not see. The moons were also bright tonight and lit up the plains in front of them leading down toward a wooded area. Miles sat down beside her and when she asked him about the tribe he mentioned before, he told her about his homeland. His land was far away and the people he grew up with were now gone and only buried in his memories. He told her that he was brought up as a warrior in a tribe bred for fighting. The weak were cast out or even executed when they were young if they did not grow up the way that pleased the clan. They were always at war with another clan on the other side of their land, and told her the history of the battles the two clans had, always over food or territory. But his tribe was finally killed off and the other clan still lives somewhere. But now he told her the other clan has stopped all their fighting ways after their soldiers were all killed in the Battle of Osiris. Now they are villagers and farmers just like everybody else.

"I was out hunting when it happened. I came back to find my village burned down to the ground. The smell of the fire and burning bodies could be smelt from a mile away. I did not even get to say goodbye. Women and children were not given the decency of quick and painless deaths. They were raped and thrown on to the fire to burn, killed if they tried to escape. I didn't see my family die but I knew they had. I found worthless jewellery they owned in the ashes afterwards. The only thing I found intact was my father's sword buried under his house where he kept it. He did not even get it when they attacked. I like to think that he knew I would come after it and find it knowing where it was and use it to seek revenge on the people who killed them. I vowed to become a mercenary after that. To build up my training while doing nasty jobs for rich people and one day have my revenge."

"I'm sorry to hear that Miles. So I guess that would make you the last member of your tribe? Did you ever know who did that to your people?"

He looked up remembering what someone once said to him.

"You know I was in the Battle of Osiris Acarlie?"

"Really? Were you?"

"Yes I was. Not many people other than me survived. It was a horrible night that haunts me to this day, but I'll tell you this. I only went knowing that the soldiers from my rival clan were there and wanted to find and kill them thinking that it was them who did it."

"But what happened then?"

"While there I was stationed with a leo named Valadad. Valadad was a good soldier and when I told him why I was there he spoke to me and convinced me of not going through with it because I had no proof and would be killing a lot of soldiers who would be fighting with me against Feydon. So I didn't and since then have been thinking he was right. Even though we were rivals they might not have done it but then again he might have only said that to keep me from killing the army. I guess I'll never know."

"Why? What happened to Valadad?"

"He died trying to defend some of the troops. Shame. He was a very strong fighter but that's the thing with war. Even the toughest and biggest can be brought down by a single strike, arrow or bullet, but enough about that," he said as he got to his feet again.

"Come Acarlie, follow me and bring some warm clothes."

"Where are we going?" she asked.

"We're going hunting and I might need you so hurry up."

Acarlie ran back to the tent and silently picked up her warm cloak without waking Sheeria and hurried back to Miles who was already heading along a path leading down the hill the cliff was overlooking and headed on to the plains. When they reached the ground they looked around in the perfect silence, with just a couple of wild lizziers silently running into the bushes. There were a few trees growing in the plains and Miles had to climb on one to pull down a large branch. It only took him a second to climb up there and a minute to find a good branch and tear it down making a noise that unsettled the scene while Acarlie waited down on the ground for him. When he got his branch he took Razor and started cutting off the twigs and sharpening the end turning it into a spear. She could see that he had done this many times before and admired the handy work of it all and how quickly he managed to do it. He then put his blade in its scabbard and tied it to his back so it would make less noise than dangling around his waist. He led her into the woods and whispered to her not to talk as soon as they entered and told her to watch where she stepped in fear that she would scare away all the prey. She did as told and said not a word as they walked in, watching her feet, being careful not to step on twigs or crunchy old leaves. She could see all sorts of other predators hunting like they were. There was what looked like a small wild cat with jet black fur crouched down in silence, waiting for them to pass by before carrying on with its hunt. Only because of its huge black eyes that reflected the light of the moons was she able to see it, but did not say anything but smiled and silently wished it a good hunt. Further down, the forest became darker and only when this happened could they both see the beauty of the forest when all sorts of plants began to light up with natural luminous glows from them. They both stood and looked around at the wonder before their eyes. Large leaves glowed white, blue and silver as the moonlight came down from above, piercing the leaves from the trees covering the ground. Vines, illuminated with an orange glow spiralled up some of the trees, strangling them as they climbed up and even Miles couldn't help but move to some different vines that dangled around the bushes and grew tiny glowing white acorns that glistened, lighting up the bush like christmas tree lights. Acarlie crouched down as she saw some flowers that were open when all other flowers closed during night time. Their petals like everything else there were glowing colours of silver and blue. She slowly went to touch one and as soon as her finger touched the petals it reacted and closed in recoil like it was in pain. But only a couple of seconds later it opened again giving out a yellowy glow which all the other flowers copied. Soon the floor was lit up and all the wildlife hiding around them scattered at this. She marvelled at this. It was a defensive reaction making all predators flee when they want to be hidden or blinded by its lights. Miles then pulled her to her feet and gave her an angry look as if to say, *don't touch anything*! Then took her away from the light back into the darkness where they needed to be.

Later on she saw a small monkey swinging through the trees on its own hunting mission. It dangled from the trees and looked down at her. Its eyes were as big and black as the cat's were earlier. Being that big for hunting purposes and under its arms were thin pieces of skin. He then showed her how they worked when it saw something moving around the floor and leapt from the branch, opened its arms and legs and glided down silently to sweep up a large insect crawling and quickly climbed up the tree. She smiled up at it as it too looked down at her while nibbling on its dinner. Unfortunately for the cute monkey however, a large white owl swooped in without a sound and gripped the monkey and without a scream, it disappeared again taking the poor unsuspecting animal to its nest. Miles however was more interested on another animal. A brown rabbit was hopping around noisily. Why it wasn't sleeping safe in its burrow was its problem. Right now it was breakfast. Miles signalled Acarlie to stand still crouched down behind a tree peering out at his prey. He judged how far he would have to throw his spear, took his stance and without making the rabbit aware, threw and watched it fly through the air. Suddenly a strong gust of wind came from nowhere and redirected the spear to fly upwards and crash by a nearby tree spooking the rabbit which ran away out of sight. Miles then broke the silence by crying out in disappointment and looked over to Acarlie who was standing there giggling at him.

"What did you do that for? I thought you weren't allowed to abuse your power outside the arena?" he asked.

She stopped laughing, "Maybe I wasn't abusing my gift," she said walking past him and brushing his shoulder. "Maybe I was saving an innocent rabbit from death."

"Hey that's not fair," he called out to her in protest.

As he caught up with her they both heard the sound of motorbike engines coming from outside the forest. They ran to the end of the forest and when they came to the plains again they could see a campfire with motorbikes gathered around it. Their engines still turned on and their riders sitting around the fire screaming and laughing noisily disturbing the whole forest. The riders sat in dirty leather jackets each with their faces smothered in what looked like dirt, engine grease or even blood. They were drunk and acting like rowdy fools.

"Who are they?" Acarlie asked him.

"I don't know but let's go and find out. Stick to the bushes and in the shadows. Let's see how close we can get," then slowly and silently he moved around the edge of the woods until they were about fifty yards away from them. Miles told her to stay where she was and bravely came out from the shadows and as quickly and quietly as he could he crouched and ran to another tree not far from them. They were too busy and drunk to notice him as he peered over and eavesdropped on what they were saying. All Acarlie could hear was the occasional grunt or laugh and cheer from them all once in a while as they drank more and chewed on the food they were eating. She could see their jackets clearly, leather with metal studs pierced through them and metal chains dangling from shoulder pads making them look bigger than they were. They were mainly bald and the ones with hair had it cut short and scruffily like they had done it themselves with rusty scissors. After a couple minutes Miles came back and Acarlie asked him what they were talking about.

"They are excited about someone that is travelling around. I think they mean harm to them," he said as he crouched back behind the bush they were hiding behind.

"Who do you think they could be talking about?" she glanced back up in fascination of who these strangers were.

"I don't know. All I could make out is that someone around here is travelling around with a large cat-like creature," he explained.

"I wonder who that could be," she said. "Maybe we could help them? If we found them before they do. We could warn them that they are in danger."

"But there's no way of finding them. These riders have got a much better chance of catching them than we do."

When he said this Acarlie suddenly saw a light in the corner of her eye and looked back into the forest and saw that something had disturbed the glowing flowers again and was heading toward them. She pointed at it and Miles saw as well and ducked behind a bush a few meters away. She was just about to follow him when she saw the footsteps of a rider coming behind her from the forest.

The only place she could go was behind the large tree she was against as the bald rider came from the bushes. He was still unaware of their presence and rocking from side to side as he tried to keep his balance in his inebriation.

"Hey guys!" he called out to his companions. "There are these flowers that light up when you touch 'em, come see guys!" His words were slurred but clear enough for them to hear him. They shouted back angrily, "What are you doing! You're supposed to be scouting around, not playing with flowers, you girl!"

He stood, trying to keep his balance, high and intoxicated. "Now come and sit down, you big drunk bastard!" they continued.

"Hold on a minute, I got to take a piss," he said then turned to the tree Acarlie was hiding the other side of. She suddenly froze in fear that he would see her and couldn't even move her head around to see Miles. Her heart pounding and promising herself that it would be fine and he wouldn't see her. She heard the rider's urine hitting the other side of the tree and his drunken sigh of relief and nearly jumped up as she saw a puddle of it running down from the tree and just past where she sat. All the rider would have to do is tilt his head around the tree and see her there and raise the alarm but he didn't. He just shook and finished up and Acarlie nearly threw up as the small drops of urine splattered on the leaves around her but put her hand around her mouth to make sure she made no noise.

"Are you done yet sissy!" one of the riders called to him as he grunted and nearly fell back to the roaring laughter of the others around the camp fire.

"No. I want to check what's over there now!" the drunk shouted back, pointing toward the bush Miles was hiding behind.

Acarlie decided she had to do something and without the rider seeing, put her hand to the trees and used the wind to push the tree tops strongly to one side. The riders got all excited with this and quickly called for their companion to catch up with them. He ran from the tree screaming with joy like a tribal hunter chasing his prey and they all started their engines again and turned and disappeared following the direction of the wind. Soon it was all quiet again and Miles came from around the bush.

"Wow, thanks for that. I thought you weren't going to do anything then."

"You could have helped me. That was disgusting Miles. It nearly touched me!" she shouted.

"It's lucky I didn't, otherwise he would have got suspicious. You did well Acarlie. You saved both of our skins."

"I wonder why they got so excited with the wind though? It was almost like they wanted it to happen."

Miles looked out to where the riders had disappeared to. The sound of their engines were only echoes in the night now and slowly disappearing. "I think what's more important is where are they going and are there any more of them? We should keep our eyes open for any more of them. There might me more on the lookout. We should head back to the campsite now and tell Sheeria. Maybe she can shed some light on these people," he told her then walked back into the forest back to the glowing trees and plants. As she followed she smiled as she looked back up to the trees and saw to her surprise a monkey standing on the branches again peering down at her. It had a small wound around its belly that matched an owl's claws. She was happy for that was the very same monkey she saw previously and had somehow survived the owl attacking and taking it away. It looked down at her as it did before and called out a noise she thought was a thank you when she realised the owl's nest must have been in the trees she moved to avoid the riders and had also saved this small monkey from dinner by knocking it away or scaring away the owl. Either way she knew the monkey was grateful and waved back at it, "You're welcome," she said and Miles turned back to her.

"What was that? Why am I welcome?" he asked her and she turned to him as the monkey glided down and disappeared into the darkness.

"What? Oh, nothing I was talking to the…never mind," she said and carried on walking.

Soon they were nearly back to the edge of the wood and Acarlie saw the wild cat again. This time it was not hiding but in the open making lots of noise as it caught a mouse and was pulling at it with its claws, shaking the squeaking mouse and rolling with it in its mouth, tearing flesh from it and once it was not moving anymore started eating it. It looked up at them and took no notice and carried on with its hard earned meal it just caught. Miles looked at it jealously and Acarlie heard him mutter to himself, "Even a stupid cat can catch dinner." He saw another rabbit hop along behind some bushes. This one different from the one Acarlie saved earlier and was unsuspecting to the predators around it. This time Miles crouched and took out Razor. With one swipe of this he would cut it in half he thought and tried closing in on it but the rabbit caught his smell and fled leaving him to chase behind. All of a sudden a flash came from the trees and a huge tumble as something fell on the rabbit. Acarlie jumped with this and let out a cry. Sheeria stood up from where she fell with the rabbit in her mouth, took it out and quickly twisted its neck killing it humanely and threw it at Miles's feet. He stood there shocked not knowing what was happening.

"You humans don't know anything about hunting. You're too noisy and your odour can be smelt all over the forest," she told them.

"How long have you been there Sheeria?" Acarlie asked her.

"I have been behind you ever since you came into the tent to get your cloak. You didn't think I would let you come out here on your own did you? No, I have been quietly stalking you all along. I even made a couple of mistakes but you didn't notice at all. You were too keen on everything else around you. All the pretty flowers or local wildlife. That's not how you hunt."

"Ok, stop rubbing it in Sheeria. I get it, I'm not a hunter," she playfully pushed Sheeria and smiled.

They started laughing together while Miles took the rabbit from the floor and began walking back to camp.

"But Sheeria, if you were there all along then you would know of the people on motorbikes we saw, right?" she asked as they began their way back to their camp.

"That's right I wasn't far from you. I saw everything."

"Why didn't you help me when I could have been caught?"

"I would have if you had been caught but I had faith in you and you did well. I'm proud of you." Sheeria always did know the right thing to say sometimes. Acarlie loved her for that.

"Thanks. Well, what do you make of the riders?"

"I think they were looking for someone when they witnessed the weather change so they headed back to wherever they came from to either report back or to call more to the scene. Whatever they were doing they were on orders to move as soon as they saw any activity."

"That was all very strange, but I'm glad it's over now. I just want to get some sleep," Acarlie said realising what time it was and how tired she actually was. All this hunting and sneaking around really drained all the energy from her. It had become an interesting first day of her pilgrimage. The tigian smiled and threw her arm around Acarlie as they walked out of the forest.

"Also one day you will have to teach me how to hunt how you do Sheeria. I still can't believe you were there the whole time and both of us were unaware."

"I'm afraid I can't teach you to hunt like me. You're too old and have already been taught by elders."

"I guess that means that you will have to do all the hunting then?" she suggested with a tired smile.

"I guess so. Unless your master hunter boyfriend can help me next time. He seemed like he knew what he was doing, breaking sticks from trees and chasing rabbits," Sheeria joked and pointed to Miles walking back in the distance. Acarlie laughed and slapped her in the shoulder for saying it, being happy that Miles was too far away to hear. When they got back she saw Miles was already in his tent and the rabbit was wrapped in tin foil waiting for morning. She was smiling still when she tucked herself back in but was still a little concerned about the riders. There was somebody out there travelling around with a big cat that was in danger but she found herself far too tired to worry all night and eventually dropped off to sleep.

9

At first glance the great city Hiro was magnificent and beautiful to look at. The sun would come up over the horizon and its light would be taken and deflected by great glass buildings reaching high into the sky on to the whole city. Trees and street lamps decorated the side of roads in turn and stretched out as far as the horizon could reach. On the streets below mechanical car-like pod shaped vehicles would race up and down carrying passengers around the city while the richer folk would have a carriage pulled by various lizziers on designated roads. Its ruler, King Kerry was located in the biggest building there. It was a monstrously large but well-crafted mix between cathedral, pyramid and skyscraper rather than a simple castle and was considered one of the biggest buildings on the planet. The city's elemental arena was not the simple coliseum like in Eloma but was designed like a great glass sphere. This magnificent city was not only perfectly designed by some of Sphere's greatest designers and architects of their time to withstand all sorts of natural disasters but was all held up by nearly a hundred huge stone pillars reaching half a mile up from the ground. Hiro was one of the great and ancient cities of Sphere and over the millenniums had suffered with the world changing and the ground level rising. Unlike every other city that changed slowly to their surroundings Hiro stayed and eventually the ground level entombed it and so the builders decided to build upwards and create two cities. One on top of the other. This new Hiro where the sun could see was now on the same level as the ground around it but had been dug below it giving it a better level foundation for the support of the pillars. This was excellent for whenever a flood would arrive which would drain down a certain sewage system, straight down a hill out of harm's way and of course there were many roads that led out the city so travellers or tourists could come and go. But underneath the great and grand city was the darker side of the city. Under the false ground the upper class people walked on and down on the floor was the slums and lower or working class people. Before the city was finished this slum was Hiro and the builders built upwards and so made a whole city again and forget about the city they grew up in so the folk left down in the old town would call the slums *True Hiro* for it was there first. True and original Hiro was now covered in darkness as its sky was stolen from them by the rich folk and would only see the sunlight briefly on sunny days on certain hours. Some people who were too poor to leave the city would go their whole lives down in True Hiro and would eventually grow ill and pale from lack of sunlight and would eventually be brought up to the upper level's hospital until they were healthy enough to be taken back down. This was known as the True Hiro Sickness and was something every single person suffered from eventually. Millions of years ago when the First Divide happened the humans covered themselves from radiation from the energy of a different sun and sheltered themselves from light. Back then there was a method they used to generate false light and even false rain, the same idea was recycled and used again here and right now it was raining.

Down on the dark, night time streets of True Hiro. In the murky cold streets as the artificial, recycled rain poured down on the busy streets the people walked past one another with the occasional group of girls or business men chatting to one another. Walking past the bright shop lights of sleaze bars and tobacco selling merchants walked a lonely aeomon. His long messy hair tied up and wrapped up in a cloth over his head covering it from the rain and wearing handmade leather sandal-like shoes someone had given him unlike all the other folk who had shoes, trainers or boots. He wore a long overcoat and an old rucksack he found a few years ago which has served him well. He walked silently like a ghost. Not that he was invisible but simply unnoticed by all the other people there. Something he had been doing for a while now and was beginning to be very good at.

He turned from the streets down a muddy alleyway passing various merchants whispering to him as he walked past.

"Do you want some sniff pal?"

"Do you want some smoke pal? It's the best gear around, grown up top."

"Got some lovely girls pal, they love aeomon."

He ignored them all and walked from the alley onto another street side. The street lights and the passing of cheap vehicles slowly driving past were the only sources of light other than the lights in the shops or the electric signs flickering outside them. He briefly looked up into the darkened abyss above his head. The stars never showed down there. Not even the source of the rain showed but total blackness, a sky-less hell constantly cold and forever dark as the light was consumed by the giant lid above his head. Dust and pieces of litter were blown around as the rain continued to fall soaking the people bitterly as they only tried to get to and from work but this aeomon was on a job of his own for he was hunting. He walked down the end of the street, turned a corner and walked into a convenience store and knowing exactly where he was going went to a fruit stand and took an apple and carried it to the storekeeper. The storekeeper smiled and nodded in recognition at him and asked for the right amount to pay for it. The aeomon pulled out some coins from his pocket and handed them over to the storekeeper who even told him to go and get a second one for free. He smiled and nodded as if to say, "*Thanks*," and went to take another; showing it to the storekeeper as he left. He stood outside the building sheltering himself from the rain while he ate one of his apples, eating it right down to the core and throwing the core away in a nearby bin.

His next destination was a nearby butchers. He slowly crept up to the window blending in with the crowd of people and looked in the window and saw only the butcher in the window on his own.

Up on the shelf he saw a large joint of gammon. This was his hunt and his dinner but he would have to take it quickly and without being seen. He had spent all his money on the apple and this was his best chance of eating tonight. He was not too worried though for he was a thief by trade. He had been doing it all his life and was quite good at it. He hadn't stolen from this store in months and the last two times he had he was undiscovered. He walked in and looked at the oily, fat butcher chopping into meat and thought to himself even if he was seen this guy would never catch him. At first he walked in trying not to make eye contact with the butcher and walked around looking at the various meats as if he were shopping when actually he was biding his time and deciding how to do it. Luck was on his side when the butcher suddenly dropped the knife he was working with, cursed himself and went into the back room to clean his knife. Now was his chance. He quickly took the joint of gammon and went to exit but he saw over the counter that the stupid butcher had left the till open. He slowly walked up to it and was about to reach over when he thought to himself stop. This gammon would keep him going for a few days and would not be worth gambling it for a little money but before he turned around to go he heard the butcher coming back. He jumped behind the back of the counter and silently prayed to himself that the butcher wouldn't discover him. Every second passed slowly then as all he was thinking was what he should do, stand up and hand it in and leave it? Make as though all was well? Or go to the till and pretend he forgot his wallet or just make a run for it. But the butcher made it easier for him when he cursed again and said, "Forgot my keys for the till. I got to start locking this thing," he then turned around to pick them up.

This time he didn't hesitate and stood up and slowly went to exit without making too much noise. He got up to the door when he heard the butcher call out, "Hey! Are you gonna pay for that!?"

He turned to see the butcher looking straight at him on the other side of the store. His keys in one hand and a carving knife in another. This plan had completely backfired now and he was caught. In a split second he decided what he would do and ran out of the store. He heard the butcher call out his two sons and before the aeomon could look back he heard the back door slam open and two boys chase after him. These two were about his age, maybe a little older and so now he knew he had to run for his life. He didn't even have enough time to put the gammon in his rucksack and carried it like a football in his arms as he charged past the public, darting down the alleyways and jumping over fences but the two lads were persistent and did not give up the chase. Aeomon were generally better at some sports than humans like jumping or climbing because of their tail but because of that they walked a little forward like a hunchback and so could not run as fast. He knew this and knew the only way he would escape the two humans would be to go on the rooftops of the houses and flats and as soon as he was in familiar ground he turned a corner and up a ladder onto the top of some council flats but the boys were only a few metres away and were catching up fast. He reached the end of the flat and just like he had many times before, jumped off the flat and onto the tiles of a house and ran across them. The boys jumped too and had to gain their balance once they landed, which gave him some extra time. He was coming up to the part he was looking for. Between two abandoned houses spaced too far apart to jump he had left a plank of wood between them shortly before as an emergency exit. He had used this thing many times before and had got him out of many predicaments such as this and used to practice running across it with a bunch of mattress on the floor when he was young. He heard them calling after him and so he quickly and carefully ran along the wooden plank and turned to pick it up from the other side but once he turned, he saw the first boy trying to place a foot on it. He quickly kicked off the end and let the plank fall to the floor leaving them separated from one another. The boys were cursing and throwing pieces of tile at him but he just smiled in victory and held up the joint to them then disappeared down to the floor.

He got back on the streets and put the gammon in his rucksack. This had been another successful steal but he shouldn't go to that butchers for a while now and stay on the other side of True Hiro for a while. He went down his home ally and sighed relief as he walked up to the security door of his block of hidden away flats thinking of how he would freeze half this joint and eat the other half in a week or so in sandwiches. But the smile was suddenly wiped off his face when a familiar face came from the door. It was a policeman from the city who knew he was a thief and would search him. Beside him was a trainee policeman, still wet behind the ears. The thief then knew it would all be over. All that work and running for nothing. Hopefully they would take it back and be done with it.

"Well, well, well, what's this then?" The policeman said sarcastically. "If it isn't the nameless mute. Off stealing again were we now? Looks like I caught you this time."

"Is this an old offender then?" asked the trainee.

"Oh yes my boy. This monkey here has been stealing from shops ever since I joined the force, and every time he got away with it. Well not today. Empty your bag boy."

'Monkey' was a racial slur said against aeomon because of their tail but they were actually apes just like humans were. The thief knew this but did as he were told and opened his rucksack and took out the gammon.

"Wow, nice ham. Did you pay for this then m'boy?"

The thief nodded his head.

"Liar! I've had enough of you this time monkey and now you're going to pay," and he whistled to some more colleagues walking around the corner trapping the thief.

"What are you going to do? Maybe he is innocent. You can't just punish him without trial," the trainee said to his superior.

"No he did it all right, I know he did. He always does. I can see it in his eyes. We're going to do what we have wanted to do to him for some time now."

"What's that boss?"

"This boy is seen as the lowest of the low. Even us hard working slum folk look down on these people. He's not even human. The only shred of dignity he has is the look of his people but we're going to take that from him."

They all knew what that meant. An aeomon's most treasured thing was their tail. It was not only a limb but a symbol of individuality and pride, and without it they were not any more aeomon than they were human.

"No! You can't do this to him," the trainee started in the thief's defence.

"What, take something from him for once? He is nothing boy. He can't even speak in his own defence, can you monkey? Go on; tell me why I shouldn't take the only thing you possess?"

The thief stood still silent knowing he was unable to speak, opened his mouth but could only say, "aaah."

"You see? Taking this tail wouldn't degrade him anymore than what he already is. Now what else does he have in this bag." He took the bag from the thief and took out the apple.

"Oh, stealing an apple? That's it! I don't want anything to do with this. I never signed up for this. I'm going back to the station. Don't think the boss won't hear about this," the trainee said and walked away trying not to look in the thief's eye for shame.

The thief knew as do we that he never stole this apple but when you are mute and unable to talk it's hard to convince people otherwise. The police men from behind him grabbed him and pinned him to the floor.

"How do you want to do this boss?"

"We'll chop it off clean then dump him outside the hospital. They can sort him out from there. I hope you feel a lot of pain boy because I'm going to enjoy this."

They held him down so he couldn't struggle and covered his mouth so no one could hear him scream.

10

Acarlie woke to the smell of cooked rabbit. She exited the tent and helped Sheeria pack up while Miles was cooking breakfast, boiling the water and skinning the rabbit and peeling some carrots and parsnips and making a quick stew to warm them from the fresh and moist morning dew. When all was packed they sat and ate the rabbit stew. Miles sat sulking to himself still upset that it wasn't him who caught the rabbit but soon shrugged it off and forgot about it, admiring his cooking and boasting it would taste even better if he had the correct spices to contribute to the meal. Their journey was another long one, passing endless trees and trying to avoid roads in fear that they might run into more riders. After hours of a tiring journey they had nearly eaten all their rations and needed a place to stay again. It was late in the evening when Sheeria caught the smell of a burning fire and led the others the way her nose guided her. She had them going for nearly another hour before they climbed over one last hill and in the distance they saw an old run down desolate city. There were small fires burning somewhere in the city and they all could smell the food cooking.

"Do you think there are people down there? We should go down there and try and find some refuge," Acarlie said.

"I don't know Acarlie. We don't know what is down there. We should carry on toward Lachine," Sheeria replied squinting her eyes out into the distance to see anything that might suggest a safe refuge.

"But Lachine is past this place. If we go through it will be quicker and we may get some supplies," Miles added then saying what they were all thinking. "I'm very tired and need to eat some proper food. We should be welcomed since an elementalist will be passing by."

"That's right, Sheeria, let's go. I'm sure the lizziers need some rest too."

"Oh very well Acarlie. We shall only pass through. I have never seen nor heard of this town so if we can we'll get some rest and supplies and leave for Lachine as soon as we can. I think we should each be careful however. We don't know what's before us."

The city looked much more abandoned up close and was very unsettling. Every window of every shop and house was smashed in. The shelves empty and the street lamps flickering every once in a while giving the whole area an eerie atmosphere. The city was totally silent as they walked in and along the first two streets of high but empty buildings. Soon it was night again and the eerie feeling was greater. Still there was no sound and everywhere they looked, they only saw empty buildings and overturned, burnt-out vehicles. The further they walked, the more it looked like this city had been hit by a nuclear weapon. Some doors were still open from where people had to leave in a hurry and even a telephone box was smashed open and the telephone hanging from it. Dust and grime cluttered the streets and built in dense handfuls in corners of black filth and spread up the walls in water stains. There were not even any birds here. No songs sung by passing wildlife but instead only the whistle and howl of the wind creeping in the alleyways around them. They tried looking for some lights but couldn't see nothing and now even Sheeria couldn't smell anything other than dust and the wind blowing paper and various other pieces of litter around this forgotten city. Acarlie walked on ahead to see where they could go when she caught the smell of something terrible. On the corner was a big bin and when she lifted it she nearly screamed as she saw the whole bin was filled with human remains. Their skin shredded and torn. Once living and breathing but now nothing but food for the flies and maggots crawling around their rotten flesh. Sheeria came up and nearly gagged as well at the smell of it.

"They have been chewed on. Given to something that couldn't eat all of it and left in the rubbish. We should leave this place immediately Acarlie. This is not a place for an elementalist."

Miles came and looked inside in disgust then looking at Acarlie, "I don't think refuge and hospitality will be granted to us here. We should go back the way we came."

"No, we must carry on and go through. It is the quickest way to Lachine. Whatever has happened here, happened a while ago. Maybe we can go through unnoticed," Acarlie suggested but had to cover her mouth with her hand to try and block out the terrible smell.

"Or maybe that is what these poor folk lying in these bins believed," Sheeria said. Just after she said it they all heard the sound of motorbike engines again coming quickly closer. They hid themselves and their lizziers behind the bin of rotting flesh as they watched the riders ride past them shouting and screaming to themselves. Again not noticing the travellers hiding from them and continued on their way.

They came out from their hiding place watching the motor bikes disappear down the direction they had to go. She couldn't help but feel very scared at this moment and wished how Argo would have been there to comfort her. But he wasn't. He was back safe at home with Barry in the comfort of the school she was already starting to miss. But this was bound to happen and she knew it would. So she took her lizzier and carried on walking through like nothing had happened. The others followed with Miles trailing behind thinking to himself before he spoke his mind.

"Hey girls. How long do you think this place had been deserted for?"

Acarlie glanced up at the tall, windowless buildings looking down on them all and spoke over her shoulder while still pulling the reigns of her lizzier, "I don't know Miles. Years maybe. Maybe more."

"What's your point?" Sheeria asked now and looking back and raising an eyebrow but keeping an ear out for the riders again.

"Because I think it's been years since anyone has lived here too."

"You're still not to the point," Sheeria stated.

"My point is that those bodies have only been there in that large bin for a week. Maybe two or three. If they have been there for years then they would have decomposed by now," he explained. Acarlie nodded understanding what he meant.

"Maybe they are travellers Miles."

They passed another dark alleyway with the cold night wind now whistling like a deathly warning. Sheeria walked past and sniffed the air and listened closely but could sense nothing over the smell of rot and decay.

"Doesn't that bother you more so Acarlie? If that's what people do to travellers..." he started but Sheeria cut him off instantly.

"Stop scaring Acarlie Miles. We are going to walk through this place, safe and unnoticed. It was a mistake coming here. With any luck we..."

She stopped mid-sentence as the wind changed. She sniffed from her large tigian nose. Acarlie noticed and stopping the march.

"What's wrong Sheeria?"

Sheeria scanned the area around them. Her ears twitched and her pupils dilated in her concentration. Eventually she saw and heard nothing and relaxed, "Nothing," she said.

They continued walking down the dark streets, shrouded in darkness and the biting cold of the deathly wind. Shadows moved from the darkness, careful in their step, wary of the ever hearing tigian admits their walking prey. They watched the travellers with beady red eyes. Their teeth broken and sharpened to rip and tear flesh as they crept from shadow to shadow, disappearing into the void of darkness of silence. Acarlie soon came to a crossroads. Light was a stranger here. The electricity was down and stretched down in blocks of dark and deserted buildings. Trees that were once tall and full of life were now black gangly skeletons that reached from the ground with pointy, grotesque wooden fingers to cut the air. Their leaves decomposed and scattered to join the debris that danced in the wind.

"It's getting too dark to continue forward. We should make camp here," she suggested and having to pull her cloak tight to her as the cold wind crept down her back and gave her a chill.

"If we camp here we do it with no fires. Predators will be able to smell and see our fire for miles. I say we make shelter in one of the buildings," Miles suggested.

Acarlie turned to face him but screamed as she saw two hands with long black fingers with pointy nails creep from behind his shoulders. Before he realised what was happening a figure appeared from his back and sprang up and bit down into his neck. He screamed, reached up and pulled the slippery, naked figure off him and threw him to the floor, drew Razor from its scabbard and stabbed its chest. The short, black figure whined and wailed in a screech that alerted the whole block.

"Shut that thing up!" Sheeria shouted and pounced on it herself before Miles had a chance and twisted its head breaking its neck. Acarlie panted in shock and horror as Miles stood holding onto a bleeding wound on his shoulder, "What on Sphere was that thing?" she asked looking down at it. It lay before them slightly shorter than a human with a bald head, red eyes and its skin looked oily, black from dirt and grime. It had a tail that resembled an aeomon and long uncut nails turned to claws on hands of five fingers. Out from the silent darkness leapt another, screeching in feral wildness and landed on Acarlie to pull on her hair and bite at her skin. She screamed horrifically and tried to push the naked wildling off her. Sheeria quickly grabbing it from behind and picking it off her and throwing it away when more appeared, trapping them and pouncing like wolves to prey. Miles slashed and cut with his perfectly sharpened sword, kicking them away but they only screeched for reinforcements, hunching on the ground like monkeys and slashing with sharp nails and teeth. Miles's lizzier was pulled away from the group and separated. The wildlings jumped up and pounced on the poor lizzier. It screamed as they bit into its long scaly neck before falling. Once on the floor they climbed over her, dug deep into her flesh and began tearing her apart and feasting on her insides. She moaned and Miles cried but could not reach her for fear of himself being consumed by these small beasts. Blood flew all around and the sound of her moans became the tearing sound of flesh and the crunching of breaking bones as they managed to pull her limb from limb and carry her away in portions. Some parts of her needed to be carried by two or three of them as they descended back into the abyss of the night. One was pulling on Acarlie's hair while she screamed and kicked trying to drag her away but she managed to punch it and throw it back. It hissed at her and pounced again but flew sideways when a crossbow bolt from a side pierced its skull and sent it to a twisted heap on the floor. The small wildlings all turned their attention now and hissed at the darkness before crawling away. Sheeria ran to Acarlie and held her in her arms while Acarlie shook and whimpered in her fright and shock.

"What's happening!?" Acarlie cried and clutched onto Sheeria's fur tightly.

"Halt!" Came a sudden and strong voice from the darkness around them. They looked to see nothing but from out behind an overturned M.V came a young man covered from head to toe in leaves and sticks, dirt and dust and carrying a crossbow. This man looked different from the riders and looked more like a survivor than a savage. He approached them slowly holding up his crossbow steadily and cautiously.

"Who are you and why are you here? If you had any sense you would leave this place immediately and never turn back."

Miles stood forward still holding onto his bleeding shoulder to answer him but it was Acarlie to speak up first.

"Help us! We mean you no harm. We are only passing by to reach Lachine…" she stood up and finally let go of Sheeria. Her legs still trembled but she composed herself and walked toward him.

"Stay back where you are!" he called back to her and she carried on.

"I...I am on a sacred journey to reach Lachine. My name is Elementalist Acarlie. I am an elementalist from Eloma and I..."

As soon as she mentioned the word *Elementalist* he lowered his crossbow and they all saw many other people coming out from hiding places around them, all dressed like he was.

"Elementalist? Prove it. Prove to me that you are an elementalist."

She felt relieved when she saw more of them were there. There must be a group of survivors here she thought. She thought for a second how she would prove to them and then went down to her knees looking for all the dirt and dust on the cold, concrete floor. She then gently moved her hands across the floor and a small ball of wind carrying millions of dust particles arose from the floor and she gently guided it to float to his feet and fall over his boots. He and all the others around him were suddenly convinced and came to her.

"You must come with me at once Elementalist. All three of you. We shall take your lizziers to a safe spot but right now we must take you to our leader. He must see you immediately before the Night Feeders come."

"Lizziers!" Miles cried in despair. "Where were you when Kelly was being torn into pieces? She was my lizzier. She was a damn good lizzier!"

"Miles, please," Acarlie pleaded and went to Miles. She could see his upset and despair of losing his friend and sympathised with him. "I'm sorry what happened but we can't afford not to trust these people. Please, I don't want to be here for another minute. This place scares me."

"I know but—"

"Miles!" Sheeria cut in silencing him. "We are leaving this place with these people. If you want to speak to them about your lizzier then do it later. Right now we have to get the Elementalist away from this dangerous place."

Miles, still holding onto his wound bit his tongue and silenced himself. They didn't have any time to ask any questions as the camouflaged people came and took their lizziers and ran with them down the alleyways. They were guided down the streets and the man with the crossbow led them to a manhole. He stopped and looked to the tops of the buildings. Acarlie looked up and saw some more people on the tops of the buildings, looking around and finally giving a thumbs-up signal to the man with the crossbow. He lifted the manhole and climbed down a ladder and signalled for the other three to come down with him. Miles was the last to climb down and when he did the people behind him closed up the manhole and quickly disappeared. Within a couple of seconds the streets was as empty as it had been only a short while ago and back to being the desolate and lonely street with the echo of screams whispering in the air. The smell of the sewage was terrible but none of them complained. The man looked back at them and said, "We are not safe yet. Stay close to me and don't make a sound, not even a squeak. If you start speaking or shouting once we're down here I'll kill you myself. Do you understand? Nod if you understand."

They all nodded clearly so he saw. He then nodded and turned and led them away. Acarlie knew not to make any noise but all she wanted to do was to say how bad this place stank but kept to her silence. They walked along muddy dirty sewage pipes running under the city and occasionally they passed some other folk who just like their guide just patted each other on the shoulder and carried on. After walking for a while, the man signalled them to stop and put his finger to his mouth. He pointed to a small vent that led back onto the streets where shadows and humanoids were running around up there like crazy animals screaming and shouting not making any real words but more like feral wild noises. Blood trickled from the drains above and Acarlie looked back to see Miles was deeply upset knowing it was the blood of his trusty lizzier that now stained the walls in long streams and drizzled down to the filth under their feet. He led them slowly underneath the feast above them and silently down another ladder, down more pipes which now they could see was like a maze only the residents knew the way and finally to a huge metal door. Instead of banging on to it the man went to a brick in the wall and pulled it out and stuck his hand through. The three didn't see but on his wrist was a tattoo of a bar code and he shook hands with the man guarding the door after having it scanned. He pulled his hand back through and put the brick back. The door was opened slowly to make as little noise as possible.

11

Once the door was closed the man spoke again. Thanking them for their cooperation and led them round what was his home. Something had gone terribly wrong in this city. Whatever those things were above they had obviously taken the city from these folk and forced them into hiding. Only soldiers and trained hunters and scouts would go outside and scavenge for food. He led them down more ladders deeper until they reached the ground floor and there they saw the community of people. From the number of people that lived in the city only a few hundred remained. All forced out of their homes, torn away from their loved ones and made to live deep down under the city away from the beasts above them. The underground village was huge but dark being a giant dugout cavern that stretched into blackness the light didn't reach. As far as they could see were tiny huts spaced closely together made of mud and pieces of scrap metal. An air vent above them blew some fresh air around but the smell of dirt and sweat was unmistakable. Many of the village's lights were hanging from the ceilings giving a dim orange glow to the place with many of the bulbs flickering once in a while. Dirt covered the walls and in some dark spots a watery sludge fell from the ceiling and walls leaving puddles of black water that some kids were playing in. Many of the men here were miners as they walked past them with their pickaxes and helmets. It was clear that these people had lived here for some time, even years at a time. Some kids had really pale skin from lack of direct sunlight but they still were running around joyfully, playing and chasing each other. There were only a handful of shops. Some that only sold food such as butchers and bakers and some selling warm clothing. The rest were huts and homes stretching all the way down the large cavern.

The man led them through the centre, past all the workers, miners, women and children and straight into a large hut that looked like a headquarters of whoever lived there. He didn't stop to tell them anything about the place. He seemed too much in a hurry and burst through the main door and into the hut with only one large room with some people sitting and working on the side. In the middle, sat in a large grand chair showing his importance, was a man. He was at the time reading some files that one of his workers gave him previously and when he saw his companion charge in with three strangers he stood up immediately.

"Travis, what are you doing? What is the meaning of this? Who are these people?"

As he walked closer Acarlie noticed that under his long unwashed hair was a dirty cloth covering up his left eye. The man looked tired. Like he had worked all his life and was now on the verge of retirement. His pale skin covered in wrinkles and mud showed his age but this might have been work and stress related she wondered. He walked up to the man carrying the crossbow named Travis and waited for a reply.

"Begging your pardon sir. This is very important. I wouldn't have brought them here otherwise."

"What's wrong my friend? You look very nervous."

"Sir, these people were spotted wandering around outside by myself and Bravo Team. We saved them from an attack from the Night Feeders but it was brought to my attention that the young pretty one before you is an elementalist. It seems the young man and the tigian are her Guides."

Now the look from the man suddenly changed and he understood immediately why Travis was in such a hurry.

"Is this true? Are you really what he said you were?" he asked turning to Acarlie.

Acarlie then stood forward and looked up to the man in front of her, looked him in his eye and said, "Yes sir, that's true. My name is Acarlie and this is Sheeria and Miles. We have come here from Eloma only to pass through to reach Lachine. We were on our way through when we were attacked. We lost one of our lizziers in the confusion but were fortunate as this man found us and escorted us here." She gestured to Travis, turned back to him and smiled in gratitude. The man looked happy with relief then patted Travis on the shoulder.

"Good work Travis. You got them all here safe and unharmed," then he called out to all the people around to go and leave them in peace with the new arrivals. In a matter of minutes of standing up and shifting around, the room was empty apart from Acarlie, Sheeria, Miles and the man standing alone in the dark and dirty, open room.

He introduced himself first as Mack and took their names again and gave them a place to sit then firstly began telling them what had happened. "Don't worry, you three are safe now. Before I tell you why you are here let me tell you what happened to us and why we are down here.

"We were all town folk once. Just like you, living under the sun and getting on with our lives peacefully and quietly. We were a peaceful community trading with all the biggest cities around the country but we were overrun by savage creatures that destroyed our beautiful city and killed many of us. For several weeks we ran the streets just like they do now fearing not to stay in one place for any time and soon we found a place down here where they could not find us and we have been mining here making our space bigger for nearly ten years now. I myself was a checkout boy for a small store when it all happened. It was late at night when the first of them came, stealing from our garbage or fridges and we only took notice by arresting or banishing them from the city. But within a matter of days their numbers doubled and doubled again and soon we all knew that this was a serious problem.

"At first came the rape and theft reports. Soon after came the murders and after that came the reports of these creatures murdering and eating people. The city went into panic but nothing could be done. The police were all gone and we tried and tried reaching out for the closest city to us Lachine but we were never answered."

"What happened to the police?" Miles asked them still holding onto the bite marks on his neck. "It's not contagious is it?"

Mack chuckled even in his grief of telling this tale, "No son, you're quite safe. They may have bitten you but you're not going to turn into one. This isn't a ghost story, this is real. The police tried forming and attacking them but were overwhelmed in a matter of days and had to resort to fleeing and surviving on the streets like the rest of us.

"Finally, after weeks of moving from building to building and not staying in groups larger than ten came the final attack. Like a wave these creatures suddenly came flowing in and many people were killed in a matter of hours. It was a night of terror I would wish upon no man to ever witness. Women and children were seen tortured, molested, killed then eaten by these beasts and these sights sent the people who witnessed them mad themselves and they either killed themselves or others around them. The Night of Blood is what we all call it now, a date that changed the way we will live forever.

"We finally, after days of wandering around surviving the terrors of the night found refuge down here and it was my father who restarted the community. Since then we have remained down here hiding from the monsters that took our home."

"These creatures you speak of, what are they?" Acarlie asked him.

He looked to the floor with discontent. They all knew well that he was unhappy with the knowledge of who the creatures were and was reluctant to tell them.

"We called them 'Night Feeders' or 'Demons'. After a study of them we have found out that these are aeomon that have done this to us."

"Aeomon? Surely you must be mistaken? Aeomon are peaceful creatures that have been an ally to humans for centuries now," she pointed out.

"That's true but something has happened to these aeomon. Their minds are blank. They cannot speak to any other thing apart from themselves. It's like they have been turned into demons by something. Their skin is darker and their eyes look like they have no soul inside them. They run only on instinct and evil intentions. I hate to think of what they do up there when they are not chasing us."

"What about the riders?" Miles asked. "We saw some riders when we first came here. Humans on motorbikes. They rode through the city, why don't they do anything about the demons?"

"Yes the riders, they are part of the clan too. They are humans with the same interests as the aeomon but they are smarter, they talk and communicate. I have spoken to one of them only once and that's when they took my eye from me," he said pointing to the cloth covering his missing eye.

"Bastard ate it in front of me. I would have been dead if my father and his men hadn't rescued me, and sadly they took him away from me.

"The riders seem to be the leaders of the clan since they have the power and intellect. They ride around and throughout the city hunting out any passers-by or escapees."

He also went on to tell them about young teenage tear-a-ways who have tried to flee from the city to find help and never returned. They all sat and listened patiently to him tell his story and how the city, now only the population of a small town, had learned to survive by hiding.

He told them about the mazes of tunnels that none of the creatures had found their way around yet and made it back out alive. The rules and regulations of survival and how they farmed. He went on to tell them that years ago they tunnelled so far that they found themselves outside the city and tried to escape from there but the riders shortly found them. So they built a huge electric charged wall to keep the demons out but also kept themselves in. This space was soon used to grow food and cattle and even a safe place for children to run around in feeling the sun on their faces.

"But why haven't they climbed over yet or why not just charge down here with their whole clan and sniff you all out?" Miles pointed out.

"Because they don't want to. The truth is…the farming complex outside to us is what this whole underground village is to them. We are to them no more than cattle. They want to grow us so they won't run out of food supply."

When he said this they all sat in silence, shocked by this revelation. How terrible it must be for the children growing in fear that one day when they are strong enough to go outside, like Travis does. They are only harvest for the demons that conquer the ground above them. How terrifying for the mothers knowing that they are bringing up their children only to be snacks to be eaten as soon as they reach adulthood. But it was Sheeria who stood up and pointed out what should have been said when they first arrived, "What has this all to do with Acarlie? Why has she been rushed down here so quickly and why is it so important to you that she is safe?"

"I'm glad you asked because it makes this part easier for me. We know that for some reason these humans and aeomon alike are very superstitious and they believe…,," he paused and tried to say as subtly as he could so Acarlie wouldn't become afraid, "…that by eating the flesh of an elementalist, they would gain their powers. They eat all different kinds of things but they seem to believe that the blood and flesh of elementalists are sacred and holy because of the things they perform and choose to believe that only by eating them…they would change themselves to become one of them."

"What!?" Sheeria cried in anger. "Are you telling us that they not only eat people, but they especially eat the sacred elementalists of Sphere!?" In her anger she spat and roared nearly shaking the hut they stood in but Mack stood firm and true.

"I'm sorry but yes. Many have passed through. The first was from Eloma like you. Tristan was his name."

"I knew him. He left for the pilgrimage when I was only a child and in training," Acarlie pointed out remembering the man and shuddering when she thought about what he had faced.

"There have been many each from Eloma or even more experienced ones from around the globe but they have all met the same horrific fate. My father used to try and save everyone but not many apart from you have even made it this far down here where it is safe. I have been carrying on with my father's work to the best of my abilities. I truly have but I also have my people I have to look out for. Some of the elementalists would give a good fight but whenever the riders and scouts would see the forces at work they would go on a wild rampage of excitement. But everyone has met the same fate. They would be caught and tied up. All the demons would gather and celebrate in their blood, sharing every part of their body among the masses. No one has ever survived. We pray that one day the great Lord Zane would pass by and vanquish the demons forever." He spoke of Zane with a smile and a glint of hope in his eye like he generally believed that he would come. Acarlie sat for a moment to take in all what Mack had said when it hit her that this was the reason why, when the riders the night before saw the wind change so suddenly had darted off all excited. They must have been waiting for her all this time. That is what they meant by someone walking around with a large cat-like creature. It was her they were speaking about. Somehow they have caught word of her beginning her journey and now are only waiting for her to arrive to have their way with her, and there she was, stood under the ground they live on. Her heart raced as she tried to think how she could get out of this situation and realised the danger she was now in, the terrible fate she could face simply by trying to escape. She paced up and down in an uncomfortable moment of fear and confusion trying to come up with a way of escaping or just surviving. The others could see that this news distressed her so Mack said finally, "Have no fear Elementalist Acarlie. I promise you safety across the city above us and will give you all the help you need to escape from the snake-pit that is our lives." He walked up to her and put a comforting hand on her shoulder, "I know the sacred task put upon you and will give my life if it were to see you across to safety."

Acarlie didn't know how to take this and looked cynically towards him. "I thank you for the gesture, but a promised word means nothing in the situation you have put me in."

Mack backed off a little and let Acarlie speak. "Right now everyone here is in danger, especially me. You plan to get me away from an inescapable city when I myself will be the enemy's main priority?"

Mack nodded, "Please have faith in us Acarlie. We have been doing this for years."

"Without any success," she added and silenced him. He winced knowing her words were true. "Yes…without any success…but right now we're the best chance you have."

She stood staring at him and his one eye still gleaming even with his face scarred, wrinkled and dirtied. He was right, they were only travellers and knew nothing of the city above them. She finally sighed and accepted his proposal with a silent nod and looked over to Sheeria who remained silent for her. Mack stepped forward and over to the door leading outside, "Thank you Acarlie. Now all three of you, I must insist you all get as much rest as you can tonight because you will need all your strength. Zack!" he called out and a tall man walked in from behind the door. "Would you please see to it that they are rested. Show them to a bed and give them some food. Acarlie, I would like to see you here tomorrow. I will send for you."

Zack was a tall, broad man in his early thirties with the look of experience in his dark eyes. He had some small facial scars hiding behind his scruffy black hair and beard. A sign that he knew what he was doing when scouting outside with the likes of Travis and the others. His eyebrows were thick like two caterpillars sitting on his eyes and his brown eyes were aged with wisdom and awareness but with a vacant look of despair and tiredness. These were eyes that had seen many dark things and had begun to despair and almost accept their life was damned if it wasn't for the strength for the body they possessed. He wore dark green, thick trousers with large pockets. The knees were ripped and legs stained with mud and blood. His shirt was plain black and looked a little short and showed off his muscular arms. The right sleeve was torn off completely, the collar was stretched and small burn holes and scratches were scattered across the tattered old shirt. To his side was a large knife and a bow was carried on his back. Something he learned to keep by his side at all times. Acarlie looked at the tall man Zack who was seeing Sheeria and Miles out of the door then turned back to Mack to thank him then followed the others who were led to what would be called a hotel if this were a real city rather than some horribly smelling huts made that barely stood the strength of the little wind that blew down there by the vents above them. Their beds were no more than three mattresses made of straw and leather placed on a dirty floor. They were given some spare blankets that were dry but stained with mud and old dirty water.

But how was Acarlie supposed to sleep? Not for the cramped, horrible hospitality that they were given. No, they were grateful for all that these people were doing for them but the thought of the monsters that were yet to face her scared her and kept her awake. The voice of Mack saying, *No one has ever escaped*, churned around in her mind over and over again. Soon after her relentless tossing and turning Miles sat up and spoke to her.

"I know you are afraid Acarlie. We all are. Even Sheeria must feel the cold chill of fear once in a while but you must put it aside and get to sleep. Otherwise you will not have the energy to escape it, and forever we will stay down here, sleeping on these beds of straw and hoping the demons above us never come down."

Acarlie turned and smiled to Miles feeling more safe but still with the unsettledness of fear and paranoia, "I can't sleep Miles. All I can think about is those aeomon and humans above us who want us dead. What possibly could have happened to these men to have changed them into what we saw out there?" She sat up and sighed as the memories of their attack came flooding back. She shivered when she caught a glimpse of their faces. "I have seen and met many aeomon in my time and I have never seen anything like that before. They were not...aeomon, nor were the humans...human. They were like animals, wild and feral, like there was not a shred of sophistication, of thought or of anything civil in their minds."

Miles could clearly see the demons in her mind were keeping her awake by the way she held her hands over her head and tried to shake them out. He reached out and touched her shoulder and pulled her towards him. She pressed her head against his chest and wrapped her arms around him.

"It's going to be ok Acarlie. I'll cut my way out of this city if I need too...I'll keep you safe, both you and Sheeria."

Acarlie smiled hearing the comforting words of the solider in her arms and nuzzled against him.

"Thank you Miles."

He said nothing more but stroked her head and waited for her to sleep before lying her back down and sat in the silence of the hut and listened in the cold, damp darkness around him. All he could hear was the steady breathing patterns of the sleeping Elementalist and her Guide and distant footsteps of the town's people still awake. He closed his eyes and breathed in. When he opened his eyes he looked at the ceiling. Above him was only some old wooden beams with dry straw over their heads but somewhere high above them all were the monsters above them. Their enemy now knew they were here and were only waiting, planning and hiding in the darkness of shadows of this forsaken city. Tomorrow would be a day to remember.

12

The next day they were fed properly and given time to ready themselves, but the overwhelming tension on the whole experience still shook Acarlie and she remained silent for hours. Children ran past her as she sat up against a wall with her head on her knees.

"Are you the elementalist everybody has been speaking about? The one that is going to escape from here forever, away from the monsters?" Acarlie looked up to a young girl before her with innocence in her eyes and a gleam of hope Acarlie dared not to destroy.

"Yes, I am her who you speak of. The one who will get out of here," she lied with a brave smile for the young girl.

"Will you bring some people here to help us?"

Acarlie smiled at this and said, "Yes, I will bring a whole army with me to kill the monsters and give you back your home."

The little girl smiled so much then it nearly brought Acarlie to tears with that lie, knowing very well that the chances of her really getting out are poor. She was not as powerful as the previous elementalists who tried and failed. What hope does she have? The little girl who believed the white lie ran around her friends screaming the news that this all mighty elementalist would escape and bring back an army to free them all and they all then got as excited as she was and ran around loudly, dancing and jumping, dreaming of a life without fear, something Acarlie knew then she had taken for granted. It was Zack who came and sat down beside her then and spoke to her for the first time. He tried to speak some words of encouragement and advice, for he knew she was afraid and didn't want to upset her.

"I know you're scared Elementalist but please try not to worry too much. It will cloud your thoughts when you need it most."

Acarlie looked up at the man. He was a large man with a strong composure to himself but looked down on her with compassion and patience. There was a kindness in his eyes that Acarlie felt comforted by. He looked like he knew what he was talking about and decided to take his word for it.

She nodded,"Please, call me Acarlie. It feels weird being called Elementalist," she said pulling her black hair away from hiding her face and with a small band she always kept, tied it to her hair keeping it back. The layered pieces of hair that wouldn't reach fell back down to her fringe and over her face. Zack gave her a comforting smile and nodded.

"Will you be up there with us?" she asked him.

"Yes, so will many of us. We will try and help you the best way we can. It is not only because we have failed before that Mack wants to help you so much."

"Then why is it?"

"Because you have the best chance of survival because of your gift. If we can see you out here safely, we trust you will help us in return."

Acarlie said nothing then. She just put her head back on her knees and tried not to think about it. They all knew this was a lot of pressure to put on a single person but it needed to be done. She really was their only hope. Soon afterwards Zack took them back to Mack. They never knew how long they were down there because with all the artificial light they found it hard to tell the time. Mack never said much as they left, only to stay close to Zack and follow his instructions. He whispered something in Zack's ear then wished them luck before seeing them out. Acarlie asked him why he wouldn't be joining them and his only reply was, "I must gather all my people who can and will fight. Have no fear Acarlie, I will not let you down. Just promise me that when you do escape, send help for us down here."

"I promise Mack, we will not forget about you."

Then they were escorted back up the ladders to the huge metal door and told to stay silent as before as soon as the door opened. Zack led them through the sewers, pointing at puddles and drops or something that would make any noise at all.

The sewers were deadly silent but soon Zack caught the sound of something hustling around nearby. They came up to a T-junction in the sewers where the sound of splashing water and grinding of teeth was heard that could not be human, for all the grave warnings to remain silent they would go through before passing through the sewers. He signalled them to stay still then and peered round a corner, then turned and silently moved around the other side and vanished around another corner. Acarlie and the others knew then he had gone around an alternative route. They all stood silent looking at one another not knowing what to do other than stay still and silent. But it was Acarlie who moved forward to peek round the corner at what was nearby them. She crouched and slightly poked her head around being careful not to be seen and saw another demon that Mack spoke of. It was the size and shape of an aeomon, tail and all. It was squatting naked with its skin oily jet black like it had been burned or mutated. Its eyes were red and head was bald. Its hands holding on to a squirming rat that it had caught and was trying to kill it by smashing it on the floor and biting into it. It continued doing this until the rat stopped moving and the demon started eating it regardless of the diseases it may have carried. The rat squeaked once and burst like a ripe tomato as the demon bit into its belly and leaked blood to trickle down its throat. Acarlie waited and watched this creature for a short while when she saw Zack appear behind it. His knife ready and waiting for its first kill of the night, slowly creeping towards it. Without a sound he covered the demon's mouth and brought his knife to its throat, slicing it across and bringing the demon to the floor silently. His hand now covered in blood signalled for the others to follow him and he picked up the demon and headed forward. They never knew why he did this until another man crossed his path, saw the dead body and took it from Zack and threw it over his shoulder, patted Zack on the shoulder and disappeared back to the underground village. They then realised that this was another rule the people had to live by. The bodies of rotting flesh would catch the attention of the demons and bring them down to their homes. So they would carry the dead and dispose of the bodies properly.

Zack found the correct ladder and took them to the surface and back out into the night air of the dead city. The cold but fresh air felt good on their faces and they could see that it pleased Zack too. He had led them back out onto the street in the dead of night and kept them in the shadows, taking them around big bins mostly of dead flesh like before. This time with the others silent and listening they could hear the cries and shouts of the demons nearby and said no word to another. One street at a time Zack lead them. He kept close up to the buildings and took the darkest of alleys, stopping every time he heard a bump, scratch or distant call of the lurking enemy. His hand was at all times holding firmly onto his bow and the other hand he used to signal the others behind him. As safe as Acarlie felt with Zack, Sheeria and Miles protecting her she had never felt so tense and scared. This was like nothing she had ever done in her sheltered life. Before she would maybe creep outside her dormitory and past the elders when she should have been asleep in her youth but never did she have to feel the fear of being caught of something that would jump on her, rip her to pieces and devour her. Her breath caught in her throat every time Zack held up his hand signalling to stop and clutched onto Sheeria. Zack would not move but stayed down and listened and looked out with his keen eyes into the inert city. The place was deathly silent, even the wind and vermin stayed away from this place and nothing but the silvery moonlight dared to enter with them. Zack squinted and waited before finally continuing on guiding them.

Their journey went safely until they cut through an alley and a young boy not much younger than Acarlie and Miles came up and whispered a hello to Zack.

"These are the people we are trying to help boy. Let the others know because we will need guidance from the rooftops above."

"Right you are Zack. I'll go tell them now."

The kid seemed wet under the ears with these instructions as he ran loudly not caring for the demons around and went to shout up a wall. Zack saw that the boy was being too loud and noticeable and would alert the demons scouting and hiding in the darkness. But he couldn't stop or shout to him and concentrated on keeping Acarlie, Sheeria and Miles safe and in the shadows behind one of the large city bins. The boy called out to the others hiding above them in all but a loud whisper but it wasn't enough. He was too inexperienced in this job and should have been with someone who could have stuck by him and taught him properly because the people above him never said anything nor even showed their faces and soon the boy knew why. The boy suddenly knew he was being too loud and turned around to look at Zack hiding. Knowing where he was the boy made eye contact and saw Zack only slightly waved for him to quietly move back to him in hiding. But as Zack did this he noticed the boy was now not looking at him. His eyes fixed on something behind them at the end of the alley.

Standing at the end of the dark alley, staring at the boy with wild, hungry eyes was one of the demons. He didn't even need to call as two more came beside him, saw the poor defenceless boy and walked toward him. The boy was smart though and did not give Zack's position away by looking at him which would endanger the other three and turned to run. Acarlie could do nothing but watch as Zack steadied her from moving, holding her and making sure she made neither movement or made a sound. The three demons walked past them all without noticing, concentrating on the boy who had now turned to run but was cornered by another two coming from the other way. The boy, now trapped drew out his blade to try and defend himself but this only turned the demons into a defensive mode that immediately sprang up and pounced on him. Acarlie watched in horror as the boy screamed, knowing help wasn't coming. The demons grabbed and ripped at his limbs and bit into him like dogs to a steak. Blood soon sprayed up as vital arteries were cut and torn and the boy screamed now in pain, something that all four of them there would never forget the sound of. The demons finally managed to rip off one of his arms and throw it aside to carry on. Now as they were still ripping and clawing and biting at him, Zack knew they would not notice them and started moving back down the alley. Acarlie and the others followed, leaving the poor slaughtered child behind. They had to leave the boy behind, who now screamed no more, was not a person with feelings and opinions anymore. He now only existed as raw meat for the demons and a story to scare the kids for years to come.

Acarlie was covering her mouth the whole time as they now escaped from the alley and ran down the empty dark street and into one of the shops. Its windows smashed and the shelves empty and dusty. They stopped to take a breath, sobbing now Acarlie could not hold her silence anymore, "They...they killed him, tore him apart like vicious animals, and we stood there and watched...we did nothing but stand there and watch him die."

"There was nothing we could do," Zack said. "He knew the dangers. He knew the risk. That's why he never ran to us or called out to us. He believed in you so much—"

"Oh stop it Zack, stop it!" Acarlie snapped now, with eyes full of tears. "Stop talking like I'm this amazing saviour of your village. I'm no more experienced than any of the others that have came and died here. What is it that I have that the others don't?"

But Sheeria was the one to speak now, looking out the window and seeing many of the demons now creeping toward them.

"Zack, they have found us. If you know a way out of here I suggest you take us there now in a hurry."

"Sod all this creeping about. I'm sick of it all" Miles now said as he drew Razor from its sheaf, "If they want to take us then they're gonna have to get through me first." He stood outside the building and made it clear that he was ready for a fight. Acarlie tried to call out for him to stop but he did not listen. The demons were the first to attack, trying to pounce on him but he quickly slashed at them. His blade cutting through their skinny limbs easily and sent them screaming back from where they came. But he was still heavily outnumbered and would only be able to hold them off for a short while. Acarlie and the others never knew this but what she said before was wrong. She *did* have something that the other elementalists never had. Something that the demons had never faced before, and that was a tigian named Sheeria. She pounced out from the store to help defend Acarlie with Miles. Her hands were big enough to hold one of the demon's head in the palm of her hand which gave her a very good advantage as she picked up one of them and lifted it up. As it was struggling in her hand she threw the demon face down to the floor. A large crunch was heard as its skull cracked on the ground and the demon started furiously twitching in its death. She grabbed another and swung it around and threw it straight into more of them with enough force to knock them all down, then picking another up by its foot and as if it only weighed a few kilograms, swung it up and smashed it down on the floor. It squeaked as its rib cage burst open and sent blood to splatter on the concrete around it and roared so loud she started to scare some of the demons around her. They suddenly started to hesitate about attacking and everyone which did had either a swipe of her sharp claws across their face or ripping out the bottom of their stomachs. Miles cut down demon after demon which crossed his path but more and more came and it was after he slashed one demon across its throat and left it gurgling in its own blood when he heard the sound of motorbikes coming in the distance. Their engines whirling and droning, drowning out the silence of the night and calling the attention of everything in the city to them. He called over to Sheeria and Zack, warning them of what was to come.

The demons now started jumping onto the tigian trying to over-power her by numbers and soon Sheeria would be worn down and too tired to fight back. She found herself surrounded by them.

They tried to pounce on her back, encouraging another to follow but she was too strong for even three of them on her back. She grabbed two of them clinging on to her back and smashed their heads together and threw them back into the demons standing in front of her, reading them, working out the right time to make a move. She did not stop clawing and throwing her attackers. They pulled at her orange fur, bit her, punched her and kicked at her until she bruised but she remained strong in her resolve to protect Acarlie. Soon however the first of the human demons appeared, stinking of gasoline and blood and to the charging sound of the bike's engine. She knew she could take the aeomon and even some of the humans on but if they kept coming there would be nothing she could do. The rider stepped off his bike and pulled out a metal pole ready to start pummelling her with it. She just finished biting into an aeomon when she looked up to see the human. His hand holding the pole raised but before she could blink, from out of nowhere came an arrow, piercing the human between the eyes. She looked to see Zack. His bow raised and sending more arrows to the aeomon around her.

When Zack stopped firing his arrows he saw that this would be a losing battle very soon and ran back to the shop to Acarlie hiding under a counter, something he told her to do previously.

He pulled her up. Her face pale, her limbs shaking with absolute fear and tears in her eyes. Her eyes were facing down at the floor like she was going into shock.

"Look at me Acarlie, look at me!" he shouted shaking her arms. She looked up at him.

"Listen to me! You have to go, run away as fast as you can. Try and get to the higher levels of the buildings. Do you understand Acarlie? You have to go!"

He let her go and saw that she had taken in what he said.

"I…I can't abandon Sheeria…I can't. She wouldn't abandon me and neither would Miles. I just can't!"

"Don't you see? They're fighting out there for you! They're giving you a head start. Now go!"

He pushed her toward a back door and watched her run away on her own in the dark alleys she had no idea were leading her to and turned back to the other side. The demons were still mounting up and Miles was fighting against one of the humans when he saw Zack and tried to call for help. Zack saw the mounting odds stacking against them as more and more wild aeomon and humans began pouring from the corners of the city, screeching their war cries and waving sticks and pipes as weapons. He turned and ran away, hopped over a fence without being chased by the demons now fixated on Miles and Sheeria.

"Come back here Zack, you coward!" he heard Miles call from afar, "COWARD!"

13

The streets were dark, cold and frightening for Acarlie as she ran through the back streets on her own. Fires were still blazing in some places made by pyromaniac demons and the smell of death was unmistakably strong, fogging up the air and in some corners made Acarlie change direction rather than run past it. She ran uncontrollably and without direction around the city. She didn't know where to go or where she was and soon she was completely lost. The sound of Sheeria and Miles fighting was now long gone and she knew she was totally alone. She ran until her feet and lungs burned. She stopped running to catch her breath back and hid in a tall building. There was a security desk in the front of it and she ran and hid behind it, pulled her knees to her chin in the cold and wept. She wept until her eyes were sore and her hands were wet from wiping her face, thinking about the terrible things that just happened and the questions in her mind raced. *Where are Sheeria and Miles? What has happened to them? Why did Zack leave me to run alone? He knew I didn't know my way, and oh, what will happen to me if they ever find me?*

A sudden loneliness struck her and she found herself trembling. She was lost in this city of death and now the two moons high up in the sky comforted her no more with the promise of light but mocked her being so safe in the sky and away from the evil she was centred in. She thought about Eloma again and wished to herself she was back at home in the school under the stadium. All these years she wanted to leave that place and now only a few days after leaving she wished she was back with Argo and Barry in the comfort of her own room, in her own bed again and to the feel of warmth of heating and security once more. She then thought about when Mack whispered something to Zack. Could it be that he told him to run at the sign of danger? What if all the people wanted to do was exchange her for their freedom?

She thought until her tears had dried and she knew she had to get away. The demons didn't know where she was. If she stuck to the shadows and ran in one direction, she would eventually find her way out. She couldn't go back down into the sewers, she would get lost in the tunnels before ever finding the village. No, this was the best option she thought and decided to get to her feet again and run back out on the street.

She ran until her legs tired again and she had to walk. Everything around her was silent again. The air was stagnant and still and only fear was her companion against the isolation. She walked lost and alone in the tall, dark city with no sign of a rising sun for hours. Her companions gone and her guide fled. She walked with no compass nor stars and only her naïve sense of direction to guide her further into the lost and dammed concrete jungle. Shattered windows scattered broken glass on the dark grey pavement around her feet which crunched and tinged when stepped on, alerting everything around her and rolling, windswept trash soon sung her position if she stayed too long. The shadows behind her began to twitch, stretch and morph. Her stealthy stalkers prowled behind her slowly, taking their time. She was unaware of their presence until she heard one climb up onto a balcony and knocking the dust off onto some metal bins below. She looked up in horror as the demon was staring down at her. Its red eyes beaming down on her, calculating her, waiting for her to act. She did not hesitate and ran for her life. Behind her she heard the demon call out to more with a blood curdling screech that sent a chill through her bones and made her blood feel cold. More appeared then, overwhelmed with excitement as they started screaming to each other like monkeys and began chasing her. She turned into an alley and remembered Zack telling her to get to higher levels of the buildings and saw a door to her left. She threw herself at the door, bursting through it and slamming it behind her and looked immediately for some stairs. She found some down a corridor and started running up them, missing two and three steps at a time. When she got to the top of the stairs she had to turn a sharp corner and climb some more. She heard the door she had entered burst open again like it had been charged at, as the demons, now inside the building started running for her, reaching the bottom of the staircase when she was only half way up. The chase wasn't over yet though she thought while she was desperately running up them. The demons called and screeched to her as they ran up the stairs. Some were only grabbing the metal railings and jumping over them. The stairway corridor was narrow and every corner was sharp which gave the demons an advantage, using their tails to jump higher than she could and climb the stairs quicker. At the top she found a door she opened and closed behind her. She looked for a lock or something she could barricade the door with but couldn't find anything. She was on the roof of the tall building now and had to catch her breath before carrying on. She looked around and found herself trapped on the roof. The only way of escaping was another part of the building that stood higher to her left. She tried running and jumping but could not reach it. The only other way was back down the stairs or straight down, which to her was out of the question. She soon heard the sound of the demons getting closer to the door. Soon she thought they would burst open the door, but something else made her jump out of her skin. From the ledge she couldn't reach behind her jumped a shadow in the corner of her vision. She looked in horror believing that the demons found another way up and saw Travis standing before her.

He helped her to her feet and she hugged him tightly.

"Thank goodness I found you. I thought I was going to−"

"It's not over yet Elementalist. Here, let me help you up," Travis said. His words were hasted because he knew he didn't have much time and helped Acarlie up the ledge.

"Now remember Elementalist!" he called up to her from the bottom. She looked down and listened to him, "You must escape at any means necessary. There is a window to another building behind you…"

The door smashed through and demons were now on the roof with them. Travis pointed his crossbow at them and shot at them, catching one in the stomach and another in its shoulder but there were too many of them. "…Jump through it!" he finally roared as the demons jumped over him. Acarlie could only stand and watch as he threw them off his back but was being nudged to the edge of the building when his foot tripped and he fell over it to his death, pulling down two of the screeching demons with him.

She looked around and just like he said there was a small glass window adjacent to the end of the building's platform she stood on. She ran to the end and looked down and had instant vertigo as she looked at what could potentially be her death in only a matter of seconds but the demons were now climbing the ledge so she had to make her decision quickly. She took a few steps back and wished herself luck, ran and jumped as high as she could, hoping she didn't miss and was heavy enough to break the glass. Her jump was straight and true as she smashed through the glass onto an open room of the building. The room looked to have been cleared out years ago, open and unstable. The soft, old floor shook when she struck and rolled. She knelt with her scratched and bleeding arms stretched out and shivered in terror as she felt the whole floor tremor beneath her. Her heart raced so fast she could not think of what to do but whimpered in pain and fear and the floor broke from under her and sent her screaming down to a lower floor in a great crash of dust and rubble. She hit the floor again and rolled in agony and hit a wooden door. She lay dazed and injured until she could hear the sound of screeching and wailing aeomon still contempt in the chase and began to try to jump after her. Instead they fell with a slam and crashed down in a broken heap. She whimpered and forced her legs to lift her up and staggered through the door to find a way out of this building quickly. She again found more staircases leading up and as much to her burning thighs' dissatisfy started sprinting up the stairs, turning when she reached the end to climb the next case with the demons screeching and calling behind her once more. They found a way from one building to another and continued chasing her up the stairs getting closer every second. She eventually reached another door leading onto the top of another building and back into the cold night air. This time she had somewhere to run to as she saw a lower landing she could jump to. She ran and jumped again but misjudged her landing and fell hard on her leg. She screamed loud hoping her leg wasn't broken and got to her feet again and started limping away. She found another lower landing. This time climbing down to it and made her way to the edge. This time she really was trapped. She now had run out of places to run and had the choice of facing the wrath of the pursuing evil or jumping from the building and dying like all the rest of the elementalists that walked into this city. She felt like she couldn't breathe when she saw them approach. Their red eyes glowing with excited hunger and howling in success of the chase. Her eyes began to burn and she stepped back until her heels clipped the edge of the building and cut into the sky. Her blood froze and she stepped forward away from the edge. Her whole body tingled in horror from the bottom of her feet and up to her gums and behind her ears. She began to weep and break down as they slowly approached. They got her to the edge of the building but did not jump for her. They waited, staring at her with their evil, red eyes. They were waiting for something, trapping her and making sure she could not move anywhere. She stood there trembling. Her tired legs wanted her to crouch down but her adrenaline and fear forced her steady on her feet. Her muscles weak and her body was exhausted, her mental composure shattered by her surrounding doom. She could run no more, she wouldn't even have the energy to defend herself when they did attack. This tension was now too much for her. She decided if they were going to kill her then she wanted them to get it over with rather than making her wait. She started shouting and taunting them, "Come one!" she wailed finally feeling sick of the tension of the wait. As she screamed she felt hot tears burning her cold cheeks, "Kill me!"

Some demons tried to approach her but she still had a trick up her sleeve; she was an elementalist after all. As they snarled and approached she swung her arms to one side and a huge gust of wind took the nearby demons off their feet and sent them falling down off the building and allowed gravity to sentence them for their sins.

"Who's next?" she croaked as she was increasingly running out of energy. She fell to her knees in her exhaustion but again forced herself back up. The demons finally acted and stood apart from one another revealing a large demon, a human. His bald head and ripped leather jacket were stained with blood. His teeth rotten and broken were smiling at her evilly. In one hand he had a cloth, in another a bottle, she knew this was chloroform. She tried to resist him as he took control of her but he was too strong and she was too weak to put up any fight. He put the bottle to the cloth and then the cloth to her mouth. She smelt the sweet smell of the toxic liquid as it turned to vapour and slowly she lost consciousness in the tall humanoid demon's arms.

She woke slowly. Her head swimming and aching terribly. She slowly tried moving her arms but found them bound. They were stretched either side of her like she was being crucified. Her feet were firmly on a platform and she found herself being tilted forward with her arms slightly back. She lifted her head to hear the sound of screaming demons, only yards in front of her. When she looked around she saw that she was in the middle of a large central park with dried mud where grass once were and dead, twisted tree barks scattered like black skeletons. Buildings were all around her and overlooking a massive crowd before her. She was tied up on the middle of a platform overlooking the demons like she was going to be sacrificed. To her left was Miles, bound up like she was, still unconscious but slowly waking. His head was covered with blood, bruises and cuts. He looked exhausted and she wanted to call to him but was still too weak to do anything. To her right was Sheeria. She was bound differently from them too. Her wrists were cuffed and supported by metal chains. The chains ran back behind a quickly made wall of scrap metal and anything they could use that was sturdy. Like the other two, her hands were separated and on either side of her but her chains were being held back by two demons from either side of the wall behind her. They pulled at her chains while she was pulling all she could but even when she tried to go around to one side of the wall her opposite hand was immediately pulled back. As strong as she was, she was helpless, being taunted by some of the smaller demons getting close to her and running away laughing, throwing stuff at her. Her roar now did nothing to the demons as they knew there was nothing she could do. In front of Acarlie was a human demon, his hands raised. She knew he must have been the leader. He called out to the other demons with an almighty scream of victory which the others in their masses followed. Next to him was a fire and what looked to be meat hanging over it cooking but to her horror, beside the fire was the clothes and the crossbow of the man who had saved her life previously.

Travis, now dead and gone was being cooked over the fire. The large human demon took parts of his carcass from the fire and threw it into the crowd in front of him. She watched as the demons started fighting over pieces of his body, grabbing his arms and ripping them in two, running away and eating them in solitude. This was the end she thought. They were going to toy with her and torture her without any remorse. They would even get thrills of hearing her screams as they cut her open and feasted on her insides just like they were doing to poor Travis. She couldn't even cry now. She felt like there was nothing she could do and no one to help her. She only hung her head in defeat realising the end of her life had come and what a terrible demonic way she would go. Now even the people from the underground she believed had forsaken her would not help her. She heard Sheeria who had seen her awake try and call for her.

"Use your power!" she called over, her hands still bound, pulling her up against the wall.

Sheeria looked over desperately to see Acarlie, who couldn't shout so she mouth the words,

"I can't." Because her hands were bound back there was nothing she could do with them.

"Help me," she mouthed again and began to weep and Sheeria tried with all her strength to pull herself free. She managed to take a few steps forward but was pulled back hard, falling on her back, then back to the wall. Miles soon woke up and started moving, struggling to free himself but found he was unable to do anything.

"Silence!" boomed the voice of the large demon leader. Everything stopped. Even the feral, wild demons stopped what they were doing and concentrated on him. He called out to his followers slowly and loudly so they all could hear him,

"Now we will finally taste the flesh of the Elementalist. May the magic in her blood pass through into us like it was told to us by the masters!"

The crowd roared and Acarlie thought to herself, *who told them this? Who are their masters?*

He drew out a knife and held it high for them to see and took a step back and looked at Acarlie

"Stop!" Acarlie shouted out. "You have got it wrong. There is no magic in me and there is no such thing as magic! You will kill me for nothing!"

"Shut up witch! That's what they all say. They all say the same thing about no magic, all of them but our masters tell us you all would say that. They tell us you all lie. You all lie to save your magical blood. They tell us if we eat the elementalists we will become like elementalists and become Gods, that's what our masters tell us!"

"Who are your masters? They are wrong! Who are your– ARGHH!" She screamed as he used the knife to cut under her forearm. The blood flowed down the blade like the lubricant oil of Miles's blade Razor. The demon took the knife to the edge of the platform and held it high, then run his tongue across the knife, licking the blood from it and screaming in triumph.

The crowd roared at this with excitement and wouldn't stop. The sound could be heard from a mile away she thought when she saw a shadow moving from somewhere behind her. She twisted her head to see Zack. He had not forgotten about her nor abandoned her but he was not moving toward her. He was going somewhere far more important. The demons hiding behind the wall holding onto Sheeria's chains didn't know what hit them. Zack crept up behind them and stabbed one in the back. The others were quick to realise but the one who was quicker to realise was the tigian who now had enough slack on her chain to reach around to the other chain and pull so hard the demon holding it crashed through the wall and lay before her. She quickly found a key on its waist and used it to undo her cuffs. The tigian was free.

The large demon leader tried to call for help but now she was free the demons were scared to face her again. He got out a metal pole to face her and charged at her. She was ready to pounce on him but didn't need to as a shower of arrows came flying from the buildings above them, one of them piercing the humanoid demon in his chest, knocking him to the floor. Out on the top of the buildings came the face of Mack and a hundred of his men. It seemed Zack did not desert them but ran back to get reinforcements. All while the demons were all gathered in one place to witness the death of the elementalist Mack and his people had enough time to gather, set a trap and attack them when they weren't expecting it. The demons still outnumbered the humans but this time the humans had prepared an inescapable trap of barriers with archers behind them. They had the high ground, the time to perfect their archery and most importantly what they had this time which they never had before was the tigian. Now the demons being outflanked panicked and were too scared to fight, they could not reach the humans and were more worried about the continuing arrows and crossbow bolts that rained down on their heads. Zack ran to Acarlie and untied her. When she was free she fell in his arms like she did with Travis and hugged him tight.

"Oh, Zack thank you. I thought you weren't going to come. I thought you all wanted me dead so you could make your escape."

"It's ok Acarlie, you did well. You kept yourself free for long enough for us to gather and arrange ourselves. Now wait here, I need to free Miles."

"I'll help you free him," she said and together they ran to Miles and unbound him.

They hugged each other tightly, "I thought you were dead," he said to her.

"I thought you were dead too," she told him back.

He stood up and stretched his arm. "Where's my sword?"

"Over there by the fire Miles," Zack said pointing to Razor lying by Travis's clothes and weapons.

Miles grabbed his blade and joined Sheeria in the fight once more, hacking his way through the crowd of trapped demons too scared to attack him back. Sheeria was flying through the crowd, simply picking them up by their shoulder and throwing them away making her way to the little demons who were taunting her before. She grabbed onto one of the small ones, no bigger than a small child and bit into it. Its whole chest nearly fit into her mouth and she tore it away and spat it out, slashing at another's ankles and when it fell she stamped on the poor little demon's head. Some demons were brave enough to jump on her and bite into her fur but this only made things worse. Put a few monkeys into a cage of a very upset lion or tiger and the result of which is what was happening here, just on a bigger scale. Every swipe she made with her sharp claws threw them back and if she pinned them down they had no chance. The ones who tried to escape were shot down by archers above them.

"Aim for the riders!" Mack called out to his men. "The riders must all die! And protect the Elementalist!"

The riders who managed to reach their motorbikes without being shot only started racing toward the tigian. With their leader dead they had no direction and only knew to fight. But the archers were patient and well skilled with their arrows and managed to pick some of them off.

Zack started leading Acarlie out of the danger zone of arrows and into a back alley. The archers on the ground helped her over the barrier while Zack fought and killed some of the nearby demons who were hiding and seeking shelter, then hopping over to Acarlie. He led her to some ladders on the outside of a block and followed her up. When they reached the roof the archers welcomed her to safety with a blanket to throw over her.

"How many people are here Zack?" she asked him in relief she was finally safe.

"Every man, woman and child who can hold a bow and fire it properly. The hunters and the scouts are the ones on the floor since it's more dangerous there but rest assured. You are safe now. Soon it will all be over and you can leave this place without fear. Now please go to that man over there. He is a medic and he can look at your arm. I have to help the archers."

He pointed to a man who was standing on the edge of the building with his own bow and started firing down at the demons, aiming for the humanoid riders.

Sheeria was still fighting uncontrollably like a wild animal against the decreasing number of demons around her. Miles too was simply swinging Razor at the demons, cutting off limbs and sending them away crying and mutilated. One demon jumped on his back and bit into his neck drawing blood. He fell to his knees and before he could pull it off his back an arrow shot through its face. He thought to himself just how good the archers were and thanked that at least one of them was watching over him, protecting him and pushed the dead weight off him. He didn't know where the arrow came from but knew the archer was still watching so he stood up and raised a hand to say thanks, picked up his blade and carried on. The demons surrounding Sheeria were fighting in desperation but they were too weak to do any real damage to her. But Sheeria didn't take into account how the riders were now approaching her. From out of nowhere a bike came charging through the demons, falling over and smashing straight into her. She rolled over to see the rider standing up from where she lay. She heard another come straight for her but before it could do any damage it seemed all the archers had seen this one coming and every arrow in the air was aimed at him. The arrows flew straight into him killing him instantly. The ones that missed pierced the other demons by accident and the bike was sent screeching across the floor beside her, sparks from the scraping metal lit up the floor as it skidded out into more demons. She climbed to her feet still feeling a world of pain all over her body from the bike that hit her and looked at the rider.

She recognized him as the rider who was urinating against the tree Acarlie was hiding behind.

"There is the last rider! Everybody, kill him!" Mack ordered his men.

"Actually I think the tigian has this one sir, look!" one of his men said back and pointed to the tigian as she slowly got back to her feet. The rider was staring straight at her, ready to pounce. She was growling at him waiting for him, hoping the archers would leave him be. He screamed at her but his battle cry was nothing to the roar of the tigian. They jumped into one another. He tried to hold her back holding her throat but she pulled his arm back and bit into his neck. With his flesh in her mouth she pushed him down to the floor, twisted his neck violently and felt him go limp in her mouth. With his neck now broken and a huge gash in his neck the last rider was defeated. She got up to look at the demons, now without any riders to guide them they started running away from them and fleeing. The battle was now over and the archers gave an almighty cheer as the demons fled or hid, cowering in the corners.

Miles limped over to Sheeria who fell to the floor and sat down in exhaustion, "I did it. I saved the Elementalist."

"Yes you did Sheeria. You're a damn fine guardian and guide. I'm glad I'm on your good side," he said as he sat down beside her.

"You fought well too Miles, thank you," she smiled and patted his shoulder, surrounded by the aftermath of the night and the great relief of not just their terrible night they had survived but the ten year torment and horror the people of the city of Plainess had ended.

14

After a decade of torment and fear finally over the city Plainess finally felt a sense of relief and a forgotten security. The leader of the city however was still not finished with his operation and sent many men and women out in groups into the decaying city to hunt down any remaining demons. Another group was sent to find any kind of radio equipment needed for calling help but came back with no results. A broken radio box, the wires removed by the human demons and looked to be thrown down to the smaller demons as a toy to be thrown and smashed. Mack knew their options were still limited. The demons would return once they have gathered again and found a new direction and leaders, more aggravated and willing to war with the survivors. Fleeing the city was an option that came with uncertainty and danger. He could not risk the lives of his people by fleeing now. He knew their best chance was to make a camp out in the city, to make a secure perimeter with sentries and guards watching in shifts while they waited for help. But with no radio equipment the only option was to send out a small party to the country's capital. Once again Acarlie was asked by the city to help. She was already on her way to Isolies and now Mack asked for Zack to accompany them so they may speak to the country's president and arrange for help. A small and welcomed favour for Acarlie since it now gave her a strong archer. Their journey was made paramount and gave them no rest however, Mack wanted to send them along their way as soon as possible rather than waiting and risking an early retaliated attack from their enemy. The goodbyes were quick and their lizziers were returned. Miles was given a fresh female lizzier with only an apology for the death of his previous, all were packed with enough food and blankets for them to reach their next city.

The sky glowed pink in the early hours of the morning as the sun began to rise and darkened to a blood red as they passed the final broken, grey building and took in the valleys beyond the evil and dammed city. Sheeria caught a quick glimpse of Zack as he finally saw what was beyond the city. His eyes looked to see diamonds before him. The sun dazzled in his eyes and his chest expanded as he finally breathed the soft, fresh air of morning freedom. The sun rose into the red sky, small lines of white clouds rested upon the sun's shoulders and reached out into the sky, the red tint turning purple and finally sky blue far above them and shined down over their road before them. Valleys of grasslands stretched out into the horizon. Hills overlapped one another and far forests spacing for miles across the land all glowed the greenest of greens for his eyes had only seen the blacks and greys for so long he had forgotten colour. Even the shadows cast from a tree beside him seemed warm to him. Shadows had always been both a comfort to like a security but also a warning of danger but now shade seemed welcoming to him. He smiled like a child as they journeyed and remained silent but took in everything that he had missed. The early songs of birds and the whistling of wind became like music to his ears like an ancient and forgotten song of his childhood and the smell of fresh grass, morning dew and even moist mud came to him like the perfume of a deceased mother to a child grown. By the time the sun ruled the sky with a magnificent yellow glow they were now a few miles from the city and all around them were fields and the old, stony path before them with trees on either side. A small hill leading to a wooden bridge that crossed over a stream crossed their path and so there did they decided they were far away enough to finally rest from all the excitement of last night. There was shade under some trees and soft grass on the bottom of the hill where they camped. They let their lizziers drink from the stream while they laid down their heads on blankets and ate some biscuits the city packed for them. Acarlie felt so tired and laid down her head and stared up to the trees above her and watched the leaves above her dance and sway and allow the bright blue light of the sky beam through the gaps and down on her in a hypnotic and therapeutic image. The sound of the stream was soothing to her and within minutes she was asleep. Miles took the first watch and made a small fire while the others slept. He sat up against a tree but also found himself drowsy. He also was exhausted from the fights last night and needed rest and so drew out his blade Razor and got to his feet to practice silently for the next hour.

They journeyed for two short and uneventful hours with Zack leading them along an old path and telling them stories of his childhood, of the terrible night the aeomon flooded his city and a particular time only a few days previously where himself and the deceased crossbowman Travis fought through the city for days in an attempt to rescue a band that were trapped by the demons, (A story for another day readers). Acarlie listened to him intensely and eagerly. She loved stories when she was young, especially ones that were true and told from the characters themselves and Zack has a very gifted story teller. As the sun still beamed down on them she wondered how her story would sound if she ever had to tell it one day. She always dreamed of her pilgrimage and even though the first chapter of her journey was one of darkness and peril the warm sun glowing down on top of her and the fresh air gently filling her lungs promised her a happy and wonderful story filled with optimism and love. Now fully rested and with food in her belly she could take in all the sights and smells of the world around her. The hedges they walked beside all grew black berries she picked as she went and ate one at a time like a child discovering them for the first time. They tasted as sweet as the smell of the yellow and purple flowers that grew in an open field to their other side. The pollen from the flowers however was thick in the air and she soon remembered her hay fever as her nose became runny and her eyes began to itch but she didn't mind. To her it was a small price to pay for such an experience after being in her home town all her life. After a while however she began rubbing her eyes until they became swollen and teary and an itch on the roof of her mouth would not stop unless she rubbed it with her tongue which only lead her to sneeze every time. Sheeria eventually caught her rubbing her eyes and warned her to stop.

"Acarlie, you should stop child," she said pulling Acarlie's hand away from her eyes.

Even with her eyes red and beginning to swell Acarlie smiled and looked over to Sheeria, "I can't help it. They're just itchy."

Sheeria laughed lightly seeing what Acarlie had done to herself, "Just try to ignore it for now Acarlie. We will be passing the field soon and will be arriving in the city. You don't want the people to see you like this."

"Is it bad?" she smiled up at her.

Sheeria laughed through her nose when thinking of how she could describe the red mess she had made her eyes look, "You look like you can't see."

Acarlie giggled and went to rub her eyes again if Sheeria wasn't there to stop her, "Feels like I've been cutting onions, but really itchy."

"Just leave them alone child. We're nearly there."

The city Lachine was overcrowded with many people. It was like a giant industrial city. It was much bigger than the city they just come from and was the capital of the country they walked in called Isolies. Whereas Hiro was the capitol city of Racoves, the country which Eloma was in. They were both on the same continent called Tranapa but it was because Lachine was closer to Eloma than Hiro that their journey led them here. The buildings all stood tall and proud overlooking the land of plains beyond it. A beautiful city brimming with all sorts of life and people, each running round like in a trance on their everyday working lives. Acarlie was welcomed gracefully as soon as it was established that she was on an Elementalists' Pilgrimage, they gathered around them and some were reaching out to try and touch her while others were cursing her like football fans of another team came into their city.

"Go back home Elementalist. Billy will beat you, you have no chance!" They called out in a jokey tone but they all knew they wanted her there as much as she did. They wanted to see the battle and even gain some money by gambling on the outcome, for it was not every day an elementalist would walk into the city and challenge their favourite home born elementalist. There were children or even young adults who as soon as they heard the news about Acarlie arriving were running home or to their friends to shout the news with such electric excitement that the parents would be excited themselves. The word got around in a matter of hours and the city started brimming with excitement and joy.

Whenever an elementalist would arrive in another city it would always bring excitement like this because it meant a bank holiday would follow it a day or so later, the people of Sphere all lived for the Elemental Battles, a reason why the elementalists were loved so much. Every male, female, employee or manager of every race would take a day off on the day of the battle to go and watch the fight with their families and friends in the great stadiums. Since everything was closed every other working class person who couldn't afford the expensive seats up front could still take the day off and stand at the poorest spots for free and watch it on a big monitor that would be set up outside the stadium. Some people made a living off the E.Bs by selling food, beverages or even souvenirs to the mass audience that would make a day out of the great battles of elements and if an elementalist would become known by the world would even start to have a following of fans on their pilgrimage bringing tourism and trade to the cities. The elementalists were one of the greatest means of business on Sphere and were loved by all. In any case she felt very welcome by the people and was happy to be directed onto a bus leaving her lizziers behind and travelling toward the governor's office. Days before when she was arguing with Sheeria about what smart dress to wear was in vain as she left her dress with the lizziers with the guards and forgotten all about wearing something smart when meeting important people. They were told that the president of Isolies was unavailable at the moment and was instead taken to a large building made with many sheets of glass windows everywhere on the outside reflecting the blue sky all around it. They walked past the reception on the ground floor and were directed to an elevator to the higher floors to reach him. The elevator took them up slowly which gave them enough time to take in the sight of the whole city. Sheeria and Miles, as the two travellers of the group took their time and pointed out certain buildings like hospitals, what they assumed might have been the city's elemental school and down on the floor, hiding behind another building was the stadium. This one was of the same shape as the coliseum at Eloma with thousands of seats around the outside overlooking the arena. This one looked very modern with strong metal foundations, like a real expensive stadium that stood out from the other buildings around and shone magnificently in the sunlight. Acarlie smiled in wonder that soon she would be in the eye of the crowd again and remembered the battle she had at home with Barry, hoping her next battle would end quickly and painlessly with the crowd screaming and chanting her name once more.

The office they were brought in to was smart, neat and tidy and they were greeted by a smiling and happy governor. He walked up and kissed Acarlie on both cheeks in a warm welcome. He was a large man with a white halo of hair around his head and rosy red cheeks. He wore a light grey suit with a red tie to match his chair in his office. He seemed a very jolly person but not too keen and interested to hear of what had just happened to them, like he was far more interested in something else, something that was unsettling for Sheeria. Here they were coming into a beautiful, large office, blood-stained and with Zack trying to speak to him but all he was doing was talking about the next battle.

"Oh, how wonderful it is that you have come..."

"Sir–" Zack tried to interrupt, stepping forward but being held back my Miles lightly.

"...And we haven't had anybody that has journeyed from Eloma in such a long while. Oh this will be exciting..."

"Sir I just want to say–"

"...Oh yes, we will have to take you to your quarters right away. Ah yes, this will be splendid." The governor paced around the room with a wild excitement. "Tomorrow the people will be gathered and brought to the stadium, yes, yes, yes. We shall start the decorations and ready the city for the opening of the stadium for the public right away, ready for tomorrow." He spoke quickly like he was talking to himself. He was trying to hurry them out of the room quickly, maybe because of their appearance Acarlie thought. They had just walked into this very smart place, looking like tramps off the street. Acarlie wished she had left Miles and Zack behind now, maybe the governor would take her more seriously if it were only the elementalist and her guide but this was important she thought. The message about Zack's home city had to be passed along to help them as soon as she could, but every time one of them tried to speak he interrupted them or moved around his office. Not one of them wanted to be rude and just blurt it out. They had just walked into his office after all and feared what he would do to them. This was the first destination of Acarlie's pilgrimage and needed to make a positive impression if the world was to take her seriously. They all relied on Acarlie to do all the talking for she would have been the leader after all.

"Sir, this is very important. There is a–" Acarlie tried to say but was interrupted again.

"Very important you say? Well oh my, you will have to get in line. I have some other people who have urgent news for me and they were here first. Oh yes, yes they were. I have had to make them wait for you because we never knew you were coming. Brucie would you mind taking the Elementalist umm..." he gestured a hand in front of her waiting for her to fill in the gap.

"Acarlie. And I just wanted to say that–"

"Yes of course. Please take Elementalist Acarlie to the Away-side's Quarters and give her enough food, time and space so she may be ready for her battle tomorrow. Now if you will excuse me Elementalist Acarlie, please go with this man. He will take you to your quarters. We will talk as soon as the match is over."

"You know why that is a bad idea!" she quickly said hoping it would be enough to make a point.

"Don't worry, there are four of you and I'm sure you will do fine. Now please, I have somebody here that wishes to speak to me immediately, good luck, I'll be watching."

The door was closed almost in their face and Miles was the first to speak out.

"What a jerk."

But it was Sheeria who was most upset. "This is completely unacceptable! You can't send an elementalist away in such a manner. This is considered rudeness in the highest fashion. I'm going to go back in there and–"

"No don't, let's just go and get ready. My mind needs to be clear for my battle anyway. We shall speak to him after, come let's go," Acarlie said pulling on her arm.

Acarlie walked over to Zack. He was the one who needed her most after all.

"I'm so sorry Zack, I'm sorry I couldn't help you there. I promise, after all you have done for me, I shall get you the help you need."

"That's ok, Acarlie. I know it was out of your control. He was really eager to let us go though don't you think? I mean even if we had absolute urgent news he still wouldn't have thrown us out of his office like that. It's like he *really* didn't want us in his office."

"Well, look at the state of us. We're not exactly presentable for talking to a governor of the whole city are we?" Miles added and they knew he was right.

"Oh my goodness, Sheeria, you know what I've forgotten?" Acarlie realised and asked Sheeria.

"Yes, your dress. You left it back in your bag with the lizzier. We could go back and get it if you want."

"I don't think it makes much of a difference now. I shall get it after and talk to him in an appropriate and decent manner. I can't believe I forgot that!"

"I don't know. I still think that even if you dressed like Queen Angel herself, he would have still wanted us out that office as quickly as he did."

"The governor is just a very busy man sir," said the man escorting them back down the corridor, "please don't feel offended if he had only a short time to speak to you. He is like that often. He is just a very busy man."

"You see, he's right. You're making a fuss over nothing Acarlie. We should just get you ready for the battle now. Also remember that was only the governor, it's the president that you will really need to speak to. It's just a shame we could not see him instead. I expect we will though, word must be reaching him now that a new elementalist has arrived in his country."

"Yes Miles maybe you're right. We're just making a fuss over nothing."

They were led away and something else distracted Sheeria from following.

"What is it Sheeria?" Acarlie asked her.

"Look over there," she said pointing at two figures walking down the corridor to the office they had just came from. One was a man no older than Acarlie herself, wearing a purple cloak and beside him was, "… A Leo…"

15

"But sir, you must listen to us," Raiden protested to the governor, his head bowed down to him. He may not have served him but he knew the governor was a man of power and he had to be subtle with him. "It is of the utmost importance that we speak to the President of Isolies immediately."

"I'm sorry Leo but there is nothing I can do for you. Oh no, nothing at all."

Raiden and Val were sitting in the governor's office trying to make some communication to the president. The governor sat down shaking his head and trying to explain to them how much of a bad time it was to suddenly try and get hold of the president.

"Why can't you just tell me what is wrong and I will pass the message on to him?"

Raiden kept quiet rather than answering him. He knew that if he told him what was wrong the governor either wouldn't believe him and send him out of his office immediately, or worse, would send him and furthermore the city into a panic. If they ever found out the consequences would be dire. Val didn't know what to say to him and was not accustomed to speaking to political leaders like Raiden was and instead just blurted out, "Look, the information we have is for the President's ears alone. Unless of course you have a skyship you can lend us?"

"Ho ho, oh no my boy. We don't have skyships here, oh no. I can't help you there but I do have a good piece of news for you."

Raiden looked up now wondering where the next words would lead. The large, balding man leaned forward over his desk until Raiden could smell his musk from where he sat and smiled over at him.

"The reason I had to keep you on hold for a short while longer was because a young elementalist has just arrived in the city," he said suddenly leaning back into his red chair with his arms out like it was something to celebrate.

Raiden looked suddenly interested in every word he was saying, "Where from?"

"Eloma, isn't that great? Eloma, oh yes."

"What do we care about that?" Val answered him. "We're not here to watch some elementalist battle. We're here on very important business."

"But don't you know what that means?" the governor asked. "Haven't you ever been to an E.B before?"

"What are you talking about? What does what mean?"

Raiden knew what he meant though and answered for him, "It means the President would host the tournament. It is a national holiday and therefore would stop what he was doing and be there for his people at a time of holiday."

"So the President would be at the E.B then? How do we see him?" Val asked.

"Well since you say the information is of the utmost importance you can get some rest here in Lachine tonight and tomorrow after the E.B when the President will have some time to speak to some of the public you can say your words to him then," the old governor suggested.

"We don't have the money to stay in places around here neither do we have money to go to the E.B anyway," Raiden pointed out in his formal but deep tone hoping the governor would accommodate them because of this.

"That's ok then because I've got some passes in here that are given to foreign diplomats," the governor said pulling open his side draw under his desk and fiddling around before he finally found two passes with a piece of string around them for wearing around their neck.

"These will give you free access to any means of travel and a room in a very nice hotel on the edge of the city. There you will also be given free meals and finally a free pass to the First Class seats in the stadium," he said while signing the passes, stamped them with an authentic seal and passing them over to Val.

"There you will sit and watch the E.B and then you will also have the first chance of seeing the President, oh yes. I doubt he will like the urgent news after the fight mind you, oh no. But if you say it is as important as you make out then he will have no choice wont he?"

"There are three of us," Val said blankly while taking the pass.

"I'm sorry, what did you say?"

"There are three of us. You have only given us two passes. What about our other companion?"

"Well where is he?" the governor asked gesturing a hand to an empty space next to Val.

Raiden spoke in then, "He is a Caster."

The governor then smiled and clapped his hands together once he worked it out. "Oh I see, oh yes. So he will be in the local hospital and elder temple then? Ok then not a problem. Here is his one. Now don't lose these. If anyone sees these they will likely try and steal them so keep them safe. Now please go back down to the reception on the bottom floor and show these passes to the young lady behind the desk and ask her for the bus or tram that will take you to your hotel. I have to get to work now and ready the city for the E.B tomorrow. All night it will take, oh yes. I must get ready right away for it ever to happen."

They both stood up and thanked the strange governor for his help but still couldn't help but think that he just wanted them out of his office as soon as he could. They got into the elevator and descended back down to the ground floor.

Val was looking at the shiny pass around his neck while Raiden stood still, arms crossed and peering out of the glass elevator. It was still high noon and the city was still overexcited about the E.B happening tomorrow. Val however still felt a little uneducated about what an Elemental Battle was and felt the urge to ask. "Raiden have you ever seen an E.B before?" he asked still fidgeting with the pass around his neck.

"Yes, only once while I was young. I was in Toshiro at the time. The power there is of diamond and I saw an elementalist from Hiro who has the power of water be defeated by the host," Raiden explained with his back against the wall and closing his eyes from the glare of the afternoon sun against the glass elevator.

"Did you enjoy it?"

"Actually I was horrified. It was my father who took me and my brother. I must have only been eight human years at the time. I was only a cub." Val never noticed since Raiden kept his eyes closed but once he remembered the age of eight he remembered his father again. The last vision he had of his father was walking out of the door while Raiden was being carried in a fit of tears in his brother's arms. Raiden sighed and forgot the memory.

"Why were you horrified? All these children look as if they can't wait to see the fight."

But Raiden did not answer. He only kept his eyes shut, his arms folded and remembered what happened all those years ago and chose not to speak about it. Val didn't understand why and turned away from the subject instead. He began looking out onto the city, marvelling at its size like a child seeing the world for the very first time. The city stretched far out into the horizon until distant buildings began to almost look as blue as the sky. The city seemed to move with all the activity below them. People and vehicles all made their way around the ground way below them and seemed to make the city look bursting with life and untold stories. Val looked down at the mass amount of people so small they looked like fleas on a dog's back and wondered which of these people walking along the floor was this elementalist, what he looked like and what his element would be. They reached the bottom and walked over to the desk and met up with Zahied there who was waiting for them with a small file of papers in his hand.

"Hi, I wasn't long in the hospital. There was nothing there I haven't already learned and in the temple I found this file of healing techniques. I photocopied them and came down here to wait for you. How did it go?"

Raiden passed him his free pass with a frown. Zahied sensed that frown was because this pass only meant they could not see the person they wanted to and would have to wait longer.

"We have to see an Elemental Battle tomorrow before we can speak to the president," Val told him.

Zahied's face suddenly turned to a smile when he heard that they would get to sit and watch an Elemental Battle for free tomorrow and suddenly turned as excited as the people around town would be. Zahied told them that he had seen a few E.B's before in his time but never had the chance to see one in a first class seat. Now he didn't even need to pay for one. The three of them at this point all had different opinions of what would happen tomorrow. Zahied was excited and happy he could get to watch one while Raiden was reluctant to watch it and would rather just wait to speak to the president and Val who didn't understand any of it, wondered what all the fuss was about. Raiden walked up to the front desk to the young receptionist and asked the way to the hotel they had to stay at. She smiled at the leo without a thought of either fear or discomfort or gaping at his size like a weird creature or a freak, like a lot of city people did to him. This was something that made him smile ever so slightly for the first time in days. He couldn't help but like the young human for this. Normally while walking through a city or town, people would stare at him and young human males or even tigians who wish to make a name for themselves would always stare at him with evil eyes. Often when he was young and was invited out for a drink with friends, young drunk males would confront him and try and pick a fight with him. It seemed like a status symbol to pick a fight with leos and those who managed to win in a fight with them were classed as hard men not to be messed with. In his youth he loved this and for many years long ago he would use this and his hatred for humans who wiped out his race to circulate bars and wait to be confronted just for the thrill of fighting. However after a while he began to tire from the fights and as he grew older and wiser his will for scrapping and fighting faded, but still would have to defend himself some nights. This happening after so long taught Raiden to be quiet when on a night out, being the biggest around meant he would have the most trouble and often blamed for the outburst as well. This is also why he moved to Walton and away from the city folk. But for some reason the girl at the desk did not gape or stare and spoke to him like he was just another normal person and he liked that. He took her instructions and thanked her before leaving the building.

Another few hours passed until they finally reached their hotel. It was actually a tavern which made Zahied smile as he thought he could get a drink and it was a secluded, very homey place, hiding behind some trees just on the outskirts of the city overlooking fields of green crops and miles of plains and trees yonder. It was now coming up to evening and they were all feeling tired and hungry and just wanted to sit down and take the weight off their feet and eat some decent food for once. Inside was almost like a palace. The floor's carpets were red and vacuumed. Even Raiden wiped his feet when entering. The walls were made of stone and in two fireplaces fires were burning warmly around the tavern. The front counter was a bar with a gentleman wearing a suit who greeted them. The passes were shown to him and he showed them firstly to some rooms above them. The rooms were like the tavern, magnificent like a room fit for a king.

"So how will you be paid for these rooms?" Val asked.

The man in the suit answered in a well-spoken and polite manner, "The passes you have around your necks have a bar code and a number on the back. We would scan these and the government would pay for them."

"In that case bring me up some dinner and a drink menu please," Zahied said quickly seeing his chance for a free meal and drink and went for it quickly.

"Right away sir," the man turned and walked back down the corridor. He then turned around and added, "Oh, and sirs? If you wouldn't mind me asking. How did you get these passes? I ask because normally people such as you don't get these passes. They are for royalty or politicians only."

"We have been told to stay here then go to the Elemental Battle tomorrow," Raiden answered.

"Really? An Elemental Battle you say? That's great news. I must go and tell the others quickly. Thank you for bringing this to our attention."

They each had a room separately but decided to sit in Raiden's room and rest. When the food arrived they sat and ate juicy steaks with finely cooked vegetables in oils. The first good meal Val would ever remember. Val savoured every bite of his delicious dinner because he knew he probably wouldn't get another one like this for a while, while Zahied sat and drank from a bottle of wine the service brought up for him. After his meal Val went and sat down outside just as the sun was going down. He only came out for some fresh air but found himself staring out across the fields and onto a road going across it. He sat and watched as buses and pod-like vehicles whizzed across. Lizziers pulling wagons would also pass and he even saw some flying vehicles flying not too high from the floor just above the other vehicles. He looked up again and saw the two moons again, now nearly covered by clouds peering over the horizon. *What a strange world this is,* he thought to himself. *There are so many strange things here like large glass buildings, flying vehicles, lizziers, casters and elders and most of all elementalists.*

Tomorrow he would see his first ever elementalist. He wondered what these men will be like.

Acarlie's room was a beautiful wooden laminated floored room with a huge queen size bed in the centre. Vases of flowers decorated the room and the room had a large wooden balcony that overlooked a private lake. This was all the Away-side's Quarters to give them the feeling of peace and tranquillity before their battle the following day. Her dinner was a whole five piece banquet brought up to her with all the fancy trimmings that only a king would enjoy regularly. She ate with her companions around a dinner table as they all chatted about their night previously and joked about how close their encounter was. Even Zack was light-hearted about the events. He explained that he knew that Mack would have the situation under control if there would be any problems but he would still sleep easier when the president had sent reinforcements down to his city he called *Plainess*. They sipped all the expensive wine until there was hardly any left and they had to order some more, apart from Sheeria who decided not to under the circumstances.

"You should not really be drinking either Acarlie. It would be better if you kept your mind clear for tomorrow."

Acarlie was in the middle of a giggling fit she shared with Miles when she turned to Sheeria, "But it would be good for me to drink just a little Sheeria. I would not like to stay up all night and worry about the battle. That only makes things worse. Plus…you know…"

Sheeria looked down at the floor then avoiding Acarlie's eyes. She knew it would be hard for Acarlie to finish her sentence and so she wanted to make things easier for her. She thought fast to change the conversation and stood up.

"Yes Elementalist you are right. I do not want to worry you anymore. It is my duty to ensure your pilgrimage goes as easy as I can make it without putting you against your will. Just promise me you will not drink too much tonight. A little will be good but even a little too much would have an impact on your performance."

Miles then leaned into the conversation. His eyes slightly misty from the wine and holding up his glass in a drunken manner, but he spoke formally, "Don't worry Sheeria. I will make sure Acarlie does not drink too much. She will be safe with me."

"Yeah that's because you will drink it all yourself and leave none left for us!" Zack joked and they all shared the laugh except Sheeria again, who wanted this drunken night to finish for Acarlie's sake but she wanted what was best for her and if Acarlie wished to drink then she would not get in her way.

"Very well then Miles. I'm going to retire to my quarters now. I trust that you will ensure that Acarlie sleeps well and enjoys herself."

Acarlie knew what Sheeria was doing then and knew she was only doing the right thing. She thanked her then wished her a good night.

"Yes good night to you too Acarlie. I shall see you in the morning. Have a good night. Good night Zack, Miles," she nodded to the others.

"Yes good night Sheeria, and sleep easy. The Elementalist will be ready and willing for tomorrow morning," Zack waved giving her the guarantee so she would not stay awake worrying about her. Zack knew as much as Acarlie did how important she was to Sheeria and knew the safety of the elementalist was paramount but also that it was important that Acarlie got a decent night's sleep even if that meant with the help of a little drink rather than a sober night awake worrying about her fight.

Throughout the next couple hours the sun retired and the two moons took rule of the sky. The temperature dropped and a silent, cool wind swept throughout the room. It was eventually Zack who stayed away from heavy drinking and watched over the Elementalist while Miles carried on drinking like all young men do. He joked and laughed with them in a steady lightly drunken state and watched as the two youngsters giggle and flirt with one another and remembered his past when he first met his wife; how they used to play and flirt with one another and that only brought him to a sadder thought when he thought of the fate she encountered. The terror he witnessed as she was one of the many victims of the *Night of Blood* all those years ago and decided to take the subject away from his mind and continue on with the conversations with the other two.

After another half an hour, the scene had died down a little and Acarlie was pouring herself another glass of wine when Zack stood up realising his responsibilities, "Actually Acarlie don't you think it is a good time to retire soon?"

"Ok Zack let me finish this one more glass then I will see myself to sleep," she suggested but Zack had heard this sort of thing before and knew what to do.

"Ok then how about this?" He then took a large swig from Acarlie's glass and gave her it back only half full and took the bottle away.

"You only finish this half glass and I take the bottle. Not that I don't trust you of course but because I have made a promise to Sheeria that you would be safe."

"You just want to drink the rest for yourself," Miles added. Zack understood the jest and carried on the banter, "Yes you're right Miles. Now I'm going to my bedroom and finish off the bottle myself!" He held up the bottle as if in triumph that his plan worked to get the rest of the alcohol still drunkenly acting the part to amuse the young adults. Miles laughed and patted him on the back. They all knew he was again doing the right thing and saw him out the door before finally being left alone.

"Well, I don't know about you but I want another bottle. Would you like some?" Miles asked her.

"No, I will be fine finishing my glass and getting some sleep. You can go though."

"Ok then I won't be long. Wait here," and he left the room briefly while he ran to the reception to take a bottle for himself.

When he came back Acarlie was standing on the balcony looking over at the lake. She was leaning over the balcony gazing out onto the empty private lake while sipping the last of her red wine and closing her eyes and enjoying the relaxing buzz from the alcohol.

Miles put the bottle down and joined her outside. He smiled as he saw her and stood beside her, leaning up against the barrister supporting them. They both looked out onto the lake. The wind was so silent and gentle that the lake sat like a mirror to the stars above them. Four bright silver moons now smiled from both above and below them.

"It's beautiful this lake isn't it?" she said as more of a conversation starter than a statement.

Miles stood for a moment staring out then adding, "It is quite pretty. The trees around it are peaceful and there is no one around to clutter or litter up the place. I guess there is something like this in every town or city with an elemental stadium. Something to relax the visitor's side before their battle. It wouldn't be sporting if they just gave us a small room somewhere in the centre of the city, with no space nor time to ready yourself."

Acarlie smiled and looked over to Miles and admired his silhouette in the silvery glow of the moonlight. Even when inebriated he stood tall and handsome, like a knight from the stories she used to love when she was young. He was tall and strong but she enjoyed seeing his more sensitive side.

"Yes, it is also very spiritual. The preparation before a battle I mean, and I suppose they have made this private lake so the elementalist can find their inner selves in such a tranquil environment," Acarlie replied.

He turned and leaned his back against the banister of the balcony and reached for his bottle again, "What do you mean by *inner selves*? Is there a special place in the human body that you must find in order to use the elders' gift?"

She smiled at him then walked back into the room to sit on her bed.

"No Miles don't worry about that. It's far too late for me to even try and explain to you what took the elders themselves years to teach me."

He nodded at this then walked back in, closing the doors to the balcony, closing the curtains for her, having a sip of his wine then sitting on the bed beside her. There was a small awkwardness in the air, but they both overcome it soon enough.

He was looking down at his bottle when he said, "Well...I wish you the best of luck on your victory tomorrow."

She felt the nerves in his tone then and added, "Well I also wish you luck on your mission," she smiled trying to catch his eye, "your mission of revenge."

He looked up then finding the words to subtly say thank you to her but when he did their eyes both met in that way young drunk teenagers always do. A million thoughts went through her mind then but the only thing she could instinctively do was lean forward toward him. She found he done the same until their lips were touching. As they kissed she felt his hand as it touched her arm and slowly slid up to her cheek and they both fell down to the bed on their side and for the rest of the night they belonged to each other, like kids living for the moment, like slaves to passion.

The next day the city roared with excitement. Since it would be a holiday the only workers during E.Bs would be in shops. Not that they minded, a busy day but half worked and with much money passing through their tills. All throughout the night, workers readied the city for its celebration, shop owners called in night staff to ready the stores for waves of customers and decorations were put up all over the city for the big day. As Val, Raiden and Zahied walked through the streets it seemed like every person in the city was there too. The trams and buses were full mostly of excited children and the city had all sorts of tinsel or paper placed around it, hanging from the ceiling of the mall for all to see. A band of musicians played songs of optimism, youthful energy and love that echoed all through the city and beside them were a band of performing aeomon juggling for the children or jumping high acrobatically to the applause of the audience around them. Humans, aeomon, tigians and some creatures Val noticed but didn't have time to ask about were all walking through the city each with their own family ignoring the others and chatting amongst themselves.

"So where is this elementalist from then, the visitor I mean?" Val asked Zahied.

"The people at the café only told me he is from Eloma. This will be the first one to come from Eloma in about ten years or so, so he must be strong. Are you looking forward to it Val?"

"I don't know really. I don't know what they are capable of."

"Wait until you see it then, it's great. I actually decided to become a Caster after I saw an E.B"

"Really? I take it someone told you it was impossible for you to become an elementalist and so you became the next best thing."

"That's right Val, and I have been sulking about it ever since."

Val chuckled with him about this for several more minutes with Raiden walking in front of them leading the way. He was quiet as soon as he reached the city and had not said a word to either of them. In his mind he was still hesitant about what he was about to witness and also because E.Bs always made him think of his father and brother.

They came to the front of the stadium. A path leading up to the front gate had a long line of people with pine trees either side of it. There were large grassy spots with people sitting down on them, picnicking in the shade and watching a large monitor, waiting to watch the battle from outside. They only waited for a minute before Raiden remembered they had the passes and did not have to wait and so made their way into the stadium. When they finally found their seats Val finally caught glimpse of the arena. The floor was dusty with dry mud covering up the ground and there were scattered pieces of scrap metal lying carelessly around the floor. Weapons like metal poles and swords also lay on the floor like someone had just thrown them anywhere. They sat and watched the stadium fill up until it was completely full of eager fans and excited followers of the E.Bs. At first, to entertain the crowd, a before battle attraction had already started. Female dancers were dancing to loud and lively music with the audience's clap as a beat. Zahied laughed while he sat and pointed to each and every attractive girl performing to Val and clapped to the rhythm of the beat along with the audience and eventually Val joined in too feeling a little out of place. Raiden however remained as silent as ever and waited. Val watched as a cloaked man walked onto the arena floor centred by the dancers on Val's right side. The crowd became suddenly silent. The man lifted his arm and Val gasped as all the scrap metal and weapons lifted off the floor and floated only a few inches off the ground. The dancers, each wearing matching uniforms of short skirts, tight T-shirts and pom-poms walked in single file to the side and stood in a perfect line. With his free hand the cloaked man lifted his hood showing a strong man in the prime of his life. His other hand he threw to the other side sending all the scrap pieces of metal he was controlling to fly into the other side of the arena away from the dancers and giving them room to perform as well as exciting the audience. When the sound of the metal crashed onto one side of the arena confetti exploded from certain parts of the arena into the crowd and the dancers started dancing to the music again to the screaming crowd while the man stood still, his hands up to his adoring crowd.

Acarlie was in her preparation room like she did before back in Eloma. She was sitting down in silence in mediation but could not help but feel scared about the fight just around the corner. All she could hear was the thumping of the music and the droning sound of the crowd cheer. But this time it wasn't for her, this time it was for her opponent. This was his home city and his crowd, now she was the underdog. Sheeria stepped in again this time with Zack behind her. The guards tried to stop him but he was throwing his hands up and saying, "Back off. I'm with the elementalist!"

She stood up to greet them. She smiled at Sheeria and Sheeria saw the gleam of happiness in her eye.

"Why are you so happy Acarlie? What's on your mind?"

She blushed at this, "Oh, nothing Sheeria, really nothing. I'm just excited that's all."

Sheeria could tell she was lying but this wasn't the time for bringing it up.

A voice from behind the door came, "Two minutes Acarlie!"

She looked over to Zack. He gave her a hug and wished her luck.

Sheeria put her paw on her shoulder and they went for the door. Acarlie noticed someone was missing.

"Where is Miles?"

"Miles has been away all morning," Zack told her. "Said he

went to speak to someone important. That's all he said."

Acarlie wondered what he meant but instead had to put the thought aside and make her way to the arena, trying her best to conquer her nerves.

A tall and dark man sat in an office located in the stadium. He wore a dark blue suit with a purple, velvet underlay, white cotton shirt and a black tie. His hair was short and neatly combed and a small, pin-like moustache sat neatly above his lips. His posture was strong and he sat in his chair in his personal office in the stadium with his back straight reading a file of the new elementalist and sipping green tea from a small porcelain cup. His door knocked twice.

"One minute please Mister President," said one of his escorts who poked his head in the door.

"Thank you Stan. I will be ready shortly."

The escort closed the door and the President finished sipping the rest of his tea. His name was President Human Matri Shuian of Isolies. He had only just arrived back in the capital of his country after he was informed of the Elementalist Acarlie's arrival and was preparing his speech to his country and the rest of the world when he himself would introduce the already famous battle. Before he managed to finish his tea however he heard another knock outside his door. At first he thought nothing of it until another, much more louder knock followed and finally one of his closest escorts and guards suddenly appeared being thrown through the door with a great crash. The door splintered and split at the locks. Shuian jumped up, spilling the rest of his tea over his desk and stood in shock and stunned to see a man before him, standing firm and breathing deeply. His clothes tattered and carrying a blood stained sword that dripped red onto his carpet.

"What is the meaning of this? Who are you? Where are my guards?" he asked loudly straightening his back and standing firmly against this sudden aggressive intruder.

"Sit down Mister President this will only take a moment," the blood stained intruder ordered and stepped towards him.

Shuian did as instructed shaking at first. The blood stained man took another step forward and leaned onto his desk, "I know you are a very busy man and so this will be short," the stranger continued.

"Where are my guards?" Shuian asked.

The man held up his red sword, dripping liquid murder over his desk and said nothing. Shuian's eyes widened in horror. His mouth opened but could not find words.

"Now Mister President. My name is Miles. I am a mercenary from a country from far away. I know the game you have been playing now and I know the deal with the elementalist in this country," he said stabbing his sword into the ground and leaning over the desk. His bloody fingers staining the paper files and pushing them aside.

"What do you want?" Shuian asked. He was shaking now in fear of what would happen to him.

"What do *I* want?" Miles asked with a slight smile in his face. "I'll tell you what *I* want."

16

The stadium was lit up with explosions launching confetti over the crowd and the elementalist finally lowered his hands after his applause and took off his cloak to reveal to the audience his strong stature and broad shoulders. His head was shaved and his eyes narrow with a strong jaw with bright white teeth in his confident smile. The cheerleaders left the arena with further applause from the audience when a voice was heard from speakers in every corner of the stadium.

"And now, ladies and gentleman, boys and girls; tigians, aeomon, ursas and all other beings of Sphere please rise to address President Matri Shuian of Isolies."

Every person who was in the crowd sitting in the stadium above the arena now stood and faced a box looking over them with a tall well-dressed man standing there facing them. President Shuian still wore the same blue suit, white shirt and black tie he wore previously and now with his unexpected visitor gone he was free to continue his duties as the President. He raised his hands to address his people before him, "My people; I thank you for coming here today on this rare occasion that our wonderful nation only encounters once in a while.

"I would firstly like to thank all the workers of the city who have worked over night to ready the festivities at such short notice. You have done a grand job and have my gratitude.

"It has come to my attention that this Elemental Battle will be a special one because we have our first elementalist from the small town of Eloma in over a decade now and..."

Acarlie was standing behind a big door guarded by security, dressed in her combat clothes, a dark grey tightly worn vest and black leggings like before and waiting for President Shuian to introduce her. Sheeria and Zack were now in the awayside's seats now and Miles was still nowhere to be found but she was not thinking about him. She was only concerned about her entrance and trying to keep her cool.

"And so without further ado my good citizens. Please give a warm welcome to our contender today, from the small town of Eloma it is my pleasure to introduce to you…Elementalist Acarlie!"

The door opened and Val had to stand on his toes to see the elementalist he was waiting to see all day over the heads of the cheering crowds. When he saw her he whispered to himself, "Oh, she is a girl…"

The crowd clapped and whistled for her as Acarlie walked onto the stadium floor. Her blood tingling with nervousness like before as she went to the man standing in the middle waiting for her. They met in the centre of the arena and a silence fell from the crowd again. Even the crowd outside watching from the monitors fell deathly silent as they watched the two shake hands and walk back to their sides of the arena.

"The battle will begin on the third siren!" Shuian called out to the stadium and the first siren began followed by the second. Her tingling sensation doubled and felt overwhelmed by it but took a breath and concentrated as the third siren went which started her second battle. She closed her eyes and concentrated on the air around her, bringing her hand up level to her chest again and felt a small cyclone of wind carrying dust to circle around her as it did before and looked up to her opponent. When she did, she saw him standing there staring at her with a blood-thirsty smirk on his face and behind him, a trap door opened and she saw an electronic windmill turbine appear from behind him. Everyone gasped as they saw the tall turbine elevate from the floor and stand behind Billy facing Acarlie.

The elementalist Billy was the first to make a move as he held out his hand and from the scrap metal he moved to one side earlier he called a pole and knife to his person. They floated there just in front of him. His hand stretched out but not touching either one of them. He tensed the muscles in his arm and relaxed sharply and the pole and knife flew like fired from a gun straight toward Acarlie. She rolled to one side avoiding the weapons and stood up to stand back in her spot. She then lowered her stance with her hands in her chest and when she released them a large gust of wind blew all the dust around her to speed back to him. He stood back then shielding his eyes from small bits of dust coming for him and did nothing. The wind she had summoned impacted the windmill which started turning and making a terrible droning sound that felt like it cut through the whole stadium. When this terrible sound rang, all the metal from the side started flying toward the middle of the arena and pile up in the centre of the floor between them, crashing into one another like a strong force was controlling them. *What just happened there?* she thought to herself but before she knew it she had taken her mind off her opponent who had jumped over the metal and toward her, punching her in her chest and kicking her to the floor. She thought fast and rolled to one side again, jumping up and kicking him under his chin and pushing him toward the metal. She jumped back and tried to send him to the back of the arena again with her gift. She called forth the air surrounding her and ordered it to blow in his direction. Her plan had worked and he stepped back and tripped over the metal and as soon as his feet slipped off the floor he flew back only to climb back to his feet quickly. The wind caught the windmill again and turning it faster now and the droning sound ripped through the air almost deafening her. She simply winced when she heard it and watched Billy get back to his feet and brush the dirt from his shoulders still wearing the same smug look on his lips. This time all the metal in the middle of the arena started shaking and compacting itself smaller into the centre. She had no idea what was going on here but soon it would be irrelevant to think about. Billy now seeing the moving metal lifted his hand gently and all of the metal levitated off the floor and floated there like they were waiting for instructions, ready to obey his commands and inflict terrible pain onto his enemy. She watched in horror as Billy looked at her. His sharp eyes widened, burning with determination and murder. He raised his hand ready to attack her from where he stood and before she could blink all the metal started speeding toward her one by one. Each one seemed to be filled with more malevolence than the last. She did all she could to avoid these speeding spikes of malice but they were fast and soon she was being smashed and battered by these flying pieces of metal hatred. Her screams of pain were heard all the way to the back of the audience and they cheered and howled at her pain. With her arms burning she climbed up from where she lay and tried to blow all the pieces of metal back to Billy but when she did the turbine again turned and made the terrible loud drone and all the metal around her began to fly back to the centre.

Billy laughed now he had the upper hand. The metal was floating higher now than before. He knew he had more control over them now and sent every piece of metal he controlled to fly toward her. She tried to dive out the way but her legs were too weak and suddenly she was hit over her head by a passing pole, cracking against her skull. She felt concussion and dizziness instantly and didn't notice the large sheet of metal fly into her and smashing her into the stone wall under the crowd. Colour faded for her and she only saw the dark red of blood and pain. She tried to scream but her head swam and her vision doubled. Under her skin she felt tingling all over her body and her stomach felt suddenly sick. A damp droplet trickled down over her forehead. She only guessed this was blood. She was picked up by three poles, two under her armpits, digging into her skin, lifting her off the floor and the third under her knees. He controlled these poles and carried her to the centre of the stadium where the crowd could see and threw her down to the ground in a twisted heap and one after another she was repeatedly hit by these poles forcing her to stay on the ground. Every scream she called out only encouraged the crowd to call out even more.

There were even children pretending to be holding the poles themselves and striking her repeatedly like Billy was.

Val watched in absolute horror as he witnessed this poor girl tortured and smacked in front of a crowd of thousands cheering on her every scream.

"What in the world is happening here?" he called out to Raiden who was only standing in silence with his arms crossed like he always does. Val could see the pain in his eyes then. He could tell that he didn't want to watch but could not take his eyes off it.

"It's always a terrible shame when this happens," he finally said.

"When what happens? What is going to happen to her Raiden?!"

Zahied spoke in then, "It's what happens to every elemental match, everybody knows this. The elementalist goes on their journey to learn all the other techniques at the cost of–"

"Of what!" Val began to shout.

"Well, at the cost of their lives. If she wins her fight then the home-side's elementalist will be revived and teach her the secret in *his* style, but if *he* wins–"

"She *dies*!?"

"That's right. You only get one chance to go on the pilgrimage. You can stay home, perfect your style and not have the worry of dying in battle or you can gamble your life to become the best, the Elemental Lord," Zahied explained. Val could not believe the words he was hearing. These famous fights, these Elemental Battles that brought so much happiness and trade to Sphere were really no more than ancient savage gladiator fights where the audience would pay for blood from these special young people with gifts to defy physics.

"But why do they have to die? You say the home-side will get revived if they fail. Why not revive the away-side?"

Raiden spoke in then again. His eyes still watching the poor girl being battered by the metal poles, screaming and starting to bleed from her eyebrow and cover half her face in claret.

"It's a big thing to be Elemental Lord. You have to be the

best. If every elementalist would be revived after their match then there would be many Elemental Lords but there must only be one."

"So if you want it, you got to be the absolute best; to beat every opponent until you reach the top, learn every technique and beat the champion," Zahied finished.

Val was stunned by this horrific revelation. He now knew why Raiden was horrified when he saw the E.B when he was young. He had watched someone die just as he was now and at such a small age it had scarred him for life. He looked down in desperation at the girl, now weakening from the torture she was facing. She was now not only screaming in pain but crying for her torturer to stop, but he didn't. Val could only stand there and watch just like Raiden did all those years ago and knew he could not do anything. His mind wondered if he could stand there and let this happen.

"I can't," he whispered to himself.

"What did you say?" Zahied asked him.

He turned to Zahied and told him, "I can't stand here and watch her die!"

He then summoned his staff to his hand which appeared instantly and ran down the stadium, pushing past the cheering audience.

"Val! Come back!" he heard Raiden roar behind him but did not listen. All the while he ran he could only think about how all these thousands of people were here and *he* was the only person to help this poor girl.

Her arms were now heavily bruised and one side of her body was bleeding as she tried to cover her head from the poles attacking her in vain. She knew this was the end then and wished she was away from there, somewhere peaceful, somewhere where she was home. She tried catching one of the poles and blocking the other with it but was hit in her skull with the third. Pain shook her mind and the warm blood staining her clothes started to slow her movements. She could not do anything now but lay facing upward waiting for the final blow but it never came. Instead she saw a flash of purple and heard a gasp from the audience as it fell into silence.

It's Miles, she thought. *Miles has come to rescue me!* and she turned her head to see that it wasn't Miles but another man standing in front of her, blocking the poles away from her with a staff of his own.

He stood over her, shielding her from the other elementalist, his eyes fixed on him.

"Who are you? Don't you know the rules in an Elemental Battle? No help from outside, the rules are plain and simple?" Billy asked what everyone in the audience wanted to know.

The man in the purple cloak stood tall and shouted to him, "Well, I'm not from around here and if you want to kill this girl you will have to go through me first!"

Acarlie was shocked at what he said, as if one of her wishes had come true. Out in the crowd there was someone there to help her.

He turned to her and carefully picked her up and on her feet.

"Who…?" she whispered in pain.

Billy laughed at this, "Boy do you really want to fight me? Very well then but I warn you…" He lifted his hand and the metal staff from the young man's grip flew out his hand and toward Billy, stopping in front of him, "…I will not hold anything back."

But the man in purple only held his hand out now and the staff he was holding only a second ago disappeared from the spot in front of Billy and appeared back in his hand in a flash. Acarlie along with every person in the audience gasped in wonder at what just happened. Acarlie had never been so confused. She had been around elders all her life but had never seen a trick like this. She, being an elementalist was very open minded about the tricks of elders but nearly thought this a man a wizard herself. She could see that Billy almost thought the same though. This trick shocked him as much as it did everybody else.

"I don't expect you to hold anything back!" he called out to

Billy who stood dumb struck. He knew he had the element of surprise now and whispered back to Acarlie, "You can win this by destroying the windmill. Don't use your element until I have destroyed it, ok?"

"Yes, but how did you just do that?" she asked him but he never answered.

Val ran toward Billy who still was standing in shock at what he saw and dived into him, landing on top of him and pummelling him with punches. Billy held out his hand and a piece of sharp metal lying across the floor lifted from where it lay and shot toward the man in purple. Val saw this coming and fell to one side. Billy now jumped on top of him and strangling him with Val's own staff but Val simply lifted his hand up to the side and summoned it to his open hand. As the staff disappeared from pressing down on his throat to his hand, Billy, having all his weight pressed down now fell down on him, turning him over again and standing up.

Billy got to his knees, "How can you do that?" he called but Val didn't answer. He just swung his staff across Billy's face, cutting his cheek and sending him back down to the floor. This time Billy saw a metal piece of shrapnel and called it from the floor to his palm and when he had a good grip of it he swung it round low, hooking Val's ankles and tripping him on his back. Billy stood over him, raised the shrapnel over his head but before he could swing down the metal shrapnel was taken from behind him.

"Elementalists shall not use weapons. Rule four," the blood stained, injured Acarlie said as she threw the weapon away and kicked him to the ground. It still ached a lot when she did but stood straight and ignored the pain and wiped the blood on her face away from her eyes.

Val jumped to his feet and turned to the girl, "Keep him occupied!" He then ran toward the other side of the windmill.

Billy jumped up again and tried punching Acarlie but she

blocked with all the strength she had left in her bruised body and kicked him again in his side.

Val who now stood behind the windmill saw an opening but could not open it with his fingers. He took his staff and remembered what Amber taught him about moulding it and he folded the staff in half making it thick but shorter. He then curved one end of it and pulled his fingernails down it sharpening it so his staff now looked like a crowbar. He stuck the crowbar in the gaps and opened the door to see a panel and cogs turning. He quickly smashed the panel and when that didn't work he jammed the crowbar into the cogs, now the windmill was unable to move.

"Now Elementalist!" he called over to the girl.

Both Billy and Acarlie looked over to him but Acarlie took her chance, punched him while he wasn't looking and pushed him away from her. She tried to be quick about it but he jumped to his feet again and saw shards of metal on the floor catching light and reflecting up at him like the shards were calling to him in aid. He lifted his hands to call them but nothing happened. He tried again and failed, finally looking over to Acarlie who now had dust forming into a large ball of wind in front of her. She released the ball of dust in his direction which took him off the floor where he stood and sent him flying toward the windmill, smashing into it and leaving a huge dent in the front of it. The crowd watched in disbelief at this offence against the rules but would not dare heckle her. Instead they waited for Billy to get back up. When he didn't they stood silent. Medics came onto the arena floor then pushing past Val and treating Billy, they put their thumbs up to show he was going to be ok to the President and carried him off the floor.

President Shuian now called down from the stand where he was, "What is the meaning of this! Elementalist Acarlie you know the rules clear and plain. Why have you cheated and insulted us today?"

Acarlie was going to call up to him but it was Val who spoke for her, "The Elementalist did not cheat for she never asked me to come. I only came by my own free will!"

"Then you will be severely punished for your actions. Guards!" Shuian screamed and guards armed with crossbows appeared from the stands, aiming for Val and readying to fire on his command

"For the sabotage of our country's only true elemental stadium and rules I sentence you to—"

Before Shuian could finish his words a leo jumped into the arena and roared so loud even the tigians in the audience felt their heart skip. Raiden knew the guards would not fire on him and also that the President would not dare sentence him to die knowing full well he was a leo then turned to scratch away at the floor. While Raiden was in the audience and watching the windmill and the metal flying to the centre of the arena a thought had come to him. He found what he was looking for which was a hoop that opened a large trap door which would take two very strong men to lift and swung it open. The guards then watched in horror as the leo ripped the whole door off its hinges and threw it aside for the audience to see a large metal mechanism attached to a metal pole with a coil wrapped around it.

"People of Isolies, this is an electromagnet! The elementalist from this city uses it to control the metal he uses in battle. Tools such as this should never be used in the arena and is therefore against the rules. This is why he has kept it hidden from you! I put it to you that *you* are the cheats and *you* who have corrupted the spirit and rules of these sacred games!" He bellowed his strong words with such fire that the tall and slim President Shuian felt himself safe out of reach of the very angry creature.

"You were all going to all going to stand here and watch this young—" he held his arm back to point at Acarlie but because he wasn't looking he got scratched by another creature.

He turned to see a tigian, standing in front of her like a protective mother, standing ready to pounce on him. Her eyes burned with passion for battle, like there was nothing she wanted to do more than protect the wounded girl behind her. He stared at her angrily for only a second before turning and completely ignored the tigian's threat and looked back up to Shuian still staring down at him. He was not interested in fighting any other creature for his purpose here was far greater than the elemental battles. He knew that but still needed to speak to the President alone other than blurting out why he was really here so all the city could hear. At first Shuian laughed under his breath knowing that all of his people were around him securing his safety, "You are not in a position to barter or barging Leo! You have a choice; you will surrender yourselves, all of you and turn yourselves into custody or you will die here and now!" He held up his hand to signal the guardsman nearby him and pointed it toward Sheeria to show he meant business, but before the man could fire an arrow flew from nowhere and pierced the man's crossbow and he dropped it to the floor. Before the guards could see where it had come from Zack appeared with another arrow ready and aiming for the President. The guardsmen closest to him sprang to his side and aimed their crossbows only a few inches away from his neck, ready to fire on command.

"President Shuian, I am Zack from Plainess. A city under your control yet we have been in dire need of help from you for the last ten years, yet you never came! You never even thought to send men into check up on us. We have been plagued by demons for years now and the survival and training I have gone through has made me a good archer and right now I aim for you! Why President? Why have you forsaken us?" he screamed so loud some of the cheeky young people in the crowd shouted abuse back but he did not take his eyes off the President.

The tension in the atmosphere was now too much and it was Acarlie to stand in. She stood forward with her blood stained hands held high in surrender, "President Shuian we will cooperate with you! Zack lower you arrow. We shall leave this city and go to another to get help for you, and sirs," she looked over to Raiden and Val and said more quietly, "Please cooperate with them. I am sure we can be out of here soon, I promise."

The whole stadium became silent then and waited for Shuian to continue. Even in the middle of the breaking of the rules and regulations in front of the people of the stadium there was a sudden respect given to Acarlie. It was clear to them that Val was the intruder in this fight but she did not even try to protest innocence before them but instead cooperated with them. Shuian listened to the sound of the silence of the stadium, waiting for his next words before he finally raised his arms and shouted down so they all could hear, "Your proposal is acceptable Elementalist Acarlie. Guards, take them to their cells, except the one in purple. See to it that he shall be imprisoned alone!"

When he said this the crowd broke out in applause. It was very unsettling for Val to hear this. First off all this crowd was happy to see a young girl being beaten to death without any sympathy at all and now they sided with their cheating president with the order of imprisoning them. Val looked over to Raiden; Raiden just nodded and walked with the guards alongside the elementalist and the tigian, followed shortly by the archer into the back of the stadium where they would be taken to their cells. Val was shunted by the guard behind him and was seen out to the silence of the crowd who now didn't know if they had seen the best E.B they will ever see or they if should demand their money back.

17

"Foolish Leo!" Sheeria shouted at Raiden as he sat on a bench in their cell. They were all put in a large cell of metal walls and caged in by a wall of what was called '*Electric Shield*' which was a device that changed the light coming into the cell from soft light to hard light. It glowed blue and was translucent but was strong enough to stop an army getting through. The prisoners inside this knew this and didn't attempt any escape knowing there was no getting through the thick blue energy. Acarlie laid one side next to the bench which Raiden sat on with her arm over her eyes, covering herself from the light above their heads. Zack sat on the floor near the shield with one leg up to his chest and his hands supporting his head against the wall while Sheeria paced up and down shouting at Raiden.

"Why couldn't you leave us be and let her fight alone? Why did the human have to interfere with the battle!?

"She will be banished now, you know that! Not only is she classed as a cheat but she broke the first rule there is in the League of Elementalists, *only one person shall fight one.*"

All the while she shouted at Raiden he only sat quietly, his head low, eyes closed and his arms crossed like he was ignoring the tigian again. She continued in her fury, almost spitting out her words and snarling with ferocity, "Banished Leo! That means me too! We shall never be able to go home nor shall we ever be able to continue her pilgrimage. We will have to live as degenerates and outcasts from now on once we are free and all because of you and your human. Well, what do you have to say for yourself Leo?" she now grew angrier because of his action of ignoring her. "Speak to me Leo! What say you!?"

Raiden took in a breath after some heavy thinking all while the tigian shouted at him and his only response was what had come to him as a revelation.

"The battle was fixed," he said quietly keeping his head low.

"What did you say?" she scowled at him.

He looked up this time and looked her in the eyes. As a leo he would never have to be as frightened as everybody else would about an angry tigian. He spoke calmly but dominantly, "The match was fixed. It was biased against the favour of the Elementalists of Eloma."

The tigian took a step back not knowing whether to be outraged by this statement or shocked that he said this. Acarlie heard this, "What do you mean by that?" she asked politely. She, like the other prisoners did not know this leo and thought it strange that he was imprisoned with them while the young human had a cell to himself. She had never met a leo before and was half stunned by the size of him but had better manners and upbringing to gawp at him but instead spoke to him formally.

Raiden continued, "That windmill he used was to power the electromagnet but only to an elementalist with the teachings of wind would it have any effect on."

Sheeria was ready to pounce on him now but Acarlie stopped her understanding what this leo was talking about. She held out her hand to order Sheeria to stay back.

"He's right Sheeria, whenever I tried to use my gift the windmill turned and his power grew stronger. The more I tried the stronger he got. There was nothing I could do. I didn't have a chance like any other would have."

The revelation hit Sheeria slowly. She still looked with wide eyes of burning anger at the leo but after her Elementalist's words confirmed the leo's she calmed a little. Soon after she took in what Acarlie said did she understand. "She was *never* meant to win the fight at all was she?"

"But why would they fix an elemental battle like that? E.Bs are supposed to be fair and true. Why would they fix the fights?" Zack asked now getting into the conversation.

There was a silence that followed. Only the sound of air vents above them with conditioned air blowing droned above them while they all thought. Raiden sat back and stroked his fire red mane under his chin and scratched his cheek with his black claws before finally adding, "I think the better question would be to ask why would they fix a battle only with Eloma's elementalists?"

Acarlie stood up and paced up and down thinking, *why would they do this? It does not make sense. My town is small and has nowhere near the kind of power that this great city does. This city is powerful and rich with many humans, aeomon and all sorts of different beings here bringing trade all the time. There really is nothing my small town has that this city doesn't.*

"They obviously never wanted Eloma to win, so they must know something they didn't want Eloma to know," Raiden said trying to work it all out.

"Like what Leo? Eloma is only a small town much smaller than this. What could Eloma have that this place doesn't?" Sheeria asked still wearing a scorn on her face.

Raiden was begging to tire from the hateful tigian's tone. If it wasn't for him the elementalist would have been killed and he received no thank you from her guide but in the end only blamed it on the stubbornness of all tigians. "Not Eloma but the Element of Wind." At first they all stared at him blankly not taking his meaning. He continued, "Well let's look at the facts here. They brought out a windmill in battle, which isn't illegal by the rules of E.Bs but would be useless against all other elementalists; and the electromagnet stopped working once it ran out of power when the windmill was broke."

It was when he said this that Acarlie remembered what Elder Argo told her about her gift, she turned to the others and blurted out, "Unseen Forces!"

"What?" Zack asked and Acarlie continued.

"When I started my journey my elder and teacher told me a secret about my element. It is not called the Element of Wind but the school of Unseen Forces because it specializes in things such as wind, gravity and—"

"Magnetism!" Raiden finished for her feeling glad they finally worked it out, "So that must be it. They clearly have stolen one of your traits as an elementalist and wanted to make sure you never won as so they would never reveal the secret. I wonder what else they have done to keep you from winning." Raiden only said this last part as a joke because he hadn't been with them before but when he said this Acarlie nearly screamed when she worked it out and stepped back until her back was on the wall. She spoke with her hand over mouth covering her shock.

"The Masters! They were the masters the demons spoke about! It was them who sent the demons into Plainess. It was the only way to make sure elementalists from Eloma never even made it to their first and closest match."

Zack now stood up realising this, "Of course, that's why Matri Shuian never came to our city. He was the one to send them there and all to keep a secret, that dirty bastard I'll kill him!"

"Have I missed something?" Raiden said and it was Sheeria who filled him in on all the information on what happened to them in the last city they were in. He sat and listened quietly taking all the information in until she finally finished. He stood up and looked over to Zack, "I'm sorry to hear about all this. Once we are out of here, come with us to Hiro. If President Shuian won't help you then King Kerry of Racoves will."

"Yes, although I never asked you about yourself Leo. What is your name and why are you here?" Acarlie asked him sitting back down.

"My name is Raiden, and yours?"

"I am Acarlie, this is Sheeria and that is Zack." She introduced herself and then the other two. Raiden shook her hand gently. Her small and delicate hand disappearing in his furry, golden grip before kneeling down and shaking Zack's. For a human Zack had a strong grip in his handshake. He held tightly onto Raiden's hand and squeezed so that Raiden could feel. Raiden admired that, it was something his brother Valadad taught him about people. A firm handshake shows the person has a strong personality and is attentive to the introduction. Finally he turned to the tigian. Once they locked eyes he could tell she still didn't like him. He didn't care however and stuck his hand out, "Pleasure to meet you Tigian Sheeria," he said formally. Sheeria only stood silent at first and stared at him, almost scowling until she saw Acarlie in the corner of her eye.

"Sheeria," Acarlie whispered loud enough for them all to hear. "Don't be rude."

Raiden stood still. His hand still held out and staring at the tigian who stared back. He forced himself not to smile. The whole moment amused Raiden since he really couldn't care and was not offended by what Sheeria was trying to do and instead waited. Sheeria still said nothing at first until she eventually nodded, not taking her eyes off Raiden and stepped back to the wall. Raiden closed his open hand and turned away hiding the smallest of smirks away from the stubborn tigian and back to Acarlie, *Tigians, they're all the same sometimes, stubborn as a mule, and they say leos are stubborn.*

Acarlie wanted to apologise at first but saw Raiden grin and shake his head. Sheeria was like this sometimes when meeting new people. She was just over protective sometimes. Acarlie thought not to bring anything up and moved on. "Why are you here Raiden?" she asked him again.

He had been keeping the reason secret for days now and thought it good and harmless to tell them now. They were imprisoned and he thought and it wouldn't make any difference telling them or not.

"Me and Val over there have been put on a most sacred and important task given to us by Elder Amber."

Sheeria recognized the name and spoke in, "Elder Amber? I have heard of her, was she not once one of the key members of the High Council of Elders?"

Raiden grinned again, *so there is her voice again, and there was me hoping she would shut her trap for the rest of the night.* "Yes she was. She has retired now and lives in Walton. Now pay attention everybody because I am only going to explain this once." He sat down next to Acarlie and went on to tell them everything that had just happened to him that all began with that morning when he first met Val. They all sat and listened to him, eagerly hanging on to his every word as he told them about the mystery of Val and how he didn't know himself who he was and the staff he can manipulate, which also answered Acarlie's question on how he made his staff appear like she saw in the arena. He then went on to tell them about the elders' village and the prophecy about the black hole and how they did not have the answer to it yet but they were on their way to Aragorth to seek the ancient scrolls for information but needed a skyship to pass over there.

"And so since we cannot see the President anymore we shall have to go to Hiro and speak to our king, once we are free."

"Don't be so sure they will let us go so easily Raiden," Zack said. "Think about what Shuian has done so far to keep his secret safe. Not only has he populated one of his own cities with infected humans and aeomon, telling them the blood of elementalists is magic and they must be killed, but he has also fixed the battles so Eloma would never win. What after all that trouble he has caused would stop him from keeping us in here until we either die or give into whatever demand he wants."

They all sat in silence then, they all knew Zack was right. Right now they were powerless and were stuck in a cell and could not do anything. Acarlie tried looking through the translucent blue electric shield to see the young man Raiden called Val in the other cell. She could make out a figure sitting in a cell of his own tired, like he had tried escaping but found there was none and given up. She felt a small feeling of happiness flow through her when she thought about what he had done for her, they really were going to kill her and no one in the crowd of thousands would have saved her but he was different. He saw her in danger and went in to save her not even thinking of the consequences. The feeling of happiness ran through her blood warming it with a tingling sensation when she thought about her hero.

It was another couple of hours of sitting, waiting for someone to come and speak to them when Raiden decided to catch up on his sleep while they were waiting and the others all sat in silence, thinking of how they would escape this one. It was another hour on top of that when Acarlie finally saw somebody moving in the hallway outside their cell. She woke Raiden and they all got to their feet as the person entered who they couldn't see properly through the electric shield. The person walked to a control panel on the outside of the cell and pressed a few buttons and the shield disappeared.

"Miles! Where have you been?" Acarlie shouted with happiness as she threw her arms around her tall, broad and handsome saviour and hugged him tightly. Miles was standing before them smiling and caught Acarlie as she threw herself into his arms. His smile seemed to light up the room for Acarlie and Sheeria who was also relieved to see him. "I spoke to President Shuian after I found out about what he has been up to and made a deal with him to let you out. Quickly all of you, we don't have much time, follow me," he told the others as he made his way for the doors.

"First of all Miles," Acarlie said with her hand reaching around to the back of his waist and gesturing to the tall leo. "This is our friend Raiden. If we are to leave I would want him to join us."

Raiden straightened his back and folded his arms and looked down at the smiling human, *I never saw you at the Elemental Battle,* he thought. Like Zack, Miles had a firm handshake when greeting him.

"A leo? Wow, there is a rare sight. Only other leo I've ever seen was last year at the Battle of Osiris. Nice to meet ya pal." Miles seemed to have a particular charisma to him that seemed enchanting but Raiden was more shocked of what he said than how he said it.

"You look like him too you know," Miles added. "What was his name again?"

Raiden stood dumbfounded now. Only one leo was known to be at the Battle of Osiris. Miles began clicking with his fingers loudly while he searched his mind. Raiden wanted to say but eventually it was Acarlie who remembered Miles telling her of the leo warrior he met the year previously.

"Valadad."

"That was it!" Miles shouted and pointed at Acarlie. "How could I forget, Valadad."

"You…knew Valadad?" Raiden finally asked. The ghost of his brother now jumped into his mind, standing tall and proud with his dark fur, red mane and red eyes they both shared and the shiny, metallic blue armour he now wore himself.

"Yeah I did. He was in my battalion along with four other good men," Miles answered. A quick vision of his own friends suddenly appeared. He quickly put them aside though.

"He was my brother," Raiden admitted.

"And a damn good soldier. I was there when he died Leo," Miles now said looked up at him. Raiden's eyes shifted at looked down at the tall human. "He died heroically, saving the lives of many in exchange for his own. I dare even say I myself am here because of him." As a soldier Miles knew himself about death and the broken hearts and families it brings, hearing something like this was hard for any being, even the strong leos and knew to be delicate around his words here. "You must be very proud."

Around so many strangers Raiden didn't know how to react. He had wanted to speak to someone since the death of his brother since the day the news was delivered. In truth he was still grieving himself and now was his chance but he had more important things to worry about. He eventually bottled up these emotions and buried them deep down, "Yes I am Human," he said. "Was it you then who delivered his armour to me in Walton?"

Miles looked confused at first but soon recognised it, "Oh yeah, that really is the same armour isn't it?" He looked around at the small scratches still on the armour and even pointed to one under the breast and smiled. "I did that!" He laughed at the coincidence before looking back up to the leo and answered his question, "No, I'm sorry but I knew nothing about Valadad's possessions. He mentioned a brother once but I never believed I would ever meet him, especially here of all places, right? Speaking of which, weren't we in the middle of escaping this place? I'm sure there was something I had to do down here, right?" he winked at Acarlie.

"Actually Miles, you must free one more of us before we come along with you," she said pointing to the other cell with the blue outline of Val behind it, standing up and trying to see through. Miles hesitated but eventually nodded and walked over to the control panel.

"Miles told me about Valadad Raiden," Acarlie said. "Your friend Val, you said he had no name when he woke up."

"I named him after my brother," he confessed to her.

"You must have really loved him."

Raiden only nodded and waited for Miles to open the cell door before Val finally appeared before them all looking confused and tired.

"There you go pal. I'm Miles, put it there," Miles said putting his hand out. Miles stood nearly a foot taller than Val, with a stronger jaw and larger arms. Val felt a little inadequate compared to the tall, charismatic soldier and was unaware of what was going on but shook Miles's strong hand.

"Thanks," he said.

Acarlie walked up to him. They both recognized each other immediately, "Hello. Raiden has been telling us a little about you, this is Sheeria, over there is Zack," she said and took a step closer to him, "And I am Acarlie," she smiled up at him.

The pretty young elementalist stood only a little shorter than himself. Val was still confused by what was happening but didn't complain that he was let out of his cell. He rubbed the back of his head in embarrassment. "I am Val, nice to meet you," he said putting his hand out but Acarlie did not shake his hand but put her hands around his shoulders and hugged him. She whispered silently then so only he would hear, "Thank you for saving me." He then understood that was why she wanted to hug him and didn't read into it any more than that. As he hugged her he could still see the cuts on her head which had been treated by medics and elders after the battle but still left her clothes and pieces of her black hair stained with blood. Even after her fight though and then hours locked in a cell he could still smell the scent of her perfume on her. He was glad she was safe. He had been locked away alone for hours now but felt he still did the right thing when hearing her scream in the battle. He acted foolishly and impulsively but it saved the life of another. Her tight embrace was all reward he could ask for. He guessed that this Miles must have been her boyfriend though and let go of her, "No problem," he whispered back. "Anytime."

18

Miles led them all out through the dusty hallways of Lachine's containment centre and down hallways of dimly lit metal walls. The tapping of their feet echoed off the floor and all around them. Miles was still wearing his cream silk shirt with the top three buttons he left undone and black leggings and holding onto the hilt of his blade while they walked. Still there was an uncomfortable silence around them. They were all alone in their escape, with not a single guard in sight. For the weight of his blue armour Raiden trailed in the rear. He could not run as fast as the others but still managed to catch up with fast strides of his long legs. Zack was in front of him. His bow and quiver of arrows had now been confiscated and only had his dark green and brown clothes on his back for protection. He felt more unsettled by the silence than any other there. The further they walked the more he felt there was something wrong. They were prisoners and now seemed to be just walking away with no means of stopping them whatsoever. Eventually he stopped when he felt he could go no further.

"What is it Zack? Why are you not coming?" Raiden asked when he caught up. He put one his large, furry hands on Zack's shoulder.

"Raiden, don't you think this is just a bit too easy? I mean we're in a containment centre right? So where are the guards? Where is anybody, this place is empty? Also, how did Miles get down here in the first place with his weapon by his side? Apart from your armour everything we had has been taken from us. Only Val and his staff has managed to stay with us."

"Well the man did say he made a deal with President Shuian. It wouldn't have been hard for him to make the President hold his guards back."

"That's the other thing. I've been around a paranoid community for the last decade of my life now and so I can't help but see things differently. Why would the President not send his men to escort us out themselves? Don't you see the holes here?" Zack asked.

Raiden looked ahead to the backs of the others and sniffed the air, smelling nothing that gave anything away but squinted his eyes now understanding. He felt unsettled too now, "Hmm, I think you may be right."

"Shuian wants us all in one place together. Maybe we're walking into–"

"Now let's not jump to conclusions Zack. We don't know where we are going yet and so we need to be with the others with a keen eye."

Zack frowned, "I wish I had my bow."

"We will be fine Zack so long as we stay alert and stick close to each other. The last thing we want is to cause a panic or risk losing this treaty we have at the minute with the President. Now I don't know this Miles like you do Zack, I can't speak for him."

"No, Miles isn't the issue Raiden," Zack assured. He brought his hand to his black beard and rubbed it with the back of his wrist in thought. "Miles has been there since the beginning. I just think that Shuian is up to something."

Raiden nodded and looked back at the others now a few yards ahead of them and now signalling for them to catch up. They caught up with the other escapees and left the containment centre through an elevator which led them to more hallways, this time better lit with red carpets with gold and yellow patters and paintings of landscapes on the walls. Small red lamps sat on the walls illuminating their way as they passed.

"It is this way, hurry!" Miles said as he ran down the hall and led them into a large, well decorated room with a huge metal door in front of them which looked to be a safe door. There were side doors to them closed and the whole room was silent.

"This is a dead end Miles?" Acarlie told him.

He smiled to her, "Don't worry, it's not. I was shown how to operate these doors when I came down here. The operating panel to open the large metal door is through one of the side rooms. Just give me a second and I'll tap it in."

Acarlie nodded as Miles went into one of the side rooms to open the door for them. Only when the door opened there standing before them assertive with four guards around him armed with crossbows was President Matri Shuian. Still wearing his blue, tailor-made suit and looking smug toward them all. The shock hit Acarlie and she wanted to ask how when her answer came before her in the form of the tall and handsome soldier who reappeared beside Shuian with his arms folded and wearing the smirking face of betrayal.

"Good to see you all again. Guards take positions," Shuian said as they walked around the side of them and stood at the exit they had just come down so the others had no escape.

Acarlie was so shocked she was almost in tears and not taking her eyes off Miles as he stood beside Shuian. Zack instantly went to step forward to approach Miles but was quickly stopped by Raiden who only held out his hand and let the distraught elementalist do the talking.

"Miles…how could you?" she asked wide eyed.

Miles looked over to them. He knew he had the upper hand and did not fear any of them. He chuckled evilly and plainly told them shrugging his arms, "Money my dear. I am doing this for money."

"Money? I don't understand. Why do you want money all of a sudden?" Acarlie asked still not believing what she was seeing. Miles's warm blue eyes she began to think she loved now seemed to glow with a calculated malevolence and his once cheeky smile she always saw as a cute arrogance now really did look the picture of betrayal. She thought she knew this man and now she instantly felt she was a stranger to him. He folded his arms again and explained to her, "I am a mercenary Acarlie; and mercenaries get paid. At first I had the contract with your Elder Argo, but when I discovered all about what the President has been doing I went to him myself at first blackmailing him to pay me to keep my mouth shut. But since you won the battle I gave him a better idea," he said with such enthusiasm and pride in his words, like the devil himself was controlling his tongue. He walked round them just wanting to shout "*I beat you*" but didn't. He wanted her to know how he betrayed her but Zack took the lead here and finished his sentence.

"As someone we trusted the President paid you to lead us here to be sentenced, privately and out of the public's eye."

Miles clapped loud in sarcasm at Zack, "Well done Zack. I knew you would be the first to work it all out. You were nearly on to the whole thing when we were kicked out of the governor's office but you just didn't get it. He never wanted us in there because he had been ordered to send her to the fight to kill her as quickly as possible so she wouldn't find out the truth."

"But I do know the truth!" Acarlie shouted now turning to Shuian still standing tall and proud. His pin-like moustache now spiked up with his smug grin. "I know what you have been up to. I know you have stolen one of the traits of the elementalists as so you can have an elementalist here, but why? That is what I want I know."

Shuian tilted his head slightly to one side and told them, "Because Isolies has never had an elementalist. We are a great nation who trades with the best of them but we have never been recognized as a nation with an elemental school. Even Racoves has two schools yet as great as we are we get none. So I did what was best for my people and…"

These last words stung like poison in Zack's heart then and he exploded with anger, screaming at Shuian.

"How can you say what's best for your people? What about Plainess? Weren't they *your* people? Have you any idea of the dramas I have been through the past ten years. The families lost; my friends, my home, my *wife*!"

"To make an omelette you need to break some eggs," Shuian countered coldly and narrowed his dark eyes in an icy stare right back at him. "It was necessary."

"I'll give *you* necessary," Zack said holding up his hands to strangle him but was held back again by the leo.

"Yes this is all very touching," Miles butted in then sarcastically. He walked back to Shuian and behind the firing range of crossbow darts.

"The first elementalist from Eloma in ten years escapes the demons of Plainess, defeats the Lachine elementalist against the odds…" he said loudly to aggravate them. "…and now you're dead. All apart from the leo of course," he winked at Raiden. "Because we all know what is so special about our lion friend here."

Raiden paused in silence and stared daggers at the traitor, clenching his fist into a tight ball and fighting the urge overwhelming him to leap across and plant it in the pretty mercenary's face. Val however looked over to Raiden and wanted to ask but kept his mouth shut and turned back over to the man he thought superior to him. Miles was taller than Val, broader, better to look at and more charismatic. With Miles standing confidently behind a wall of crossbows he could do nothing but let him continue provoking Acarlie.

"Oh, and Acarlie, you and me…" he said pointing to him and her, "…It was never going to happen."

Acarlie's heart stopped then thinking about the night they had together previously. She turned red from embarrassment, "You unbelievable son of a bitch," she said. Her eyes now welling up with hot tears and wanted to hide her face from him so he couldn't see her pain. He laughed arrogantly and walked toward her again but was blocked by Val who stood in front of her. She hid behind his back and wiped her face while he didn't say a word but stared at Miles who walked up close to him until they were nose to nose.

"I don't know who you are Val but I wouldn't protect her if I were you." He looked over Val's shoulder at the hiding Acarlie and back at him. His piercing blue eyes winked at him, "The things we got up to last night–"

"Choose your next words wisely or they will be your last!" Sheeria snapped as she stood beside Val. She too felt red from anger of his sudden betrayal. She trusted Miles and considering how he was also betraying Argo's trust, an elder Sheeria had known for decades now she too began to fight the tears seeping from her eyes and wore a look of disgust and hatred for him. Miles looked up to her, still smiling and took a step back. No one said anything but stood in silence and stared at Miles who laughed again and began clapping his hands. A sound that echoed off the walls and circled all around them like the whole room was laughing at them too. "I don't think you understand the situation you are all in. We are not here to imprison you nor are we going to let you escape," he told them as he stood back by Shuian's side.

"Actually that is just what you might want to do," a voice said from the side door Shuian came from.

They looked round to see a well-dressed person in blue robes with dark skin and a bushy beard that only Raiden and Val smiled at as they recognized. He stood tall and strong beaming toward Shuian not blinking or taking his eyes off him.

"Who might you be and why are you here?" Shuian asked the stranger.

It was now Zahied's turn to stand assertive and confident while he had their attention, "Well my name might be Jonathan but it's not. I prefer people to call me by the same name my parents did, Zahied. I am with the leo and the boy in the traveller's cloak and I have some information for you that you might want to hear."

"Speak now then," Shuian spat out at him.

Zahied then spoke in a slow, strong voice making sure everybody would understand him.

"I have been following you for the last couple hours and have overheard some of the things you have been talking about," he told them using his hands to gesture like he was speaking to a large audience.

Shuian looked unsettled by this news. "That's an offence!" he said.

Zahied giggled and shook a finger and his head while grinning, "Not nearly as bad of an offence as what you have been committing. When I heard about the city you have infested and the elementalist you have cheated and imprisoned I took some actions of my own."

Now even Miles looked a little unsettled by this news as he looked at Shuian.

"What have you done?"

"Why, as the children would say I have 'tattled' on you," Zahied said with such triumph he couldn't help but smile at them.

"What! No, you couldn't have?" Shuian shouted in anger and disbelief at him.

"I think you will find I have. I have written a dozen letters and sent them to a dozen cities including the High Council of Elders in Chippenham. Your days as a city with an elemental school are over and your days as President are numbered. Once they find out you have betrayed your own people they will send for you. I have written that if the safety of the elementalist is not ensured and she is not found safe then you would have killed her, and you know the punishment for a crime as great as that don't you?"

Shuian looked outraged now, this stranger had beaten him. He could not kill the girl and could not carry on any of his plans, and so he turned to another option, *if I'm going down...*

"Kill him," he told his men and the archers pointed their arrows at him and fired...

But to their disbelief the darts flew straight through him, like he was a ghost; like he was not there at all. Miles understood immediately what this meant and shouted, "He is a Caster! He is portraying his position from elsewhere in the room!"

"That's right," Zahied said, this time appearing from behind them still with his hands behind his back and his back straight.

The guards all turned to him believing he was armed. "And this is a distraction."

As soon as the guards turned was all the time the leo and tigian needed to pounce on them, scratching at their faces and knocking their crossbows. Raiden being stronger than Sheeria had just finished ripping one guard's arm back and out of its socket but was caught unaware by the guard who managed to fire his dart at him, but the dart was only wooden and tipped with steel and so did not pierce his Leoium alloy armour but simply deflected off his chest and angered the leo. Raiden dropped the screaming maimed guard and turned to the other, grabbed him by his throat, took the crossbow from his grip and shoved it as hard as he could down the poor screaming man's mouth, pinned him to the floor and fired the crossbow into the back of the guard's neck.

Miles drew Razor and tried blindly swinging his blade around to catch one of them but failed. Val tried to step forward but Miles instantly punched the him in the nose and forced him back then followed Shuian who immediately ran back past Zahied and back down a narrow corridor and toward a presidential elevator that would take him anywhere in his complex. He typed in the code needed and entered the door when it opened. The door closed and the two stood panting and worried.

"What just happened there? Who was that man and why could he get past security and down here?" Shuian bellowed as he pressed a button, turning to Miles red with anger. Miles was not as angry as the president and seemed cool and self-composed when he answered, leaning back against the wall and looking to the ceiling, "He was a Caster, meaning he would have the know-how to cloak and make himself seem invisible to your guards. That's my best guess."

Shuian was still almost red from rage if it wasn't for his natural dark complexion, "Well whoever he is I want him dead. I want them *all* dead, do you hear me Miles? *Dead*!" He roared at him in the small but tidy glass elevator now climbing.

Miles only stood still and laughed which only enraged Shuian more. "You think this is funny!?"

"Hilarious," Miles countered.

"You won't be laughing when I have you arrested for helping the prisoners escape!" Shuian tried to threaten but Miles only looked down now and gave a warning himself.

"Try it."

The red faced Shuian turned back to the panel and pressed another button then spoke in a speaker under it. He called more guards to go down to the floor the others were on then stopped the elevator and turned back to Miles who was still chuckling.

"I'm glad you're finding this so fucking amusing!" he eventually shouted.

"Calm your passions Matri," Miles said like he was speaking to a best friend.

"You shall not call me that! I am President of Isolies!"

"Keep on throwing those toys out that pram, eventually you'll hit something," Miles said again sarcastically.

Miles sarcasm was angering Shuian in a way that made him want to punch him in the face, only when he clenched his fist Miles looked down with a confident grin and a gleam in his eye as if to dare him to try. He eventually calmed down and his combed his hair with his hands and straightened his tie and told him.

"I want you to go down there again and outflank them. I don't care how it's done just do it. You hear me?" He stepped closer and said quietly in his ear, "Do whatever you need but she must not be allowed to leave this city!"

Miles was unscathed about the news of his new orders, "Ok, but it's going to cost you."

"You can have anything you want. Just bring me her."

The door opened and revealed another corridor much like the one he was on before. Miles walked out and stood just beyond the door and looked back over his shoulder.

"Your price will be more than money this time Mister President," he said as the doors began to close, "I shall see you soon...."

The last of the guards had just fallen from Raiden's grip when Acarlie noticed President Shuian had escaped.

"Damn, he escaped," she said looking at Raiden who was now wiping the blood from his hands, "What do we do now?"

Zahied answered her then, "We have to climb onto a higher level. Shuian's office will be on the top floor. If we want to get out of here alive we have to talk to him and convince him of freeing us. Otherwise if the guards don't kill us the people will."

"Why would the President's office be in the same building as the prison?" Val asked pointing out what everybody else was thinking.

"It's not a prison down here. This place is one of the tallest buildings in the city, the presidential office is on the top and you guys were contained in his personal containment centre on an underground floor. Think of this place as a modern version of an old castle. Where you were was in its secret dungeon. The President wouldn't keep you in the public's containment centre now would he? He wanted you out of the way quietly."

"The top floor it is then," Zack said picking up a crossbow from one of the dead guards.

"There's another elevator down the end of the hallway, it won't be direct though. We will have to change over and take another if we want to reach the top floor and the only thing is that we have to change on the security's floor. I expect there will be people working today and won't be so friendly to us."

"If it's the only chance we have of getting out of here in one piece we have to take it," Val said understanding the situation. "Raiden, Zahied and I must reach Hiro to get a skyship, until then the elementalist is the number one priority, right?" he said to Raiden as he knew Raiden would be thinking on the same lines. If they got Acarlie safely to Hiro it would be more than easy to convince the king to help them on their quest. Raiden did not answer though. He stood upright facing the back hallway they first came down listening to the sound of voices and hurried footsteps coming toward them. His ears twitched, "More are coming," he said calmly in a growl staring down the hall.

"I hear them too, we can take them on," Sheeria said standing beside him but Raiden would not be convinced so easily.

"No, you must go with your Elementalist. You must ensure her safety and help her get to the top floor. I will take these on myself. I will catch you up."

Val and Zack were together opening the large metal door, just wide enough for Acarlie and Zahied to run through as the guards noticed them. Sheeria was still standing stubbornly next to Raiden refusing to leave him but still he was not swayed and took her by her shoulder and almost threw her past the large metal door with the others.

Sheeria, as soon as he let her go roared and ran back to him as he shut the door in her face and locked it from the other side. She barked and slammed on the door screaming, "Foolish leos! Foolish bloody leos!"

As Raiden locked the door from the other side he heard Sheeria's cries and curses, "Foolish bloody leos!" but ignored her. The guards had now caught up with him and now another seven guards stood where the others lay dead on the floor, their swords and spears ready in hand.

Stubborn tigians, they never know when to quit or when to run, Raiden thought to himself as he stared at the guards facing him and stood low in a defensive position, his claws and teeth now showing, *right now it's time to do what I do best…*

The others had tried to open the door to help Raiden but it was Zahied who took control of the situation and got them to move on. The hallways now were less decorated than the other ones were and were more like a hospital corridor with plain white plastered walls on one side and large glass windows on the other looking over at the city, now lit by the moons in the darkness and the light of the city at night. Zahied tried looking out the window to see the office they had to reach but the building was now too tall to see anything.

"So you are a Caster then Zahied? I am impressed, especially how you projected your image away from yourself like you did just there. But how did you get all the way down here without being detected and how did you know so much about the President's plans?" Acarlie asked him while they walked down the endless hallways, occasionally passing doors leading onto more hallways of confusingly similar walls.

Zahied explained to them all, "Well, after Val and Raiden had been arrested I couldn't do anything to stop them and because of all the crowd around me I could not try any tricks in case I was also arrested. So I decided to wait until I was alone and cast a small illusion on myself, making me not invisible but simply unnoticed to everyone. I didn't know where you would be so I figured I should stay close to Shuian and that other guy who was there, Miles. While I was standing and listening to them I heard everything I needed to know about where you were and also everything else he had been getting up to these last ten years."

"So then you sent messages out to all the cities around the world?" Val said getting in on the conversation.

Zahied laughed and said, "Actually no, I did not have enough time to write and send out all those messages. I was bluffing and it worked, they still believe it too."

"So his days as president are not numbered then?"

"No, they're not but he believes they are and that could be our ticket out of here."

Acarlie smiled at the thought of escaping out of the complex and the whole city on a single bluff but at the same time felt a little uneasy knowing that no one yet knows the danger she was in. Sheeria was still walking behind the group still angry with the leo when she stopped and her ears pricked up. She stopped the others and pointed down the hallway at two guards walking down talking to each other. There was a moment of panic about them then not knowing whether to run back or rush the two guards. When Zack realised the guards hadn't noticed them he acted quickly, opening the nearest door to them which was only a small storage closet but big enough to fit them in. Zahied however had an alternative plan and told them to close the door.

"You should get in here with us," Zack told him.

"Trust me. I will be fine, now close the door before they see you."

Zack did not know what he was up to but did as he was instructed and closed the door with his ear to it. Zahied was quick and knew exactly the trick to cast as he had been practising it for a while now and did not even need his book for it. The guards were closing in now so he had to be fast. He put his hands out and pointed in front of him. He then moved his pointed hands in a large rectangle in front of him from his head all the way down to his toes making an invisible window which he quickly stepped through and then waited to see if it worked as the guards walked up to him.

"I hear President Shuian has some prisoners down below us he wants executed," one said to another. They walked blissfully unaware of the escaped prisoners hiding from them and especially the cloaked Caster who stood before them.

"I know but why don't he just kill them in front of the public? It will send the word out that we don't agree with liars and cheats wouldn't it?" the other said walking past the door the others were hiding behind and ever so close to Zahied. Zahied knew not to touch them because the trick would instantly wear off if he did or if they heard him so he stood flat up against the wall hoping they didn't lean up against him and tried to slow his breathing.

"You just don't get it do you? The President needs them out of the way quietly so he can seem more merciful to his people if they had an *accident*. I hear they got that new guy to do the deed anyway. That guy that showed up this morning before the E.B. They said he cut down the top security before finally getting to the President who hired him to do his dirty work. What's his name...Miles, that's it, Miles. A mercenary who was in the Battle of Osiris don't you know?"

"Really? That guy was in the Battle of Osiris? Last I heard

no one ever survived that battle. I heard Feydon swept the battle ground after the fighting and murdered all injured survivors."

"No, there were a handful of survivors. He just happened to be one of them, fancy that? Honestly you should hear some of the stories I've heard about that guy already. It's only been a day but somehow some things have been said about him already. The most recent being that he was with the elementalist and helped her get past the demons through Plainess."

"Yeah, I heard that one too. What do you reckon to that?"

"All I know is I don't want to get in his way. I also heard he single handily killed a tigian with that blade of his."

The two were now standing still, chatting to each other and would not move on. Zack slowly opened the door to see the backs the guards. He tried to sneak up on them when he was held back suddenly by Zahied who appeared behind him. He looked desperate not to draw attention to them and tried pushing Zack back behind the door.

"Well I'm going to grab some coffee and have a smoke. Do you want one?" one asked the other still blissfully unaware of the hidden people behind them.

"No that's ok. I'm trying to quit. The wife says they'll kill me one day."

"Suit yourself then. I'll see you later," he said then walked on and turned round a corner and down another of the corridors while the other stood there sorting out his jacket and looking out of the window. Before he could see the reflection in the window a hand grabbed him from behind and covered his mouth from making any noise. The man went into shock and froze as his attacker's other arm swung around his neck and pulled him back to the floor. The last thing the man ever saw was the face of Zack as he violently jerked the poor man's neck to one side breaking it. Zack dragged the body into the closet and signalled the others to go.

"Was that really necessary to kill that man like that? You could have just let him go?" Zahied asked him angrily but quietly. Zack was not going to tolerate such arguments and grabbed Zahied by his collar and shoved him against the glass.

"Do you have any idea what I have been living through for the last ten years? Every one of these men *knew* it was happening and none of them sent for help. To me every one of these people are scum and by not helping they are just as bad as the one who did this to my people, so back off!"

He let go of him and carried on down the hallway. The others stood and stared at him as he walked by but didn't say anything. Val walked to Zahied and patted him on the back. Zahied stood pale with what just happened and Acarlie said to him, "Don't worry about him. He will not hurt you. He is just very upset at the moment."

Zahied nodded then, gathered himself together and looked to see Zack now walking in front of them, "Zack is right on walking. We should go quickly. The elevator is further down the hall," then closed the door hiding the dead guard and followed Zack.

A little while after that and they were still walking down the empty hallway toward the elevator looking out for it. Soon to their left they found it. Zack pressed the button and they silently waited for the elevator to arrive.

Val walked over to the glass window behind them and stood looking out of it when the thought came to him to ask Acarlie, "Acarlie, the man those men were just talking about, that Miles. He was the one who trapped us right?"

Acarlie felt stung when she heard his name and winced with anger and embarrassment. She looked to see if Sheeria felt the same way about him and answered him quietly under her breath, "Yes that was him. He was supposed to be my guide and guardian like Sheeria but he obviously had other plans of his own."

She looked at him thinking, *what's your point?* and hoped he wouldn't ask too much about him and her, but he didn't. He had another question in mind.

"They said he was in the Battle of Osiris and has done this

and that. They said he even killed a tigian on his own, that can't be right. I mean how good can he be?"

The elevator dinged and the door opened and they all looked over to its empty contents. Val turned away from the glass for just a second when something large fell smashing through the glass and on top of him. From an above floor of the complex Miles tracked them and once they were at the elevator used the time to climb outside while they were waiting and smash through before they could escape, landing on the little Val and beating him. The others were now all standing in the elevator when they saw this, "Miles!" Zack shouted and went to kick him off Val. Miles saw the attack coming and jumped to his feet, blocked Zack's kick and kicked Zack under his knee. Val saw what was happening now, reached up and grabbed Miles from behind and swung him off him, helped Zack back to his feet and pushed him into the elevator.

"Let me handle him!" Val told them as he gave Zack to Acarlie. He really had no idea of how to deal with this man but felt it more important to get the elementalist away.

"No Val there's still time, get in here with us!" Acarlie called to him.

He had no time to answer. He was pulled back from the elevator from behind and slammed up against the wall by Miles. Acarlie shouted in vain as the doors closed and all they could do was watch Val be thumped in the stomach and again knocking him to the floor then both of them disappeared as the elevator started lifting and they were no longer visible. Acarlie tried to dash for the control buttons to go back down but was held back by Sheeria. "We have got to go back down there!" she told them.

"We can't, the longer we stay the less chance we have of getting out of here. With any luck Val and Raiden have bought us some time," Sheeria told her and moved her away from the panel.

"But we can't just leave everyone who gets left behind. What if the next one is you?" Acarlie protested.

"Then you must leave me behind," Sheeria said in a tone that could not be argued with.

"They will be fine. Val is stronger then he looks and Raiden... well I think we can all agree that Raiden will be able to look after himself," Zahied said to try and calm her down.

"He's right. I don't know Val but if he can pull off that trick with that staff of his he might have a chance against Miles," Zack said as he rubbed his throbbing knee and lifted his leg up and down to get the blood rushing through it.

"Of course he doesn't. Do you remember the way Miles fought back in Plainess? He has far more and better training than Val would have. He will rip Val to pieces!"

"Then you must let him go. His death will mean your survival," Sheeria told her.

"I can't let him go. He saved my life!"

"Then let him save you again," Sheeria said, this time reaching over and putting her paws on Acarlie's shoulders trying to comfort her.

"But what about the mission he was supposed to do? What about the black hole we have been told about?"

"I still know the details and the whereabouts of the monastery. If anything should happen then I will take on his mission," Zahied pointed out but this was still not good enough for Acarlie who still only wanted to stop the elevator and go back down but her conscience knew the truth. She had to let him go. Everyone in this elevator was between her and the panel back down. A part of her knew she was just being stubborn. The truth burned inside her like acid and she felt it tear up her insides as she thought of leaving the man who saved her life behind to die so she could escape. But she had to, like all her natural survival techniques were coming into play all at once and not letting her press the button to go back down. She looked into Sheeria's apple green eyes who looked down at her gently, silently whispering the truth she already knew. She finally accepted and closed her eyes and clenched her fists still not enjoying the feeling that she knew this was wrong. "Very well. We carry on forward as planned... Val gets left behind." She sighed again and dropped her head down. Sheeria knew this was hard for her and pulled her closer to embrace her. Acarlie knew what she was trying to do and chose not to act but to gather herself together again and waited in Sheeria's furry embrace for them to reach the switching point on the security's floor.

19

Stubborn tigians, they never know when to quit or when to run, Raiden thought to himself as he stared at the guards facing him and stood on a low defensive position, his claws and teeth now showing, *right now it's time to do what I do best...*

The first guard approached him, unaware of the damage a single leo could do to a person but he was a good guard, strong and fearless, but not too bright.

"By order of the President of Isolies you have been sentenced to incarceration, to be carried out immediately. If you defy your arrest we have been given the order to use any means necessary," the guard said as he approached him. His spear held high ready to strike down on him but as he did Raiden caught the spear and pulled the guard toward him with it and head butted the man before biting into the side of his neck. The strong and fearless man was now screaming like a child holding onto the gaping hole in his neck, staggering back with an unbelieving look in his eyes before finally falling to the ground and crawling out of the way.

Raiden wanted to laugh, these men were not soldiers, nor were they equipped like them. They looked to be personal security, armed with only melee weapons and light battle gear of black body armour, useful against a group of humans and even a tigian. But compared to a tall, leo armoured in the traditional leoium alloy armour with sharp teeth and claws and superior strength they were all outmoded. The others weren't as stupid as the first man and knew they would not win this fight unless they had more numbers on their side. They sent one back to gather reinforcements who sprinted back from where he came while the others only tried stalling for time. Raiden was trying his scare tactic he often tried against humans, but one guard wasn't buying it. He stepped forward with his chin high and spoke to the leo. "Leo, you know we cannot let you pass. It will be easier for everyone if you surrendered yourself and maybe the president will go lenient on you for cooperating."

Raiden was a lot smarter than the human thought and laughed at his threat, "Somehow I don't believe the president will let me leave so freely." He smirked and continued, "But we all know here what should happen if you try, and more importantly succeeded in killing me. You would have every world leader as well as every elder in the world commanding you paid the price for a crime such as killing me of all people."

Every man now exchanged worried glances, Raiden grinned. He knew he had them where he wanted. "So here's my offer. You humans turn around and walk back while your limbs are still attached to your body. Heed my words, if you don't want to lose your lives then turn around now and I will forget about you," he said it in a threatening growl with such fire that one of the guards actually got the message, turned to his companions and bowed to them. Then he turned back to Raiden, bowed and turned around and started walking away. Raiden was always very good at this. The scare tactic was an important and very useful tactic for all leos and they had been using it for thousands of years. They figured a creature would not be a threat to you if it is scared away. But the only problem is that humans are normally more difficult to scare than other creatures since they are smarter and sometimes will face their fears. Something the leos have always admired the humans for. The man walked out and down the hallway but did not get out in time as the reinforcements arrived and the tallest commander of the group took the man by his collar and started shouting at him.

"Where are you going Dexter? Answer me!" He bellowed at him. The man was large and tall with a muscular build with battle scars all over his face and down one side of his neck. Dexter, the man trying to escape was brought back into the room before he finally shrugged himself off.

"I'm going home to my wife, ok? We're not the army and this is only a job. If I have to fight this beast then I quit! I don't fancy my chances fighting him."

The large commander walked up to him until they were almost nose to nose. He also had a scare tactic of his own, staring down at the man who was slightly shorter than him.

"If you are not one of us then you are one of them. Now kill that thing or I will kill you myself, that is an order!"

Dexter gathered all his courage and shouted back at his commanding officer, "You know what Grimman, screw you! You want this thing dead then do it yourself. I only work security like everyone else here. We're not trained to fight leos. Do you even know anything about the leos? What has he done to us anyway?"

The large man Grimman had enough of Dexter's backchat and pushed him to the floor beside Raiden who was standing still analysing the situation and counting the men he would have to fight. He had a picture in his mind of how he wanted the fight to go. He thought to himself, *none of these men have a ranged or any forbidden weapons that killed out my kind, which gives me the advantage if I carry it out properly. Swipe the large man to one side and dive into the group. They look inexperienced and a little scared, they would not know what to do. Any strike they would do would likely only make contact with my armour and that gives me another advantage. The only problem will be if the large man takes control of the situation which will give his people confidence, but if I help this Human Dexter he will likely help me.*

Overall; take out the large man, scare the people and fight correctly and don't lose focus. Fourteen people, one of those is injured and one is on my side, that's only twelve, all humans and not a tigian in sight, I like those odds….

Grimman drew his sword and went to stab at the young guard Dexter on the floor and kill him but he was stopped by the towering armoured beast that with two swipes knocked his sword from his hand then knocked him to one side. Raiden straightened his back, brought his chest forward and roared as loud as he could and dived into the group of people. Like he predicted, they only called out in fright and jumped back. The ones brave enough to swing their weapons only deflected off his armour and ducked, screamed and kicked wildly as he got hold of them one by one and slashed at their pathetic human made armour. His claws cut through the thick, black material like tin foil and left it tattered. He was quick and relentless and fought them valiantly but was not too sure of himself to let his guard down. Every swing they tried at him he either ducked, rolled or jumped as to avoid their attacks. It was like he thought; these people, like Dexter said, weren't soldiers and were not trained with fighting such oppositions. One managed to remember a little of his training and ran back down the hallway for a weapon he was trained to deal with tigians, assuming it would have the same effect. Raiden now had them all good and scared. They stood with their backs to the wall, whimpering in fear at him, not daring to take another step forward. Raiden took this as his cue as he looked at one human who was still dazed on the floor and knew it was now time to attack. He pounced on the human with both his knees pressed down on him and reached out for the next person to him who tried to run away. He caught him by the back of his collar and threw him against the wall, knocking the air from him. He then quickly turned his attention to the human still on the floor. This would be his power move. A move to scare the humans around him. He opened his jaw and bit down on his head. The other guards saw in horror as Raiden bit down with their friend's head in his mouth and tugged violently and viciously until the bones in his neck separated and the skin slowly tore away, the poor man wailing a muffled scream whilst inside the mouth of the leo. Blood now sprayed everywhere as he tugged more until he finally separated the head from its shoulders and spat it out beside him. He punched the other man's skull with enough strength that they all heard the bones break and the pair of them both lay dead, twitching uncontrollably as their nerves were now the only thing on their bodies working, in an increasingly large pool of blood. But Raiden was not finished yet and only darted to another, slashing his claws across his throat and opening it to leak hot, red liquid down his body before turning to another, who tried to run away. Raiden caught him from behind and holding him by his face pulled back hard and slammed it into the floor, so hard the floor rumbled and the man's skull cracked and started bleeding. A puddle of slippery blood on the floor diluting and mingling with the others spread across the room like red, wet carpet. Three of the guards nodded to one another in agreement, ran away as fast as they could and managed to get away safely while another did as Dexter did and saw there was no point in fighting and put his hands to the back of his head, got down on his knees and put his head to the floor. There were now only four more to deal with and the first two decided to attack together, drew their swords and charged at him swinging blindly. Raiden took a step back and tried parrying their swords to one side when one connected with his hand paw and cut it open. The two got over confident though when they saw the leo in pain and tried jumping on him. Raiden sensed their desperation and took this as his advantage and when the first dived for him he grabbed him and threw him to one side, blocked the other's attack and grabbed his sword from him and quickly slashed him back with it across the face. The other man saw what happened as he was already running back from him. With a quick look Raiden crouched low and took hold of the man by his feet and flipped him over his shoulders. When the man hit the floor Raiden took his sword and stabbed him with it hard, the sword snapped and stuck in the ground a little and pinned the dying man to the floor.

The man who ran away previously to get the weapon made for tigians came back with it. It was a long pole, as long as a sword with an open electric bar at the end, like a long taser. It was named a lightning rod. The man crept up behind Raiden with it and shocked him. The shock also conducted with the armour he had and the pain sent him crazy, it only lasted for a second but the pain seemed much longer. Raiden cried out in pain and fell to the floor, loosening his armour and quickly taking it off.

Grimman was now on his feet and went over to the man and took the lightning rod from him.

"Let's see how you like this now Leo," he said shocking him again. Once again Raiden cried out in pain and froze as the shock paralysed him. Grimman tried shocking him again but was unaware that leos had thicker fur than tigians which conducted less electricity but still the tactic was working and soon Raiden was back down on the floor helpless, with his back against a wall so he couldn't escape. Grimman laughed as he repeatedly shocked him and Raiden closed his eyes so he wouldn't see the attacks coming but when he did he heard Grimman shout out in pain. He opened his eyes to see Dexter behind Grimman holding the sword that he pierced through Grimman and twisted it. When he withdrew the sword Grimman fell to the floor like a sack. Dexter helped Raiden to his feet, when Raiden got back on his feet Dexter screamed and fell to the floor holding his side as the last person was still standing, holding up a blood stained spear and threatening Raiden with it. A berserker's rage possessed Raiden after seeing this last man who electrocuted him and now injured the man who saved him and for a brief moment Raiden felt he disappeared into his mind and let his anger control his actions. He roared and took the wooden spear from the soldier's grip and snapped it. The man again tried to turn and run but the rage fuelled Raiden simply reached out and grabbed him, picked him up from behind and slammed the soldier's spine into his knee, snapping it like a boy snaps a stick. When the man fell to the floor Raiden then picked up the lightning rod and stuck it in his mouth and left it there shocking the man who could not move and was now in deep agony until he eventually died. With all his enemies now dead Raiden stood victorious among the dead and surrendered, adrenaline pumping through his heart and his animal instincts and rage still possessing him. He dominated the room by broadening his chest again, tensing his whole body and roaring out a powerful note of victory, a tradition of his people and releasing all the built up aggression, anger and wrath still in his body after his bloody victory.

He breathed deeply after, calming himself down now feeling stimulated and self-satisfied, like he had just won a great competition of endurance and strength. The rush of battle always excited Raiden. He then turned to go to Dexter on the floor and examined his wound. He looked at it and told him, "You will live Human. You will live if you get to hospital immediately. You, Human!" he shouted pointing to the other man with his head to the floor, he looked up shakily.

"Take this man to a hospital!" Raiden barked the order at him while he put on his armour.

The man nodded and got to his feet and Raiden noticed the other man injured hiding on the edge of the floor and admired his strength, "Take him too, leave the rest. They were weak, you three were the strong and wise ones, now go."

Before he left he picked up Dexter off the floor and gave him to the other man and said to him, "Thank you Human. You have no idea what a courageous thing you have done today, go back to your family and tell your story."

Dexter only nodded and the three of them left back down the hall they came from. Raiden unlocked the large metal door and took one final look at the carnage behind him. The walls now stained red. The floor cracked and large red puddles of blood smothered the bodies scattered around, pinned to the floor, some still twitching and the lightning rod poking out of the corpse's mouth now inert. The single head lay across the red floor away from its original shoulders and now closer to the corpse with the opened throat still leaking. Raiden looked down at the human blood staining his paws and covering his blue armour. This is the substance the armour was made for. His gauntlets seemed to drink the blood of the humans now drying over it. His bottom jaw also began to dry from blood. He was a leo, a powerful and proud warrior of Sphere. Humans were his sport. His ancestors would be proud, his family would be proud.

Acarlie shouted in vain as the doors closed and all they could do was watch Val be thumped in the stomach and again knocking him to the floor then both of them disappeared as the elevator started lifting and they were no longer visible.

Val looked up to see the elevator had disappeared and tried to get to his feet but Miles kicked him while he was down on the floor. He swung for another kick but this time Val caught his leg and tripped the other leaving Miles to fall to the floor beside him. They both lay beside one another amongst broken glass trying to get to their feet before the other.

"It's over Miles, Acarlie has got away. You can leave now, just walk away," Val tried to convince him but Miles wasn't fooled so easily.

"The deal in my contract was to kill all of you, so once you are dead I will have to catch up with your friends and–"

"You think I'm going to die that easily?" Val asked him clenching his fist tight and putting up his guard.

Miles had an evil grin on his face and answered, "Yes of course. You think I have gone through all I have to get beaten by you? I have fought many people bigger, stronger and faster than you. I survived Osiris kid, what did you do?"

Val did not answer but punched Miles under his jaw and immediately sent a swift kick in the same direction hoping to push Miles toward the window and push him out but was unsuccessful. Miles received the kick and retaliated with one of his own then jumped toward Val grabbing him in a headlock and pulling him down to the floor. Miles sat down with Val's head firmly in his arms and Val tried everything to get out of it but couldn't free himself and was soon thrown about as Miles tried to snap his neck. They both struggled on the floor for several minutes pushing and pulling each other like schoolboys in a playground occasionally punching each other. Miles still had Val's head locked in his arms until Val pulled hard enough to pull Miles to the floor, then while biting into Miles's hand, he picked up a shard of broken glass and stuck it in his arm. Miles screamed immediately and let go of Val who took a second to catch his breath back then jumped to his feet, called his staff to his hand and swung it across Miles's face. Miles fell back and Val jumped on him, punching him until he was sure Miles's nose was broken. Miles, while on the floor with Val repeatedly hitting him thought enough was enough and decided to end the fight. He reached for Razor in its scabbard and slashed it across aiming for Val who dived to one side and lay on the floor. The fight to anybody else looked like it finished now with no winners because they both lay on the floor dazed looking at the ceiling, trying to get their breath back. After another minute of silence, Miles was the first to eventually get to his feet. He took a step and kicked Val on the floor and tried to stab him but Val was quick and rolled to one side and slowly got his feet. He clutched on to his staff and stood in his fighting stance. Miles grinned at him and pointed Razor to him and said, "Ok, so I can't beat you to death. No matter. I'll cut you up all the same."

With his face still soaked with blood from his bloody nose Miles started swinging for Val who blocked it with his staff one time after another but Miles was on the offensive of this fight and was slowly moving Val back down the corridor. Miles quickly grabbed Val and threw him against the window, elbowing him in the face so his head would crack the glass. Miles looked quickly behind him to see a door leading into another room, took hold of Val, turned and threw him through it. Val smashed through the door and rolled almost unconscious with his head still hurting from the elbow but he got to his feet. His vision was now blurred from the pain but it didn't stop him from seeing Miles raising his blade above his head. Val quickly called his staff again and held it horizontally above his head to block Miles's attack but the staff broke in two which confused even Miles then, who looked at the broken staff and admired his strength of breaking a metal pole such as that. Val looked at half of the broken staff in one hand wondering how Miles managed to break it so easily, then cracked Miles over the head with it without a second thought. Miles screamed out in pain holding his head now and taking a step back, then gripping Razor with both hands but now became desperate to win. He lunged in to fight with Val again who was now using the two halves of his weapon in each hand and managed to get in a few quick jabs with it, but Miles still had the winning hand in the fight. Very soon Miles had Val up against a wall again and kneed him in the groin. He struck Val again with his elbow and when Val was on the floor he knelt down on top of him. Miles panted with exhaustion now knowing he had the time since his knees were on Val shoulders so Val couldn't move.

"I just want you to know, when I catch her..." Miles said holding up his weapon. Val looked up at him with an exhausted and worried expression. Blood from Miles's nose dripped down on Val's. "...And after I have my way with her again..." He spoke with large gaps of exhaustion as he was trying to breathe while speaking to him. "...I'm going to make her scream Val...she'll scream so much she'll begin to like it! I'll have her back in my bed before the end of the night."

Miles laughed at him then went to strike down at him but suddenly was grabbed from behind and with one throw disappeared back and flew back against the wall. Miles was stunned as he was picked up and slammed up against the glass in the hallway. Miles looked to see Raiden holding him up with one bloody hand tightly around his neck, squeezing tightly like he was going to pop his head. Miles had the look of horror as he looked into the ruby red eyes of the leo, "You...you really do look just like him..."

"Raiden..." Val tried to call him whilst still lying on the floor beaten, battered and bruised but it only came out in a whisper, "...Raiden."

The leo heard his companion and looked back to Miles who still was in shock. Raiden glared at him, pulling him closer to his face. The respect he had for this human for being on the same battle field as his brother now instantly vanished and not even hatred remained, "I don't have time for you," he said then threw him out of the window leaving Miles and his blade to fall from the building onto a lower floor.

Miles fell for what felt like twenty meters. Without any armour he suddenly panicked at first but his fall was broken when he fell on a slated tile roof that was a rain shelter of a lower floor's smoking area and slipped down it. Once he reached the end he again fell down and slammed his back against the floor in a large *thud*! "Fuck!" he cried. His head felt dizzy and his vision swam. Razor luckily landed a few feet away from him. Within a minute he suddenly was swarmed by people crouching down and seeing if he was still alive. He tasted blood under his tongue and laughed looking up at the smashed window he was thrown from.

Raiden turned to Val and picked him up, "Where are the others Val?"

He gave Val a minute to wipe the blood from his face and to regain consciousness.

"The elevator. They had to go to the security's floor to switch over and go to the top floor to see the president."

"Then that's where we are going. Come Val, get to your feet. Are you ok?" Raiden said helping him up and taking him to the elevator and pressing the button.

"Where's Miles Raiden? Where did he go?"

"He fell," Raiden said looking out of the window he threw him out, expecting to see his broken lifeless body but instead only seeing a small puddle of blood from where Miles should have been lying. Raiden growled under his breath at the sight of this, upset that he did not know what had happened to him then turned back to the elevator now opening for them. A couple of minutes in the elevator and Val was now himself again but still sore and with a limp. When the elevator opened they found themselves in the security hall with bodies scattered dead around the floor. Raiden knelt down and examined the scratch marks on the bodies, "A tigian passed through here," he said standing back up.

"Then they made it. Look, there's the elevator," Val said pointing across the room to an open elevator.

"Quickly Raiden, let's go before more guards come."

They found the final elevator across the floor Zahied had left open for them then activated it and made their way to the top floor where the others would be. They hoped they were all right and that they would not be too late if anything should happen to them.

20

Zahied burst through the door back into the hallway he left the other three in to see the bodies of the deceased guards and security scattered around the floor. Zack was kneeling down catching his breath back and Sheeria was kneeling over Acarlie who was on the floor in shock. Sheeria was holding her shoulders and comforting her with blood soaked paws as Acarlie was on the floor staring with tears in her eyes at the poor deceased guards. Zahied was just as shocked as she was and wanted to ask Zack and Sheeria if what they just did was necessary but decided not to say, having Zack already shout at him previously made him hesitate. When he left them, there was no blood but many guards walking on this floor. It was important for him to find a security room and unlock the elevator door they needed to reach the roof. It wasn't difficult on his behalf. Whilst cloaking himself he simply crept past all the sentries and found the room he was looking for. A surveillance room with a single lazy human monitoring the rooms of the great building, taking more importance to a conversation to his wife on the phone rather than the escaped prisoners now making their way to Shuian's office on the top floor, or even the caster creeping up to his office since his cloaking trick was useless against cameras. Once inside Zahied simply used another one of his clever elder tricks to send the human to sleep without him even knowing his presence. It was only when he returned back to the others when he realised how difficult it might be now. These people were all dead and their murderers will be simply walking out of the city now, hopefully far away and never to return, he hoped.

"Is everyone ok?" he eventually asked and Zack who was still gasping for breath smiled with a look of pleasure on his face, like he had just avenged all those who had died over the last ten years all at once, but they both knew he still had one person to tend to.

"Yeah I am fine Zahied," he said getting to his feet and brushing himself off.

Sheeria however only looked over to him and nodded while she was still comforting Acarlie whispering to her, "It's ok, it's over now. There won't be any more of them but we must hurry."

The presidential elevator was now open since Zahied had unlocked it and hurried the others inside. Zack entered first followed by Sheeria who now had Acarlie to her feet and was escorting her to the elevator. As she walked over the bodies Acarlie couldn't help but glance down at one of them and look into his lifeless eyes which stared up at her and through her into oblivion. She choked on her breath, covered her mouth and shut her eyes wishing this never happened and knowing his eyes would haunt her for the rest of her life. Zahied couldn't hold it in anymore and had to ask them all, "What happened here? Why the carnage?"

Acarlie spoke at last trying to control her tone from blurting out, "They attacked us! There was nothing I could do. They just kept coming until–"

"It's ok Acarlie, we did what we had to do. It was either them or us," Sheeria said from behind her as the door of the elevator closed sealing them all inside.

"That doesn't make me feel any better you know, they're all dead now because of me."

Zack stepped in then correcting her, "No they're dead because of their president. They all knew what was happening to us, every one of them had the chance to stand up for us but they didn't. They made the choice to follow orders, they knew the risk."

"But what about their families? They were only following orders, only doing their job. How many families will be broken because of us?"

"You rather they kill us then?"

"You know that's not what I mean!" Acarlie snapped at Zack's remark. The elevator was now rising to the top of the massive building.

Being a Caster Zahied had always been a peaceful man who believed that the best solutions were the ones solved without violence. Violence only brought upon more violence, injuries, death; broken prides and broken hearts. Seeing a blood stained Zack so close to him made him feel he stood far on the other side of the spectrum to him and Sheeria who also, being a tigian looked like she had also solved many problems with the teeth and claws of hers but he felt he had a connection with Acarlie. The gleaming moisture of a tear on the bottom of her eye told him the truth of the matter to her. She was also a believer that death was wrong even in defence.

"Look, they were not good people Acarlie. For ten years I have been tortured by these people. They all knew what was happening and they did nothing, that's like pulling the trigger themselves," Zack told her.

"No matter what they had done, does death justify their crime? All we needed was to speak to the President–"

"He is trying to kill us, don't you understand that?"

Zahied now had to speak in order to calm them both down.

"As much as I don't approve of killing a bunch of people, I do believe in what Zack is trying to say. We all need to escape this city in one piece by any means necessary and those guards stood in our way. Acarlie, once we reach the top we shall confront Shuian and make him give us a safe passage out of here."

Acarlie took a breath and wiped her eye, "What about Raiden and Val?"

"Raiden is safe. I saw him on the monitors in the surveillance room. He was running toward the first elevator."

"What about Val? What has happened to Val?"

Zahied paused them remembering the sight of Val fighting. He chose his words carefully, "He is with Miles…they were fighting in armed combat. It looks like Miles had the upper hand."

The name sent a shudder of anger and hatred through Acarlie when he said it and the thought of him killing Val sent another chill of horror through her all at once but she knew like she did before that there was nothing she could do. Even Zack flinched when he thought of him, Sheeria too, they all trusted him but Zahied was unaware of any previous encounters with him.

"Who is that guy anyway?"

Sheeria spoke then, "He was a mercenary contracted by our elder to protect Acarlie but at the first chance he got he betrayed her, myself and Zack for only the price of money."

Zahied nodded but remembered something that Miles said earlier. He picked his words carefully and tried to find the right tone as to not upset the elementalist, "When Miles was standing before us with the President he said something. It was something about you and him 'never going to work'. What did he mean by that?"

The others wished he never asked that because it still upset Acarlie at the thought of it but still she answered, "It was because I—"

"Acarlie, don't hurt yourself by finishing that sentence. Whatever happened between you and that back stabbing bastard should be put behind you and whatever you thought you may have felt for him was not real, do you understand?" Zack interrupted then trying to save the situation and give her a clear mind. She nodded like she was ordered to. He carried on his point to make her understand, "I was with my wife for five years before I lost her to fate. You must forget about him and keep your mind on what lies ahead if you wish to survive." His big, worn, ageing hands rested on her shoulders as she stood still with her head facing the floor before she finally looked up at him and said, "Yes...I guess you are right...as an elementalist I should not let my emotions get in the way of my pilgrimage."

She sighed away her problems and tried to get her head together as the elevator climbed up to the top of the building. The elevator dinged a chime as it reached the top floor which was an open courtyard sitting on top of the building overlooking the whole city. The street lights were now only tiny specks of light from way underneath them and the night air now had a strong wind blowing coldness through them when they stepped out. Zahied immediately activated the elevator again so it would go back down to the security floor on its own where he hoped Val and Raiden would find it. They all walked away from the elevator and across the strange courtyard sitting on top of the building. There was a large shallow concrete pond in the middle of the courtyard with tiny miniature canals only a foot deep and wide reaching all around the courtyard and stretching across some perfectly placed and groomed hedges around the outside of them. In the daytime this would look like a beautiful concrete garden made by the finest designers to overlook the whole of the city but at night it was very disorienting. It was like standing on the edge of the world in a garden made of stone. On the other side of them were large rooms with large glass windows looking onto the courtyard which they could only guess were either offices for the president or were guest rooms. To the right was the biggest room of all. Sitting on the corner and looked like it had another three stories to its size and expensively decorated. They could only guess that this one would be the president's office and walked toward it when they were stopped by a familiar voice.

Out from behind a security door leading into one of the smaller rooms stepped Shuian.

"I have anticipated your arrival Elementalist. I knew that if you were to escape you would make your way up to my personal quarters of the building," he had to shout over to them as the wind was a large factor in their position. Acarlie went to step forward but he carried on, "Which is why I brought some more help to dispose of you this time."

Acarlie shouted over to him, "We just want to leave this place in peace. Please Mister President, let me carry on my journey. It doesn't have to end like this!"

Shuian laughed and called back to her, "If I am going down them I am taking all of you with me. You have destroyed Isolies's chance of ever having an elementalist and have destroyed my reign as president..."

Zahied couldn't help but snigger then unnoticed by Shuian because he knew as did the others that he was bluffing before and found it amusing that Shuian still believed it. The wind blew fierce between them and whistled and shouted with enthusiasm like a commentator before a big fight, pulling at their clothes, trying to undress them. Acarlie stood burning with resolve against the provoking wind and the threatening president and held her chin high against them both. "You got one more chance to let us go free!" Acarlie shouted threatening him now.

Shuian only laughed at her threat again, "I don't think so Elementalist. Billy!"

A window smashed from one of the rooms above them and there stood the bald headed Billy from her E.B previously, the humming electromagnet he used before now was beside him along with many swords and pieces of sharp metal. Acarlie stepped back shocked then turned to Shuian again.

"What are you doing? That's illegal! The elementalist goes through strict rules and regulations restricting them from using their gift for an offensive purpose. We mean no harm and there is no need for this!"

Shuian laughed even louder this time, "Yes that is true but we have already established that Billy here is technically not an elementalist and therefore—"

"You bastard," Zack spoke under his breath readying himself to dive aside if needed to, "I should have killed you when I had the chance."

Shuian lifted his hand and pointed it at them ordering Billy to attack them. Just as he was ordered to, Billy lifted his hands in front of him and the weapons lying by his side levitated in front of him and one by one he sent them flying toward the four of them, cutting through the fierce wind. Sheeria, Miles and Zahied dived to one side avoiding the rain of metal shards and weapons but Acarlie stood perfectly still staring up at Billy, half knowing that he would not kill her outright because he would want to defeat her properly since she beat him earlier, and half scared stiff in case she was wrong. She waited for one of the weapons he controlled to stab her. She also felt like she had just worked something out, like a darkened room within her head suddenly lit up and was thinking to herself how she could get herself out of this situation. Only she couldn't defeat him this time since he had the high ground. The other three were powerless and left hiding behind some of the concrete steps. Sheeria screamed over to her but couldn't move for Billy kept throwing the weapons, aiming to keep them out of the way. Shuian had now escaped again but could now only run into his personal quarters and had no other way of escaping since the elevator was on their side. The elevator door from behind them chimed again and out stepped Val and Raiden who quickly saw the situation and went to join the others.

"Val, you're ok!" Zahied called out to them as they ducked down and beside their companions. "The President is in there!" he shouted again over the wind and pointed to the rooms he fled to on the corner of the courtyard. "Only now we have another obstacle in our path!"

With Zahied shouting Acarlie looked away from Billy and saw Val looking back to her. A warm gush of excitement suddenly overtook her as she called to him. He got up and ran to her narrowly avoiding more shrapnel thrown at him.

"Val, thank goodness," she shouted as she embraced him feeling relived to see him safe. "I thought you were—"

"I will be if we don't get out of here. What's happening? Why is he not just killing us?"

She thought for a second as they stood there in the middle of his firing range, well in his reach, embraced in each other's arms. She then realised what she wanted to know. The recently opened dark room within her mind now burned brighter and she saw everything, she understood...

"He wants us together, to kill us in one blow," Val called.

He looked up to see the false elementalist smiling now. A large, table sized piece of metal he had saved for them floated in front of him.

"We have to go!" he called again and tried to run away but Acarlie held him tight. Her eyes widened and now a relaxing confidence made her stand still and hold him tight, now that she understood...

The chunk of metal suddenly was thrown toward them and Val went to shield his eyes from what was coming. He heard all the others screaming for them unable to do anything but when he glanced toward Acarlie he saw she had the most calm, concentrated face. With one hand still holding Val she lifted the other and pointed it toward the flying metal speeding towards them and suddenly, like there was an obstacle in its path the metal stopped before them. A large blue circle of electricity appeared in front of the chunk of metal and for only a brief second lighting up the dark sky then cracked like thunder in a deafening tone and disappeared as quickly as it came. After that quick second the chunk of metal still levitated in the air above their heads, this time however it was not controlled by Billy. Whilst standing there frozen from fear, by forced instinct she understood a part of her training about magnetism. This was a trait of her training she now fully understood. How her masters never taught it to her she never knew but could only guess that it was an ability that was unlocked only when faced with the absolute desire for it. She felt excited and wished her Master Argo was here to witness it. The courtyard suddenly fell silent. The only sound came from the wind whistling as it passed them around the cold, black night. Billy seemed the most shocked then as he knew what this meant and tried pushing it back toward her but he found out then what it meant to be defeated by the better fighter. He tried with all his might and skills to overpower her but because he was no real elementalist he would never be as strong. In one final movement Acarlie pulled back the floating chunk of metal and threw it toward him, then throwing both her hands in front of her controlling the strong wind around her to change direction and sent the large chunk of metal hurling through the air into the room Billy stood in. He didn't even have a chance to duck out of the way as the metal hit and suddenly, like a fly on a wind shield, a spatter of blood was seen flying in every direction as Billy suddenly disappeared behind the metal. His scream was sudden and weak and immediately silenced but the metal hadn't finished its course yet and carried on flying straight through the whole room and out the other side leaving a gaping hole in the foundations of the small apartment and the whole thing started to fall down. As it fell it started bringing down the apartment next to it and the weight of them both started to crack the whole of the courtyard itself as one corner opened up and let the debris from the fallen apartments fall down to the floor. Everyone screamed and stumbled as the floor shook. Sheeria, Zack and Zahied scrambled to the other side of the courtyard while Val and Acarlie tried to find their footing on the now slanted floor. Val tried to help Acarlie who was inert again and shouted to her but he saw that she was fixed to the ground she stood on with a look of blankness in her eyes. It was like she was turned off altogether and only her shell remained standing there in the midst of the peril of falling off the building altogether. Her head tilted slightly, like a nervous twitch then she looked over to Val. The darkness of death was in her eyes, not even blinking. Val thought he saw the shade of her brown eyes fade slightly to a white, maybe it was a reflection of something up here he thought. She stood like a statue, it was like she was not there at all but had disappeared somewhere leaving her physical body behind.

"I have done it. I have broken one of the sacred rules of Elementalism. I have used my power outside the arena and have killed someone in the process. I am a disgrace to my elders!" she finally said in a low, defeated tone.

"Now isn't the time for this Acarlie!" Val shouted back to her as the floor they stood on cracked a little more and slanted downwards further.

What is wrong with her? Why has she suddenly changed so? Val thought to himself as he tried to help her. One of the hedges had now fallen from its roots and slid on the floor towards him and ready to knock him off the building. He jumped as high as he could but still caught his feet in the end, tripping him and leaving him to fall on his battered face as the hedge fell to its death below. He quickly got to his feet again and held onto a piece of flooring at an angle so he could support himself. He looked up to see Acarlie now moving toward the end of the slanting floor. Every step she took closer to the edge she slid a little more into the oblivion.

"Acarlie! What are you doing!" he screamed out to her in desperation but she looked over to him with such a look of anguish. The wind was still blowing and causing her black, silky hair to whip around her face as she spoke. The words she spoke were loud and clear with a slowness to them Val did not like, "After an elementalist leaves their home there will never be any return unless they become the Elemental Lord or returned by their Alanode to be buried with a proper and sacred burial. There are no exceptions. Death is the only way."

What does she mean death is the only way? he thought.

"If an elementalist breaks the rules of engagement then they are banished and are unwelcome anywhere they go. I have only one chance to redeem myself and make up for the wrong I have done. It is a tradition what I must do! I have broken the rules and so *must* be terminated immediately."

She then took another step back with her arms stretched out to her side. Gravity whispered in her ear seductively as she walked away from Val, from the others, from life itself and towards the fall before her, ready to feel its cold and sudden embrace. Val's heart skipped a beat as he knew then what she was going to do and took a leap of faith and dived toward her. She leaned back and closed her eyes and accepted her fate and waited for the wind she had trained with all her life to carry her home, but instead she felt a hand tightly gripping her wrist and opened her eyes to see Val holding on to her. He leaned over the edge of the building. His other hand trying to support himself from falling over with her. She looked down to see the ground all the way down beneath her feet then looked back up at him.

"Let go of me!" she ordered, but he didn't answer.

His arm stretched out painfully and the floor was pushing into his chest making it difficult for him to breathe. He let out a feeble cry as he tried to breathe in and pull her to safety. He slipped forward a little and tried helping her back up but knew if he used his other hand then they would both fall. Like a big brother Raiden appeared then grabbing the back of his collar and grunting as he used all the strength he had to help pull them back up. Once Val felt confident, he used his other hand to pull Acarlie back up to her feet. Even though Raiden was normally gentle and proper with elementalists and especially women, he took hold of Acarlie and pulled her toward him and shouted at her.

"Elementalists are supposed to be smarter than this! What do you think this would achieve? Think about your Guide. Think about the man who nearly died trying to save you!"

Acarlie seemed to snap back to herself then. She was speechless and turned pale as the leo put her back down on her feet. She felt like breaking down crying but knew this wasn't the time and turned and ran back up the slope for Sheeria. Raiden followed her but the floor cracked one last time and sent a slab of flooring falling from its place and struck Raiden and made him loose his footing. Acarlie and Val turned to see the leo slide towards the end again, scratching at the floor but unsuccessfully. This time it was Acarlie to come to his rescue. She dived down toward him as he fell over the edge and as soon as she could see him falling she stretched out her hand just like she did with the chunk of metal, and suddenly Raiden stopped. The blue circle appeared again and Raiden's roar of pain was silenced by the crack like thunder. Only by the metal in his armour his brother wore before him could Acarlie control him from falling and slowly brought him back to the courtyard without even touching him. She placed him down somewhere safe where he groaned in pain as the armour he wore dug into his skin as she brought him back. They all ran to him and helped him to his feet. Acarlie ran and embraced him shouting, nearly in tears again, "Oh I'm so sorry Mister Raiden. What was I thinking? Please forgive me!"

It was Sheeria's turn to shout at her this time, "What were you doing Acarlie? How could you do such a thing?!"

"I'm sorry!" she screamed at her. "I wasn't thinking. I don't know what came over me!"

Sheeria, still red with anger hissed like an angry cat and turned away from her.

"Leave her be, she's going through a lot. Let's just get in there and talk to the President. There is nowhere he can go now," Val said trying to help Raiden up but was pushed back. Raiden got to his feet on his own and brushed himself off, "Thank you Acarlie. I'm sorry for shouting earlier. You scared me," he said in his low tone of the leos'.

He didn't wait for an answer but just turned around and walked to Sheeria to speak to her.

"Well at least everyone is safe. Come, let's go see the President," Zahied said then walked toward his room. Val sat down on the floor for a second breathing heavily and rubbing at the sores Miles had given him. He looked over to see Acarlie kneeling down in shame that she nearly killed herself and two others with her.

"I'm sorry Val," she said to him knowing this was the second time he had saved her.

"What happened to you just then?" he asked with his hand over his eye rubbing his bruise.

"I don't know Val. It was a feeling of like..." she thought hard to search for the right words to explain to him, "It was like... extreme dishonour and shame. I can't really explain it properly. Are you ok?"

He looked to her, wondering if anybody else saw what just happened. Was he the only person to see that something else happened there?

"I'm ok now. Help me up please," he said holding out his hand and she pulled him to his feet.

"Zack stop!" they all called to stop Zack. They had found him standing over President Shuian with his hands over his throat strangling him. His anger and wrath were the only things on Zack's mind and all he wanted to do now to wreak havoc on the man responsible. Sheeria stepped forward and pulled him back leaving the tall and dark president to gasp and choke for air.

"It's over Mister President. Everything you have thrown at us we have overcome. There is nothing left to threaten us with," Zahied said as he stood over him.

Shuian, still red from choking, croaked at him, "What...do you ...want?"

"You know what we want Mister President. We want a safe passage out of your city and out of your country." He had had enough with trying to negotiate with him and now moved onto demands.

"And a skyship," Raiden added from the back of the crowd.

Shuian got his breath back and got to his knees, straightening his blue suit.

"Very well, you win. You will be taken to the lizzier stables and escorted out of the city. No harm will come to you, but a skyship I cannot do, I am sorry."

Raiden growled but Zahied spoke, "That's better than nothing then. See to it that we are out of here. Oh, and by the way. I was bluffing about telling the other cities about you and your elemental school."

Shuian turned from red to white then and thought quickly, "If that is so then you really have beaten me but if I am still in command then I still have the power to banish your elementalist from taking part in any other battles. If I cannot take part then neither will you. Now go, get out of my city. Your escorts will take you to your lizziers and out of my city."

They turned and left him in his broken room, on his destroyed courtyard, in his scarred building. Only then did Acarlie turn and say, "I'm sorry this had to happen, but everything you have done has led you to this. All you had to do was let it go that your country could not take part in Elemental Battles."

She didn't wait for a reply but turned away from him and stood beside Val, who was still in a lot of pain as they got in the elevator back down the building. She looked at his bruised and cut face and his tired body and thought of how much this man had done for her in the short time of meeting her. He returned a weakened smile back at her and limped out of the elevator. She was left standing alone. This building was still a danger and now her pilgrimage looked over. She couldn't think of anything to do but follow Val, lift his arm and helped him walk. With everything he had done the least she could do was not make him limp all the way down.

21

After they were all reunited with their lizziers they took no extra time to gather supplies and were escorted out of the city, from where they rode all through the night in fear that President Shuian would change his mind and send guards out to follow them and hunt them down in the night when they slept. After the sun came up and even later then in the late morning did they rest their lizziers and decided to march to Hiro with their lizziers by their side. It was now something Acarlie and Val had quickly come accustomed to. Acarlie who had never left her village and was new to all this hiking around and Val who was still new to everything in Sphere. They now had a few days each experience of travelling and knew to keep quiet and follow the leader who in this case was Raiden. But Acarlie and Val were not the only ones to remain silent through their journey. Sheeria who was still very upset with the actions of Acarlie from the night previously had not spoken a word to her since then and avoided eye contact with her. Acarlie, who was riddled with shame with it could not dare to speak nor look at her either and prayed that soon she would be able to apologise. She also felt lost then and never knew why she was still heading for the next city; she was an outcast now, a disgrace to her way of life and felt like there was nothing for her anymore, nowhere to go and nobody to take her or her Guide in. She felt like she was only going to see that Zack made it safely to Hiro where he would finally get the help he was looking for to save his people. Tiredness was also a large factor in her mental state at the moment and she could see that Val who was marching beside her felt the same way, they both lagged behind everyone else slightly and only kept their eyes on the floor in front of them. She couldn't help but blame herself for everything that she was feeling bad for, as well as every time she thought of Miles, she felt shame mixed with anger but blamed herself for falling for him. She remembered the talk she had with Sheeria that night and wished she had taken her advice. She also thought about all the hundreds, maybe even thousands of people including Zack's wife who had died at the hands of President Shuian just to keep her from finding out the truth about his crime against the League of Elementalists. The shame for her act of attempted suicide was the worst though and how she nearly killed Val and Raiden in the process and would have left Sheeria an Alanode ate her up the most. She knew that was the real reason why Sheeria wasn't speaking to her and wondered what everyone else thought of that act of stupidity she wished she never committed. But every time she looked up at Val and their eyes met he would only smile and look back down to his marching feet. That small, insignificant, warm smile became the only piece of comfort for her as the day passed. Their march led them through one plain after another, finding paths that led them from one horizon to another passing a few small villages and only stopping briefly to feed their lizziers and asking directions from the villagers then they would be back on the road toward the city of Hiro. It wasn't until the late evening that they decided they were far enough away for anyone to catch up with them and were confident that they were now back in the country of Racoves and out of harm's way from anything that Isolies could do to them. They made camp on one of the many plains stretching out into the horizon with only a few wooded areas in front of them. It was a relaxing place and very peaceful to be away from the town's folk but the pleasure of peace and quiet came with an unnerving sense of caution from hijackers and thieves through the night. The tents were set up quickly so everyone had the chance to take the weight off their feet now as they sat on the plain of summer grown green, dry grass under the late afternoon blue sky above them with the stale and warm air to fill their lungs.

Acarlie was given the time to rest as her tent was laid out for her and she climbed into her sleeping bag putting her head on the floor and tried to shut off her mind and catch even a little sleep before the others all did. After sitting down for only a couple of minutes they found that Val had nodded off to sleep too. He simply lay down with his back to the dry grass and closed his eyes. Zahied and Zack noticed this while they were all pitching up tents and decided to let him stay. Only an hour later and Raiden woke him up though. With all the walking and riding they had just done only one hour was not enough for him but still Raiden got him to his feet.

"Rest later boy, when we all sleep. Now you must practice what I have been teaching you."

Val felt a little annoyed about this and wanted to go back to sleep but rubbed his eyes, nodded and stood up. The evening air was still warm and dry and Val felt happy about this, only his joints were a little stiff from sleeping but like a decent teacher Raiden made him warm up by jogging back and forth to a certain tree he pointed out then put Val through a series of stretches to loosen him up. For the last few days when they started on their journey Raiden had been teaching Val the art of fighting. Since he and Val were from the Walton Warriors, Raiden wanted him trained like one and had been teaching him katas that would help him later in combat. Val would be silent and listen to Raiden and copied everything Raiden showed him. Step by step Val would turn, strike, step; strike, block, turn and strike with Raiden stopping him every once in a while telling him, "Lower your stance, strike stronger, block faster."

Val was a keen pupil and a quick learner and after his training Raiden stopped him.

"Now you must learn some weapon katas. Where is your staff? I will teach you to use it properly."

"What is wrong with the way I have been using it so far?" Val asked him.

"Let's not forget that you would have been killed yesterday if it wasn't for me. Your technique is there but it is sloppy. Whatever you know about fighting with your weapon I want you to forget it, wipe everything you know about it and we will start afresh. We will do it the Walton way. Now call your staff."

With Raiden saying this Val wondered if he was trying to say that he couldn't fight at all and felt a little shamed by it. But he knew Raiden wanted the best out of him and he knew he trusted him.

He nodded and did what he was told, "Yes, Raiden," and called his staff by holding his hand out and instantly the staff appeared in his hand in the way it always does. Raiden then began to teach Val a series of simple movements, showing him the correct stances and applications on how to use his staff and then sat down on the warm grass. Val practised these series of movements over and over again with Raiden closely watching him.

"Raiden can I ask you a question?" Val said putting down his staff and turning to Raiden.

"Yes, what is it Val?" Raiden said, his arms crossed like they usually were.

"You spoke once of you training me to fight like you."

"I am training you to fight like me. What do you think all these katas and techniques are?"

Val shook his head, "No I mean like *you*...like a leo."

Raiden then uncrossed his arms and gave him a look of surprise, smiled then said, "So you want to fight like a leo do you?" he said walking up to him, lifting his arm and shaking it loosely.

"Human arms are too weak to fight like a leo." He let go of him took another step and carried on, "but it has been done before..." He stepped back with his chin to the blue sky, again the face of his brother appeared in his mind and he remembered something he said years ago. There was a time, long before Val was born that Raiden hated all humans and never saw himself of even speaking to one. But Raiden was past a century now and much wiser, "... Very well then I shall teach you the ways of the Leo. Seeing how you fought Miles I think this will be good for you."

Raiden took a step back and covered his face hiding a secret smile Val saw. This was the first real smile Val ever saw Raiden pull, a smile of happiness. Something Val would later remember for the rest of his life. Raiden took off his armour and laid it down beside him and said, "Now the first aspect of the art of Leoism is striking fear in your opponent's hearts. Whether that foe is bigger or smaller than you. To do this successfully you need a stance. Now then let's see your scare stance."

Val stood in the only stance he knew and that was the one he was being taught as a Walton Warrior, his legs bent and his back straight, guard up with the look of readiness in his eyes.

"You call that a scare stance? You couldn't scare an aeomon with that stance. It needs to be more brutal. You need your body language to say to your opponent, *come near me and I'll rip your bloody eyes out!*"

To show him what he meant Raiden suddenly pounced back on all fours and straightened his back and roared in Val's face, a chill of terror shook Val as he suddenly changed himself from Raiden to a wild beast Val felt scared of.

"Do you feel that? Do you feel that fear inside you? There is no threat here, no enemy in front of you, no near death experience. It is I who is putting the fear into you, whether that means shouting or screaming in the faces of your foes. You must tell their inner selves that you are not to be messed with. Try it, try and scare me."

Val felt a rush of energy through him and he used it to run forward, jumping toward Raiden and landing in front of him.

"AHH!" he screamed like a war cry with his hands clenched into fists held low and spreading out his chest, bending his legs again this time further apart. To a leo this was still a feeble attempt but Raiden did not laugh since he knew Val was trying and said to him, "Good, you seem much more feral this time. To a human you may seem a worthy opponent but to the likes of me or Sheeria you are still only meat. You need to show more strength. It is all about presentation. You are not proving to your opponent that you are stronger than them. You just want them to think it, even to consider it. Now spar with me, take your staff and remember the technique of using it, use that and what you have just learned."

Keeping to the same mind track Val called his staff and screamed again and swung at Raiden, Raiden ducked away and pushing Val's shoulder away took a step back to give himself room.

Val quickly turned and rolled to the side and pounced up at Raiden, dropping his staff and clinging onto Raiden's fur, his feet pressed into Raiden's chest leaving him to fall on his back. Val rolled when he landed, turned back and dived again into Raiden calling his staff and readying it to strike Raiden when he was down.

Raiden only swiped his arm across, pushing Val away from him and getting to his feet.

"Yes that's more like it Val, I can feel it now. Let go of customs and teachings and become the animal inside you!"

Val screamed again and dived forward but his time Raiden caught him and slammed him into the floor knocking the air out of him.

"But don't let anger and adrenaline take control of you. It's hard to master but you must keep under control at *all* times. Even a second without thought could be the one your foe was waiting for. You must never be angry in combat just like you must never be scared. Fear and anger are emotions that bring even the best fighters down by an opponent who has control of the fight. You must put your emotions aside in every battle and every fight."

Raiden picked up Val and brought him to his feet. Val, still a little shaken took a second to recover when a third voice spoke in, "Teaching a human to fight like felines? It can't be done Leo," Sheeria stood in front of them watching them with her arms crossed like Raiden usually does.

"The reasons for teaching him are my own Tigian. He wishes to learn and I feel he needs to know," Raiden told her with a *mind your own business* tone.

Sheeria then changed her tone and walked over to him friendlier, "Please stop calling me Tigian Raiden. My name is Sheeria and I feel like we have got off on the wrong foot."

Raiden still felt he had little to say to the hot headed Guide but was patient with her, "Very well Sheeria. I will also ask you to stop referring to me as Leo and call me by my given name. What do you want?"

"Only to ask you two things. Firstly if you wouldn't mind accompanying with me to a hunt? Acarlie is awake now and my Elementalist will need supper soon if she is to gain the strength to address the King of Racoves."

Raiden nodded agreeing with her, "Yes, we all will need food soon. I will join you on a hunt."

Sheeria took another step, "My second question was…" another step. "Why are you here? A journey as dangerous as this I mean and I know very well of the reasons of why you should not be here now. I apologise if I seem rude but I am only concerned for the leos."

Raiden then bit his lip and clenched his jaw, took a breath and said to Val, "Lesson is over today. Take my armour to the camp and wait for me there. We shall return with supper," he then turned and walked off toward the forest beyond them. He stopped and said over his shoulder to answer Sheeria, "I once told someone who asked the same question that if I should die then the leo race would be grateful that I died for a cause as great as the one I am on now."

"That's no answer Raiden," Sheeria countered. "The leos were all proud and honourable but would they really want you here or would they want you safe?"

Raiden grunted in disapproval of her statement and walked toward the wooded area.

"Wait, what's going on? Sheeria what is wrong with Raiden?" Val asked suddenly worried for Raiden.

She looked down at him and said, "Well, have you seen any other leos around yet other than the one you travel with? Raiden's health is of dire importance to the whole planet because… he is the last of the Leos. Raiden is an endangered species who many people already thought extinct. He is the only ray of hope for all of his kind."

"Is this true Raiden, are you the Last Leo?" Val asked but Raiden was gone. Maybe he was embarrassed of his answer? Maybe he was gone to remember the rest of his kind? In any case Val knew the truth now and it saddened him. This revelation answered a few unanswered questions for Val like when Raiden went quiet whenever Val asked about other leos or what Miles said about not wanting Raiden dead. He thought how incredibly lonely it must be for Raiden being the last of his race. Maybe that was why he smiled when Val asked to be trained like a leo? Sheeria went to catch up with him but was stopped by Val, "Let me ask you a question this time Sheeria."

"Speak."

"Are you and Acarlie going to be ok?"

Sheeria scowled a little but still answered him, "My Elementalist will be hungry. It is my job to see that she keeps well. Any decision that she makes will be the decision I make too, until her service is complete."

"When will that be?" he asked again.

This time Sheeria could not bring herself to answer and turned away from him and ran towards Raiden walking off into the distance. This only made Val realise the worst. *Until she dies*, he thought to himself as he picked up Raiden's armour and carried it to his tent where he found Acarlie.

Acarlie was sitting down beside a camp fire with Zahied and Zack. There was another person there too, a traveller who was just passing by that Zack and Zahied had befriended and offered to sit and dine with them. He was short with a traveller's cloak on not much different from Val's and had short jet black hair, unwashed, greasy and messy with a short black beard covering an unwashed, dirty and tired face. He was sitting comfortably on the floor with the others and enjoying a conversation with Zahied who was telling him their story so far, although in his words the number of people they encountered was exaggerated a little and the Elemental Battle seemed so much more explosive when Zahied told it. The man listened filled with awe as Zack also recounted his part of the story and told him about his city, the demons, riders and Acarlie, the heroine elementalist who came from the small village near to them and saved them all from the evils the city possessed. Whenever the two spoke about Acarlie as *The Elementalist* the traveller's face went cold and they noticed his eyes drift away from them whenever they mentioned it.

Acarlie was sitting beside them in silence, her legs crossed and her hands on her thighs and rocking ever so slightly, staring at the fire with misty and clouded, tired eyes from where she had just woke up recently. Val did not need to guess to know that she was cold and took off his cloak and put it over her shoulders as he sat down beside her.

"Thank you Val," she said smiling over to him. "Have you seen Sheeria yet?"

"Yes I have. Sheeria is out hunting with Raiden and I can only guess they will come back soon," Val said while looking into a pot of what looked like soup in it that was cooking over the fire being stirred by Zahied. Zahied took the hint and with a small ladle he poured some in two plastic cups that he then gave to Val and Acarlie. With both hands Acarlie reached out and nodded a thank you as she took the hot soup and sipped it, sighing with comfort as the hot liquid sank down her body. She felt warm immediately.

She asked Val again, "Is she still mad with me?"

Val, now sipping his own soup said, "I think she still might be a little pissed off but I'm sure Raiden will calm her down before she gets back. You just better get a good apology ready for her when she comes back anyway."

Acarlie tensed her jaw and nodded.

"Why did you do it? What happened back there?" Val asked her again.

"I...I still don't really know what came over me. When I saw that Billy being struck by that chunk of metal I threw at him I froze. I felt an overwhelming amount of instant shame and it was like all I wanted to do was to end my journey there. I have been trained all my life by my elders and have heard a story of traitors of the elementalists who all have gone against the teachings. They are scum who do not deserve the gift we all have received from birth…" she paused then staring into her soup, "…and now I am one of them…I do not deserve the blood I am blessed with."

"But what about what happened in Plainess? Didn't you use your gift there?" Val asked remembering the details they told him previously.

"That was different. We are allowed to defend ourselves against people or creatures outside the arena or to help innocent people up to a certain amount but when I stopped that metal… Billy was powerless against me and didn't stand as a threat to me so when I stuck him down…"

"I understand but wasn't Billy a false elementalist anyway? I mean when the other cities find out they might thank you about it," Val said trying to encourage her to see the bright side of it.

"This only makes it worse though Val. I don't know how he managed to control the magnetism with that machine. He may have only been a caster like Zahied but to the teachings if you are not an Elementalist then you are a civilian, an Innocent."

"Well he defiantly wasn't innocent. He tried to kill all of us."

Acarlie shook her head, "No you miss understand me. An Innocent is what people who are not born with elemental blood are known as by us."

"Oh, I see," Val said and sipped more of his soup. He tried to think of something more he could say to her to lift her spirits. She sat with her chin resting on her knees and stared at the fire like the world rested upon her shoulders. He may have known nothing about these elementalists but he knew enough to understand that they were like everyone else. They may have these incredible powers but still were human, with problems and fragile emotions.

Acarlie sat still for a moment thinking of what to say to him when she finally said to him, "There is something I would like to ask you Val."

"What is it?" he answered with a comforting smile.

"When we were contained in the city Raiden told us all about you and your sacred task. Where are you from Val?"

Val sighed as he answered, "I don't know. All I remember was waking up against a tree overlooking a sea and then Raiden found me shortly after, only a pair of shorts and my staff next to me." Acarlie could see the question troubled Val. He fidgeted uncomfortably, picking up a small twig from the floor and began digging the dry mud with it like a pencil.

"That brings me to another question Val. Your staff, how do you do that thing with it?"

"Once again, I don't know how I do it but I know that I can manipulate it to any shape without adding any more mass to it. It is somehow linked to me I think, like it is a part of me. But I was thinking, where we are going there will be a lot of old scrolls and information there. Maybe some of my questions will be answered there. What about you Acarlie? Tell me about your training." He moved the conversation along so he wouldn't have to think too much about it again and threw the twig into the fire.

She smiled then as she finished the last of her soup.

"I was chosen from birth by my elder to be trained in Eloma, school of the Element of Wind and Unseen Forces." She then bit her lip remembering herself having the same conversation with Miles once when they first met back in Eloma.

But Val was different, instead of being cheeky and talking about the old Ultra-soldiers Val asked another question.

"So if they chose you from birth, where are your parents? Are they back in Eloma? Did they get to see you grow up?"

This question struck a chord in Acarlie's heart and echoed within her whole body, *my Parents...I haven't thought about them for so long*, she thought.

"My parents were demoralised. It's something that happens to all and every parent who gives birth to children of elemental blood."

She could see by the puzzled look on his face that she would have to explain to him more detailed, "They were put down by the elders. *Demoralisation* is seen as an honour by all parents who see it as a better chance for their children to grow up and become famous by becoming an elementalist."

"The elders killed your parents?" Val asked now shocked.

"The elders *were* my parents, just like any adopted or surrogate parent," she explained to him. "They fed and loved me, taught me about the elders' way of life so I would become a sacred Elementalist. I honour and love the elders that took me in."

This information was a little unsettling for Val as he heard this but he saw that it did not affect Acarlie and put it aside.

"Can I ask you one more thing? The last battle you would have, with the Elemental Lord, there can only be one elemental lord right? So if you were to beat him—"

"I would have to kill him. The last fight is always to the death. It's the only way to make sure."

Val nodded and chose not to ask another question on that subject in case it upset her.

Val looked around him to see some small flies start to fly around the fire. He was amazed to see that these flies glowed with all colours of the spectrum and glistened as they flew around the fire.

"What are they?" he said pointing at them.

Acarlie laughed a little and said, "Why, they're Wiggiflies silly. Have you never seen them before?" then she remembered his condition then explained to him. "Wiggiflies are born at noon and live only throughout the night before dying in the morning just like mayfly live only for a short time in the day. The little lights they emit are reflections from the sun. What they do is soak up the light in the sunset and carry the light with them through the night to keep them warm."

"They're amazing. I'd like to see them in the night when they light up."

"You think that's amazing? Would you like to see how they react to my Elemental Kata? It's about time I practised anyway," she smiled and brushed her hair behind her ear.

"You have a kata?"

She nodded, "Yes I do. I will show you if you like. Wait here, I must quickly go and prepare. I will be back soon."

She then got up and stretched out her legs and went into her tent.

While he was waiting he shuffled over to Zack and Zahied and the new guy and asked them, "Hello, who is this guy? We haven't been introduced yet."

Zack put his bowl of soup down, "Of course, Val this Ceasier, he is an Alanode. Ceasier this is Val."

The rugged unshaven man stuck a stubby hand out that Val shook firmly.

"Nice to meet you Ceasier."

"Likewise Val, thank you for having me here with you," he said politely.

"No problem, I just don't quite know what an Alanode is," Val said hoping someone would answer him.

Zahied finished the last of his soup and stirred the pot over the fire adding, "An Alanode is a Guide of a deceased elementalist, a failed Guide if you were."

"Oh, I'm sorry," Val said but Ceasier smiled and said back to him comfortingly.

"It's ok. It is something I need to get used to."

"What was your elementalist like?" Val asked and this time he twitched a little.

"My Elementalist was actually my wife. We grew up together in Donolan and before we set out on our journey I asked her to marry me so I would always protect her on every step," they could all see that it slightly hurt him to speak of his wife in the past tense. He covered his face as all men do and took a deep sigh, "...But I failed her."

"Look if you don't want to speak about it you don't have to mate," Val said to comfort him.

"No I must get to terms with it so I can carry on with my life," he said.

"What happened then? Was she bested in an Elemental Battle?" Zack asked.

"Actually no, no she was a strong and smart elementalist in the arena. It was actually outside the arena. We were camping out just like we are now, the two of us. I was out hunting and when I was coming back she was sitting with two travellers. She was only talking to them while brushing her long beautiful red hair when one of them pulled out a knife. I ran to help her but was too late."

"They killed her?" Val asked him.

"No she killed them. I was relieved at first but then she suddenly changed into a pool of despair. I remember I was holding her trying to calm her but she kept crying and shouting out, '*I have gone against the teachings, I have gone against the teachings.*' It seems that she killed them after they admitted defeat and would have left. I remember the crying like it was yesterday. Such a sound coming from the one I loved has kept me from sleeping for such a long time now and her torn up crying face will never leave me..." he paused again controlling himself then carried on. "Soon after that when I thought she would be ok she took my knife from its sheaf and rolled on top of it. My knife, the one I swore would protect her. The one that was supposed to save her took her from me, my beautiful Lucureral."

Val felt incredibly bad for him but could not help but see the resemblance of what happened yesterday with Acarlie and asked him.

"I'm sorry to hear that, does this happen to many elementalists?"

It was Zahied who answered him though, "Yes, all of them."

"*All* of them, really?"

"Yes all those who defy the teachings try to...you know," Zahied said thinking nothing of the question and sipped on his mug of soup. This was too much of a coincidence for Val and he immediately starting thinking, *why would all those who go against the teachings kill themselves?*

He sat thinking for a while as the others changed the conversation along and started talking about other things but Val sat there in the same mind set. He sat there rubbing his chin in deep thought, thinking about the facts he had, from Acarlie wanting to jump to hearing of Ceasier's wife killing herself thinking to himself, *but why would every elementalist do it? Surely one would be an exception.* But then he remembered Acarlie's blank face when she killed Billy, the way she turned off then and became someone else.

He stood up slowly, "Excuse me guys I need to think for a while," he told the others and walked a little further away where it was quieter and he could think in peace. He sat down on the floor looking over at the horizon, the sun was now setting a red shade across the sky with the wigiflies roaming around him, flickering light like droplets of water. Still he wondered why they could all do this to themselves and why they turn off before they do. The answer came to him when he thought about what Acarlie told him, *the elders must have something to do with this,* then he thought about the way the elementalists grow up and realised it. *Conditioning, brain washing!* He thought. *They condition the elementalists to kill themselves after they abuse the rules they have given them.* The more he thought about it the more it made sense. The elders obviously were scared of humans who could use the same power they could. So they take them at birth, kill the parents, teach them how to use their powers within a set of strict rules and send them off to their deaths. If they die in the arena then all's well, if they become Elemental Lord then they die when they are bested and if they try and escape they go outside the rules and are forced to kill themselves through the conditioning that they teach them from birth. Only by living with the elders in the stadium do they escape death, imprisoned and under the watchful eye of the elders and all they do is make up some sacred thing about elementalists and sport, tell them their parents are saints and are Demoralised rather than the truth of being executed so they could not protect their children from them. It all made sense to him now but how could he tell her this? She would believe the elders above him, like she said, they were her parents. As a leo Raiden would not listen to him since the leos answered to the elders as a species and Sheeria would definitely not listen to him. He thought it best to keep it to himself since everyone treated the elders as sacred people and would upset everyone he went around accusing them.

"Hey there you are. I have been looking for you!" Acarlie shouted over to him happily and running over to him.

"I'm sorry I just needed to think about something," he told her.

"Oh really, what's that then?" she asked innocently.

"Oh…nothing, don't worry about it. So let's see this kata you told me about."

She walked passed him to face the sunset, "Ok, sit there and watch this. It's actually a grand honour to see an Elemental Kata you know?" she said finding a large piece of level land on the grass in front of her carrying his staff with her.

"I bet it is," he still knew the truth but could not bring himself to tell her.

She took a couple more steps in front and placed the staff down on the floor.

"Ok, now be very still and quiet. I must concentrate and need to focus."

Val nodded and stood up to watch her.

She stood there in front of him with her back turned to him, looking into the sunset and shook her arms and legs to loosen herself up and ran her fingers through her black, silky hair. Taking her time she breathed slowly and closed her eyes and concentrated on the soft, warm air gently blowing against her. She felt the dry grass on the hard ground on her bare feet and felt goose pimples on her arms as her blood rushed through her body cold and quickly. When she felt the tingling in her fingertips she slowly raised her hands to the sky and began her kata. Her first moves were slow and loose like in tai chi, very spiritual and meaningful, reaching out from one side to another, circling and turning with elegance.

Val soon saw the wind around her begin to circle around her at the speed she was going, small pieces of dust were carried from one place to another as they flew around her. She picked up her pace and just like the kata he learned from Raiden she threw a punch, then another. The wind from around her suddenly picked up as well and circled around her, high above her head like a small cyclone. Every punch she did was perfect, with precise timing and the wind perfectly obeyed her by going exactly where she punched, sending a quick gust in the direction. She kicked and turned and kicked again, blocked and reversed with every move also guiding the wind around her to twist and turn and change direction, carrying the small pieces of loose grass and wiggiflies to cyclone in a clockwise direction around her. Soon she was well into her kata and it was like she had totally forgotten about him. The wind kept circling her carrying the tiny wiggiflies to zoom around her with small flowers and other dust particles. Her movements became fluent and more of a dance with quick snaps of her fists and legs when she attacked the air in front of her. She then took a step back and straightened her stance and held her hand up to her chest and the staff lying beside her levitated from the floor and started twisting and turning like Val himself was holding it. Val watched in awe and wonder as he watched her dance so beautifully that it was like the planet itself was dancing alongside her. The flowers and loose grass picked up off the floor and went soaring around her as she quickly twisted and turned guiding the staff to attack without even touching it. In the light of the sunset it was amazing to watch. The wiggiflies reflected the blood red light of the sun and coloured the wind as they were caught up in the cyclone sending streaks of light of all colours of the spectrum to fly around her and all under the warm sky as the sun was setting. The sky slowly turning from golden yellow to orange, crimson to violet with single stars beginning to appear like tiny diamonds. Val stared frozen to the spot and watched her toned, thin body throw punches and kicks to the shadows and her hair whipping around her beautiful face as she turned from one position to another. It suddenly felt to him like the two of them were the only two people in the world and nothing else existed, only him and the beautiful Acarlie performing her kata like a dance in the sunset.

How can I let someone this beautiful die like the elders want her to? he thought to himself as he watched her. Now he even felt himself feel a little lighter and he saw more pieces of Sphere, flowers and grass levitating from the floor and floating around her ankles as she slowed down now, the wind dying out and settling around her. *I can't, I can't let this happen. Not to her,* he vowed but had no idea of how he would do such a thing.

She now stood perfectly still again in the same spot where she began with her back to Val and facing the setting sun. She bowed to the wind as it dispersed and scattered the wigiflies all around the sky above them. The dust in the wind dispersed and Val's staff now gently lowered to the dry grass again. Val looked up at the wigiflies as they flew in every direction like tiny multi-coloured fireworks just above his head to join with the soft, blended colours of the sky as the sun declared its retirement. The sky had never seemed to vast and open to him as it did now. He realised then how insignificant he was, how beautiful this place was but somewhere out there behind the enchanting reds, oranges and violets and dark blues was something without colour, a black so deep even hope was a stranger, a hole of pure despair in space and time, hungry and waiting.

He looked back down to her. She took another sigh and turned to him smiling, "Well? What do you think?"

"That was beautiful Acarlie," he said blankly still in wonder at what he had just seen.

"I'm glad you think so. Elementalists are supposed to practice their kata whenever they can, it keeps them sharp." She picked up his staff and walked over to him.

"I thought you were not allowed to use weapons?" he said taking his staff back.

"Not if we are touching them. It's a loophole we from Eloma benefit from but up against some of the strongest elements it doesn't make much difference anyway. Did you see the grass around my ankles by the way? I am slowly learning to control the gravity as well."

"Oh, was that what that was? Yeah I saw it," he tried to smile but still every time he looked at her he could only see the elders' conditioning in her. That she would die on every path she took as an elementalist. She led the way back to the campsite when she asked him, "Val what will you do once your mission is over? I mean, you don't know your family or where you come from. Where will you go?"

Val thought for a second again, "I don't know. I guess I will go back to Walton with Raiden."

She thought for a minute then said, "Then let's make a promise, you and me. When you finish your mission, will you stay with me on my journey? I will help you find your home once I am Elemental Lord," she then had a thought of Miles again and was a little hesitant. "…Just don't leave me…"

He looked over to her smiling back at him with her big dark eyes and natural beauty. Val thought this was the only opportunity he had to possibly save her without her knowing and took hold of her, turned her around and held on to her shoulders staring into her brown eyes. "If I do then I want you to promise me something first. Promise me that you will never again try to harm yourself. If ever the thought comes into your mind, forget your teachings, forget your principles as an elementalist, forget your elders and just remember me as I am right now telling you not to do it. Promise me Acarlie."

She looked and saw the importance in his eyes and knew there was only one answer to it.

"I promise," she said looking up at him. "I promise I will never attempt to harm myself under any circumstance ever again."

He sighed a relief and followed, "Then I promise too, once I am done I will stay by your side."

"Then it's a pact then," she said and gave him a quick hug tightly.

"You won't regret this!" she said running off back to the camp site.

"Neither will you," Val said to himself wondering to himself if this counted for saving her for a third time now.

He got back to see Raiden and Sheeria had returned with food and were sharing it out, even to the traveller sitting by the fire. He saw Acarlie and Sheeria smiling next to each other and guessed that Acarlie had apologised to her. He sat next to Raiden who handed him a piece of cooked rabbit with a look of pride in his eye. His pupil Val, named after his brother and taught to fight like a leo.

"Eat up boy, we finally reach Hiro tomorrow, you will need your strength."

Val nodded and ate what Raiden gave him. He was still concerned about him being the last of his race but he decided that if it was ok for Raiden then it was ok for him.

Hiro tomorrow, he thought as he sat in the company of his friends eating a good meal under the warm setting sun. The stars now began to appear and join them and decorated the sky while the fire kept them warm as the sun finally slept.

22

It was high noon in Racoves when the six travellers finally reached the capital city Hiro. They had their first glimpse of the great city after they rode their lizziers up a large wooded hill leading to another long plain and in the distance they could see the tall towered buildings and even King Kerry's palace sitting patiently awaiting their arrival. They started passing some of the city folk once Sheeria told them they had entered Hiro who guided them along the quickest path and within a few hours were walking on the concrete floor of the great city with hundreds of people surrounding them. Once word had reached the city that a new elementalist had arrived a carriage was sent for them. Acarlie was welcomed warmly by the city and flushed red once she found out King Kerry himself had sent the carriage for her and her Guide. She accepted the present and soon was on her way toward the king's palace guarded by the royal security. Zahied was trailing behind the group of lizziers now beside Raiden. Val was beside Zack a few yards in front and Acarlie and Sheeria's lizzier were given to the royal security. The city around Zahied seemed full of energy. The roads were quickly closed and allowed them a straight path to the king. The people clapped when they saw them pass, stopping what they were doing and watching them all slowly trot past. Acarlie would often wave to the children and smile like she were a princess herself.

"Does this happen often?" Zahied asked Raiden over the din of whistles, claps and cheers.

Raiden looked around at all the smiling faces, some were even pointing at him.

"Look a leo!" some said, lifting their young children to sit on their shoulders, "The Elementalist has a Leo friend, wave!" The children waved and Raiden just lifted his hand and nodded shyly at the crowds.

"I don't know Zahied. This is my first time escorting an elementalist to a king myself," he confessed.

"Of course, sorry Raiden," Zahied said waving at a group of young women. "I guess I'm a little excited at the moment. I feel like Val at the moment."

Raiden chuckled and tapped his heels into his lizzier Bluey to catch up with the others. This was Zahied's first visit to Hiro. He had seen many pictures and heard much about this great city but was surprised how many trees were here, even though they were in the centre of a city trees were all around them, lined one by one on the concrete and beside the great River Green that flowed through the centre of the city. Their road took them on a large bridge that crossed the Green where Zahied could see all of the great famous towers and buildings all reflected in the dirty river. Even Raiden trotted back now and pointed out the Spike, the tallest building in the country poking out from the shoulders of two buildings.

"This is your first time in Hiro?" Raiden asked.

Zahied laughed, "Yes, I know my history of the country and a little about the Green," he confessed looking down at the great river under the bridge with ships and boats full of tourists all boarded.

"Named because of the county Greenwitch where it originates?" Raiden smiled.

"Named because of the colour it's turned from all the filth in the city being thrown in the river," Zahied laughed.

"Hey what are you guys talking about?" Val asked now appearing from in front of them.

"Just about the river Val," Raiden confirmed.

"It makes me think though, it can't be a real river since the whole of Hiro is a city sitting upon another city."

"What's your point?" Raiden asked. Val pulled back and tried listening to what Zahied was saying.

"Well, it's got to be a canal right? Man-made if there is another city below us."

Raiden laughed out loud, "You're over thinking it Zahied, just enjoy it." Again Raiden trotted forward and beside Zack when Val now pulled up beside him.

"What's this about another city?" he asked.

Zahied smiled and gave Val the quick lesson. "There are two cities you stand on now Val. Hiro and way below us is another city, where all the crime and violent residents are, True Hiro they call it. They have been hidden from the sunlight for decades and have rarely breathed the clean air up here. It sounds the perfect idea doesn't it? The top half is clean, tidy and punctual. No crime and no death. All the dirt, scum and criminals are on the lower parts of the city, where they are too poor to buy themselves a place up here. So the city still shines like brand new as all its troubles are out of harm's way, safely swept under the carpet."

"That sounds terrible. You mean to say under the city itself is another city, where all the criminals and thieves are? With children having to grow up not knowing what sunlight is?" Val seemed shocked and disgusted with the idea.

"That's right Val, not my idea of a perfect society but it gets the job done. I've always wanted to see this city, especially the shield."

"What shield?"

Zahied pointed up to the sky, "This city is built in a perfect circle Val, it's for the electric shield. That's the great thing about this city. It was made in such a way so if any attack was to happen then a large electric shield would rise up from the outside of the city where the line is and would curve and meet itself in the centre making the city into a dome so no one could get in or out."

"But what about the homes living outside the dome? Wouldn't they have any protection?"

"I guess that was the price they had to pay for living up here in the sunlight. Down in True Hiro they would be protected. They say when the giant dome is active you can see it for miles and miles, especially on a clear night. The dome lights up and glows bright blue. Once it's activated no army can penetrate it, especially since the universal treaty when the forbidden weapons were outlawed after the Leo Divide."

Zahied looked back to Val who now looked at the ground, "Is there a way to the city below us?"

"Yes, a great circular elevator in the centre of the city that winds down like a corkscrew. No one goes down there though, it's dangerous."

They crossed the bridge and were back on the road now. Zahied now was beside the carriage to see Acarlie and Sheeria still sitting comfortably and waving at the crowd as they passed. Soon the king's palace came into their view. The city seemed too clean and tidy to be a city. There were no tall buildings stuck next to one another with alleyways cluttered with bins and litter, homeless people or even graffiti on the side of the buildings. No, this place seemed perfect and new. Some of the buildings were made a very unique way from one another and would have archways or concrete pillars holding up extensions to the roofs of some of the finely crafted buildings each lined with coloured neon lights. The city was also very green and growing with life, apart from the trees man had made in the concrete floor they left areas of soil to grow grass and bushes if they desired. It gave them the feeling of tranquillity as they walked down past the busy streets of rushing people as it felt like they were also walking through a national park. As far as he could see were tall square built buildings each with great glass windows placed perfectly next to one another with roughly the same amount of space in between one another and at the end of a long road was their destination. A place that Zahied never dreamed he would ever set foot in, King Kerry's palace. This building was monstrous in size and easily overlooked the whole of the land from the top, this building was more of a giant cube or pyramid than a castle. It seemed to Zahied when he first heard of King Kerry that he would live in a cliché castle with towers and dungeons but this was more like a home for an emperor. Zahied had to stop at one point just to take in the sight of this amazing building, the light from the afternoon sun reflecting off this giant palace and casting a shining radiance all over its city. The inside of the palace seemed even more bewildering. Their lizziers were taken to the royal stables and they were escorted inside. After nearly an hour of walking around from one corridor to another and waiting for security to let them pass they finally came to a courtyard high in the castle overlooking the city below. The floor was paved with red bricks and the ceiling was of glass letting the morning sun through, many large coloured flower baskets hung from the walls and gave the area a peaceful mood. The tall security guard escorted them to a room and asked them to wait in it, when Acarlie walked over to him.

"Is there a place I can change into proper clothing before meeting the King? I do not want him to see me as I am."

The man smiled and pointed over to a smaller room adjacent to them, "Certainly, there is a room over there. You may change there if needed."

"Thank you," she then turned to the others. "I won't be a minute, Sheeria will you help me?"

Sheeria nodded and walked into the room in front of her. The security then walked down to the end of the courtyard, past the giant flowers and to another door. "The King is through here. I will tell him the Elementalist is here to see him, please remain where you are and have patience, I will return shortly."

Zahied went and stood by a large window to gaze out upon the great circular city, sure enough he had a view of the whole city. Only the Spike, the tallest tower in the country over looked them and he felt he could see the tops of every building for miles, all the way out of the city until in the distance he could see the hills and woods they passed which now seemed blue in the horizon meeting the sky. *This truly is incredible. Here I am, a Caster in the halls of the King of Racoves. I wish I could capture this moment.*

The door adjacent to them opened again to reveal Acarlie standing before them in the dress she packed for herself back at Eloma. The dress was white with flowers on it; there were blue and green lines going sideways and swirling on it. The dress itself reached from her shoulders all the way down to her ankles and looked to be made of a very finely woven silk with the bottom half of the dress shaped like only half a skirt with the left side reaching down her left ankle but the right side only came down to the top of her thigh. Val thought she looked a little strange in it and could see that she had a little difficulty walking in it. Her right step was normal but she was obviously not used to walking in a long skirt as her left leg seemed a little slow but she walked up and down the courtyard asking the guys how she looked. When she came up the Val she asked him posing to one side, "Well, what do you think?"

"You look great Acarlie. Your dress really suits you," Val said nodding. He may not have been from around their home and didn't know where he was really from but he knew the rule of when a woman asks how they look when in a nice dress.

"Aww, thank you Val. You know you're more right about this dress suiting me than you think," she said cutely and blushing slightly with her head tilted to one side.

"What do you mean by that?"

She pointed to the little black flowers and lines of blue and green telling him, "The lines are supposed to represent the wind. The flowers are being blown by them, this dress I chose because it would represent the element I have studied."

When he realised what she had showed him he smiled saying, "Oh yeah, I see now. That's really clever Acarlie."

"Well actually it was Sheeria who picked it out. I wanted to take something shorter but she said I had to get something presentable."

"Well you should thank her then because I think she got the right one for you."

She blushed again with delight at his compliment, "Maybe I will then."

The other door opened and the security escort came back out with four other guards who stood either side of the door. They held spears in the right and in the left were large oval blue electric shields attached to their arms. Val recognised the blue shields as the same substance that was used as the prison cell door back in Lachine. He knew then that this would also be used as the dome to protect the city Zahied had told him about.

Their escort stood to attention and addressed them, "All will stand to attention for His Majesty King Kerry of Racoves."

Raiden was the first to stand to attention then and signalled Val to stand beside him. He then whispered to him, "Do as I do," then waited for the king to enter.

King Kerry stood in the room. He walked in slowly after throwing his royal cloak over him and looked at the six travellers standing in his kingdom. Raiden immediately knelt down to the floor which Val quickly followed, as did the others. Val looked to see more of a warrior than a king. His face had a terrible scar down his right cheek and his right eye was half closed. He had a shaven head with a long bushy, black goatee beard on his chin. Even to Zack he seemed more like a cleaned version of the man-demons back in Plainess. His big build gave him a strong walk and he looked like he had seen the heat of battle many times before but he walked in with a great welcoming smile on his face and when he saw Acarlie he opened his arms and embraced her.

"Ah, young Elementalist Acarlie of Eloma I am overwhelmed with pride as I finally see you have begun your pilgrimage. Tell me, how is old Elder Argo?"

Acarlie did not answer just yet but got down on her knees with her nose nearly touching the floor and nearly shouting, "Your Majesty, I come first of all to beg you to help my friend Zack. On my journey to Lachine I passed a city overrun by aeomon and humans who were changed and mutated into demon-like creatures. They had taken his city from him and his people and then forced them down into the sewers. I have already gone to President Shuian of Isolies but he was the one who ordered them there in the first place. They are still trapped there my king and have no help from the outside world, their president has forsaken them and has forgotten about them and they need your help my king. Please help these people."

This was all very sudden for the king as he stood bewildered looking down at her.

He looked over to the others, "Is this true?"

Zack stood up, "Yes King Kerry, it is all true. For ten years my people have been trapped underneath our own city by demons. It was all a hoax played by our president. Lachine had stolen one of the traits of the Element of Wind and put the demons there to stop them from ever entering the city knowing full well that my city would always be the first stop for elementalists from Eloma. My people have been waiting for me to return with help from the outside world but when I found out there would be no help from my president I came to you. Please help my people."

This came even more of a shock to him and he seemed angry at the same time, "You mean to say that after all these years Lachine had stolen from one of my towns. This is an outrage!"

He then did the maths and realised. "Ten years? That's about how long it has been since Eloma has gotten anywhere in the Ele-mental Battles. My friend," he reached out with both hands and held onto Zack's shoulders, "your people shall suffer no more, ser-geant!" he called and one of the shielded guards stepped forward.

"Yes, Your Majesty!"

"Take a skeleton crew and the last of the skyships. Rescue mission."

"Yes, Your Majesty right away!"

Kerry turned back to the travellers, "My men will need a guide though."

Zack stepped forward, "I will gladly show them the way."

"When can you leave?"

"Right away Your Majesty, my people have waited long enough already."

"Then say your goodbyes, you will leave immediately."

Zack was now the one to look a little shocked and over-whelmed with gratitude at the same time.

"Thank you, Your Majesty."

He first walked over to Acarlie and hugged her tight. Val could see the happiness in both their eyes.

"We have done it Zack."

"No, you have done Acarlie. I can never thank you enough,"

He then hugged her close and whispered to her, "I am sorry about Miles Acarlie. I'm sorry I wasn't there when you needed me."

Acarlie remained silent then only with a discomforting smile.

"Forever will your name be remembered by our people. Yours too Sheeria, thank you."

Sheeria hugged him too saying, "This is not goodbye Zack, we will meet again."

Zack nodded and went to shake Zahied and Raiden's hand before finally reaching Val. He gave him a quick manly hug patting him on the back saying, "Good luck on your mission,"

Then leaned over to his far ear and whispered something no one else would hear, "Look after her."

Val did not answer and kept the whisper secret by only nodding as to say *I will.* Zack quickly took a step back and bowed to them all and thanked them all one more time and to the king before being escorted out of the hall and back to his own mission of saving his people.

Kerry was all the while standing smiling then spoke to Acarlie again, "Thank you for bringing this to my attention Acarlie, so how is old Elder Argo?"

Acarlie answered him still with a little trouble in her face, "Elder Argo is fine. I'm afraid he won't be so happy with me though. You see at the last city we were at, the President's last wish was to banish me from the League of Elementalists, so I'm sorry for misleading you Your Majesty but I cannot take part in any more Elemental Battles."

The king looked a little upset but he then pointed out, "But if Lachine never had a real elementalist then President Shuian never had any real authority to make such an action. I am your king Acarlie, Elementalist of Racoves and I say you shall battle. It has been ten years and I am not going to let him take any more from me."

Her eyes widened then, like her soul had just been given back to her, "Really?"

King Kerry smiled with a gleam in his lame, half opened right eye, "Yes Acarlie, who am I to stop your journey? I have been waiting for ten years now to see two elementalists from my own country battle. The city will be told immediately. All of Hiro, True Hiro and all of Racoves shall watch this fight. The Away-side's Quarters are down the bottom half of my home. It is well secluded where you cannot be bothered. Please stay there the night while the city gets ready for you. Preparation will start immediately," he said waving his hand to another guard behind him who stepped forward saying, "This way please," and showed her the door.

"Thank you Your Majesty, I will not let you down," but before she left she turned to Raiden, Zahied and Val.

"I guess this is where we separate then, thank you for all your help."

"You're welcome Acarlie. I wish you good luck," Zahied said and bowed for her.

She smiled and turned to Raiden, "Raiden, thank you for all your help, I couldn't have done it without you."

Raiden only bowed down, "No I thank you Acarlie, for helping us get to see the king. Without you we would have probably been sent away by now. I wish you all the luck on your pilgrimage." He held his hand to his heart but Acarlie instead hugged him. She only came up to his chest when she did but he just returned the hug by wrapping one arm around her softly before letting her go. Sheeria said her goodbyes to both Zahied and Raiden while Acarlie turned to Val. She now stood in front of Val, they both stood with an awkward silence. Val didn't know she would be leaving after this and didn't expect to have to say goodbye to her so soon on their journey. It was something he never even thought about until now. They were only escorting Acarlie, Sheeria and Zack to the king and here they were at the end of their crossed paths. He began to feel tense, like he knew this wasn't meant to happen, all the promises he made with her and she made with him but here she was.

"Well...Thank you for helping me Val. If it wasn't for you..." she also felt the sting of having to say goodbye to him and wanted to say the right thing to him. Val still remembering what would happen to her as an elementalist and didn't know what to say. He promised he wouldn't leave her in exchange for her safety. *Has she forgotten our promise? Is this really where we go our separate ways?*

Everybody was now watching him in an awkward silence. He could feel Raiden's stare and reminded himself of why he was really here, the black hole. He eventually just held his hand out silently and felt her warm, soft hand when she shook it. Val looked up at her who shook his hand with a look in her eyes to say *'how can you let me do this? How can we end it with a handshake?'*

She reluctantly pulled back, "Well...goodbye Val..." she said. Val seeing the pain in her eyes had to pull himself back from embracing her, *she is doing the same* he thought to himself, *this is how it has to be*.

She silently turned to the king again, bowed and followed Sheeria out of the room controlling herself not to look over her shoulder to Val one more time as she left and just like that Acarlie was gone.

"This only leaves you three," said the king as he approached,

"Yes Your Majesty, I had come here to−" Raiden began to say but was taken back as he saw the king himself bow down at Raiden's feet.

"You are a Leo."

"Y...Yes I am," Raiden said. "What of it?"

King Kerry stood up and looked Raiden straight in the eyes then tilted his head to the right for Raiden to see his scar. Raiden then understood immediately.

"You are trained as a leo."

"What's going on?" Val broke in.

"You must forgive Val Your Majesty. He is new to this world and does not know much about Sphere."

King Kerry nodded and looked over to Val showing him the scar, "This scar boy is no ordinary battle scar or childhood accident, it is the marking of the Leos' training. It was given to me by my master before he left for battle."

He walked back over to Raiden and inspected his face, "You look like him too. You have the same eyes."

Raiden then looked even more shocked asking him, "What was your master's name?"

The king smiled as he reminisced his old tutor before he left for battle, "I was tutored by a leo called Valadad, the Last Leo I always thought."

This was what Raiden expected but still felt the sting as he said his name.

"Valadad was my older brother. I am now the Last Leo."

"Then as the brother of my master and the last of your kind, I am in your will. What can I do for you Leo?"

"Please Your Majesty, call me by my given name, Raiden. This is Zahied and Val over there is named after Valadad. He is my protégé."

"Then we have something in common Val," the king smiled over to him. Val now understood the presence of the king and why he looked more like a brute than a king. It was the leo training in him. Val could see that Kerry could put the fear into a man's heart if he wanted to and wondered if he would look like him when he was older.

"Your Majesty, I've travelled from Walton to be in your presence. We tried the President of Isolies for help but with no success. The great Elder Amber has given me and my companions a sacred task to find the monastery in Aragorth for scrolls to help us find a solution to a very important and potentially massive global disaster."

"Why Raiden? What is going to happen?"

"Elder Amber has shown me and Val that somewhere out within the depths of space is something called a black hole. This black hole is the product of extreme and out of control gravity. It is slowly edging itself toward the planet. We at Walton had a meeting and could not think of any answers to solve this problem and could not simply pass the burden onto another country nor could we scream the news to the rest of the world since it would cause global panic, maybe even another divide the likes of which Sphere has never seen."

The king looked a little scared then but asked them, "And what is it of me you needed?"

"We need a skyship. Only a skyship would carry us there over the waters dividing us."

The king's face suddenly dropped, "The last of the skyships have just been sent on a rescue mission to help your friend and his people."

All three of them felt it then, the only skyships in the country had just been sent away and now there was nowhere else to turn to.

"What will we do now then Raiden?" Val asked.

Raiden paused before answering, "I don't know Val, this was our last resort."

"There will be ships coming back though. The skyships with your friend aboard will return in a matter of days, also I have some ships stationed for trade ported in Angland. They too will be arriving in only a few days."

"We don't know how much time we have," Val said.

"Then you should try the slums."

Raiden looked up then, "What was that?"

"We often have visitors come here to Hiro. When they come they keep their skyships up here in the ports and they often stay down in True Hiro. Seems it's cheaper for travellers down there."

"Then that's where we'll go!" Raiden said as he sprang out of his failure. "There is hope yet. Your Majesty, can we have authorisation to go to True Hiro if it means looking for a skyship?"

"Certainly. Here, take these signed permits with you. We give these to foreign diplomats. It will grant you entrance to many places. Just keep them close to you all times and don't let anyone from True Hiro see you have them or you will likely be knifed for them."

He handed them from his pockets three permits similar to the ones they received in Lachine, bar codes on the back and all.

"Your Majesty thank you for all the help you have done for all of us today. We have been through a lot just to be here at your presence and you have done more than enough for us," Raiden said as he bowed down again with Zahied and Val following him.

"You're welcome Raiden; anything for the brother of my old master. Good luck on your journey and if you don't succeed then return to me. I shall see to it that you *will* reach your destination one way or another."

"Thank you Your Majesty," Raiden said and bowed down one more time.

The king all shook their hands before they were finally escorted out and back on track with their sacred mission.

They were walking back down the hallway being escorted by the security, Zahied leading, Raiden following and Val dragging behind. He couldn't stop thinking about Acarlie and the fact that she could once again die tomorrow again and with the crowd cheering at her pain. He remembered what it was like last time when they first met back in Lachine and the way she was being beaten by the other elementalist. He thought about the way he left her just moments ago and remembered all the conditioning, remembered himself saying he would protect her, remembered the promise...

He stopped suddenly realising what he had just done, when Raiden noticed he turned around.

"Come on Val, we have to get down to True Hiro quickly,"

Val looked up at him, "I...I can't go with you Raiden,"

"Why not?"

"Because...I have to make sure the Elementalist is safe,"

Raiden walked over to him, "We don't have time for this Val. The Elementalist's safety is now in the hands of her Guide, the way it should be."

"That's not it Raiden."

"Yes it is Val. You have done your part in ensuring her safety as have I but it's over now. We have a much bigger problem to deal with," Raiden seemed more agitated now and looked tired of the conversation.

"I know the mission we have to do is important Raiden but–"

Raiden growled now, "I don't have time for your games now Val! I have not come all this way to lose you now because you are thinking about your dick!"

"That's not it Raiden!" he shouted back at him.

"Yes it is of course it is! I'm not even human and I've seen the way you look at her, forget her Val!"

"No, I can't forget about her, she needs me!" Val protested.

"That's Sheeria's problem!"

"You don't understand Raiden!"

"Then tell me Val; tell me why she needs you," Raiden stated bluntly feeling annoyed with the argument now.

Val paused then. He knew full well that Raiden wouldn't like to hear what he had to say. Leos were loyal to the elders and so should he being trained as one. He didn't know what Raiden would do if he told him about the elders conditioning Acarlie. He knew he wouldn't believe him.

He croaked out and barely whispered, "I...I can't."

"How convenient, Val this discussion is over. We will go down to True Hiro and find a skyship as planned."

But Val was too stubborn to let it go, "No Raiden, you will go. I have to go to the Elementalist."

Raiden nearly roared with anger and disgust them, "Fine! Stay here, do what you want Val! The mission carries on as planned with or without you. The planet means more to me than you do boy, you should think the same about the girl too!" Raiden finally shouted and turned back and walked to catch up with Zahied.

Val stood behind, on his own watching his best friend walk away and quietly muttered to himself, "But I don't think the world's more important."

Val didn't know what to do then and quickly became lost. He didn't know where Acarlie was and also didn't know where Raiden was but he knew where Raiden was going and decided to ask directions once he was out of the king's palace of how he would get down to the slums. He was directed to the famous large corkscrew elevator Zahied told him about at the end of the street that he boarded all alone with the exception of the man at the control panel.

"I don't know why you want to go down there boy. It's rough down there," the man said as he was pushing the lit up holographic control panel buttons.

Val, still in a sour mood only spoke back to him in a snap tone, "I just do ok. Now do your job and take me there."

"Ok buddy. It will take a while, it's a little over half a mile down you know, so don't go in the centre of the platform and don't go too near the edge."

Val felt like snapping at him again but realised the man was only doing his job and his caution was something he had to say. Being a very strange design the large circular elevator sat still as a platform with two circular platforms. Val stood on the outer and the central part was lined off with a railing. In the centre was the top of the corkscrew. When the elevator started the inner circle began spiralling downwards like a screw and with many unseen bearings between the two circular platforms the outer part Val stood on remained in the same position. Val watched as the city ground slowly became the ceiling as he descended into a darkness with a large mechanical whirl of the elevator. He looked down, over the railings to see loads of massive concrete pillars reaching up from the darkness below and supporting the floor of the city above them.

"Oh, great it's raining down here again," he heard the man say to himself and looked up. At the top near to the white hole of light now surrounded by giant beams of concrete and metal were thousands of small, office-like fire extinguishers that stretched out as far as he could see in the limited light, each one spurting out water and raining down to this city in darkness so far down he could see nothing but the giants legs of the pillars disappearing into a shadowy void. Within a minute he was cast into darkness, being too far away from the ceiling and still many minutes away from the floor there was nothing but the cold, stale air, soaking from the artificial rain and the elevator's conductor beside him. He shivered as cold water founds its way down his collar and ran down his back like a watery snake and kept his eyes down at the deep void below him. The blinding darkness lasted for ten minutes before he finally saw small lights, shapes of buildings morphed from the darkness and into reality. Some lights moved in straight lines, turned sharp corners and carried on. He guessed these were motorised vehicles or M.Vs as he heard Zahied call them once. Soon he heard distant sounds of a city, movement, crying, high pitched screams either out of joy or horror, he couldn't tell. The sounds of many engines and passing-by vehicles and distant sirens. After that colour took shape, the light came in neon lights of blue, purple, red and green and other colours of shop signs. He began to pass the first of the tall buildings and windows began to reflect more of the light. Now when he looked up the white hole of Hiro was now gone and nothing was above him but the artificial rain that now appeared to fall from nothing but darkness. He finally felt now he was in a different city, now he felt he was in True Hiro. The elevator stopped on the wet, concrete floor of the loud and sinful city. Two other men wearing the same suit as the elevator conductor came up to him. They were armed to prevent anyone else getting back on it.

"Just one!" the man on the elevator called to them.

"What are you doing down here boy!" the other man shouted over the rain and other various noises of the city.

"I just need to find someone!" Val called back.

"Do you have a pass?"

"I have this!" he pulled out the slip the king had given him and showed him it.

"That will do fine, look after it boy, don't show it to anyone."

"Where can I find a bar or something?" he asked.

"I will take you to one, follow me!"

Val got off the elevator then pulled his cloak's hood up over his head to shelter him from the rain as he followed the man. He was led down onto the streets of rushing people. If it weren't for the street lamps, MV's and lights in shops it would be pitch black down there. He looked up to see blackness and could not even see the ceiling anymore, only the rain pouring down on him and the light pollution from the nearby street lamps glowing a dirty yellow. It felt like the darkest of nights where not even the sky could be seen but felt strange because he knew the sun was out and shining brightly for the rich folk above him, only half a mile above them but felt like they could have been on a different planet now. The city down here was much more closed in as well, with the buildings all stuck close to one another leaving only dark alleys cluttered with litter and dirt. The man stopped at a crossing at the road then pointed out a bar at the end of the block, "There is a bar there, they will take your bar-code as currency as will that noodle stand over there. Not many other places here will though so be careful."

"I will, thank you," Val said then walked away from him. As he passed the noodle stand in front of him the smell of it drew him closer. His stomach growled and reminded him how long it had been since he last ate. There were many other people sitting there as well eating silently. He went and sat next to a man about the same height and age as him who was just finishing a small bowl of noodles. The young man had a large cloak on covering him from the rain and had taken a wet rag off his head to reveal a freshly cut head of dirty blond hair. Val sat silently next to the man and looked at a menu above the man at the counter's head. The man sitting next to him finished his bowl and held it forward silently to the man at the counter as if he was asking for more.

"No more for you Aeoman, no more," the man said in a strange accent Val hadn't heard before then turned to Val. "What can I get you sir?"

"I'll have whatever this guy was eating and another one for him too," Val said and gestured to the silent man beside him.

The man at the counter looked puzzled, "How will you pay?"

Val signalled him to lean forward and flashed the pass the king gave him.

The man at the counter smiled, "Ah, yes very good. You must be an important person, no?"

"I guess so," Val said quietly after the man pulled out a scan gun and scanned the bar-code of his pass and passed it back to him, then getting two bowls of noodles and giving one to him and another to the silent man next to him.

The silent man smiled and held up the bowl and bowed his head.

"Ah, Dude says thank you sir."

"I'm sorry, what?" Val asked bewildered and the man at the counter pointed to the silent man.

"Dude, he says thank you," he repeated.

"That's his *name?*"

"Yes, Dude. His name is Dude. He says thank you."

"Can't he speak for himself?" Val asked again a little puzzled.

"No, he is a mute. He has been here ever since he was a small aeomon. He never could speak and used to play with a young boy who used to just call him 'Dude'. That boy died a few years ago of lack of sunlight, the True Hiro Sickness, lots of people get that down here. Since the aeomon could not speak we all call him by the name the young boy did; Dude."

"Oh, well, you're welcome Dude. So you are an aeomon?" Val asked and looked behind the mute, "where is your tail?"

When he asked this Dude just looked back down at his noo-dles and ate silently.

"No no, he not Aeomon; he AeoMAN. When an aeomon has a tail lost they become known as neither Aeomon nor Man, just Aeoman, that's the technical term anyway," the man behind the counter explained while cleaning a glass, lifting it to the light and checking for smears. "A lot of people, elders and tigians often still call them Aeomon though since that is still their species."

"Oh, I'm sorry then Dude. I'm not from around here. You will have to forgive my ignorance," Val said as he started eating his noodles.

Dude, the quiet aeoman only looked up and waved his hand and nodded as if to say, "*It's ok, don't worry about it*".

"Why are you here then stranger?" the man at the counter asked him.

"I'm looking for someone, my friend, a Leo."

"No leos down here stranger. No leos anywhere anymore."

"No he should be down here somewhere. We're looking for someone with a skyship."

Dude then looked up and started pointing at himself and pointing into the bar at the end of the street.

"What's he saying?"

"He's trying to say he knows where you can find someone with a skyship."

"How do you know?"

The man at the counter smiled, "Known him for a while now. Just know what he's saying. You will too once you get to know him. Just ask him over wise. You know what a yes and no are in body language don't you?"

"Yeah, is that what you're saying Dude? Can you take me to someone with a skyship?"

Dude nodded and put his thumb up then paused for a second then started pointing at his noodles.

"Ok, we'll go after we eat, thank you," Val said finally then sat with this aeoman eating his noodles in the rain before they finally finished and got up, thanked the man behind the counter and set off down the street into a nearby bar.

23

The city down in True Hiro was packed with people either working, selling things on the street whether that be illegal or not, but people really didn't mind so much as they do in other cities and towns. Yes, there were law enforcers down there just like another city and the prison for both Hiro and True Hiro was down in True Hiro. But the people were more tolerant of some of the smaller crimes down there because they were dammed to darkness already and were already prisoners of their community and so such crimes as prostitution, drug dealing and even petty theft were often overlooked because it was seen that they were only trying to make a living in the world. The police and law enforcers were bad down here too. If they didn't overlook your crime then they would deal out their own punishment. Dude was one to suffer from such an act when he was caught stealing previously and had his precious tail removed from him. But he couldn't tell Val that. The reason for Dude being a mute was the same story too. He was caught as a child by the police breaking into some offices and generally messing around like all boys do. When he was caught he didn't exactly 'come quietly' as they say and kicked up a fuss until the enforcers had enough, held him down and brought a knife to his tongue. Ever since then he found it very difficult to talk and gave up on the idea and started using body language to communicate with others. It also was a psychological problem that grew gradually as he did. Ever since he was young he knew the truth as all aeomon did. Aeomon were looked down on by the humans and seen as inferior beings and were never given the same respect as the other evolved species. Also, as a thief he was looked down on and seen as scum of the underground city and so with these problems with him all his life he grew tired of the silence of people ignoring him and became invisible to the streets, walking silently amongst the other people unnoticed and going places where no one else did. He became a ghost, a phantom of the slums and his inability to speak made it so much easier. He began to see himself as the lowest of the low after a while and became his own worst enemy and having lost his tail made this much worse. His tail was his link to his ancestors and family. It was a symbol of individuality to him and always gave him hope that one day he might make it to wherever he came from to be with his own kind again. The aeomon were a proud race and when an aeomon was seen without its tail it was frowned upon because it meant that the aeomon had forgotten its heritage and wanted to become a human. Dude knew this and now with his tail missing he would not be accepted back into the home he had been dreaming of all his life. Depression quickly took hold of Dude and soon everyone saw the constant tired look in his loveless, lonely eyes but did not take pity or show any empathy or remorse but carried on with their own problems. Suicide became an often and welcome thought in Dude's mind. The thought of throwing himself into the passing MVs crossed his mind more than once when he walked the streets. But he couldn't tell Val that.

Dude led Val across the busy street in the pouring, artificial rain. The word of tomorrow's Elemental Battle had reached True Hiro and the authorities had already started getting the city ready for it. The people could not watch the E.B from down there and so they had a large monitor screen in the middle of the city so everyone would gather and watch it from there. Many legal and illegal trades would make a lot of money at such an event and so everyone was excited. As Val watched the people setting up equipment for tomorrow he thought about Acarlie again. Because the elemental battles brought trade every time he realised that wherever Acarlie would go she would bring trade with her, this would also bring happiness. Wherever she would go she would bring a smile to the people and it was a celebration every time she entered a city, but at what cost? Tomorrow she would have to go through all the same pain as she did in Lachine. These people didn't love her. They just wanted her for business and for entertainment. They just wanted to see her beaten until death, even her guide would only stand there and watch her die. Maybe he was the only one who cared for her safety. Maybe he...

Dude patted on the door disrupting Val's train of thought when they reached the bar. Inside was full of drunken men and hard working strippers and dancers, having lost all their self-respect and dancing for the drunken men throwing money at them to the sound of sleazy music and cigarette smoke clouding the air. Dude stood still in the smoky, dark bar peering through the fog of cigar and cigarette ash until he saw what he was looking for. A tall dark man sat lounged back on a private table with a few of his cronies sat beside him. He wore a smart tailor-made suit with a wallet full of notes he was throwing at the woman dancing on his table. He had a chiselled face with a dark smile. His moustache and short goatee gave the people the impression that he traded in some illegal form or another. Dude patted Val on the shoulder and pointed to the man and took him across the room toward him. When the tall man saw him coming he sat upright and called over to him, "Ah, if it isn't the mute monkey. What can I do for you today my quiet friend, another woman perhaps?"

Dude only showed the man Val and gave Val a push in front of him.

"Oh, I see then. Given me another customer have you? What can I get you friend? I got all sorts of women here to suit your desires," he said with a croak of smoking too much and his voice was the sound of temptation and sin but Val stood before him.

"Actually I'm looking for something a little different."

"Is that so? Well not a problem. It's not often I get a request like that but it can be arranged, you must understand though that my selection of men is a little more...limited."

"I'm not here to negotiate for sex for neither man nor woman. I want to ask you about something else."

The man took a large pull on his cigar then waved for the stripper to leave his table. He pointed at a chair by the table. "You wish to do business with me then? Sit down, both of you."

Val sat down as did Dude and waited for the man to take another pull on his cigar then glaring at Val through the smoke he blew in his Val's face.

"What is it you want?" he asked them.

"A skyship. I need passage across the waters to a place called Aragorth."

Everyone around the table started laughing then at the two young men in front of them. Even Dude had a troubled look on his face and scowled at Val as if to say, "*You never told me that part.*"

The laughing died down and the man sat back in his chair with his arms stretched behind, "That's a long way friend and you don't look like you got the money to pay me for such a trip. Now piss off before they find your corpse in the trash."

Val slammed his fist down on the table and leaned forward, "What do I have to do then to get passage of your ship?"

With the music still playing in the background a tense silence fell over the table. This act impressed the pimp and he sat back smiling and thinking something to himself, "Maybe there is something you can do for me, both of you. After the E.B tomorrow we leave for Anavrin to a country called Walshraw. You two will accompany us there. There is something I must have."

"Let me guess. We have to steal it right?"

"If you want admittance to my ship then you will do whatever I ask of you."

"And what if I say no?"

"Then you get no ship."

Val thought about his offer for a minute then said, "Ok then. I'll do it but the aeoman stays out of it. He has nothing to do with this."

"No, this will be a two man job and he is in it as much as you are. Besides, you will need his help since he already knows the trade," he then leaned forward suggestively. "I want you both back here after the Elemental Battle. Not a minute later, is that clear?"

Val looked over to Dude who only nodded then turned back to the pimp, "Ok then, we'll be here after the battle tomorrow."

"Good, now get out of my face," the pimp waved his cronies to escort them out of the bar.

"Can I get your name?" Val quickly put in before he was escorted out.

The man grinned and pulled on his cigar again. The red and yellow glow lighting up leaving dark lines across his gaunt cheek bones.

"You can call me…" he paused while he thought of an alias to be known as, "…Gendrick." He then only needed to nod to his men who grabbed Val and Dude and threw them outside. Val landed hard on the stone floor and turned defensively, "Screw you goon!"

The man only kissed his teeth at him and said, "See you tomorrow bitch."

Val went to step back in the bar and was about to call his staff when Dude put his hand on Val's shoulder and shook his head. Val sighed, "Maybe you're right Dude. I should leave them."

Dude nodded and gave him a comforting pat on the back.

Now he stood in the street with nowhere to go and had to ask himself, "Well, what am I supposed to do now?"

Dude heard him say it and waved over his shoulder as if to say, "*Follow me,*" and led him down the alleyways and up to a hidden block of flats and to a security door. When they entered Dude showed him up the stairs since the elevator was broken and into a small, one bedroom apartment cluttered with possessions and second hand furniture. Dude moved some old rubbish and clutter off his torn sofa for Val to sit. Val looked around and felt sorry for this young aeoman. The place was dimly lit and even if it was cleaned the only word he could use to describe it would be 'dingy'. But it was Dude's home, and he was good enough to allow Val to stay so he knew not to say anything. He sat down in silent thought while Dude disappeared into his small, grime ridden kitchen and moved a heap of unwashed crockery aside to make Val a hot drink. Val knew he had to do something that could help Acarlie but found himself lost for any ideas. He closed his eyes, sighing and pondering.

The next morning Acarlie was sitting patiently in her given room. It was much larger than the last one she stayed in with a balcony that overlooked the whole city. She had been meditating for the whole of the previous day and resting herself so she would be in peak condition when her fight would begin. Sheeria walked into the room having washed all the clothes they had worn the previous days and had just washed herself and eaten. Acarlie was standing out on the balcony taking in the fresh morning air when Sheeria stood behind her.

"Is something troubling you Acarlie?" Sheeria asked her.

"No Sheeria, I was just looking out onto the city. I was hoping to see the others. I hoped that they would walk down the street sometime. Have you seen them anywhere?"

"No, I haven't seen them. Don't worry about them, I'm sure they found the ship they were looking for and have probably already left the city by now. It wouldn't surprise me that Raiden and Zahied will be a hundred miles away from here now."

"And what about Val?"

Sheeria hesitated this time, "You should forget about him most of all child. You have your first real important battle soon. You cannot stop to think about him."

But he is the reason I am here, she thought to herself but just answered, "Yes, you're right Sheeria. He is gone now and I need to accept that."

"That's my elementalist. Now are you ready for your battle child?" Sheeria said while wrapping a blanket around Acarlie's shoulders.

Acarlie sighed and forced a smile to her guide, "Yes, I am ready...."

I'd just like to see him one more time, she thought to herself.

The door knocked then and Sheeria went to open the door. Like a wish had come true, Val stood in the doorway, still dirty from the city below.

Val expected Sheeria to be more protective over Acarlie but was pleasantly surprised when Sheeria smiled and welcomed him inside.

"Hello Val. What are you doing here?" She asked him.

Before Val got the chance to answer he had to catch Acarlie as she threw herself onto him and embraced him tightly.

They smiled at each other and let each other go, "I have come here to wish the Elementalist good luck."

Sheeria nodded, "Very well then. Acarlie, I will return in two minutes." Acarlie nodded and watched Sheeria walk out of the room.

"Thank you for coming Val. I thought you weren't coming..."

She took Val's hands and looked up at him but his face was different as soon as Sheeria had left. He seemed more concerned and worried.

"I just wanted you to have these Acarlie, to ensure your win."

He took from his pockets three little star shaped shurikens he made by moulding his staff down.

Acarlie looked down at the weapons in shock and looked back up at him, "But you know I can't use weapons Val. What were you thinking?"

"You told me once that Eloma doesn't need to touch a weapon to use it. Also back in Lachine, Billy used a windmill as a tool against you. These don't have to be used as weapons Acarlie, merely tools to ensure your victory. Take them, please."

She could see the concern in his eyes and took them for that reason, "Val, I don't know if I can use them," she started to stutter.

"Yes you can Acarlie. You're a smart girl, you will figure out how to use them." He then put his hands on her shoulders, "Just remember our promise Acarlie. Remember our pact we made, ok?"

The way he said this made her feel more worried and had a feeling there was more in his words than he let out, "Where are you going to be?" she asked him.

"I have made a deal with someone for a skyship. I have to go away for a short time though."

"What about your side of the promise Val. The part about not leaving me?" She asked looking up at him.

"I'm coming straight back Acarlie. I just needed to know you would still be here when I get back."

"But if I win then the day after I would have to go straight into the next city, and anyway aren't these star weapons your staff? What happens if you need it? When you call it won't it disappear from me?"

"You let me worry about that. I just want you to concentrate on staying alive today. I will come back, ok? I will come back."

Acarlie took the shurikens from Val nodding reluctantly, "Ok Val, just make sure you do come back. I don't want to leave you behind again."

"Just remember our promise. Whatever you feel, don't do anything to yourself."

Sheeria opened the door again to see Acarlie standing with her head low and Val looking back at Sheeria.

"Is everything ok Acarlie? Are you alright?"

Acarlie forced a smile and hid the shurikens behind her back, "Yeah I'm fine. Val was just leaving."

Val understood what she was trying to do and took a step back, "Yes, I wish you the best of luck Acarlie." He then gazed a sorry expression to her silently so Sheeria wouldn't understand it, "I will see you soon."

Sheeria closed the door behind him and Val stood there in the hallway taking a breath, *I hope this works*, he thought as he started walking down the hallway.

"What was all that about?" Sheeria asked Acarlie.

"Oh, nothing. I'm glad I got to see him one more time before the fight," she said. She wasn't lying either. She really was glad that she got to see him one more time and felt secure that he came all the way to try and help her and ensure her safety but she felt really worried and remembered what he was saying about making a deal for a skyship and wondered if it would be the last she saw him. She remembered what he said and had faith in him.

"Come now then Acarlie, the arena awaits you. You must make your final preparations before confronting Logan."

The arena was a huge glass sphere with the audience all crowded around it and sat in a stadium surrounding it. There at one of the highest points in the stadium overlooking the whole arena was the king. He sat proudly looking down at the arena as the perimeter of the outside was filling with water. Sat next to him was his queen, a beautiful slim woman who did not show her age at all and in the seats in front of him were Raiden and Zahied. Having unsuccessfully found a skyship Raiden retired from the hunt and later that day went back to the king where he and Zahied were given a room that night and access to the royal seating in the stadium. Raiden was still upset about having to wait for a skyship, to loosing Val and to having to sit through another Elemental Battle, something he still never liked watching. Zahied however didn't seem to mind. The day previously he had visited the local libraries and hospitals for documents he could put in his book and stayed up that night studying them. The thought of sitting in royal seats was an honour for him and he thanked the king and queen a dozen times before he actually sat down. Down on the local seats every seat was taken. Outside the stadium, the parks were packed as well with a large screen set up so the people who couldn't get in could still watch this already famous battle.

Down in True Hiro there was the same vibe with one large monitor set up and a few other smaller ones set up on the tops of buildings so the really poor could watch from work or home. The whole of Hiro and True Hiro boomed with excitement and wonder as for the first time they would watch two people from the same country battle for honour.

Acarlie was the first to walk into the arena to the cheers of the crowd. She walked in the arena bare footed since the floor was made of steel and not dust or stones like the previous ones she had fought in and was well polished and smooth for her feet to walk on. All around the outside of the arena was water circling around giving her the uneasy feeling that very soon this calm and peaceful element would be her enemy and be trying to take her life. She looked up out of the glass sphere to see the king and his queen sitting proudly above her and bowed down to them, much to the crowd's pleasure,

"Such respect this elementalist has," they said to one another.

"Such beauty and admiration for someone as young as her."

She looked up to see Zahied and Raiden sitting close to the king as well but no Val and she felt a little worried by this. *Where is he?* she thought and hoped he would be ok.

There were seven small mechanical devices floating around the sphere with her. They were the size of a football and had a lens in the centre of it. These were cameras made for the monitors outside as so everyone could see it at a different angle. The cameras zipped from one side of the arena to another, high and low to see the happy faces of the children, mothers and daughters waving to the cameras to the people outside and many young men and boys flying flags and banners of the Racoves flag and signs with either Logan or Acarlie's name on them. One banner that stood out most for Acarlie was an old couple holding up a big cream banner with painted writing saying, *WHOEVER WINS WILL DO US PROUD...RACOVES!*

One of the cameras then floated above her head and peered down at her. The ball-shaped camera moved slightly getting the best angle and the lens in the middle centred on her. She looked up and into the camera thinking to herself, *I hope you're out there Val.*

Back down in True Hiro and Val had met up again with Dude who showed him the way to the giant monitors where they found a place to sit and ate some of the noodles being carried around in little trays and sold to the people. Val watched as the crowd in the stadium screamed, smiled and waved and heard the jealous remarks of the slum people waving fingers at them.

"Piss off!" they called out to the monitors.

The monitor then turned around and hovered above the elementalist's head and looked down at her. The crowd suddenly cheered when they saw her for the first time as she stood there looking up and into the monitor.

"She's beautiful" the jealous drunk shouted.

"Back off buddy, she's mine," another shouted back to him.

Val only stared up at the monitor as he saw Acarlie looking up into the floating camera. It was like she was looking up to him, *I'm here Acarlie. I'm watching you*, he thought to himself.

Acarlie waited for the audience to calm down then the announcer's voice lifted their spirits again and announced her first. When the voice announced the arrival of Logan the crowd screamed filling the stadium with noise. Logan stepped out of the other side of the arena. He was dressed in a wet suit and his hair was gelled back and he looked more like a surfer that an elementalist. He smiled and waved to his adoring fans then stepped forward to the centre to finally meet Acarlie.

"I've heard a little about you Acarlie. I must say I have been looking forward to this match."

"Me too Logan. May the best elementalist win," she then shook his hand and walked back to her side of the arena.

She took another breath and thought about Val one more time before she cleared her mind of him and concentrated on the battle as the three sirens sounded, starting the battle.

24

The crowd sat silently on the edge of their seats as they watched the elementalists stare at each other for a brief moment. Logan held out his arms and closed his eyes and Acarlie watched as some of the water from each side of him jumped out of the small little canals and began circling in front of him like a sphere of water. She brought her hand to her chest again and closed her eyes and felt the circle of wind rush around her, as if answering to her call and joining her as her partner in their battle. Logan suddenly punched the water ball and it shot across the massive glass sphere toward Acarlie. Acarlie opened her eyes and swung her hand aside in the same technique she did with Barry back in Eloma and the ball of water changed its direction and splashed up the side of the dome. As soon as this happened the crowd opened up with a roar of cheer and applause. Acarlie then ran in and jumped to kick Logan while he was stationary but Logan dived out of the way and reached out for the water again. The water obeyed his commands just like the wind obeyed her's and lifted out of the small canals. Since water was liquid and could take any shape it wanted he had the ability to change the water into weapons. He immediately used the water and twisted it in front of him turning it into a whip then swung his arm back as he whipped the water to Acarlie. With a *crack!* the whip exploded with water as it struck Acarlie, soaking her immediately and leaving a red mark on her arm. He whipped it again and it connected with her face. She screamed and fell to the floor holding her wet cheek. He whipped again while she was down and the crowd cheered every time it made contact with her, just like in Lachine. Acarlie got to her feet quickly and limped to one side narrowly avoiding one of Logan's water whips and pushed her hands forward and blew the water away back into the stadium's glass sphere. She then tripped Logan and tried chopping his neck with the edge of her hand. Only he was stronger than he looked and only blocked her and threw her to one side and got up. She instantly dived forward again with more aggressive attacks, trying to get him on the floor again and try and attack his throat. Sometimes she was successful and managed to trip him or throw him over her shoulder to the ground but every time she did he only struck her back or threw her away. Soon she started to become out of breath and slowed down when she realised that was what he was trying to do to her, tire her out and give the audience something to cheer about. Make them think she might actually win then easily take her out when she was tired. After realising this she changed her strategy and turned to a defensive position. He noticed this and tried attacking her with shots of water fired from the canals in her direction. Some hit her and sent her back a few paces and the others she managed to avoid then attacking by sending strong gusts of wind in his direction. He then decided it was time to pull out the big cards and held his hands out to one side again. Acarlie noticed that at the end of the glass sphere behind him where the canals met there were two dams there rumbling and when they broke open she nearly screamed as water started gushing through and within seconds the smooth steel floor was flooded and reached her bare feet and rising to her legs. She was now shaking with coldness and needed to close the dams. She noticed that they were made of metal and therefore she could move them back into place. She held out her hand and concentrated on one door at a time. The crowd watched in wonder as the metal dam started moving back in place slowly but Logan saw this and tried to fight it and use the gushing water to force the dam back open. Acarlie looked up to see the pain in Logan's face as he couldn't hold the force anymore and pulled back in pain letting Acarlie close the first dam but the other one was still wide open and the water was now up to her waist. She tried to close the other dam but Logan turned the water into little balls and shot them towards her. When she avoided these projectile water pellets he then turned more water into another whip and struck her into the water she was standing in. She found herself safe from the whip when she was under the water but could not use her power so well when under it. When she came back up the water was up to her neck and soon had to swim to keep her head above the water. This was exactly what Logan wanted her to do. She had no choice and knew he could win. She looked up to see him not swimming in the water but standing on top of it. Like he had made it solid for himself. He tried whipping her a few more times but she only held her breath under the water. This was another thing he wanted her to do and simply walked over to her bobbing head and pushed it under the water. The crowd watched in horror as there was nothing she could do now to protect herself. While she was under the water she could not control the wind and was now only strug-gling to free herself from Logan's grip as so she could catch some of that precious oxygen only just above her. She twisted herself around and freed herself of Logan's grip then gasped a breath of air and tried swimming away but when she looked back she saw Logan was still standing there laughing at her.

"You have lost Acarlie. You are defenceless now. This sphere will be full soon and you will have no oxygen to breathe. What are you going to do?"

Acarlie, refusing to give in thought of Val again. She remem-bered the day she performed her kata in front of him and had an idea. She took a deep breath and swam down to the floor. Even under the water she could hear the gasps of confusion of the crowd. When she reached the floor she concentrated on everything around her and hoped she could pull it off. Being underwater she didn't feel it at first but when she opened her eyes she saw the water at her feet suddenly came upwards and over her head. A mass confusion came from all over Hiro as they watched this strange phenomenon. The water inside the glass sphere lifted up off the floor and floated loosely like a giant bub-ble inside it, then Acarlie too started floating upwards. She knew then she had done it. She had mastered the gravity inside the sphere and now with all the air in her lungs she floated upside down back up to the floating bubble of water above her. The first thing she noticed about floating in zero gravity was that it was like being under water, only with the joy of being able to breathe. She slowly floated upwards and turned, seeing the opened dam. She now had the time to close this without being interrupted and held out her hand and closed the second dam so no more water would come in. Logan appeared from the bottom of the floating water above her and she knew he would have the most deadly move with him. She knew that if she released the gravity or if he controlled the water to smash down on her the pressure would kill her instantly. The only thing she could think of doing was using the shurikens Val gave her. She pulled them out from behind her wanting to throw them at Logan when the thought of Val telling her popped into her mind, '*use them as a tool*'. She twisted and turned while floating in the sphere and threw the shurikens and threw the wind after them to enhance their power to stick them into the glass sphere itself. They each struck into the glass walls of the dome which instantly cracked. Everyone man, woman and child in the stadium and watching on the screens knew what this meant. The crack spread further up the glass sphere and scared the rich audience so close to it. Acarlie looked up to see Logan still floating above her with tons of water above his head ready to be smashed down and shatter the whole sphere and send huge glass shards to fall on top of them. His face went pale and she could see him mouth the words, "*You wouldn't dare.*" Acarlie gave him a cheeky wink and a small grin of mischievous pleasure then spun her hands around followed by the rest of her body, twisting with her hands above her head like a floating ballet dancer leaving a cyclone of wind to circle her and reach up into the water above her and separate it like an upside down cyclone. This also caught Logan and the cameras and they started circling around her slowly.

"Don't do it!" he called to her but she knew she had the upper hand now and wasn't about to let it go.

In one final move she released the gravity inside the sphere except for where they floated and the tons of floating water fell to the floor. The cyclone reaching up through the water acted as a vertical tunnel and made the falling water pass straight through them without touching them. When the water struck the ground the glass immediately shattered all the way to the top and Logan looked up whilst still floating uncontrollably to see the top of the glass sphere shatter and a rain of large shards of glass fell towards them. Using the wind and gravity Acarlie managed to dodge the glass or send it away. Logan however was defenceless and his precious water now below him was ineffective. The audience screamed as they saw their stadium destroyed but thankful no one was hurt. Even the closest were only soaked from the water that spread itself around. Acarlie slowly floated herself down to the floor by gradually realising the gravity and putting it back to normal. At first everything was silent for her. She took a breath and relaxed herself but when she looked down she saw blood diluting with the water and circle around her feet. She heard the crowd scream and looked around, following the blood around her feet and saw Logan lying on the wet floor with a large shard of glass piercing his stomach. His blood diluting into the water and spreading out, turning it red. Medics and elders rushed in to help him, fussing over him and the elders performing tricks to revive him. The medic turned from him with a great smile on his face and looked up to the king. All the cameras floating around him watched his reaction. He put his thumb up. Logan was going to be ok. The whole of Hiro and True Hiro erupted into screams and applause the likes of which Acarlie had never heard before. She even looked up to see Raiden who never liked these matches giving her a standing ovation with the happiest look on his face.

True Hiro was so loud with cheer. One for the fact of it was such a good fight. The other for the fact that she destroyed the stadium and soaked the rich people with her that it was like they wanted the rich folk above them to hear their cheers from way down below. Dude was jumping and clapping and shaking his fist in the air now and only Val was sitting down watching her on the monitor waving to the cheering crowd and to the camera to the people down there. *I have done it, she is still safe*, he thought to himself.

Acarlie was overwhelmed by the way they cheered for her then and she could only stand in the middle of the broken arena and wave as Logan was taken out to be revived. A camera came and floated by her again and she looked into it waving, *thank you Val*, she thought.

After the battle Val and Dude went to the bar and met up with the pimp who named himself Gendrick and his crew to be taken to the upper level to the skyship. They paid the man at the elevator to take them up and to keep it quiet that they were coming. This was the first time for Dude to see the sunlight in all its glory in so many years that it burned his eyes and he lay down on the floor covering his face with his hands. Gendrick, still smoking a cigar and covering his head with a fedora hat looked down at the seemly crippled aeoman and laughed, "Of course. How could I forget? This monkey has been in the dark so long his eyes will not be ready for the light yet."

He then snapped his fingers and one of his cronies stepped in from behind him, "Give him some dark goggles. I don't want my master thief blind and unable to do any of my bidding."

The big bulky bald goon answered him like a moaning child, "But boss, I don't have any dark goggles on me,"

Gendrick scowled at him, "Then gives him *your* glasses."

"But boss–"

"Do as I say!" the pimp snapped at him, "We need him to see properly. You will get another pair."

"Yes boss," he finally said and reluctantly took off the pair of dark sunglasses and handed them to Dude who reached up for them and put them over his eyes like he was reaching for a cure when poisoned. Val helped him to his feet and looked at Dude in the sunlight and saw how pale he really was and wondered what would happen to him if he stayed down there all his life and never saw the sunlight he himself had taken for granted. Dude's skin was so pale Val thought he was nearly transparent. He was skinny and nearly frail if but the lean muscles he devolved from running and stealing. They were led up to a skyship port and finally for the first time Val saw what a skyship actually looked like. The ship was much larger than he thought with the nose of it shaped like an aeroplane with the cockpit looking out from the top of the nose. The skyship had metal wings on each side with two smaller wings on the side of the nose with two propellers on each one. On the top of the base of the ship was the deck with two doors at each end that looked like they could be sealed up like a submarine hatch. The end of the ship was very big and made the ship look like it had a large cargo hold with another two small wings at the tip of it. The ships he always imagined at first were small and thin and this sight really changed his view on what a skyship actually looked like. The bottom had large fold away thrusters that he could only guess lifted the ship off the ground without the use of a runway. It sat there magnificently with its door open on the side and a ramp for them to walk on,

Val went to the pimp and asked him, "So what is it that we have got to get for you?"

"It is a blade my boy," Gendrick croaked while still smoking.

"A blade?"

"Yes, a very special blade called *Fireshaver*. It's kept by its owner in his mansion in Walshraw. We will take you there and wait for you to infiltrate the building, steal the sword then bring it back to me."

"And then I get the ship."

"Yes, and then I will take you to your destination on the *Scarlet Arise*. Anywhere you want to go. She will take you."

"The Scarlet Arise? Did you think of that name?"

"No, she was named by the Anglish army. This ship used to belong to them."

"Let me guess. You stole it," Val increasingly felt sick with the tall dark man beside him with every breath he took.

"Hey, they can have it back whenever they ask for it. Once they find it that is," Gendrick laughed followed by a small chuckle of the large hulking men behind them.

"So is this like an attack ship or something then?" Val asked.

Gendrick laughed once at his question and admired him for asking it, "No, there is not a single gun, turret nor cannon on this ship, none of them do, they're forbidden weapons. Don't you know anything boy? The Scarlet Arise was made a scout ship for their army and is made only for speed and agility. I guarantee you this. The Scarlet Arise is the fastest ship in the sky."

"Ok, whatever. How long will this take?" Val asked.

"A few days there and back," the pimp said checking the backs of his finger nails, "Oh, and I'm afraid I'm going to have to keep you bound until we get there," he said suggestively to him and signalling to his men.

"Why is that?" Val asked but he was struck behind his knees by a weapon and when he fell to his knees they threw a black bag over his face, tied him up and carried him inside. He thought he heard the distant sound of a leo roaring but it was silenced by the sound of Dude suffering the same treatment as him and thrown beside him. He felt the skyship take off the ground. *What have I got myself into?* he thought to himself.

Raiden had just finished watching the battle when the king came to him after.

"I hoped you liked the battle Raiden?" Kerry asked.

"Yes, it was a great fight wasn't it? Acarlie is quite an extraordinary elementalist. I think the stories of this battle will be told all over Sphere."

The king laughed, "Yes, and every time the story will seem greater until it will be a legend."

"At least that way she will always be remembered Your Majesty, don't you agree?"

"Oh my yes, and what a grand way to be remembered. The first elementalist in ten years comes in and defeats Hiro's elementalist and destroys the stadium along with it." He was laughing a little too happily for someone who stood in front of his destroyed arena.

"Aren't you upset about the destruction of the arena? Won't there be someone who has to pay for it?" Zahied asked the king then.

The king looked over to Zahied and smiled at his worthy question, "I can't say I'm not a little upset about the destruction of my arena, no. But it will be worth it soon enough. All across the globe people will now know of Hiro. This stadium will now be a tourist site I imagine, and once it's finished it will be greater than before. This time I will not make it out of glass no?" he laughed it away standing before his destroyed stadium and Raiden knew he would be right. It may be destroyed but the money itself it will take to rebuilt it will be nothing compared to the years of support it will now have after today.

"I say Raiden, I was waiting to tell you this after the match because I knew you would leave as soon as I told you," the king said. "There is a skyship docked in the port at the end of town. You should go there and see if there is anybody you can talk to about renting it. Your pass I gave you shall give you admittance."

Raiden's smile turned to an immediate serious frown once he heard and bowed to the king,

"You were right to tell me now Your Majesty. I will go there at once. I will return if I do not succeed. Excuse me Your Majesty," he then waited for Zahied to say goodbye to the king and his queen and they both set off out of the stadium and through the city crowded with still excited people, asking only for directions to the docks. When they reached the docks they showed the admittance passes and ran out onto the port and finally saw a skyship they had been looking for. The only problem was that they were a little too late and they saw people already boarding, and one of them looked all too familiar.

"That's Val!" Raiden shouted, pointing to the figure of Val walking in talking to a tall dark person. They tried running for them but were too far away and watched in horror as they saw Val get struck from behind and tied up and thrown in the ship along with somebody else. Raiden roared as loud as he could and tried to catch up with them but the door closed and the ship lifted up off the floor and flew away. Raiden cried up to Val but he knew was already too late. Val was gone on the only skyship in the city and there was nothing he could do.

25

"You lost the boy!" Sheeria shouted at Raiden as he stood with his back leaned against the palace walls with his arms crossed and his mouth shut. He was still upset that he had just lost Val to the mystery people who had taken him away in the skyship. They had returned to the palace to rest since they had nowhere to turn now and tried to figure out a way of finding Val. There they met up with Sheeria again. Acarlie, who had won her last battle was taken away by a revived Logan to a secret and isolated location in the city where she would only have one night to learn the basics of mastering the Element of Water. This was something all journeying elementalists would do and ensured the progression of them. Once they learned the element of which they had just defeated they would practice this on their pilgrimage to become better. This did mean though that because of the years of practice their home element would always be their strongest point and were taught to practice this the most. It would seem like this would make every fight easier as they journeyed along and a lot of people thought so but the practice along the pilgrimage was a very important thing to do if they wanted to become Elemental Lord but it was also very tiring. A lot of elementalists would learn three or four different elements and would try and learn them all at once and become very tired and that would be their downfall in the next battle. Also a lot of elementalists would practice their new learned elements and forget all about their home ones, which would always be their strongest ones and again this would be their downfall. Finally were the elementalists who wouldn't practice their elements at all and would be too weak against the Elemental Lord. It was a hard road to walk and the practice and sufficient rest must be taken in order to beat the Elemental Lord. While the winning elementalist was with the defeated elementalist teaching them the secret the Guide would always have to stay behind and wait where instructed and in Sheeria's case it was the king's palace. It was nearly nightfall and Acarlie had been gone for several hours when Raiden and Zahied had arrived to find her there waiting for Acarlie and had told her the news.

"How could you lose him?" She shouted at Raiden again who still only leaned back with his eyes closed trying only to ignore her rant.

"How could you be so careless Raiden? Why was he not at your side?" she barked.

Raiden spoke heatedly then, standing up tall to step the hot headed tigian back. "He wanted to leave!"

"And you let him go!? How could you do such a thing?" Sheeria, unlike many other creatures was not scared by Raiden and stood up to him still only slightly shorter, this being a tigian thing but also because of her stubborn temper that made Raiden think she would stand up to him even if she were as small as an aeomon or porcus.

"You do know what will happen to him out there don't you? Sphere's divide Raiden! You're supposed to look after him! He doesn't know anything about the world outside him."

Raiden knew he had failed then but still felt the sting when she said it, '*Sphere's Divide*' was a curse said by the people of Sphere when they would be angry or upset like Sheeria was. It was said because the divides were the most terrible parts of Sphere's history and would always bring countless deaths from war. There had been several divides in the history of Sphere and every time it meant the wise but arrogant elders would battle with the intelligent but selfish humans. Zahied only sat quietly on the other side of the room watching the two felines at it and couldn't help but admire Sheeria for not only standing up to the huge Raiden but to give him a lecture as well.

"How is Val supposed to survive out there on his own? A child has more chance than him of surviving on their own—"

"Val is not a child though," Raiden broke in. "He is a man Sheeria! A fighter who can protect himself," Raiden pointed out but Sheeria only snapped a correction.

"He is a *boy* Raiden! And how can he protect himself? Look what happened with Miles. If you were not there then he would already—"

"I know what happened with Miles Sheeria!" he shouted back at her but she only stood unscathed at his roars and glared at him the whole while.

"I don't know what else to say to you Raiden. He was your responsibility just like Acarlie is mine but you don't see me giving up on her as soon as she says she wants to leave. That was a careless and a *foolish* thing to do." She finished her lecture and started pacing up and down the large decorated room of the royal palace leaving Raiden to stand there defeated and staring at the floor.

She thought for a minute and asked him, "Where did he go?"

"I told you, I don't know. We saw him boarding a skyship."

"I mean before that. He said he wanted to leave right? So where did he go?"

Zahied who understood the question then stood up and followed in, "Hey yeah, he said he wanted to help you and Acarlie. He said she needed his help, that's what Raiden told me."

Sheeria thought for a second and remembered Val coming to see Acarlie, "Yes, he did come and see her earlier this morning but I don't know what he might have told her. I gave them their privacy."

Raiden looked up now, "So you think he might have told her where he might have gone?"

Sheeria nodded and carried on, "It's a possibility you will have to rely on. Is there not any way we can check where the ship might have gone? Will the port authorities not have any records that tell us where the ship's destination would be?"

"That's a good idea Sheeria, I shall go now and return and..." Raiden said but Zahied broke in, "No, I'll go Raiden. I can ask the workers there and if needed I can get in there unnoticed and check myself. It won't be good on the king if his guest was caught snooping around the port authority files after hours. When will Acarlie arrive back here Sheeria?"

"It could be anytime from now to the morning?"

"Then I've got plenty of time. I'll go now and return later, hopefully Acarlie will be back then." Zahied said as he threw his cloak on and patted Raiden on the back comfortingly.

Sheeria went and sat down and said to Raiden, "Come now Raiden, there is nothing we can do but wait for Acarlie and Zahied to return. You should rest yourself now."

Raiden who was still blaming himself for Val only nodded silently and sat beside Sheeria as she switched a television on and took the time she had to relax.

It wasn't until the next morning that Acarlie arrived back in the room with the others. Zahied had also returned a few hours previously and took the time to sleep. Sheeria and Raiden were already awake when she came in the room with a huge smile on her face. She looked up at Sheeria and said softly, "I have done it. I have taken my first step in progressing as an elementalist."

Sheeria smiled with joy when she heard the news, "Congratulations Acarlie," she said as Acarlie walked in the room and gave her comforting hug.

Acarlie turned to see Raiden smiling at her too but could also see a look of trouble in his face and asked him what she had wanted to know for a while now, "Where is Val Raiden?"

"That is something we wanted to ask you about Acarlie. We heard Val came and saw you yesterday before your battle and hoped he told you where he might have gone."

Acarlie's face dropped then when she found out and only stared in shock as Raiden told her of how he saw Val beaten and taken aboard a ship.

"Did he not say anything about where he might have gone?" Raiden asked her.

"No, he only said something about making a deal with someone for a skyship and that he would return. So is Val in danger?"

"I don't know but the way he was bound suggests he won't be in a position to bargain as to how he could return so quickly," Raiden said and Acarlie covered her mouth and sat down.

Zahied stepped in then, rubbing his eyes from waking a moment previously, "I checked the flight records at the skyship port last night but could not find anything. The ship was a private ship owned by outsiders and didn't need any record of its destination."

"Then what are we going to do?" Acarlie asked them but a silence entered the room and only Raiden had the courage to end the awkward silence.

"We have to carry on without him..." the words leaving his mouth even stung him but he knew it was the only way.

"You cannot mean that?" Acarlie asked him shocked at his suggestion.

"It is the only way. We still have a mission and you still have your pilgrimage to attend to, whatever Val got himself into can't get in the way of the planet. We move forward...Val stays behind."

"Raiden!?"

"It has to be done. Our last chance of finding out where Val went was with you Acarlie. There is nothing we can do now. You must carry on with your pilgrimage and Zahied and I shall wait here for one of the king's skyships to arrive and when it does we shall go to the monastery without him."

"How can you say something like that? You can't be serious about leaving Val behind?"

"He's right though Acarlie. We must travel to Mecroyles and to your next elementalist," Sheeria pointed out and Acarlie turned around to her.

"I'm not going to leave him behind again Sheeria."

"Val is their problem Acarlie, not ours."

"That still doesn't make it right Sheeria, Val wouldn't leave us behind."

"Were you not listening? He already has left us behind," Sheeria pointed out again and it only made Acarlie remember Val last speaking to her and what he said.

She walked over to Raiden who was now standing at a window and staring out at the city below; she thought of what she could do when the idea came to her.

"Raiden, will you and Zahied accompany me and Sheeria to Mecroyles?"

"What? Why would you ask that?" Sheeria asked her.

"No, I'm sorry Acarlie but I still need a skyship to get to Aragorth. If I go with you then I will miss another ship," Raiden said to her.

"Then tell the king to radio in and send a ship straight to Mecroyles to meet us there. I will need a ship there anyway."

"But waiting here will get us one quicker and we can be back on our way earlier," he said stubbornly.

"Doesn't Val even matter to you at all?"

"Of course Val matters to me," Raiden finally admitted. "Of course I want to see him safe and well but I still have a very important mission to fulfil and I can't spend my valuable time looking for someone who can't be found."

"Do you trust him?" she asked him and turned him from the window and looked so he could look in her innocent human eyes, "...Yes Acarlie, I do," he said softly realising himself that he did trust Val.

"So do I, and he told me that he was coming back. Now if you come with me, you will get the skyship you have been waiting for. We will come back here and search for Val. If we do not find him then with my help it will be easier to find him on a skyship, right?"

"She's right Raiden; with the help of an elementalist it will be easier to find someone since they have access to all the mayors and presidents of every country," Zahied pointed out. Raiden considered her idea but asked her, "But what about your pilgrimage?"

"I will not abandon my pilgrimage. Only postpone it while we look for him."

"You...you would do that for him? Postpone your sacred pilgrimage you have been training for all your life if it meant finding this one person. Is he that important to you?" Raiden asked, lowering his voice so to make his question more personal to Acarlie.

She nodded to him as she did and answered him clearly, "Yes he is."

Raiden considered her proposal for a minute when Sheeria stepped in, "Come on Raiden, admit it, you need Acarlie more than she needs you. If she wants to find Val rather than completing her pilgrimage then I will stand behind her and together we will find him, with or without you."

"Very well then, the mission goes on hold until we have found Val. We shall arrange with the King to send one of his ships directly to Mecroyles, the city we head for. Once there after the Elementalist has her next element we do not rest until we have found Val and have him back with the rest of us," Raiden spoke out to the others then in a leadership fashion and Acarlie smiled, brought her hand to her head and saluted to Raiden

"Yes sir!"

26

The morning air was fresh and the sky glowed a warm yellow as the group now set out from the king's city towards Acarlie's next elemental battle. Their destination was now miles to the east. Their lizziers were gathered and restocked with new blankets, food and some small medicines offered by King Kerry and Logan, the High Elementalist of Hiro. Zahied breathed in and welcomed in the fresh, cool morning air and admired the vibrant mixing colours of the sky above them, lifting their spirits and readying them for their next journey. Their first destination was to a monorail station on the outskirts of the city that would take them speeding across endless green fields of farm land and forests to the docks at the coast of Racoves. Like a silent bullet the monorail shot through and over the country, past many forests and wooded reserves and villages with tiny people in the distance who disappeared as soon as he saw them. Life itself was presented to him whenever he travelled like this, like everything outside was still moving and at an accelerated speed while he inside froze in time and simply watched, safe inside this raised, speeding train. Zahied had travelled on many monorails and trains like this before but still admired the view of the ever changing landscapes as it seemed to fly through the land. Tunnels carved through highlands darkened instantly, the speeding sound popping his ears as the monorail entered the tunnels and into a black abyss outside the windows. He loved travelling. The darkness from the tunnel ended in a flash of light revealing the world once more to Zahied and sound seemed to also return now his ears adjusted to the sound of the quiet carriage and woke him from his thoughts. He eventually pulled himself away from his window to see Raiden taking the time they had to catch up on more sleep whilst sitting next to Sheeria who only sat gazing out of her own window at the fast moving scenery. Acarlie was sitting next to Zahied and looking bored and had since taken one of Zahied's books to see herself what he had been learning as a Caster.

She smiled up at him, "Have you learned anything new?" she asked.

He grinned as she put the book down, "Actually yes I have. The spell I had used before in Lachine about projecting myself and concealing myself from the eye. I have been studying a technique made by ancient casters where they copy and project an object of their choice to divert an enemy away from them for a limited amount of time."

"Wow, sounds cleaver Zahied. Have you practised it anywhere yet?"

"No, I have only been reading about it so far. What about you and your new skill? Have you not practised it yet? What can you do with the water now?" he asked her.

"Yes, I have been practising it all last night. Logan is actually a very good tutor and made it easy to understand. Now what I can do will never be as good as how he does it but I can control the water to my bidding so I can direct it in any direction or use it as a weapon like he did. It is not advised though and I was only really taught to use it as a tactical move or a defensive move since the wind will be my strongest point and I should use that as a weapon."

"I must say I was impressed with the way you dealt with Logan back in Hiro. I honestly thought you were defeated then. How you beat him in that force battle to shut the first dam door was remarkable."

Acarlie chuckled at his compliment, "Thank you Zahied. Yes, I have always shone out in my home town at the force and mental part of the element but never at the physical parts of it. I suppose it's because I am a girl."

A stewardess then walked past and offered them some refreshments. Zahied took some water and a bag of dried fruit while Acarlie just took a bottle of water from her. Zahied smiled and watched the stewardess walk down the rest of the carriageway and couldn't help but stare at her behind as she saw to the other passengers.

Acarlie watched Zahied do this and laughed at him, "Men..." she commented.

Zahied grinned as he turned back, "What? What did I do?"

Acarlie carried on chuckling and then asked him, "Don't you ever get the urge to quit your pilgrimage as a caster? Settle down with a wife and raise a family?" while sipping her water.

"Oh yes, I would be lying if I said I didn't but it's not the way of the Casters. Our pilgrimage for knowledge comes first before any sexual desires and some remain celibate and a stranger from any physical touch. It is something that comes with the job I suppose."

"Then what do you expect to do once you have learned all you want to know?" she asked him.

"I will start my own school and teach others who wish to learn. All this pilgrimage stuff is nonsense to me. What I want to do is find all the data I can get and store it in here," he said patting his forehead with his finger. "Then write it all down so it will make the journey easier for casters in the future. What about you Acarlie? Don't you ever want to be a mother?"

"No, we elementalists are not allowed to bear children. It is a rule we must live by. Once an elementalist becomes a mother or father then their pilgrimage is over. When the child is born the elementalist is then Demoralised by their masters so their child will become the next elementalist. The Elemental Lord must never have children neither, nor shall the elementalists who choose to stay at home and train. We must set an example for the people of Sphere and work hard to please them."

"Well what about love then? Surely you must be able to love someone?"

"It has been known before for an elementalist to have a husband or wife. Normally the spouse is a guide but usually we never live that long to see ourselves have any children. It was our wise masters who have taught us that."

"I see then, but don't you ever want to just have a child anyway? You know, just go away somewhere safe and raise your own family?" he asked her again.

She twitched like she didn't understand the question. Her eyes glazed over and she said blankly and out of character, "I don't understand. The elementalist must never have children. They must set an example for the people of Sphere and remain on their pilgrimage until death departs them." Her sentence she said like she had recited it a thousand times before and wasn't thinking at all of what she was saying.

Zahied was a little a confused by her answer but just nodded and said, "I understand. We're not so different you and I Acarlie. We both have our vows and tasks to accomplish do we not?"

Acarlie smiled as she unknowingly awoke from her blank stare, "Yes we are alike Zahied aren't we? Every place we go brings us a new gift that we must learn and master until we have completed our goal."

Zahied lifted his bottle of water and toasted Acarlie happily and they sipped their bottles both staring out of the window at the city they were now passing over.

The hours passed slowly and eventually after the long train ride they reached the docks on the coast of the country. There they boarded a large, steam powered cruise ship. With no sails but with five large funnelled air vents pouring smoke out onto the dock. The ship looked colossal to Acarlie while she formally met with the captain to gain a free boarding for her and her guides. Within another two hours, when the sun was setting a lazy orange glow over an endless blue ocean the ship departed with its four unexpected visitors. As payment for the voyage Acarlie was promised to spend one night meeting the crew and passengers with Sheeria and the captain of the ship at her side while Zahied and Raiden slipped away from the commotion of Acarlie's new found fame. Zahied stepped out onto the mile long deck to feel the salty fresh air from the sea against his face and listened to the sound of the ship crashing against the waves.

Night fell over them quickly as the giant, boat-like hotel drifted on a lonely path in an everlasting horizon of constant but calm water. Joined only by Sphere's two moons who peek-a-booed between dark clouds that danced across the sky before disappearing and lighting up the horizon with the universe's heavenly lights. Sheeria, after eating a fine meal of raw fish and meats walked from the hall onto the deck to catch the fresh sea air when she saw Acarlie standing on the side of the ship, leaning over the edge and staring into the horizon of the clear black, starry sky. The two bright moons reflected by the calm waters giving a symmetrical portrait of wonder for Acarlie to stare at. Sheeria knew she wasn't staring at the scenery though and thought of speaking to her when she knew what she was actually doing and thought of a way of helping her. Sheeria walked back into the hall full of rich, tidy people dining at small wooden circular tables, with silk table cloths and silver knives and forks placed in front of them. She walked across the great and expensive looking hall to find Raiden who found himself uncomfortable around all these rich folk and sat with Zahied in a corner eating a plate of hot meats in gravy.

She sat down next to him, "Raiden, I need your help, come with me," she said to him blankly.

"What is the matter?" he asked her as he shoved the last of his dinner in his mouth.

"Acarlie misses the boy. I need you to talk to her."

"You're her guide," he pointed out while swallowing his meal and washing it down with a thin and clean glass of water his large paw-like hand had difficulty handling.

"But you are the closest link to him. Go and talk to her. She needs comfort in these parts of her journey and worrying about him will not help her in her next battle."

Raiden nodded after that while wiping his mouth with a napkin and stood up.

"She is out on the deck Raiden," Sheeria said as she started looking back into the ship's menu sitting folded up in the middle of her table.

Raiden found Acarlie standing in the same place Sheeria had seen her, staring from the side of the ship out into the water in front of her. Raiden sighed when he saw her and went to step forward to her.

"I worry about him Raiden," she suddenly confessed softly, sensing him there.

Raiden breathed and clenched his jaw and joined her at the side of the boat and stared out into the night.

"I do too Acarlie. I worry if he is safe from those men," he said softly but his deep voice only croaked. She dropped her head when he opened up to her like that and asked him, "Who is he?"

Raiden sighed again, "I have been asking that myself ever since I have known him. The truth is I don't think anybody knows. It was like he just appeared one day with that staff of his by his side, and the skyship wreckage behind him."

"Do you think he will be ok?" she asked him again.

He looked over to her and asked her, "Do you?"

"I want to Raiden but I can't help but feel like he really needs us right now and we're not there to help him." She looked back out to sea again and listened to the sound of the waves thinking maybe they might know.

"What you said before really struck me you know, about trusting him. I do trust him, it's everybody else I don't trust," he told her quietly.

"I know…me too."

"Look, I have only known him a little longer than you have, so we pretty much know the same about him right? So you have to keep your chin up and trust him to handle that situation on his own."

Acarlie soaked in his words and nodded, "You're right Raiden. We're a team and sometimes a team member has to do something on his own, this is just Val's turn right?"

This was the first time Raiden heard her say *team* and didn't really agree with it but he agreed with her if it was going to cheer her up.

"That's right Acarlie. Now how about we go back inside and let Val deal with this one on his own?"

"Yes Raiden, let's go," she finished and rubbed his shoulder, "Thanks," she said then walked back into the ship to eat with the others.

Before Raiden followed he looked out into the darkness himself, *I DO trust you Val*, he thought to himself then turned around and entered the ship.

The ship arrived in the country Calmaron a day later and they got off the ship and back on their lizziers. They took a load of supplies from the ship and stayed on the roads at first where the rich folk all disappeared in front of them in Mvs. The ground was much damper in this country and the trees and bushes were a darker shade of green with smaller wildlife running around but the roads were all the same for the travellers who took their time with this journey and stopped every couple hours to rest and eat. Sunset came too quickly again and a cloudy, gloomy sky soon took the sun away from them. They ate one last time and wrapped their lizziers up in large blankets and set up a small camp. Raiden insisted they camp away from the roads and further down beyond an overgrown field was a small, muddy wooded area where they had their last meal before putting the fire out when the night sky came again. The cloudy night sky brought darkness and coldness to them and they gave Acarlie an extra blanket to sleep with. Sheeria advised that they take turns guarding the campsite since they were in a new land and did not know the wildlife or the people around here. They were to switch members waking them from sleep and staying awake for two and a half hours since there would only be three of them on guard, Acarlie was the only one who had the privilege of staying asleep all night. They set up a small secluded watch point to sit. Zahied was the first to watch, then Sheeria, then Raiden.

Raiden slept roughly knowing subconsciously he would have to wake soon and woke easily in the middle of the night when Sheeria shook him awake.

"Is it my turn?" he whispered to her rubbing his eyes.

"There is something I think you should see," she whispered back and whilst very cold he got out of his tent and followed her to the watch point. It was like a large burrow in the bushes at the edge of the wooded area overlooking the overgrown fields of lumpy grass and old broken concrete roads.

They lay down together silently in the dead of the night peering out into the darkness, "What am I looking for?" Raiden asked.

Their conversation being no more than a whisper because of sound travelling further at night, Sheeria pointed out into the darkness and onto a faraway hill in the distance and whispered to him, "Can you see them?"

Raiden looked to see a large, single file army of soldiers marching through the night, their marching footsteps could be heard in the dead of the night.

Raiden nodded, "Yes I see them," he moved a little closer and tried to make out their armour.

"They're Septurian. Feydon soldiers, most probably from Alpha. It looks like they are marching from the direction of Mecroyles."

"What do you think they were doing there?" Sheeria whispered again.

"They're carrying wounded. Look, in the stretchers. There must have been a battle there."

"But why would they go to Mecroyles? They have nothing there they want."

"I think the better question is where are they going Sheeria? Look," Raiden pointed. "If they carry on the direction they are going now, over the waters they will reach..."

Sheeria understood where he was pointing now, "Hiro...? They're heading straight for Hiro...."

27

The Scarlet Arise was a beautiful ship that silently flew over the dark ocean like a snowy owl over its hunting ground. The ship was originally made in Angland and was supposed to be used as a scout for a fleet of skyships produced for war and battle and is the only ship in existence that could fly over water, float on top of it and travel under it. The ship was stolen from the Anglish army by the very crew that piloted it now, a finely executed plan with no flaws and the speed of the ship made it an easy get away as well. The only question was why these thieves would hire Val and Dude to steal something for them when they very clearly could do the job themselves? Val lay on the floor of the ship bound and blindfolded silently wondering how long the journey would take and what would become of him. Lying beside him was Dude again. Also bound Dude was only lying still and not making any sort of fuss. Maybe he had been in a situation like this before Val thought to himself. There came heavy footsteps from behind them. Unable to turn they both could only lie down and listen to what was happening on the ship. The footsteps circled them and finally the man walking around them spoke and they both instantly recognised the voice as Gendrick who was the leader of the crew holding them on the ship.

He spoke to his men sitting round the two prisoners watching and guarding them, "I think they have been bound long enough men." He knelt down and spoke in Val's ear, "If I release you and keep you in a room where you can sleep and eat will you remain as good tempered as you are now or will I have to be cruel and keep you in these binds for the rest of the journey? I am not a cruel man whoever you are but I will be when needed," he held Val's head up waiting for an answer. Val who knew this would be his only chance and this offer would only come once shook his head only hoping Gendrick saw him.

Gendrick grinned through dirty un-brushed teeth and stood back and ordered his men to lift the two and brought them to a brig-like room. Their bonds were finally removed and were given the time to use the bathroom before being sat back down in front of the pimp. He lit up a cigar and blew the smoke in their direction whilst still holding his evil grin on his face, "Thank you for your cooperation boys. I'm glad I could finally sit you down like this as so I could tell you about your mission."

"There was no real reason to bind us in the first place really. We already were cooperating with you and agreed to steal this sword for you all along, the fact that you tied us up suggests that the deal you have with me is no longer valid," Val said.

"The deal still stands boy. I just needed to know you were not going to steal my ship from me. Also I wanted you to know that I meant business and if you try anything stupid I will throw you overboard. Now the other reason I released you was so we could discuss what you will have to do once you are on dry land again."

"Ok then," Val said lying back on the floor and stretching out his legs, "You say we have to steal a sword?"

"Yes, the blade Fireshaver is in the care of a Baron called Dimitiry Taylor; an antiques dealer and collector of many things who lives in Walshraw. A few years back he came into the possession of this blade and has been showing it off ever since. He believes the blade to be a symbol of power because there have been countless legends and stories about the blade bursting into flames. Children all over the world have heard of Fireshaver and bedtime stories exaggerate and empower the legend of this actual antique artefact."

Val looked stunned at the pimp whose eyes now opened wide as he spoke about this sword in disbelief, "And do you actually believe in children's stories? You have brought us all this way across the ocean; bringing me away from my mission because you want a sword that you only heard about in bedtime stories?" Val asked him cynically.

"The stories are only exaggerations of the actual truth behind the blade's history boy. It is documented and a fact that more than one king has been overthrown by a man who carried this blade. This one blade and its owner at the time sailed across the waters and took part in the very first divide that took place, we are talking millions of years old now. The body count of this blade must be remarkable. Also the fact of how Fireshaver is this old but has not yet rusted and turned to dust is an enigma, not even time could destroy this blade. Millions of years on and this blade still stands today, it's just time for its true owner to stand up and take it from him."

"And what will you do once you have this Fireshaver?" Val asked him again.

"That's not for you to know boy, you are only here to retrieve it for me. The deal was only for you to bring the blade to me and then for me to take you where you wanted to go."

"Ok then that's fine, what do I want to know for anyway? To be honest I think you're an idiot and this Fireshaver stuff is nonsense. The fact how a few kings have been overturned by some men carrying the same blade is possible but how you say it is millions of years old and still stands today is unbelievable. But what do I care? I'll get this sword for you, no doubt about that and what you do with it is up to you. Just take me where I want to go after."

"Yes, that's the deal boy."

"Good then, now where does this Baron Dimitiry Taylor live?"

"He lives in a manor house on acres of his own land secured by his guards at night. The night will be the only time acceptable to acquire the blade for me because the Scarlet Arise could set down on his own land without going through the legal landing procedures that we would go through at a port. This will also be good for you since we will practically be dropping you off outside his doors. You will both use the night to sneak into his manor and find and retrieve the blade he owns and bring it back here."

"Where will he keep the blade?" Val asked.

"I spoke to the Baron only once and he tells me that he loves this blade so much that he trusts no one with it and keeps it safe with him in his master bedroom. There will also be his personal security you will have to get past."

"This sounds like a mission you yourself have no idea how to execute. How are we supposed to creep through a man's house while he is asleep with his security wondering around and go into his room and steal his prized possession?"

"Let's not forget that you will be accompanied by a master in this profession," Gendrick said referring to the quiet aeoman sitting beside Val with his knees in his chest and wrapping his arms around them.

"This monkey has pulled off bigger stunts like this before and without any help, so trust me when I say stay close to the monkey and do exactly what he wants you to do. We arrive within the hour so use this time to eat what we give you, you will need the energy. You will remain in this room until then," the pimp then took another puff on his cigar then stood up and walked out of the room.

Val sat back against the wall and sitting on the wooden floor and thought to himself, *This whole thing is ridiculous. How am I supposed to go to this mansion and take something from a heavily guarded man and bring it back to a psycho who believes it's magic just so I could get passage to the monastery?* He sat there rubbing his fingers into his eyes and looked over to Dude who was sitting beside him thinking along the same lines. Val saw how quiet Dude sat then, like he was used to sitting this quiet and did not do anything but sit perfectly still and stare at the floor without even blinking. Val realised that life must have been hard for Dude who was constantly looked down upon by every other being on the planet and resorted to stealing just to keep himself breathing at the end of the day. Val could now see from the look in his cold eyes that Dude was depressed. This was something that has probably been with him for some time now, even when their food was brought in to them Dude only took the bowl from them and turned from Val so he couldn't see him eating and ate quietly in the corner of the wooden empty room. Val finished the bowl of food given to him and turned to Dude who now had his back to him,

"Dude, I'm sorry about dragging you into this. I never meant for this to happen to you," Val said carefully not wanting to upset him anymore. Dude only turned back to him though and nodded and patted Val on the shoulder once then sat back against the wall.

Val joined him and asked him, "So what did he mean that you have been in bigger stunts like this Dude? Have you worked for this guy before?" he asked.

Dude only put his two fingers up in the shape of a V in the direction of the door the pimp walked out of. Val comforted him with a laugh, "Yeah, I know Dude, I know."

In the dead of the night the ship finally landed on dry land, a dark grassy field overlooking the manor over its horizon. Gendrick was the first to step out followed by some of his men escorting Val and Dude out of the ship. Gendrick was smiling when he stepped on the grass, "There is always something special about stepping on foreign land for the first time isn't there? Makes me feel like I've crossed off a country I've never been too, don't you agree?" he said turning to Val as he stepped out onto the grass.

Val was still sore from being bound for no reason and the idea of this whole thing annoyed him, "Let's just get this over with, you want your sword and I want my lift, the quicker this is done the better right?"

"That's the spirit boy, now over the hill behind me is the back of Dimitiry's mansion. We will turn off the engine as so we won't make any noise and give you a better chance of getting in. You will have one hour before we leave without you, understand?"

Val pushed past him, "Good, I doubt this will take long but ok, come on Dude," he then signalled his companion and together they walked away from the ship he so desperately needed towards the back of the Baron's mansion sitting peacefully in the centre of his land.

One of Gendrick's men turned to him, "What do you think boss? Do you think he will make it?"

He replied with a scowl, "Either way we win, they get it then all's well. If they don't then we answer the Baron's distress call and steal it ourselves, but as from tonight, I will own that sword," he grinned evilly at his own plan and walked back toward the cargo door of the ship, turned and looked back one more time before shutting the doors where he now could only wait for Val and Dude to return.

They ran through the field of now damp grass edging toward the mansion looking down at them. A large brick wall blocked them and Dude climbed up quickly and helped Val up before jumping down and onto a patio just outside the back door. When Val looked down he saw Dude not looking at the door but all around the outline of the house and when he found what he was looking for he pulled Val to one side and pointed up to a surveillance camera looking down at them both. The camera suggested that they had already been caught but still they carried on, because they would be flying away in a skyship they did not care for the fact that they would be caught by police tomorrow when the surveillance footage would be given to them. Val looked round at the door and found that they were locked and not a way in. Dude however was looking for another passage inside. He looked to the side of the mansion and found that there was a tiny window opened ajar. This window was far too small for a man to enter and so high up that even the most adventurous child would not be able to reach up to there, but for a skinny aeoman this sort of feat was not a problem. He signalled for Val to follow him and pointed up to the window; he then pointed at Val. Val guessed that Dude wanted him to stay put whilst Dude climbed in.

"Ok," Val whispered but Dude instantly punched his arm and put his finger firmly to his lips. Val understood and nodded and watched as Dude started feeling along the wall trying to figure how he could climb into the window from where he stood. Around him there was nothing he could stand on and nothing to climb onto. There was a drain pipe that ran down from the roof of the mansion and ran down the corner of it but this stopped halfway down and went back into the mansion, so he could climb up it if he got half way up the building already. There was a window above him that he knew he could climb on and from there he could climb to the top of it and reach the drain pipe, but there was still no way he could reach this window on his own. He pulled Val to the building and stood him with his back against the wall and showed him to put his two hands together. Val understood what he wanted to do and bent his legs ready to boost Dude up so he could reach the closed window.

Dude stood a few steps back and ran toward Val and lifted his leg up ready to jump. Val caught his foot and threw him up to the window and watched as Dude caught the end of the windowsill and quickly climbed up on the narrow sill with his body against the glass. Whilst up there he found a tiny foot space on the wall he used to lean on then had to jump and silently grab the bottom of the drain pipe as it went back into the wall. Dude found his grip and one hand and foot at a time climbed up the small pipe. Val knew that this now was a dangerous place for Dude to be and if he fell there was no way Val could catch him and would seriously injure himself or worse, but still he climbed. When Dude was near the top of the pipe where the window as adjacent to him and reached out from the pipe he was climbing onto and when he reached the open window he pulled himself towards it, stretched himself out and yanked himself into the building. A few silent, cold and tense moments later and Dude appeared again and held the door open and after Val entered the building he closed it silently again. Val took a step forward in the mansion. His heavy boots gave a quiet step on a marble floor but was quickly pulled into the shadow by Dude again who sat him down and made him take his boots off. Val didn't understand at first but cooperated with him and took off his boots and gave them to him. Dude took them from him and tied the laces together and threw them over Val's shoulder where they would no longer make any noise in the deadly silence of the mansion. Dude led him back into the hallway where they would go up the stairs and look for the master bedroom.

It was Dude who heard the noise first; footsteps coming from the ground floor towards the stairs. He quickly pushed Val into a small shadowed spot, to hide behind a large indoor plant then when he heard another two footsteps he had no choice but to silently dart up the stairs and find the closest corner he could and waited in the darkness. From around the corner came two of the security guards, walking together in whispered conversation between themselves. Val held his breath and crouched perfectly still as the first walked by him, brushing past the plant he was hiding behind. He stopped and shone his light up the stairs then looked to his friend, the other guard now stepped forward beside him. Val tried not to breathe now, his heart thudding through his chest. He knew that if he held his breath for too long then he would finally exhale loudly and they would discover him. He slowly let his breath out covering his mouth, not taking his eyes off the guards who were still standing just in front of him, deciding whether to go up the stairs or not. The thought of escape filled Val's mind then; to call his staff and strike them both in the back of the head and run up the stairs but he didn't. He only sat there frozen in suspense. His blood now rushing hot and his heart seeming to beat so fast he was sure they would be able to hear it thudding away against his ribcage, but they didn't. He concentrated on his breathing.

"What do you reckon?" the second guard asked the other.

"I don't know; just saw a shadow move up there when I shined it with my torch."

"Could be a ghost," the second guard said again, he obviously wasn't taking his job as seriously as the first.

"Oh behave mate, I was just making sure. It is our job you know?"

"Then go and look then, I'll stay down here and keep an eye on the kitchen."

"Yeah, because I'm sure the first place a thief who breaks into a place like this goes to is the fridge."

"You'll never know until you find out right? I'll see you later mate, good luck finding the ghost," he said patting him on the shoulder and turned back.

"Oh, piss off then," the first said then started walking up the stairs.

Val felt the wave of relief then as the guard now shone the light upstairs and took no notice of what was behind him. Now it was Dude Val was afraid for. What if the guard found him? He didn't know what to do. Should he stay where he was or go up and help Dude and risk being found? He could only calculate the different outcomes of going up as getting caught or not, then again he thought they're going to be found out sooner or later and went to step out of the shadows. He stepped out from behind the plant, the stairs in front of him and the guard, still unaware who was in the mansion, walking up them. The guard got to the top of the stairs and shone his light to his left then right in the upstairs hallway. His left was clear, all the doors on the hallway were closed, including the door that lead to the master bedroom; just like how it was when he checked it an hour ago. His right was all clear too apart from one of the doors for the storage cupboard was left slightly ajar; not how it was when he checked it an hour ago. He thought nothing of it but his colleague was not doing his job properly and went to close it. He stepped forward and took hold of the door when he decided to check inside to see the face of a stranger holding a hammer. He had no time to scream or make any noise as the stranger in the cupboard swiped at him and felt the cold steel as the hammer struck his face. He stumbled back and looked at the stranger as he stepped out and noticed he was only an aeomon and knew that wouldn't be a problem. He went to make any noise he could but instantly noticed the aeomon nod at someone over his shoulder. Frightened, the guard turned around to see nothing but a metal staff swing and suddenly everything was black.

Dude caught the guard as he fell unconscious after Val struck him with his staff and tried fitting him in the cupboard behind him but couldn't. Instead, Dude, whilst still holding the under-arms of the heavy man, nodded at Val to open the door closest to him. Val opened the door without looking inside and grabbed the feet of the guard and together they carried him in the room.

The room was darker than the hallways. Closed curtains shut out the light from the moons and suggested to them that someone was sleeping in there, probably close to them. Dude looked up to see a bed and pointed for Val to see, the person on the bed was lying down. A young and pretty girl was lying unconscious and naked with her hands chained apart from one another to a long chain connected to the bed, dry tears smeared the make up on her face and her right arm had a syringe hanging out of it. Dude stepped forward to inspect the drug induced, sleeping girl. It was clear from everything around her that she was here against her will, and her body had been abused by whoever occupied the room with her previously and had left her there to recover. Val also now forgot about why they were here and looked more concerned of the poor girl before them. As Dude removed the syringe from the girl's arm Val realised then how terrible this place actually was. It was no wonder Gendrick and his men wanted no part in the stealing of the artefact. This mansion was a centre for human trafficking. *These women are lured, tricked and raped by these sick perverted bastards*, Val thought to himself.

Dude got to work and searched the unconscious security guard for keys and unchained her and found her clothes, put them on her bed then tried waking her up. Val stopped him when he realised she might give a scared scream and alert the others. Dude however had slightly different morals than Val had and pushed him away and started helping the girl back into her clothes hoping she would wake soon and escape this evil and dark place. Val rubbed his palms over his eyes as he tried to think of a way of escaping but nothing came to mind. He was only here for a sword so he can get passage on the skyship to the monastery for information that only might help about the inevitable black hole and now he had this on his mind. He wanted to leave her, to just grab the sword and run back to the ship and just get back to Hiro; this wasn't how he wanted his trip to go; this wasn't how he imagined it. He sat down and remembered the village in Walton, the waterfall he looked at, the way the grass was bright green and full of life. He remembered Theydon the leader of the Walton Warriors and wished he was back there with Raiden but he wasn't. He was stuck here hidden away halfway around the world in a human trafficking centre searching for a mythological blade for an insane man. He slowly realised that this pimp who made a deal with him must have connections to the pimps in this building, which would be why he knew about it. He had been tricked, all this time Gendrick knew about what was happening here and decided to say nothing, maybe there was no blade at all, maybe he had already left without them. He thought about Raiden then, like his older brother and teacher. He wondered what he would do, what a leo would do? For he was just like Raiden, he was a Walton Warrior, he was a leo. He stood up and went back over to Dude who had finished dressing the girl and was leaving the keys with her for her to save any others in this deadening night. Val placed a hand on Dude's shoulders and gave him a look of concern but also of worry and fear. He nodded and gestured back to the door and waited for Dude to reply. Dude still felt an overwhelming sympathy for the girl who now looking to stir from her sleep. She, in a moment would have a story of escape of her own, they didn't have the time however to wait and witness it. They left the room as silently as they entered.

Once the room was still and silent as before the young girl opened her eyes. She was suddenly dressed, with keys for her escape in her hand and an unconscious guard at the end of her room. This would be her only chance to escape...

The fear of being caught suddenly gripped Val again as soon

as he was back in the hallway and knowing that there would be more guards still wandering around this place and together they tiptoed along the hallway. Val's boots still hanging around his shoulders and leaving his staff in the room with the girl. One by one Dude opened the doors whilst Val looked out for people around them but safely nothing, all Dude kept seeing was more chained women like the girl they met. They were all sleeping in a drugged coma with dirty, naked men hugging on to them as they slept beside them. Bedside tables were covered in white powder, empty syringes and half empty bottles, whatever happened to these girls the two intruders were too late to stop. The mansion's silence now seemed to have a different feel to it now they knew the truth, only a few hours ago the halls would have been filled with screams and sexual demands of the men holding them, now tired and their demands sated it was like the walls still screamed out in pain. One thing was for certain though, the men and women here would be far too drugged to wake up, and it was only the guards that Val and Dude really had to worry about. They found another staircase and at the top of it another hallway. Once again they could only find the master bedroom by peeking in every door, this time only seeing a bathroom, an empty sitting room and finally they came to the end of the hallway. Before them were double doors that must have been an important room.

Dude opened it slightly and looked inside then waved for Val to come in after him, this time he didn't even shut the door behind him but pushed it right up against the door frame so it would look closed from a distance. Val crept up to the bed and looked at the owner of it to see a tigian sleeping, his head rested on a pillow. His female tigian companion asleep beside him. The room here was fit for a king, the queen sized bed, ornaments and expensive antiques and vases scattered and placed around the room. The walls were placed with various old worn armour and weapons rusted beyond recognition, like they should have been in a museum. This baron tigian was clearly an antiques dealer but it looked more of a hobby than the real profession he dealt in. It was clear he was a collector, of antiques and artefacts and of people themselves. All Val wanted to do was to find this sword and run as fast as he could and escape but without knowing what he was looking for it seemed pretty hard. The room was massive and well spread out, nearly all of the antiques in this room were ornaments or vases. He guessed it was the female tigian's idea to keep them in the bedroom with them. There was a manikin wearing armour Val instantly recognised as Leo armour and was a double of the armour that Raiden wore, this could have been a collecting thing since the leos were practically extinct or maybe could have even been the baron's personal armour since he was a tigian and could wear it unlike any human could. It was Dude to point out a sword placed on the wall high and clear for them to see. Val went closer and inspected the blade. It looked more like a katana, the blade was very thin and sharp with a long hand woven handle which were meant for two hands to make the weapon stronger. The hilt of the weapon was metal and shaped like a small wave of fire. Val stood on his toes and looked closer in the dark to see the engraving *FIRESHAVER* wrote along the steel of the blade.

This is it, this is the blade we have been sent here to retrieve, Val thought as he held up is hands and slowly lifted Fireshaver from the rack and took its scabbard from below and took a second to study it. It seemed to gleam in the moonlight as it lay in his hands. It felt too untrue to be millions of years old as it looked brand new. The weight of it was unbelievable to, and it was so light he could balance it across the edge of his hand.

"It's a beautiful blade is it not? Almost like it was made by Sphere herself," a deep voice of a tigian said from behind them. The lights came on and the two swung round to see the tigian, up and out of his bed, standing by the light switch, throwing a cloak over his shoulders…

28

Sheeria was the first to step into their next town, Mecroyles however was in a burning ruins. Once they all entered Mecroyles they could smell death from its gates as soon as they approached. The smell of burning flesh was terrible and filled the morning air with misery and desolation. The sight of the town was heart breaking, the buildings and temples had burned down to the ground and only a handful of survivors had gathered around a pile of burning corpses to mourn their deaths together. Children clung onto their dead parents and buried their crying faces into the lifeless bodies, begging them to get up. Sheeria sighed and closed her eyes, trying to block out the scene. The sight of the broken town pierced her heart like a fiery arrow and burned with a passionate empathy, this scene was all too familiar to her. Again an ancient memory of a fire much like the one before her burned bright and flashed past her eyes. She forced the memory aside. She watched Acarlie fall to her knees in agony covering her mouth with her hands. The fire was still burning as people were one by one carrying more recently dead, saying goodbye to them and throwing them into the fire. This way they could all have the same sending. Even elders were gathered around the great fire as it burned high and prayed for the dead to have a peaceful passage back to the planet where their soul would be recycled and born again as another being. They were not greeted until they walked right up to the fire. The dead bodies that were still burning were staring at them with dead eyes, their bodies crying out in misery that they never said goodbye to their loved ones gave Sheeria and the others a chill as they could only stand and watch. A small brown haired boy approached Acarlie and spoke to her formally in a sad and depressed tone.

"Are you here to mourn loved ones?" he asked them.

Acarlie looked down at this boy, his face was damp from dried out tears and his eyes were sore, matching Acarlie's eyes which started to cry from a mix of sympathy and the hot fire burning her eyes.

"Where is your elementalist young man? My name is Acarlie; I am an elementalist from Racoves on my pilgrimage to become the Elemental Lord."

The boy did not answer, but started crying again, covering his face and turning from them. Acarlie knelt down and tried to ask him again but she was lifted up by Sheeria and moved to one side. She then knelt down herself and turned the young boy around.

"Who do you cry for, young man?" she asked him subtly rubbing her paws up and down his shoulders to his elbows. The young boy rubbed his face and tried to catch his breath but his words were still hard to understand as he only stuttered amongst his tears. Sheeria then held him close to her and rubbed the back of his head as he returned the comforting hug, his face buried into her shoulder, shuddering every now and again.

"It's ok young man. It's ok, just take your time," she told him gently.

Acarlie watched Sheeria and remembered the way she used to do this for her when she was young. As a tigian grows much older than humans Sheeria always seemed the same age all Acarlie's life, it was one thing Acarlie loved about Sheeria. She was a strong warrior, smart and wise but her female side always shone through when it was needed and comforting a child was like a gift to her. She remembered all the times Sheeria used to hug her like that when she was young and tired of being an elementalist. She started off more like a nanny to Acarlie back in her home with the elders in Eloma, a tigian the other kids used to be scared of but she was always there when they needed her. As she grew older Sheeria became like the mother Acarlie never had and apart from the female elders she became her female role model. Finally after all her growing up Sheeria, who had been watching over her since she was a baby was her most trusted and dearest friend.

The boy finally stopped crying and let go of Sheeria, "My friend," he said. "I cry for my friend, she was the elementalist of this town. She was much older than me though. We used to train together."

"What is your name child?"

"Will."

Sheeria nodded with sympathy, then asked him again, "Will, does this mean that you are the elementalist of this town?"

The boy sniffed, wiping his eyes and nodded to her.

"Are there any other elementalists here?"

"No."

"You are the only one?"

"Yes."

"Ok then."

Sheeria, still kneeling down thought for a minute then asked him again, "Could you get the elders of your town please? We would really like a word with them."

The boy nodded and walked off around the fire. Sheeria stood up and turned to Acarlie.

"If he is the only elementalist then I don't know how you will acquire the next element. He is only young and learning himself."

"I know, there is no way I could battle with a child to acquire the next element. What will I do?" Acarlie asked.

"We will have to ask the elders Acarlie, they will know what will happen," Sheeria said.

They only had to wait for another few seconds before the elders approached. Together Acarlie, Sheeria and Raiden all knelt down and bowed to them, only Zahied didn't kneel down but bowed his head as he was not an elementalist, guide nor leo but knew to give respect to these sacred beings.

"Elders I am Elementalist Acarlie of Eloma, my master was High Elder Argo," Acarlie said still knelt down. "With me are my Guide, Tigian Sheeria, Leo Raiden from Walton and Human Zahied, a travelling Caster."

"Rise Acarlie of Eloma and companions," the elder spoke in a soft, old voice.

"I am Elder Haloer. I was the High Elder of the elemental school here in Mecroyles. I know why you are here and I must bring you the news, an Elemental Battle is out of the question for obvious reasons."

"Elder Haloer, what happened here? Who was it that did this to your town?" Acarlie asked him.

"It was the army of Feydon, they marched in last night and started pillaging our community and torching our homes; none of us had a chance. We were all out numbered."

Sheeria quickly felt a sting of shame. She glanced over to Raiden who returned the look. They decided not to tell Acarlie of what they witnessed the night previously.

"Feydon did this? But why would they? There is nothing that you have that they don't."

"I don't know why they did this but it looked like they were looking for something. They marched away after only a few hours last night in the direction of which you came. Did you not see them?"

Acarlie paused and turned round to see Raiden and Sheeria silent and looking guiltily at the floor.

"Can you give me a minute please Elder Haloer? I must speak with my guardians," she said then walked away from the fire so Raiden and Sheeria would follow her. She led them back down a broken road of which they walked up previously where no other town's person was and looked at them sharply.

"You knew this had happened hadn't you? You saw the Feydon soldiers didn't you?" she asked them.

Raiden remained silent and Sheeria answered her.

"We knew not to tell you Acarlie, you are on your pilgrimage and have been side tracked enough already. We couldn't let this get in the way of your path."

"But you know it's my responsibility as an elementalist to help communities when in trouble like this. Why did you not just tell me?"

Sheeria remained silent then, together Raiden and her knew not to tell Acarlie since this would side track them from their mission. But they both knew Acarlie would act differently. Not only was she human but she was also naive like a child and didn't know much of the world outside her school. She cared too much and they both knew this. She finally stood forward and told her, "Yes, we knew about the soldiers Acarlie and yes, we knew not to tell you. I know this is a terrible tragedy for these people but this is nothing to do with us Acarlie. I'm not arguing with the fact that some services may be needed from you here, but we cannot stay long, these people have to help themselves."

Acarlie burst out in anger then, rushing forward and hitting Sheeria in her chest repeatedly,

"How could you!? We could have been there for them. We could have saved them!"

Sheeria stood silent and allowed Acarlie to continually strike her before finally opening up and explaining, "We saw them last night, marching from Mecroyles, carrying their wounded. You were sleeping and needed your rest. We decided to wait and let you see for yourself rather than ruin your practice and meditation in the morning. You are an Elementalist Acarlie, your purpose must be fulfilled and to do that you have needs and we were assuring them."

"You're my Guide Sheeria! You're supposed to follow my decisions and examples. You knew I would want to help these people, now you have made me look insincere for showing up a day late!" Acarlie snapped at her.

"We were too late already Acarlie, when we saw them they were already leaving. There was nothing we could do," Sheeria told her.

"There was plenty we could have done, there still is!" Acarlie shouted.

"Acarlie—"

"Enough!" Acarlie snapped back at Sheeria again holding up her hand. Sheeria stood silent.

Acarlie looked up at them, "I am going to help them and if you wish to continue with me on my pilgrimage then you will help too."

"I don't have time for this," Raiden said bluntly and turned to walk away feeling impatient with the tantrums of an elementalist.

"Don't walk away from me Raiden! As an elementalist I am trained to live as an elder, which are your natural masters. These people need us Raiden and–"

Raiden now swung back around and snapped back at her, "And what about Val, Acarlie? Does Val not matter anymore now that there are other problems at hand? Wasn't it you that suggested that we put your pilgrimage on standby until we found him? Now you're going to forget about him just like that! These people need help, I'm not denying that, but it's not them that needs you, *Val* needs you."

There was a quick silence then as Raiden finished his sentence and put Acarlie in her place. The realisation of her error struck her immediately and she stood stunned and staring into the eyes of Raiden. She looked down to the floor and back up to him, she knew then she was wrong. The second he mentioned his name Sheeria thought about him tied up in the back of that skyship again, with no food or water given to him, beaten and taken to a strange, faraway place he would not know, and that's even if they allowed him to live. She saw Acarlie thought the same thing. Acarlie silently cursed herself for forgetting about him and asked herself how she could do such a thing and took a step back and turned from Raiden so he wouldn't see that he upset her and went to cover her eyes. With a motherly reaction Sheeria immediately stood beside her to comfort her, snapping back at Raiden, "They were harsh words Raiden. You didn't have to make her cry you know."

"But he's right Sheeria," Acarlie said bringing her hand away from her face, "Val is still missing and we have to find him. What do I do Sheeria? As an elementalist I am obliged to offer my services to a community that might need me but Val needs us more than they do, who knows what they have done to him."

Sheeria had known Acarlie all her life. It was a shame however how she was never introduced to her birth parents. But it was knowing this that made Sheeria care for Acarlie and all the other elementalists growing up as orphans. Sometimes even the sacred and wise elementalists needed guidance, it was one of the reasons where the term 'Guide' came from. "Acarlie, as much as it pains me to say this; this is their problem that they have to solve themselves. If any help is needed then they will get it from the other nations. We must concentrate on our own problems rather than keep helping others."

Acarlie thought for a few seconds. She hated the idea of leaving a town that had been destroyed and just carry on as normal, but it seemed like she had no choice, then she realised something and asked them, "Wait, you said you saw the Feydon army marching right? Well, where are they? Where were they marching to?"

Raiden and Sheeria exchanged glances and Raiden told her, "When we saw them they were on their way towards," he paused, "...Hiro."

The shock took her back instantly again. Hiro; her own country's capital city was now in danger of meeting the same fate. She felt like crying out again but now no sound came out. She felt lost, like there were too many things she had to do all at once. She had to help these people in this town, she had to warn Hiro of what was coming and she had to find and save Val.

Elder Haloer approached them again and asked Acarlie, "Miss Acarlie, I'm sorry for interrupting but we are in a rush so if you could follow me we can start your lessons as soon as possible."

Acarlie said with a puzzled face, "I don't understand Elder Haloer. What lessons? There is no elementalist here to teach me."

"That is why we elders are going to teach you. We have just lost all but one of our elementalists and since you are here we must keep our school alive by passing the teachings on to you. You will not have to battle and the lessons will be twice as long but we shall make you strong in the art of the Element of Sphere."

Now her path was clear again, she thought this really was a miracle and a gift from Sphere and she bowed down and thanked the elder.

"Thank you Elder; this is most generous of you to teach me without an Elemental Battle."

"Well, under the current circumstances we all have no choice, now please follow me. Tigian Sheeria and Leo Raiden; it would mean so much to me if you could help with the town's folk whilst Acarlie is with us. Please go and see the young elementalist for directions, people will have plenty of work for you, when Acarlie is ready we will send you back on your way."

Raiden and Sheeria both bowed down, "Yes, at once Elder Haloer," Raiden said and together they both wished Acarlie luck as she was taken away from them to a secret part of the broken school where she would learn the next element. In the meanwhile Sheeria and Raiden caught up with Zahied again by the fire and found the young boy so they could help him.

After hours of heavy lifting, carrying more hidden bodies and broken pieces of shrapnel to the fire the town started to look much tidier now, only much less of it. Some of the houses that were still standing were made into temporary shelters for the community where food and clean water were supplied. Sheeria, Raiden and Zahied made themselves useful by helping the humans with all the heavy lifting, carrying beams of wood to the carpenters and helping them put up more shelters just so they had somewhere to sleep that night. The sun was about to set in the late afternoon and it was like the day itself was exhausted from all the hard work that had been done today having a cooling breeze sweep through and the warming dry heat of the sun now fading leaving a blue tint to the air. Sheeria and Raiden sat side by side eating together whilst Zahied sat with some of the men he had been working with and was in conversation with, telling them and the children around them the adventures he had been through so far with Raiden and the others. The children sat in awe and hung on to his every word like story time in school.

Whilst sitting beside him Sheeria noticed Raiden was troubled as he sat eating the food provided for him.

"What bothers you Raiden?" she asked him.

Raiden flinched then and answered her quietly, "The misery of this place is familiar to me," he said in his familiar deep voice Sheeria had now grown accustomed to. He tried to speak in riddles for her but she knew exactly what he meant. He meant he had been in a position like the one this town was in before.

"I understand what you mean Raiden, the Last Divide, the one that–"

"No you don't understand Sheeria, I don't want to talk about it," he told her whilst standing up and walking away from her. She left her unfinished meal on the floor then and followed him away from the humans. She knew he was only being difficult for her. She found him leaning up against a lamp post looking at the still burning fire of carcasses; troubles filled his eyes as he could only stand there and remember seeing the bodies of his people burning in a fire just like this one. She walked up behind him and he knew she was there. She stood waiting for him to speak first.

"You keep trying to get something out of me Sheeria. Why do you persist?" he asked her.

"You know why I'm asking Raiden, stop being difficult for me. You know as much as I do, silence is not the way, we need to talk about it."

"We don't need to talk about anything–"

"Raiden!" she stopped him there, "You are acting like a child. I know this bothers you because of what happened to all the other leos in the Last Divide a century ago now. I know you witnessed it, you are not as young as you make out."

He turned round so he could look her straight in the eye and tell her.

"You know nothing of what I went through a hundred years ago Sheeria. The things I saw then, the monstrous act of the ancestors of the people who live today..." but he stopped when he saw that Sheeria was highly offended by what he just said and nearly turned pale if it wasn't for the orange and black stripy fur covering her. He saw the anguish fill her face like a horrible and forgotten memory suddenly came back to her that had been repressed for all these years.

She didn't take her eyes off him and whispered in her shock, "How dare you...?"

Raiden saw then that he upset her and wanted to turn round again and leave her there but he didn't. He respected Sheeria more than other beings on this planet. She was strong but also smart and kind, aspects hard to find in other beings. He knew then he was in the wrong and stood there awkwardly waiting for her to continue.

"You're not the only one who suffers from then, you know?"

With a sentence like this Raiden knew then there was only one thing he could say.

"I'm sorry Sheeria. You're right; you would be as old as me and would remember what all the humans in this world wouldn't, what their ancestors did to my race. What happened to you?"

Sheeria knew now that he could talk about it and knew she had to start him off and told him what she hadn't spoke about in nearly a hundred years now.

"Once when I was young, before the Leo Divide I was a young mother to a cub. The humans took my cub away from me when they went around torching the leo villages. My husband tried to save him but was killed himself by the forbidden weapons the humans used. My cub was murdered just like a lot of other tigians then who were caught up in the fight between humans and leos."

"Yes, I still don't know why you tigians were not there when we needed you," he said.

"For your information Raiden we tigians offered to help the leos when this all happened but the leo leaders were all too proud to take help from a species they considered inferior to them. It was the last mistake the leos ever made and eventually led to the downfall of the race. My child was burned in a fire just like the one before you, so don't tell me that I don't understand what you feel because it was part of me that burned that day too."

Raiden apologised again and turned back to the fire and started to tell her.

"When it all happened I was young, maybe as old as you were. The humans developed the forbidden weapons that could shoot the leos from a distance. We never had a chance, the kingnines they used tore us apart and the humans mercilessly killed the women and cubs and burned them all. I, my brother Valadad and few survivors managed to escape after being told we were too young to fight for our race and made to flee by the elders who protected us. We always knew we were the last of our race and soon we began to fall one by one until it was only me and my brother left."

Sheeria then understood another thing about what was upsetting Raiden, stood behind him as he gazed into the fire and put a paw on his shoulder. "Tell me about your brother Raiden. What was he like?"

Raiden clenched his jaw when she asked him but found himself answering her, something he didn't want to do.

"My brother was always stronger than me, always looking after me and stepping into any fight that came my way. He always used to say that we were the last two left and that we should look after each other but when the Battle of Osiris started Valadad insisted that he joined the army that needed help. I tried to convince him otherwise but he was adamant on joining and made sure I never followed him. He sent me to Walton where the villagers took me in and gave me a home while he died on the battlefield. His armour was the only thing sent back to me by one of the survivors who knew him. I never met this soldier though."

He paused as he tried to find the right words to finish off his sentence, "I tried to save him Sheeria, it's because of me that I'm the last one left, I'm...the Last Leo."

Now unlike anything a tigian would do Sheeria turned Raiden around and wrapped her arms around him, it was more like something Acarlie would do, like she had learned compassion, something humans outshone in.

"You may be the last Raiden, but you are not alone," she said to him as she held onto him tight and together they both remembered the loved ones they had lost all those years ago whilst embraced in each other's arms.

"Your cub Sheeria...Is this why you became a guide?" he asked her and she let go of him and opened up.

"In a sense yes Raiden, after my cub was taken from me I drifted Sphere alone for a while until I made it to Eloma and befriended the elders there. They gave me a home while I worked for them, bringing up the elementalists and helping them with their studies and battling, it turns out that mothering was my prime spark in this world. I just wish I could have used it when I needed it the most with my own child.

"Soon I watched one elementalist after another leave the town and go on their journey and one by one I would never see again. Every time I heard they didn't make it was like losing another child over and over again and every time it would tear me up more and more.

"Then came a special child to the school, a bright spark and wonderful little child. She was always filled with energy and one of the brightest students that ever came to the school. She and I grew closer as she grew up and over time I watched her grow into a woman. After all the children I had lost in the past I knew I couldn't send her off to her death, to die like every other student that I brought up and watched grow strong. I tried to convince her again and again but she was adamant about leaving and so instead I asked to be her guide. It gives me a purpose again and I watch over this little girl like she was the cub taken away from me and I would rather die than become an Alanode, a failed guide to her."

"You really love her don't you?" he asked.

"The same way you love Val Raiden, I know now why you call him Val. We both have something in common. We have both taken a human for the lost family we couldn't protect from this world, we have taken them as a child and as a brother so we could be given a second chance for us so we can protect them..." and for the first time ever Sheeria noticed a gleam of moisture in Raiden's eye. He shut them firmly and tried to turn from her but she held him close again.

"It's ok Raiden, you have nothing to hide from me. I know you miss Val and as soon as we can we will have him back, Acarlie will make sure of that. I know you worry about him."

Raiden nodded, "That boy will be the death of me," he said.

"I think Acarlie and Val is the problem though, we both know the way they look at each other. They care for each other Raiden."

"I know but what can we do? They are both young and won't listen to reason."

"We will have to watch them like we vowed to Raiden. Together we will see no harm comes to them."

Raiden nodded again then turned back to the fire, this time he pulled Sheeria close and swung his arm around her shoulder. She laid her head on his shoulder as they stood side by side and together they gazed into the fire.

29

Dude ducked as a chair was flung through the room aiming at the two thieves. The man in purple was still a stranger to the mute but already he sensed that trouble seemed to follow this enigmatic character. All he wanted was to go home and back to his run down flat in his dirty city but now he was faced with an angry tigian and his wife now waking from the commotion.

"Look, I'm sorry to do this but I need this sword a lot more than you do and–" Val tried to begin while dodging the chair but was silenced by the tigian.

"This is not a matter of who needs it the most Human. It's a matter of belonging and it belongs to me, now return it to me immediately!" the baron said again and looked for something else to throw at his two burglars. Val looked and saw he had to escape from the room and walked towards the baron pointing the sword at him. The tigian saw the threat and suddenly put his hands up. Val edged round him until both he and Dude were back in the hallway staring back at the baron.

"You are making a big mistake Human. This is your last chance; return the blade to me and I shall see to it that your friend will be able to leave here unharmed and to live to tell the tale."

A part of Dude hoped that Val would take this option and at least this way he could just return back home.

Val however thought carelessly and laughed at his threat, "You forget I am the one with the sword, and I am the one out of your room, come on Dude, run!"

Dude felt Val grab his arm and started sprinting for the stairs again but did not expect the baron to chase after them and pounce on him and let out a mighty roar that would surely wake anybody that was asleep in the mansion, drugged or not. Dude whimpered under the weight of this tall creature and reached out silently for Val who looked to panic and run back down the corridor. He wanted to call and cursed his severed tongue he couldn't. With the mansion now seeming to wake the tigian gripped Dude by his hair and slammed his head against the floor and cursed.

"It looks like your friend has left you to die; a pity."

He again slammed the poor aeomon's head and then dragged him back into his chambers.

The following ten minutes were painful and torturous for the mute. With the baron's men now awake they went to work on punishing Dude to about an inch of his life. Every strike seemed to bruise his fragile, pale skin. He had been caught a few times stealing before and even had limbs removed but never had a beating such as this before. Blood began to spit and dribble from his mouth and his eyes became so swollen he could barely see. The thought of Val leaving him however hurt him most and eventually after a few more strikes only waited for the final blow to end him. He was being held in one of the rooms on the top floor of the mansion. They made sure they beat him until his body was weak and his face was covered in bruises and blood. A strong nose kept it from breaking but his ears were bloody and swollen. His chest and stomach also beaten made it hard for him to breathe as he was placed on the ground and made to look up at the baron before him. The tigian baron had him held down by his drugged men and was sitting down in a chair in front of him not saying anything at first and just staring at him like nothing had happened. He bit into his nails and sighed looking around his house thinking of how he could punish this intruder. He finally said, "You know it took me a long time to get where I am today? I had to do things I never thought I would do and mingle with a lot of people I should never have, but it was these little hobbies like collecting that have kept me alive today," he paused looking back at Dude. It seemed to Dude that his words weren't going anywhere and that he was just rambling along like a lonely old man but this only exacerbated the tension in the room and soon Dude became fearful of what this tigian would do to him. The two men holding Dude were stretching his arms out and laying him on his front and kneeling on his back giving him enough slack to lift his head up and look at the baron but in a very uncomfortable way.

The baron continued, "Do you have any idea how long a tigian lives for Aeomon?"

He waited for a reply but Dude never gave him it.

"I'll tell you then, the longest recorded lifespan for a tigian are roughly two hundred and fifty years, more than triple the life span of a human, which is a long time to live bored and unamused. I had been looking for this sword, this Fireshaver for one hundred of them. That's a good portion of my life just searching for this artefact, only for it to be taken from me by a boy and his aeomon. Now I'm only going to ask you once, where is my sword?"

Dude remained perfectly silent as always and said not a word, the baron was unaware that he was mute and unable to talk but still took offence to his silence.

"You do know what sort of house this is don't you? The law never walks past my land and that makes me king of my own laws. You have stolen something very valuable to me and I want it returned."

Silence filled the room again as Dude lay there helpless.

"Your silence is testing my patience Aeomon; do you want to die so?"

And again silence, this time even the men holding down the aeomon felt the uncomfortable presence and felt pity for the creature beneath them, but only the baron started to become angry with him. He slammed his fist down on the table beside him, cracking the wooden base of it and frightening the aeomon then began shouting, "You're not doing yourself any favours by protecting your friend. Tell me where my sword is and I promise your death will be quick. You will even be cremated and set free in the air but I swear if you do not talk soon then your head will remain in a jar where the sword used to sit, being an example to others."

Still Dude remained silent and he started to get nervous and wished he could speak to tell the baron he couldn't. A nervous sweat began to drip from his forehead and his stretched limbs began to ache. He opened his mouth and blurted out the only sound he could.

"Ahh."

The tigian quickly looked down at him and stepped forward, "Do you mock me?" but peered down at the helpless aeomon who held his mouth open and the tigian saw the severed tongue in his mouth and said, "So you are unable to speak then are you?" he then looked back to where his tail should be and saw the surgical scar from where it had been removed, "It seems to me that as an aeomon, you did not wish for this tail to be removed and maybe your missing tongue and tail is the result of something similar to what is happening tonight. You are obviously not a very good thief are you? But I'm afraid I will not simply remove an organ from you. I'm going to take your life as my trade, maybe your silence will persist when you feel the pain of death," he then stood up and looked at his men and ordered.

"Kill him."

The men lifted Dude up off the floor and carried him away.

"We will have to find Fireshaver elsewhere," the baron said again finally.

One of the men held onto Dude as the other went to open the door. He gripped onto the handle and began to turn it. As soon as the catch was away from the door the door swung open and a man standing in the doorway struck the man and knocked him to the floor holding his mouth in pain. The other man dropped the aeomon and only had a brief second to look at the man in a purple cloak in the doorway swinging a metal staff at him. A whole wave of relief swept over Dude, all the hate he suddenly had for Val had vanished. Val had obviously run back to the ship and ordered Gendrick to bring him back to save Dude. All that was needed now was to escape. After striking the other man down Val helped Dude to his feet and looked up to see the baron in front of him, now that his patience was totally gone the baron seemed like an angry beast. He didn't say a word but snarled at him staring at his sword on Val's back. Dude weakly stumbled to his feet and when he found the strength he stood up and looked at the baron who was now eyeing Val who was staring at him right back, unafraid of his fear stance. Dude knew he was unarmed and grabbed the old sword from Val's back and held on to it with both hands. Fear and desperation overwhelmed him. At first he didn't care for this sword and only wanted it for protection in order to escape but as soon as he held it the metal of the blade began to burst into flames. This act suddenly surprised everyone in the room, especially the battered and bruised mute. There the beaten aeomon stood, holding onto a blade of fire. His hands were not burning however, and he only gripped on to the blade tightly and hoped not to drop it. The men on the floor stood up now, looking at their boss for confirmation on what to do but the baron didn't take his eyes off the sword.

"The sword of fire! I have only heard legends of this happening, they say that you cannot choose Fireshaver but Fireshaver chooses you when you are ready. I have been studying that part of the legend of the blade for a decade now believing it to be only that."

Val listened to what he said and told him, "If the blade chose Dude then it doesn't belong to you, and therefore we have stolen nothing from you!"

The tigian snarled and spat at Val, "The blade is still mine!" then leapt toward them. The baron almost flew into him and knocked him into a wall behind him and went to slash at his face but Val saw this coming and ducked his swipe, quickly side stepped away from the wall and struck him with his staff. A man suddenly grabbed him from behind and held him tight. The baron who stood in pain against the wall rubbed his strong chin where Val had struck him and snarled again. Thinking quickly Val remembered the training he had with Raiden and roared one of his own and with all his strength he pivoted and threw the man holding him over his hip, quickly turning and swinging his staff again across the baron's face, this time knocking him to the ground. He then pounced on the man on the floor and like a leo he began shouting and assaulting. It was like he had found his rage Raiden had told him to look for and whilst beating the man he remembered Raiden saying '*don't let anger and adrenaline take control of you,*' and rolled back, calling his staff again and noticed the baron was already back on his feet and this time swung it low and connected with the baron's shins. The baron fell forward and caught Val on the way down and together they roared and snarled at each other like two tigers fighting.

Dude was fending off the other guard who held him before, swinging the fiery sword from side to side backing the man off him. He was still shocked at what was actually happening here but didn't want to stop and think about it and carried on keeping eye contact with the man in front of him who was backing up as the swinging blade of fire got closer to him. He looked over for only for a brief second to see Val and the baron face to face and screaming at each other trying to scare each other. In this time the guard used it to jump towards Dude with his arms out to grab and take him down but was unaware of how quick an aeomon's natural reactions were and screamed as his arm was quickly sliced off by Fireshaver. He lay on the floor in agony with Dude standing over him white with shock. He lowered his hand and didn't see when the fiery sword only needed to touch the curtains next to it to catch alight. Dimitiry looked over from Val to see his curtains now caught fire, his guard now missing his hand and the aeomon standing over him unaware of the fire, looking down at the crying man. Now fear came into the baron's feline eyes and he screamed and went to scramble over to Dude.

Val, who had his back to Dude and the fire only saw the tigian scream in fear, called his staff and lifted it as the tigian went to scramble over and struck his nose. The baron felt the instant sting of the staff and only swiped his paw, knocking Val back and pounced for Dude. Dude only had a split second to see the baron coming and quickly lifted up Fireshaver for the baron to run into. The fiery blade cut straight into the baron's side and away from him leaving a terrible wound. The baron screamed in pain and fell to one side gripping his wound. Val who now saw the chance shouted to Dude and grabbed him and made a quick escape of the room. The curtains now completely on fire and burning the ceiling, the handless man and the baron on the floor and the other man getting up to help them escape of the toxic fumes now alerted the whole mansion. In the hallway Val turned Dude away from running back down the stairs and said to him, "Follow me Dude, the ship is waiting for us on the roof, this way quickly!"

A few moments later and the baron was standing outside his mansion and could only watch his home burn and light up the night sky. Over the flames a skyship hovered with two smoky figures climbing up a rope and he nearly cried as the ship's doors closed with them in and started to fly away. His house would be gone in a few hours now and his precious blade he had searched so long for was now stolen from him. He stood defeated amongst his men and turned to his female tigian companion. She scowled and told him the final news, "The women have escaped dear."

The news upset him but with what he had just experienced he didn't really care much, "When?" he said still gripping onto his wound.

"We don't know but it must have been when you were seeing to the thief. You were so absorbed with that ridiculous sword that you forgot about the real job you should have been taking care of."

The baron sighed, he knew she was right and now he had nothing. Everything he had worked for was now gone, taken from him all in one night by a human and an aeomon, shame overwhelmed him, but at least he still had The Bastard Camp...

The pimp laughed at the two smoky figures safe and well on his ship and turned and winked at Val. "Well there you go, the monkey is back on the ship and so are you, now where is my sword?" he said eager to lay his hands on it.

Val looked at Dude sitting against the cargo door beside him and nodded to him.

"It's ok Dude, give him the sword and we can go home."

Dude handed the blade to the pimp who stared and admired it, the flames of the steel were now gone and only blood remained staining its steel.

"It's beautiful isn't it? Yes I have been wanting that baron to slip up with this sword for some time now, and now it's mine."

"That's great, I'm happy for you. Now, could you take us back to Hiro to drop Dude back home then take me—"

"No, you won't be going anywhere boy," the pimp said slyly.

"What do you mean?" Val asked.

"You altered the deal remember? You wanted us to wait for the mute, and you said that 'I won't get the sword until the silent aeomon gets back safely on the ship'. Here he is and I have the sword, which sounds like a deal to me."

"That's not fair you son of a bitch!" Val shouted and went to stand up but one of the pimp's men swung a heavy punch at Val which connected perfectly and in one Val was unconscious. Dude only sat there panting and fearfully looking down at the man who saved him. He was already beaten and weakened and so wasn't expecting one final strike from Gendrick's men to also knock the sense out of him.

All was black.

30

Val gained consciousness the same way he lost it. A fist swung and connected with his face bringing him out of his dream and back into the real world. The first thing he noticed was the pain that he felt all over his body and as he opened his eyes he noticed his left eye was too swollen to open and he could only see out of his right. His face was sore and bruised all over and his mouth was bleeding over his chest. He tried to move his hands to clean himself and rub his sore face but found his hands were tied behind his back. He felt his legs and buttocks and felt them in pain but still in one piece. He looked down out of one good eye and could see that he was sitting in a chair, his legs tied together and his hands tied behind his back. He slowly tried looking around him to see where he was and felt heat from a hot sun turning the inside of the ship into an oven. He looked up to see he was still in the same room they were contained in before, only now they were tied to chairs so they could be beaten. Another fist struck his face suddenly but Val was still too dazed to work out where he was or what was hitting him. He looked at the floor and saw his feet, firmly on the blood stained, laminated wooden floor of the ship. Just in front of them were shoes attached to feet attached to—

Another fist struck his face, again this time harder than before and now he felt his face bleeding from the beating and knew he had to wake up quickly. As he looked up he saw the man before him, his fist raised and about to strike him again.

"Stop, stop, I'm awake!" he pleaded with him but couldn't stop the man striking him again this time nearly knocking him over still attached to the chair. The chair rocked from one side to another. Val tilted his head up so he could see the man now, it was one of Gendrick's cronies punching him, the pimp behind him finally telling him to step aside.

Gendrick stood wearing a light leather vest with a simple white shirt underneath it. He now wore a fedora-type hat and black shorts. It was clearly very hot outside. He walked up and knelt down in front of Val and smiled at him, "Glad you're back with us boy. I thought we were going to lose you there."

"Where am I?" Val croaked still in pain and trying to understand what was happening.

"Where you are is unimportant boy. What should you really be asking?" the pimp asked him. Val knew he was clearly toying with him and only wanted Val to play along. He looked to his side to see a familiar face sitting in a chair beside him. His hands and feet also bound and his head leaning against his chest in an unconscious state. Val recognised him immediately as Dude, the aeomon who was with him when he was knocked unconscious back when he was made to steal a blade for the pimp. Dude was breathing heavily which suggested to Val that he was either trying to breathe through broken ribs or having difficulty breathing because of the heat inside the ship. Val looked back to Gendrick, kneeling down in front of him and answered his question, "What is going to happen to us?" he croaked again and watched the pimp's evil smile turn into laughter and stand back up. He stood in front of Val and drew forward the very same blade he made Val and Dude steal from the Baron, the sword named Fireshaver. He held it high and admired the perfection of the blade, from the woven long handle to the long, thin but strong metal of the blade then held it to Val's neck.

"Well I never thanked you properly for getting the blade to me you know, and as my present back to you I wanted you to meet the blade for yourself, a more personal meeting, something that only a few people in the world's history have had the privilege of doing."

The way he spoke suggesting that he was going to kill Val with the blade he stole for him only angered Val. He felt like shouting up at the pimp and telling him to stop talking and get on with it but he didn't, the heat inside the ship clouded his mind and the pain in his body only left him sitting there looking up at the sword helpless. Gendrick and his men stood there over the two captured young men and were suggesting different ways of killing and disposing of the bodies, the suggestions were rejected from the pimp.

"What's there to hide," he told his men. "Out here there is no law, people die out here every day and no one gives a damn. We could just kill them and leave them for the kingnines to chew on, who's going to stand in our way?"

As he finished his sentence the door opened and one of the pimp's crew popped his head into the room, "Boss you should come and see this, some pirates were caught trying to steal the skyship. We got them tied up and waiting for your presence."

The pimp beamed then, the idea of killing the local pirates was something he was waiting for. Killing the pirates would send a message to the other pirates that he was not to be messed with and that was good for him because to the pirates it meant strength, strength bought respect, respect bought trade and trade meant business that would pay off greatly for someone in his position. He owned the fastest skyship in the sky, he owned the strongest blade and now all he needed was to have the pirates at his side. He signalled his men to leave the tent then looked back on to the unconscious Dude and the beaten Val, still firmly tied to the chair, nothing sharp within his reach and no way of escaping the chair in which he sat before closing the door leaving the two alone in the increasingly hot room to slowly cook them like a large oven.

As soon as the door slammed shut Val looked to Dude again. His face was just as beaten as Val's and he was still breathing heavily which had to be a bad thing for him.

"Dude," he tried to whisper over to him, "Dude," but nothing. Dude was too far under and that meant Val had to try and escape without him. He looked all around him and other than Dude sitting beside him the room was completely empty. Gendrick and his men must have emptied the room knowing that Val had no means of escape there. His hands were firmly tied as were his feet and there was nothing in sight he could reach to try and free himself with. He tried to think fast, knowing that soon the pimp would be back bloodthirsty and wouldn't toy around with him this time, it was amazing how he wasn't dead already. The thought of screaming came to his mind but he knew this would only catch the ears of the Gendrick and his men who would come back and silence him. After calculating all he could in the hot heat of the room he knew there was no way of escaping unless someone could save him maybe. He hung his head and thought of Raiden again and how he wished he was back in Walton with Theydon and the other Walton Warriors, how he needed them now. He thought to himself what would Raiden do in this situation? Break from the ropes, go on a rampage and kill the pimp and his men? No, Raiden maybe but Val was too weak and human to do that. He groaned in defeat and thought about his journey so far with his friends and felt empty when he realised that it was here that would be where his journey ends and so far away from them. He thought about Acarlie and remembered the first time she hugged him when they first met when he was released from the containment centre in Lachine. He remembered the smell of her perfume. He remembered all the times she smiled at him, the way her brown eyes gleamed with delight when they made their promise together, the promise he could not keep now and knew he had let her down. The promise he made kept repeating over in his head. He would not be able to save her from the elders' conditioning he realised about the night she showed him the elemental kata, when they sat down and he told her about his mission, his lost memory and his staff... His staff!

The second his staff came to his mind a whole wave of hope overtook his grief as he now had a chance of survival, only he with his staff could get out of this situation if he tried. He leaned forward and opened his hands and called his staff. As soon as he felt his staff in his grip behind him he tried with his bound hands to break it in half, then in half again and moulded them together and into a knife-like form. It wasn't razor sharp but maybe sharp enough to cut through the rope. He positioned it in his palm and furiously started rubbing it against the rope binding him. He rubbed until his hand was sore and hurt from the awkward movements but still carried on until small pieces of the rope began to cut and this gave him even more drive to continue before it became so loose that he could pull his hands apart. With his hands free he shaped the knife even sharper now and began at his feet, sawing at the rope, cutting away a little piece at a time until he was free from the chair in which he sat. He knew he didn't have long then and had to escape before the pimp came back. He thought up a plan quick and turned to Dude. His plan needed Dude and if he was still bound when they came back the plan would fail. Val sprang to Dude and tried lifting his head and patting his cheeks repeatedly saying, "Wake up Dude, please wake up."

He tried opening his eyes with his hands but saw that Dude's eyes were rolled far into the top of his head, shaking slightly.

"No, no, wake up Dude, come on wake up!" Val shouted now and started slapping Dude to try and wake him. After a few more knocks Dude began to wake and looked at Val, unable to speak still but Val knew what Dude wanted to know.

"Listen to me Dude, we have been held captive by Gendrick and his men. I'm going to free you, ok? Hold still." He moved behind him and started cutting at the rope binding him. When he was done he began cutting the rope at his feet until they were both free and Dude was about to stand back up but Val stopped him and sat him back down, "No Dude listen to me. I think I have an idea but I need you to be strong," Val said putting his hand behind Dude's head and gently pressing his forehead against his. Their bruised faces both tired and their bodies ready to die had to be strong here and Val knew this if they had to survive. Val took the untied rope at Dude's feet and placed it on his feet giving the illusion that his feet were still tied and told

Dude to put his hands behind his back then when Dude did this Val heard the voices of Gendrick and his men coming back for the room, laughing and cheering at the thieving pirates they had just killed. Val acted fast and hid the rope by sitting on them and placed the rope for his feet on his feet and put his hands behind his back again, holding firmly onto the knife, waiting for his moment.

"Just act unconscious Dude and wait for me to act. Don't freak out," Val whispered as the door started to creak open and Gendrick and four of his men entered, the illusion was now complete.

The pimp was holding the bloody Fireshaver and wiping it clean and laughing at how the pirate pleaded for his life when he cut him down when he walked back into the room. He saw Dude was still unconscious on his chair and Val still bound sitting in his. He approached and said to Val, "Good you're still here, now then..."

Bide your time, Val thought to himself as the pimp stood in front of him, *I must have him close to me. I must have him close enough to stab if this plan is going to work, just wait Val, just bide your time.*

At first Gendrick walked up to Dude and lifted his head to check his condition. Dude who was still acting unconscious just sat there lifeless and let him examine him. All Val needed was for the pimp to get in close enough. He thought he could hold the knife to his neck and make their way out of the Scarlet Arise and make a new deal of passage back to Hiro. It wasn't the best of plans and they only had one chance since they were outnumbered but this was all that Val had to work with. Gendrick walked away from Dude and now stood in front of Val. His palms started to sweat and his mind was fixed on the timing, his feet tense ready to pounce. *Patience Val, you must stay focused, you only have one chance at this so it must be perfect, patience.*

Gendrick walked up to him and got face to face with him, "So how would you like me to do this boy?"

He is going for it, that's it. Now you're close enough. Now all I need is for you to turn slightly.

"I would rather one of your men does it," Val croaked pathetically knowing that this would fool the pimp, "That one there would do."

"Which one?" the pimp said as he turned slightly to face his men behind him.

Now's your chance, go for it now before it's too late, the voice inside Val's head screamed and at that point Val sprang up and held Gendrick's arm back with the knife to his throat.

The pimp was shaken up at first and called to his men for help but Val shouted louder, "Stay back or I'll cut his throat!"

The pimp's men backed off a little, afraid of what Val would do and didn't say a word. Val sat the pimp in the chair, moving the concealed ropes onto the floor then whilst still holding the knife to his throat, took Fireshaver from him and said, "Here you go Dude," and threw it to the aeomon who sprang to life, caught the blade and stood up straight. Just like before as soon as Dude held the blade a beam of light came from it and fire began to flash and burn from the blade like it was on fire. This shocked the men even more and even Gendrick screamed as he saw this for the first time. Dude swung the fiery sword from side to side cutting the closest man who screamed out and fell to the floor holding his wound. The other men backed up against the side of the room, not knowing what to do and turned to their boss who was still shaking from fright and was shouting, "The ship! Don't burn the ship! We will all die if the ship gets set alight!"

Dude heard him and put the fiery sword close to the wooden walls and watched the men all flinch in fear and held their hands up calling, "No don't!"

This wasn't really what Val had in mind for his plan but it was still working all the same and let go of the pimp, turned to one of his men and shouted to him, "You, come here!" when he did he shouted again, "Tie him!" pointing at the pimp.

The man did as he was instructed and took the rope from the floor, and tied up his boss with it to the chair. Val had the situation in his control and he knew this but the voices in his head still kept repeating, *don't get cocky, just tie them and get out of there.*

"Good, now do him!" Val shouted again pointing at another man who stepped forward and sat down in the chair and let the other man tie him. Val went round and checked the ties were secure and when he was satisfied he looked back up at the last remaining man still standing. It was the man punching him previously when he woke up, the very same one who pushed him out of the bar back in True Hiro and the same one who knocked him out on the Scarlet Arise. Val called his staff back to its true shape in front of them and smacked the tall man around the head with it, "That's for punching me when I told you to stop!" Val shouted but the man just stood back up and dived into Val. They fell to the floor and started punching each other furiously until the man who was bigger than Val had him pinned down. Val was quick enough to bring his arm up to block his fist and was about to strike him when a fiery sword came from behind and ripped through the man's back and stuck out his chest. The fire burning silenced his painful, blood curdling scream and covering Val in a shower of blood. The fiery blade retracted from his chest and Val rolled over and laid the man down, quickly shaping his staff into a knife again and sticking it hard under the man's chin, reaching up through his mouth and into his skull. Dude helped Val up and they both stood there looking back at the pimp and his other companion tied to the chairs, the third man still holding his wound not daring to confront them. Val took his knife from out of the corpse's skull and stared down at his blood stained hands. This was blood from a person he just killed, blood from a corpse down at his feet. He felt instantly frightened and guilty. He never wanted to become this, a murderer but when he looked over to the tortured Dude he knew he had no choice but to bury these feelings down and concentrate on their own lives. He took a deep breath and now stood over the helpless wounded man, deciding against stabbing the wounded since he was cut deep and would die shortly anyway. He felt sorry for him lying there silent but breathing deep and heavy holding onto his side. Blood soaked his robes and hands and spread a large claret puddle around the room. Val only stood over the man in shock and sadness as his breathing became fainter, a small whelp came from him as the pain became too much for him and he slowly died there and then on the floor. Gendrick could only watch as Val who had just killed his men went to leave the room.

"You know my other men are still around, don't you? When they find me I'm going to hunt you down and kill you outright!" he called back at him.

Val walked back up to Gendrick and ripped a sleeve off the pimp's arm, cut it in two and used them gag him and the man next to him.

"I'm not a person to kill someone without reason. I have killed one of your men in self-defence but you two I have no reason to kill so instead I'm going to trade with you; your life for the Scarlet Arise. If you agree with the terms then nod your head."

The pimp scowled past his binds making him unable to speak and didn't move an inch, after Val saw this he took his knife he moulded from his staff only a few seconds ago and held it under the pimp's chin and spoke to him louder with more threat in his tone, "Or I can kill you now, the man next to you will then through rank I guess inherit the Scarlet Arise and I can offer him the same question. I don't think he will be as eager as you to die for the ship. So what will it be?"

Val stared at Gendrick waiting for his answer, the pimp just stared back until he finally nodded and Val took the knife away from his chin.

"Then it's a deal, the ship now belongs to me in a fair trade for your life. I shall keep my side of the bargain and spare you." Val then held up the knife to the pimp's eyes and in a threatening tone again, "And if you even think of stealing my ship back I'll make sure you never want to see a ship again."

Val turned to Dude behind him who was now putting Fireshaver in its sheaf and holding it, breathing heavily still and rubbing his wounds. Dude was clearly still hurting from being beaten by the baron's men that night and now his fresh wounds only made them worse. Val who was still in a terrible state of his own went to Dude and helped him out of the room, locking it behind them and leaving the empty ship, taking the first step outside only to be blinded by a blazing bright sunlight. Sand and desert was all around them and clear blue sky above them.

As soon as the sunlight hit him Val squinted until his eyes were closed and heard a weak scream as Dude fell to the floor covering his fragile eyes from the brightness of the sun and the sands reflecting it. Val pulled Dude back into the shade of the ship and looked around to see only the Scarlet Arise, everything else was sand and as far as he could see in every direction was only endless dunes stretching out into the horizon.

Val fell to his knees then, "What's happening? What is this place?" he asked himself knowing that Dude would not answer him. He was truly lost now. Wherever Gendrick's men were they left the ship out here in the desert, and with leaving the old captain in the ship meant Val and Dude were suddenly alone and desperate. Piloting the ship was out of the question since neither of them knew how to fly one. They didn't even know where they were. Val took off his cloak and wrapped it around Dude, covering him from the sunlight. Questions flowed through Val's mind repeatedly, questions like, *where are we? How long was I asleep? Where are the rest of the crew?* Val sat down helping the cowering Dude in the shade from the sun when he could see the smallest thing in the distance, so small in fact that even when he squinted hard he still didn't know if it was real or not. It looked like a building or a hut made of sand in the distance but the heat from the sun was causing a refraction making it almost concealed completely. There were tracks however, this was where the crew had gone, this was his only option of direction. He looked up to see the sky-ship standing before him, empty and waiting for its crew to come back, this was Val's ticket out. If only he could pilot it he could just simply fly it back to Hiro and back to Raiden but he knew he couldn't and asking Dude was out of the question and he didn't trust the pimp and the other guy as far as he could throw them. The only chance he had was to make for the building he could barely see and try and find someone to pilot them back.

"Dude, listen to me, there is a building in the distance. If we hurry we can get there soon, we have to find someone to pilot the skyship in order of escaping this place, here..." Val said as he picked up the aeoman, "I need you to walk with me. Just keep your face covered and your eyes closed. I will have to guide you, come on."

He held onto Dude's arm and started walking in the direction of the building in the distance. He knew very well that leaving the pimp was a bad idea and also if the rest of the men were back in that building then he wouldn't survive long but this was all he had. He *had* to go somewhere to find a pilot, he *had* to survive. Dude still wrapped up in the purple cloak that wasn't made to withstand heat started to struggle quickly. His breathing became very fast and deep the further they walked into this unknown desert in the unbearable heat of the sun, even Val loosened his armour and wished he was wearing sandals, as the sand was burning his feet but he became more worried about the blind Dude following him. He had been in the dark and wet True Hiro for so long that this terrain could easily kill him. Val knew he couldn't let this happen to him and was patient with him. Every now and again Dude would have to stop, shut his eyes tight and pull his hood down just to breathe the sweltering warm air around him. His hair was now soaked from sweat and he soon gave the cloak back to Val. He would rather burn from the scorching rays of the sun on his pale skin than spend another second under the hot cloak. Val tried all he could to keep Dude moving but he became a heavy burden and soon he was carrying him. Dude dragged his feet trying to walk with Val, looking up at him every now and again without opening his eyes.

"You're doing well Dude, I can see the building more clearly now, no wait more than a building, it's two or three," Val said encouraging him when he finally noticed what it was. "It's a town Dude, we're saved! It's going to be ok Dude we can make this. We just got to keep on going."

But it was when he said this that Dude fell limp and collapsed on the floor from exhaustion, dropping Fireshaver next to him and spread out in the hot sand.

"Dude!" Val cried out and fell to the floor with him and checked his breathing. Val shook Dude a couple of times and tried to sit him up without succession before he finally gave up. Poor Dude had been beaten to a pulp and now couldn't walk to save his life, the light would burn his eyes if he opened them and the sun was burning his pale skin. Val knew he was Dude's only hope of surviving and picked him up, his cloak and the sword and started slowly walking to the town in the distance.

"Why couldn't I leave him in the skyship?" Val started talking to himself. "At least the cloak and sword could have stayed behind. Ah! You're heavy Dude!"

The armour he was wearing didn't help with the weight on his back either and soon Val started to grow weak and stumble in the sand, constantly shifting the weight about on his back. Now he could see the town clearly, it had many huts and people walking around in the distance. It was like a market place. There were roads in the distance and he knew someone would see him soon but not yet, he had to keep walking. A few minutes passed with each step harder than the last. Sweat was dripping off Val's head now and he began to look like Dude did earlier. Soon the heat waves in the distance began to feel closer to him. His stomach felt empty, his legs began to feel weak and soon he had to drop everything on his back. All the colours in his vision began to blend in with one another turning into a dark blue and he felt a strong pain in his knees as he fell to the floor, held out his arms and caught himself just before he fell on his face. He shook his head and tried to gather his strength again but everything was spinning and he couldn't hear anything, wiping his forehead with his hands and turning to check on Dude beside him.

They were dying Val realised, from a mixture of dehydration and exhaustion. Dude lying unconscious now started to breathe slower. His pale skin now turning red and continuously burning in the desert's heat. Val sat back and stared out into the desert. Millions of particles of sand sat motionless in front of him without a breath of wind to move even the smallest pieces. Many hills of sand large and small sat there beautifully reflecting the light of the sun and out into the miles and miles of pure dunes in front of him. This place was dead and soon so would they. He wiped the sweat off his face and tried licking the moisture off his hands to soothe the terrible pain of dryness at the back of his mouth. This place he thought had even blown sand into his throat, this was more due to the fact that the pimp wanted him dead and didn't bother to hydrate him whilst he was unconscious. He laid his head down against the hot sand and felt it instantly stick to his sweaty face. He decided he would close his eyes, just for a moment. He immediately felt fatigued and made his body feel like it was sinking into the sand. He had to carry on, he had to survive, but he needed a minute. He felt himself relax and slowly slip from consciousness into a threatening, blackened sleep.

31

It was high noon when the tall, sharply dressed man looked from out of the window of his personal helicopter onto the ruins that was once Mecroyles. He knew this old town very well and had been there on many occasions to watch the Elemental Battles since he was young. Like a lot of people he never missed a single match and even watched the recorded battles from abroad from the comfort of his home. He tilted his head back and waited for the helicopter to position itself ready to land in an open space on the ground below. One of his men turned back from the pilot's seat and shouted over to him, "We are landing now sir. This will only take a moment!"

The man said nothing but nodded and tilted his head back again and rested it on the back of the helicopter seat. Gently the large and highly decorated helicopter landed on the floor spreading dust from the fallen buildings across the plains of the destroyed town. The door opened downwards revealing a small staircase on the inside of the door which touched the ground operated by mechanical cogs and wheels. The town's people from Mecroyles gathered around the helicopter and watched in excitement as the tall, sharply dressed man took his first step from the helicopter onto the stairs. Running his hand down the banister to the side of them as he walked and smiled at his people. His polished, black shoes touched down on the dusty floor of broken bricks and destroyed breeze blocks. The people of Mecroyles were quietly arguing amongst themselves who would address this man and finally pushed one particular man in front of them so he stood square in front of the tall man. This now nervous man did not know quite what to do and just saluted the man from the helicopter and stood there dumbstruck. He said in a nervous, shaky but deferential voice, "Mister President, welcome to Mecroyles, thank you for coming on such short notice, I–"

"Please, please..." the president interrupted him waving his hand in a comforting gesture. "You don't have to be so formal to me. I may be your president but I would appreciate it if you were to speak to me like you would anybody else."

The nervous man still dumbstruck with his hand to his head in a salute now dropped his hand like he was ordered to and took a breath to gather his nerves together.

"Now please tell me, who is in charge here? Where is the Mayor?" the president asked him.

"The Mayor died sir. The soldiers from Feydon took no prisoners."

The news affected the president since he knew the mayor of this town and was wounded by the news of his death.

"Oh, I'm sorry to hear that. What about the council then, is there any still here?"

"I'm sorry sir, they too were taken from us. Everyone was killed and only a handful of people have survived."

"Where are the elementalists?"

"Only our youngest elementalist has survived sir. The elders have taken him away from us so he can continue his work in private."

"Then who can I speak to about what has happened here? Surely there has to be someone here of authority to help you before I arrived?"

"Yes sir, that is right. There is an elementalist who was on her pilgrimage that caused her to arrive here just after the incident. In time of crisis after the elders she was the one who spoke to us and told us to wait here for you to arrive."

The thought of a foreign person coming into the country and telling his people what to do upset the president slightly. He may have loved the Elemental Battles all his life but he was still very cautious sometimes about the way that the elders' connections worked. Many human leaders were the same sometimes seeing the elementalists as human versions of elders because of their upbringing and didn't understand the teachings like some other people did. The president knew what he could trust and human technology was what he trusted and even though he promoted the Elemental Battles in his country for his people and loved to watch them in a sporting fashion he never quite agreed with the '*magic*' part of it and how all the towns from around the world with elemental schools were networked together, it made him feel like he was inferior to his own people.

"Ok then, where is this elementalist? Maybe she can shed some light on what has happened here."

The president was led away from his helicopter and across the ruins of Mecroyles, past the ashes of the fire that had now burned out. The bodies of the deceased now only existed as dust to go wherever the wind took them. He looked in a mourning state at his fallen town, destroyed for an unknown reason by an army from a city he had no quarrel with. The town schools, hospital, shops and elemental school all destroyed by either fire or some other strong powerful weapon he had not heard of since some of the buildings had large holes blown out of them and only a few were gone completely. Fire could not have caused this type of destruction to buildings such as these. He asked but received no answer from his guide from what had done this to the buildings. He thought about the last time he spoke to the Queen of Feydon. Queen Angel was her name and she had controlled the whole Septurian continent for a few years now and he wondered how she would explain herself when he demanded an explanation from her. He was led finally past one large broken building and to a door with a female tigian guarding it. The tigian stood up from the spot where she sat and immediately noticing the face of the president bowed her head.

"Mister President, it is an honour to meet you. My name is Sheeria and I am the Sacred Guide and Guardian to Acarlie, the Elementalist from Eloma."

The president smiled and waved the same comforting gesture to Sheeria and said, "I am here to speak to this Acarlie you speak of Sheeria. I hear she has been giving some comforting words to my people here in Mecroyles," he said in a matter of fact tone.

"She has only done what had been asked of her by her teachings Mister President, nothing more. This town was in need of some guiding words after the torment and she gave them what they needed."

The president only lifted a hand and tilted it to one side, "Please..." he said. Sheeria knew what this gesture meant just like anybody else would. It was the international sign for, *get out of the way and let me pass*, "Let me see her. There are some things I would like to discuss with her."

Sheeria knew her place and could not stand in this human's country and not let him pass through a door just because her elementalist was behind it. She reached out behind her and opened the door and stood aside for the president to enter. The president walked through the door and found himself back out in the open. The door he walked through was meant to carry on but because of what happened earlier the top of the building had collapsed and let sunlight shine through. There, amongst the gravel and destroyed remains of the building was the elementalist he had been told about. She stood there with her back to him in concentration, slowly stepping forward and back, twisting her hands over and under themselves, crossing them and elegantly swinging them around. He stood in silence for a moment while he watched the small particles of dust, grass and other tiny pieces of debris lifting up from the ground and circling around her as she guided them with only gestures of her hands. He had heard of these sorts of things before, an *Elemental Kata* someone once told him, but he had never witnessed one before. He was almost mesmerised from watching her as she unknowingly performed her kata in front of him. The white dress she wore with the lines of green and blue waving and black flowers laced on them flowed smoothly with her movements as she slowly twisted and turned gently and smoothly. She punched the air a few times and lifted her legs to kick slowly, being careful not to ruin her dress or rip it on the shrapnel circling around her. In the light coming down from the heavens the tiny dust particles glistened in the rays of the sun and swung around her clockwise. He understood then that she was controlling the wind carrying the dust and the pieces of debris floating around her was also under her control. *She's very pretty. So this is the elementalist who has been talking to my people, let's see if she really is as good a talker as she is a dancer,* he thought and decided to wait for her to finish her kata before stepping in and saying something. Finally she stood still with her hands close to her chest. The debris now slowly floating back on the floor and she sighed a relaxing relief knowing that she had finished her practice, something that was very important on her journey. The president stood there slightly embarrassed but cleared his throat loudly so she would hear him. He watched as she swung round, now as embarrassed as he was and stood there awkwardly smiling.

"That was very nice. Your ability to control the wind and the air around you is truly amazing and you perform it so beautifully as well. Miss Acarlie is it? I am President Sarauami, Chief Commander of Calmaron."

Acarlie only stood still, embarrassed about this and wondered how long he had been standing there. She smiled at his compliment and pushed her black hair to the back of her ears with her fingers.

"Thank you President Sarauami..." she felt like she wanted to say more but found herself silenced in his presence as he took a step forward.

"I hear that you have been the one who has been comforting the people of Mecroyles with words and have been helping them with sanctuaries."

She nodded and answered, "Yes sir, I have only been fulfilling my duty as an elementalist to help a town in need of help such as this."

"Hold on, I know you have certain duties you have to do but you must remember mine. These are my people and I don't care for immigrants no matter how sacred they may be coming and telling my people what to do, do you understand Miss Acarlie?"

She could tell from his tone that this was not a lecture but it sounded more like something he was obliged as Chief Commander of his people to tell her this. She knew she could not argue and only hung her head and accepted his words.

"I'm...sorry Mister President."

As he looked down at her he could see that she was distressed by what he was saying. He knew he didn't want this to be a bad conversation and had known that his actions would one day reach the elders and eventually come back to haunt him so he changed his tone, looking down at the beautiful elementalist before him. He knew there was business to attend to but he couldn't help but have ideas of how she could be useful to him and his country.

"Mister President, before we continue any further I must inform you of the events that happened in your town."

"I'm aware of what has happened here, my town's people have informed me about the attack from Feydon."

"If you know that, then you will also know that they continue their path Mister President. My companions have reported seeing the army passing through on their way towards Racoves, and whatever they were looking for here they did not find and now are marching to Hiro."

"What are you suggesting Acarlie? That I send my men out across the oceans to catch an army that is not in my country anymore, after the events that have occurred I want my people to be safe. Security is paramount for my people right now."

"Sir, people are in danger right now and you would willingly stay here and let them die? What happened here was only the beginning of something much bigger. Whatever it is Feydon wants they want it so badly that they would risk a divide to get it."

"Look Acarlie, I understand your job to entertain and worry about all the people of Sphere but mine is only to the people of Calmaron and more importantly Mecroyles. I can't send my people across the waters off to war when they are calling out for me to heal their wounds. I must secure my country before I make decisions that would risk the safety of it."

Acarlie turned around then knowing that he would not help her. He didn't even like her she thought, he certainly didn't like the fact that she was only helping out his people, *this is pointless, he is not going to help neither me nor the people of Hiro.*

"Well, if you're not going to help my people then I guess I should just go Mister President, like you said, you have your duties and I have mine. I thought for a minute that we would be able to help each other out."

"Well maybe we can help each other out Acarlie."

Acarlie turned back around, "How can I possibly help you? You don't even like my help. I tried to comfort your people and calm them down for you and you bite my head off."

"Actually I didn't appreciate your help since you're an outsider, but I'm actually grateful for your words calming the people down and this is what I want to talk about. Acarlie, it is clear that my town, no, my whole country is without an elementalist now..."

Acarlie felt instantly offended by what he was insinuating, "What are you suggesting? That I retire from my pilgrimage?"

"I'm suggesting that you help out a town that needs your help. Just like you say, it is your duty. Stay here in Mecroyles and be our new High Elementalist, with your knowledge of your other element you can master two elements at once. No elementalist will be able to defeat you in your home stadium."

"President Sarauami, my home is in Eloma. I feel your country's pain and I have tried all I can to help you but I have made a promise to my people that I will bring glory back to Eloma or die trying."

"But if you stay here will you not still bring glory to your home town? With two home elements at your practise, any journeying elementalist will not have chance of beating you."

As much as she disliked the president saying this she knew he would be right about her strength if she stayed here and became the High Elementalist here in Mecroyles.

"And maybe if you did stay here and become a Mecroyles citizen, maybe I can take your contributions of ideas that you may have."

So this was his real intention. She knew now what this was all about; he wanted to blackmail her into becoming his new elementalist since all but one of his were now dead, and this child would not be able to battle for some years now leaving Mecroyles out of the picture of the League of Elementalists.

"I see now President Sarauami, the only way to save the people of Hiro is to hand myself over to your school and stay here imprisoned like I was back in Eloma. You put me in a tight spot. If I stay then Hiro will get the help it needs, but I must stay here and forget about the sacred pilgrimage I have sworn to fulfil."

"Well I don't want to make it seem like blackmail Acarlie. I just want what's best for my people and you are a very talented elementalist and such a pretty one as well. The people will love and cherish you. They have only known you a short while and already they follow your words, if you stay here then everybody wins."

"Except me."

"Yes, but isn't sacrifice what the elementalists' life is really about? You are taken from birth and schooled, taking away your childhood, then sent on a voyage only to entertain the people that you have grown up knowing. Word will reach Eloma that their brave Acarlie saved two nations at once by taking a necessary choice given to her by the president himself."

The door from behind the president opened again and in popped a head of a leo, stepping through the door to address Acarlie. The president was shocked from what he saw, for all he knew the leos were extinct and there was one, large as life before him, rubbing his arm nervously knowing full well he was in the presence of the president but feeling the need to interrupt the negotiation.

"Acarlie, the Anglish have just arrived in their skyship sent from Hiro, may I remind you about–"

"There is no need to remind me Raiden, I know what I must do," Acarlie stepped away from the president and walked to the door, stopping briefly and turning around and addressing him again.

"President Sarauami, I'm sorry but I have to decline your offer of becoming the High Elementalist here in Mecroyles. Your offer was reasonable and if the circumstances were different then I would have taken it, but regardless of what has happened here I still have my oath to my people and a promise to my friends to find a missing companion. If you will not help me then I shall not help you. My ship is here now to pick me up and fly me back to Hiro where I shall warn the king myself of the imminent attack coming."

The president just smiled and nodded. He knew he needed her but was honourable enough to let her make her own choice.

"Very good then Acarlie, I am sorry we could not make a deal." He bowed his head respectfully towards her. "I wish you luck on your pilgrimage Acarlie, may we meet again someday."

"Thank you President Sarauami. We shall meet again some-day, hopefully in better circumstances." She returned the bowed gesture. "Come Raiden, show me the way to the skyship. We don't have any time to spare."

The president stood there under the broken ceiling with beams of light shining down behind him, lighting up the tiny pieces of dust floating in the air settling on his shoulder silently and he watched Acarlie walk out of the door to eventually leave his country.

Maybe I was a little hard on her, he thought as he stepped away from the spot where he stood. He peered over his shoulder at the broken wall behind him and out onto the empty, broken remains of his once great city. He was optimistic about this dis-aster though and knew that over time eventually his town would be rebuilt and the young elementalist would be strong and tour-ists would come again to watch the E.Bs. He couldn't help but wonder though what it would have been like if he managed to convince Acarlie into staying there.

The skyship Acarlie was lead to was huge, like the massive passen-ger ship she was on previously but with large propellers on the top of the ship reaching high above it and wings on either side each with more propellers and air thrusters underneath them to stabilise the ship when airborne. Acarlie was greeted by the captain of the ship. A well dressed Anglish army commander approached her. His short blond hair was barely visible as his head was covered by a beret. His posture strong like any other soldier and his grey uniform neatly ironed and creased in the right places with the Anglish signature symbol of a strange creature with the feet of a hawk, the arms of a lion and the head of a man on his collar. He approached Acarlie and politely bowed before her. She followed the gesture with a slight bow of her head.

"Elementalist Acarlie?" he asked her.

"Yes."

"My name is Commander Chez of the Anglish fleet. I have been asked by your king to fly here as requested by you, to collect you and give you a lift back to Hiro. I'm sorry I could not get here sooner but the Skycrawler behind me is not the fastest ship to sail the sky."

"That's ok Commander Chez, thank you for coming," she told him then remembered about Hiro and added, "On your journey here did you see an army marching or even sailing towards Hiro?"

"Acarlie, whilst in the Skycrawler it is hard to see anything that is below us. My pilots keep their eyes forward when flying, not downwards. If an army did pass, they would have certainly passed below us without our knowing, is anything the matter Elementalist?"

She thought for a second and wondered how far the Feydon army would be from Hiro now.

"Commander, it is of the utmost importance that I reach Hiro and report back to King Kerry immediately. We believe that a strike from Feydon is imminent if they haven't attacked the city already."

"What? Are you sure?"

"I don't have time to answer your questions right now Chez. Please escort me back to Hiro. I will explain when we are airborne."

"Very good Miss Acarlie, follow me then."

He quickly turned and pointed to some of his men that were on the Calmaron turf and shouted for them to get back on the ship and start the engines. Acarlie and the others made their short and final goodbyes to the people of Mecroyles and Acarlie made sure as an elementalist that the young Will got a message from her wishing him good luck on his training and hoping one day they would meet again as he was now back in training with his elders. The doors of the skyship closed and slowly and loudly the ship lifted up from the ground and using the power of the air thrusters on the bottom of it climbed into the air and turned its nose to the direction of Racoves and started its long journey back across the ocean to the city of Hiro.

32

The sun beamed down stinging hot rays to burn Val's skin. He briefly opened his eyes to find himself lying flat across scorching hot, white sand. The mute beside him was lying under his purple cloak since the sun was deadly to his fragile skin. Val lifted his head and slowly brushed off the salty sand that had stuck to his sweaty face. He grunted in exhaustion as he forced himself back up and almost fell again. As he sat there in the silence looking over at Dude trying to regain his strength the sound of heavy footsteps in the sand filled his ears. His head was light and his vision was blurry so all he could see in the distance was an animal-like creature walking toward him.

Raiden has come for me. Oh, praise Raiden for he has found me out here in this desert and has come to take me back, he thought to himself as he watched this creature slowly step-by-step draw closer to him. Soon he noticed that this creature was not Raiden but different. A creature that walked on four legs. A beast if he ever saw one. This creature walked on the ground like a lion and was as large as one or bigger with sharp shoulder plates slinking up and down giving it a powerful walk. If this quadruped stood on its hind legs it was easily taller than Raiden. Its body may have been the shape and the golden brown colour of a lion but when it came closer Val realised it resembled more of a dog than a cat with a long dog-like nose, large teeth and spiky ears. Val noticed though that humans must have interacted with this creature at some point because it wore a collar with metal spikes on it with flashing red lights next to them and on its head it wore what looked like a kind of helmet that covered its head and eyes. It gave a red glow to its eyes making it look like a demon from hell. Its jaw was larger than Raiden or Sheeria's and this huge beast that must have stood on four legs still reached up to Val's diaphragm, and it was walking straight for him. It's every step striking fear into Val like a hungry wolf would to a defenceless rabbit. The creature sniffed the air and loomed towards them, an aura of fear followed this ravenous, armoured beast. Val froze in fear, waiting for what this beast would do to him, hoping it would just pass him by. He waited as it walked up to him, sniffed down at Dude then turned to look at him with its evil looking red eyes and to Val's surprise, suddenly in a deep bass-like voice said to him.

"You're a long way from home Human. Why are you here?"

Val still frozen in fear just stared at the creature amazed that it could speak considering the size of its mouth. His voice was almost enchanting, not just the deep base sound like Raiden but this creature had a voice like an echoing whisper, like the tone of a wise, dying old man.

"Who are you?" was the only thing he could answer, still wide-eyed in terror.

The beast looked at him straight in the eye and said again in his seemingly elderly but strong voice, "You have never seen a kingnine before, no?" It's voice seemed to echo within Val and shake up his insides. Val shook his head and watched the beast laugh a wicked and loud laugh that trembled his insides once more.

The beast stopped laughing and looked back down at Val. "I am Zoudiva!" the beast said loud frightening Val more. "Pirate and smuggler; killer of men and hunter of lost prey in the desert."

Val knew that if this creature, this Kingnine wanted to kill him he could. Val was far too weak to fight such a creature but since he was a pirate maybe he could negotiate with it.

"Why are you out here Zoudiva?" he dared to ask him.

Zoudiva started to pace around him, every step still scared Val right down to the core of his body, even the training he had with Raiden was useless now. This beast knew the ways of striking fear into humans even more so than Raiden and froze Val to the spot where he sat. Zoudiva paced around in the sand behind him then appeared in front of him and answered, "I was sent out here by my master to scout out my colleagues that wondered out into the desert not long ago, instead I find two young men dying in the sand. Sorry, pardon me, a human and an aeomon," he said as he sniffed the dying Dude spread out on the floor.

Val knew what Zoudiva was trying to do and gathered his strength together and said faintly, "Stay away from him."

The kingnine growled when he said this, turned back to him and with a deep growl in his voice said to him, "I could kill you now Human, snap your neck like a twig in my mouth. Dare you tell me what to do? I only take orders from my master. You are weak Human, you don't have the strength to strike me let alone fight me, suppose I eat your friend? What will you do?"

He moved back to Dude on the floor and sniffed him again.

"Please don't kill us Zoudiva," Val said again. Everything was starting to spin again but Val tried to stay focused. This time Zoudiva did not growl back at him. Instead he said, "And what if I don't help you? Suppose I eat you instead?" he said and turned back to Val.

"What do you want?"

Zoudiva paused now and stared down at Val like he was thinking, "Hmm, you wish to bargain Human? Very well. What I wish is freedom from my master, to have a new master who would treat me as an equal rather than a pet."

"Your master, he is a pirate yes?"

The kingnine walked closer to him until his wet nose was touching Val, "My master is Captain Kaza Caines, pirate and smuggler."

"If he is a pirate then he will bargain right? Because I have something that he would want."

"Oh really? And what is that little human?" his old voice echoed again.

"A ship, a skyship. If you save us I will bargain with him, the skyship for our lives."

The beast walked back a bit and considered the deal.

"And if he says no?"

"He won't say no, this is an offer in his favour." Val's head swam again. He shook his head to refocus, "He can't refuse."

"Suppose there is no ship?"

"Then you can kill us both if the ship is not there."

The kingnine took a few seconds to consider his proposal before finally saying, "Very well you have a deal Human. Put the aeomon on my back and pick up your belongings, your lives for my freedom."

Val picked up Dude and placed him on Zoudiva's back and picked up the sword and his cloak and followed him through the last part of the empty desert and into the sandy town of passing people at many small market places.

"What is this place?" Val asked him.

"This is a secret pirate trading base, where smugglers come from all over the world to sell off their loot and spices and get money to carry on their pirating. The coast is to one side of us and on the other side, miles of desert that no one but you two have ever been found alive in."

"That's because the men who kidnapped us landed the ship just out of eye's view from this base, I guess to keep pirates from stealing it."

"If they did that then surely they would return soon Human."

"That's right so we must be quick."

"In here Human," Zoudiva said as he led him into a large hut which Val saw was a tavern with many merry pirates all drinking, shouting and squandering their money. The women in the bar were not waitresses nor dancers like in the bar at Hiro but prostitutes made to walk around to the pirates, flashing off their goods hoping the pirates would buy them for the night so they could eat tomorrow. This made Val think of the girl he saw to back in the baron's mansion. This is where the majority of the girls there would have ended up, slaves and whores to a bunch of dirty, sexually deprived pirates.

The tavern owner approached them and went to Zoudiva, "What have you here Zou', is he ok?" he asked referring to Dude.

"No. He needs medical attention immediately, make sure he gets it," he said as the tavern owner took Dude off his back and laid him on a table, grabbing a glass of water and forcing him to drink.

"He will be fine eventually, you brought him here in time Zou' but why?"

"Where is my master?" Zoudiva asked him ignoring his question.

"Over there at the back," the tavern keeper said pointing to the back wall where a large crowd was gathered around two tables put together. Before Val walked over to them he took a glass from the tavern keeper of his own and drank his life back.

"Follow me this way Human," Zoudiva said after he finished another glass and took one last breath before following the king-nine over to the table crowded with pirates; sweaty, drunk and merry pirates all shouting and laughing amongst the whores that surrounded them on dirty wooden tables filled with empty beer glasses and spilled wine. They laughed like they had not a care in the world, like everything they ever needed in this world was right with them in this stingy, dark tavern locked away from the extreme light outside. Women at their disposal, alcohol and the company of each other to spit at and laugh alongside each other like brothers but Val was hoping that there was something that they didn't have as pirates and also hoped he had what they wanted. In the middle of the drunken swaying loud pirates was their leader, sat there with two whores sitting around him, an arm around each one and his feet up on the table. He laughed like all his brothers as well as the whores who had accepted the life they had been forced into and now were no longer the innocent young girls from another country but changed into filthy prostitutes so used to their work that they started to enjoy the life and just forgot all about their old lives. His skin was darker than Val's but not because of dirt or freshness but ethnically, not as dark as Zahied's skin, but a golden light brown with short stringy black hair on his head. He wore a leather vest and shorts, with bangles of different metals on his wrists and woven, beaded necklaces. Over his eyes he wore dark glasses even in this dark environment, that shielded eye contact from Val and a rugged unshaven face that attracted the girls around him. He was large in size with wide shoulders that the two girls either side of him were rubbing. He had large knives in their sheaves tied to his legs with velcro showing all those around him that he was the one in this bar not to be meddled with. Val could only approach slowly thinking to himself, *I can't believe I have to do this again, approach someone I don't know and bargain with just for a ride in a skyship. This time I must do it right. I have the Scarlet and have the upper hand of the bargain. He is a pirate and cannot refuse a bargain like the one that I have for him. I just have to be subtle and watch where I step. These men will kill me if I make the wrong gesture, play with me psychologically if I seem weak or nervous. I have to be strong and present myself correctly, presentation is everything.*

"Hey Captain, look at this walking meat sack in front of us," one of the pirates laughed as Val approached them, limping like a beaten victim, Zoudiva at his side and stood in front of the table. "If I didn't know any better I would think this guy has a death wish."

The captain held up his hand to silenced his fellow pirate behind him and all of the pirates fell silent wanting to know what this beat up stranger in front of them wanted. Blood stained and still only able to see out of one eye Val just stood in front of the captain and his whores waiting for him to speak. The captain took his arms from around the whores and took his feet off the table and sat upright staring at Val, measuring and calculating him, searching for any hidden weapons before finally speaking to Zoudiva.

"Why is there a half dead man ruining my table of merry men Zoudiva? I sent you out to find the others and you come back with this."

Zoudiva looked down at the floor and avoided eye contact with his master like a dog to its human.

"This human says he has something to speak to you about. I brought him here believing he is true to his word Master."

"Is that right?" the captain said then sitting back and looking at Val. "Do you have something to say to me Dead Man? You look like you have been in a fight with a grinder and come out worse off. What's your story?"

Val stood up straight and remembered what he had to do, "Before I start let me introduce myself, I am Val, you must be Captain Kaza. I have come a long way and have something that I would like to bargain with you. I have something that you will want and I only ask for two small things in return."

The idea of a bargain silenced the captain and he then sat forward and waved his whores to leave his side. He gestured for Val to sit in front of him and crossed his arms.

"What is that I would want then Dead Man?" he asked sarcastically.

"Out in the desert is a very expensive and special skyship, it belongs to me but I have no use for it since I can't pilot it, all I need is a pilot to–"

Val's sentence was then silenced by the roar of laughter coming from the pirates including Kaza.

Val knew then he had to set it out right and asked them, "What's funny?"

Captain Kaza finished laughing then and told him in a loud drunken tone, "You don't need a pilot to fly a skyship! You need a crew!" The laughter continued at Val's expense. "And if you are looking for a crew then I am the captain of these here merry men. So then Dead Man, what is your bargain? What are we selling our services for a flight of the skyship for?"

"The skyship itself, you take me where I want to go when I am aboard then the ship is yours, no catch, no price, just my two favours."

The captain sat back now looking into the eye of the beaten and bruised Val and considered his offer. A free ship waiting in the desert, a skyship of his very own and all he has to do is take this one man where he wanted to go.

"What else do you ask of me for this ship?" he asked.

He's interested! Val thought with sudden excitement but pushed his thought aside and continued.

"Your kingnine earlier saved my life, in return I promised I would add him onto the bargain. He would belong to you no more and I would be his master," Val said firmly.

This now shocked the pirates around them and Val saw a look of anger in his eye, this Zoudiva was obviously a valued asset and would take more than a skyship to bargain with but the captain still wanted this ship and leaned forward again.

"That's now a heavy bargain you have Dead Man, now this makes your offer unfair on my half."

"Maybe the weight of the bargain will balance once I tell you the name of the ship Captain Kaza."

"Oh really, well, what's that then Dead Man? Tell me the name of this ship."

Val leaned forward this time and with his one good eye watching Kaza said slowly, "The Scarlet..." he saw Kaza's eyes widen from behind his glasses. "...Arise."

In the split second, he felt spun around. He felt his back thud hard followed by a knock on the back of his head and felt a heavy presence pressing up against his chest and a sharp pain pushing up into his throat. He found himself lying back against the table he was previously leaning over and could see Kaza now on top of him, arm forward revealing a large blade like weapon similar to the Tonfa Val saw back in Walton and pressing it hard into his neck. Suddenly Val found it hard to breathe and dared not swallow in fear that the blade would slice his laryngeal prominence off. Kaza leaned in so close to Val that the only thing Val could smell was his hot, beer sweaty breath and rasped at him, "Dare you try and fool me with a promise of the Scarlet! I'll stick your head on my mantle piece as a trophy amongst my companions and bath in your blood if you even think you can fool me with the Scarlet Arise. The Scarlet is under the control of the Anglish army and they will not let her go so easily boy!"

Val tried to push Kaza off his chest but this only made Kaza push down harder, crushing into his diaphragm. Val choked and could only whisper under his throat, "The Scarlet is not under the control of the Anglish."

Kaza loosened up his grip of his weapon sticking into Val's throat and let him continue. Val took another second to catch his breath back and continued, "The people who stole it from the Anglish were led by a pimp and his crew I found in Hiro."

"Why were you with them?" Kaza asked looking into Val's eyes wanting to see lies but could only see honesty.

"I and my companions have been seeking a lift on a skyship since the beginning on my journey from Walton. We need to get to a monastery in Aragorth. I was separated from my friends in Hiro and made a deal with the pimp on the condition that I steal an artefact from some mansion."

Kaza sneered at Val, "Looks like you were mislead by this pimp Dead Man, and taken a long way away from Hiro. What makes you think I will take an offer from you?"

"You have walked in here beaten black and blue, disrupted me and my crew's merry time and tried to take my Zoudiva away from me and offer me something I don't believe you are in the position to give away."

"Listen to me Kaza!" Val tried to shout but only a feared squeak came out, "The pimp is bound and tied in the ship. He can't escape but his crew will return soon. Once he is unbound he will take control of the ship again."

"Maybe that's what I want. Once he boards he will come looking for you and we will intercept him, try and swap you for the ship or just take it from him."

Val was stunned by the quick mind of Kaza; this was obviously why Kaza was the leader and superior to the crew of drunken pirates.

Val thought fast and remembered the pirate the pimp killed earlier.

"Your colleagues Kaza; the ones you sent Zoudiva out there for. The pimp caught some pirates and executed them when we landed—"

"Don't lie to me Dead Man!" Kaza snapped at him cutting him from his sentence.

"I'm not lying to you Kaza!" Val shouted right back at him.

Kaza finally loosened up on his grip and lifted Val back to his feet. Val brushed himself down and stood up straight.

"Now look, if you want the Scarlet Arise then you're going to need me since I know the way to the ship, if he gets back the ship then he will flee and return back here with greater numbers, because that aeoman over there..." Val pointed over across the tavern to Dude now conscious and sitting up and sipping the water that the tavern keeper had given him. "He has the artefact that we were sent to steal, so he will be back for me but he will have the upper hand since he will have hired mercenaries and the ship. Now I have made a deal with Zoudiva here and the bargain I have made is solid, I promise, but I can't keep my side of the bargain and you will never be the captain of the ship if you don't help me to help you."

Kaza, now believing Val took a step back and ran his finger down the side of his large knife's edge considering Val proposal.

"What will it be Captain Kaza? Glory of owning the fastest ship in the sky or having my dirty head on a mantel piece?" Val asked him directing a dirty, blood stained finger toward him.

Kaza looked to his men; there must have been a crew of thirty strong, forty if you included the whores that surrounded them, all looking at him for confirmation on what to do next. Kaza who felt the excitement and thrill of the chase inside him began to burn through his body, the idea of owning the Scarlet Arise to go where he pleaded, in a pirate style bargain of which the Anglish cannot deny its authenticity. It would not be stolen property but swapped with Val and he knew that once this was done the Anglish could never take it back. He held up his arm and his sharp weapon that he held with a handle and the sharp edge ran down past his elbow and further past his fist extending his reach in the air and with the other arm held it out for Val to shake.

"You make a fine proposal Dead Man, the Scarlet Arise for my Zoudiva and access to any place in the world when you are aboard. Zoudiva, it has been a pleasure to be your master for so long and I'm reluctant about this but this man here is your new master, serve him well. But know this Dead Man, if the ship is not there then the deal is off, right?"

"That's right so if you're ready I would like to take you there now."

"Very good," Kaza then turned and called out to one of his men. "Oran! Get the men assembled, we will take the sand buggies. Dead Man and the aeomon will take lead with me. Everyone else grab your weapons and follow us to our new home!"

His men all cheered then and finished the rest of the drink that they were holding and scattered around the tavern picking up weapons and flooding out into the sun like wild dogs.

"You stay with me Dead Man, come with me and show me where my ship is," Kaza finally said putting his arm around Val's neck and patting his back, leading him to the door leading outside back into the sweltering heat.

Out in the desert in the sweaty sticky heat the Scarlet Arise was still stationed in the sand in the distance out of the way of the pirate trading base. In the stillness of the dead, sandy wasteland the sound of the sand buggies with loud engines roaring and the sound of the pirates shouting and screaming their war cries cut the dry silence.

"There she is Kaza! Over there past the dunes, do you see?" Val called out over the sound of the engines pointing over to the ship in the distance.

"Yes, I see her!" Kaza shouted back and steered in the direction of it.

As all the buggies followed Kaza and Val in the leading buggy Zoudiva ran on the ground beside them. His strong legs enabled him to take large, powerful strides across the sandy floor and could keep up easily with the buggies. As soon as Zoudiva saw the ship he picked up his pace and started speeding off in front of the pack of pirates and was soon closing in on the ship like a cheetah to its prey.

"Where's he gone?" Val asked.

"He's going to give us the upper hand Dead Man! The crew won't know what hit them, and try and defend themselves, before they know it we'll be there too. It's called tactics!"

Back on the Scarlet Arise, Gendrick was standing back in the cockpit with his pilot and some of his crew. The rest were outside loading crates of cargo containing clothes, spice and weapons he would sell back in Hiro, use the money to gain more mercenaries and return back here to hunt for Fireshaver again. One of his men came rushing through the door in a panic after he was summoned, "You called me boss?"

"What's the hold up? We should be in the air by now!" Gendrick snapped.

"Boss, we are being attacked by what looks like a wild kingnine. It came charging in from nowhere and had already mauled and killed three of the men. We're handling the situation now boss."

"Just kill the bastard and get the men inside now. We're losing time here!"

"Actually boss you should take a look at this," his pilot said leaning over to look out of the window.

Gendrick looked out of the window and saw the buggies racing toward them in the sand. He squinted his eyes to see Val in the front buggy and a load of screaming, battle ready pirates behind him. He turned back to his man, "Get the men inside now, we leave now! Anyone who isn't inside gets left behind!"

"Yes boss, right away!"

The buggies were now in range and Val could see Zoudiva fighting the men there outside the ship, biting at their arms and ripping down, injuring them. The men started fleeing inside the ship's cargo doors leaving boxes and crates still out in the sand. The ship was still on the ground when the pirates' buggies reached it. The pirates jumped out and ran aboard killing all the unsuspecting pimp's men in their way. The ship's doors started to slowly close and when aboard, Val quickly looked outside to see Zoudiva still fighting one of the men. He pounced on top of him and was gouging his chest. Val knew he couldn't leave the creature that saved his life out there in the desert and quickly ran to him.

"Come on Zoudiva!" was all he shouted as he grabbed his collar and yanked him away from the man and pushed him toward the closing door. Zoudiva sprinted aboard the ship with Val closely behind him as the last person aboard when the ship started to lift off back into the air and close all doors containing all the pirates and pimp's men in the cargo hold.

"To the deck!" screamed the pimp's men as they retreated from the cargo hold and on to the upper deck of the ship. Kaza looked back at his men. He now had one of his bladed tonfas in each hand, turning his arms into deadly weapons and called to them, "They are outnumbered and have no place to hide now, the ship is ours!"

His men cheered and ran for the decking above them holding their weapons high with pure war in their eyes.

The pimp was still standing in the cockpit when one of his men came to him, red faced from exhaustion and scared of what will happen.

"What's happening?" Gendrick asked.

"Boss, it came too quickly, they're all aboard boss, all of them! The men have retreated to the deck where we will try and fight them but we're outnumbered boss and most of us don't have weapons."

"What about the weapons in the cargo room?"

"The pirates have secured the cargo room boss; the last chance we have is to fight the pirates off the ship on the upper deck!"

Gendrick slammed his hand down on the control panel next to him and cursed. He then pulled out a short sword from behind him and went to the pilot, "Keep the ship above the ground and don't flip her, we'll all be on the deck so keep her steady!" then stormed out to find the boy that caused him all this trouble.

The upper deck was now full of men, both the pimp's men and pirates, hacking and slashing away at each other in a desperate attempt to secure the ship for themselves. Men were either cut down or thrown off the ship to fall down to an uncharted and forgotten sandy grave. Kaza had sent his pilots to reach the cockpit to try and take control of the ship while he and his other men fought the pimp's men. The sound of screams and war cries was all they could hear out there in the sky and not even the ship's engines could be heard. Men from both parties were meeting the same fate from either sharp weapons cutting their flesh or being kicked off the side of the deck to disappear forever. Soon the pirates were crushing the pimp's men, as they were better fighters and better equipped. The pirates had them backed against a wall leaving their wounded behind them. Kaza was leading his men into the final extermination of the pimp's men when he saw the pimp himself reach the deck. He was better dressed than his men, sand and blood stained his expensive clothes, and with a short sword in hand. He headed for Val as soon as he saw him. Kaza intercepted the pimp's path towards Val by quickly charging toward him, arm held up to one side and clotheslined him to the floor. Gendrick fell hard and dazed on the floor when Kaza picked him up and dragged him to the side of the deck, slit the back of his ankles and left him there kneeling in front of him. All of the pimp's men now stopped fighting and watched their leader kneeling there at the side of the ship in front of the pirate captain. This was exactly what Kaza wanted. He wanted the men to see their ship being taken from them. This way they would surrender without any more of his men being injured. The pirates now also stopped fighting and everything stood still while Kaza had the pimp in a checkmate position. He held onto his bladed tonfas and standing like a giant in front of Gendrick. He waited for him to say something. The pimp knew what would happen here and knew there was nothing he could do about it now. He had lost and now only fate stood before him in the shape of an angry pirate. He spat at Kaza's feet, "The Anglish will find this ship, you know? And when they do I hope they hang you all, you dirty, stinking pirates."

Kaza just stood there and as Val watched he noticed that Kaza was like a leo or a tigian at this point. His stance suggested that he was striking fear into the pimp, Gendrick wasn't buying it but this was not only for the pimp to see. Val looked over to see fear now in the eyes of his men. They could now see that these pirates were led by a great and strong leader who had their boss right where he wanted him, ready to execute him. Kaza looked down at the blood diluted spit on his boot and looked back at the pimp and said in a loud, strong tone so the crew would hear him, "Get off my ship!" and lifted a leg and struck the pimp with a kick knocking him off the side of the ship to fall to a hard, sandy death below him. With their hope now lost the pimp's men now held up their hands and surrendered to Kaza. He looked back at these men, walked back to the door of the ship leading back into it and with his large, bladed tonfas, carved a giant *K* in the door and shouted, "This ship now belong to me, Captain Kaza Caines!"

The pirates cheered and held their weapons high, the ship was theirs. They were now pirates of the sky, nothing could stop them now, they now had the fastest ship in the sky and it was all thanks to the beaten up stranger who appeared from out in the desert.

"What about the other men captain?" one of the pirates asked Kaza.

Kaza thought for a minute and looked down at his fallen comrades dead on the floor and came up with an idea to regain his numbers.

"Bring them here!" he signalled to his men to each grab a man each and march them in custody to him. Kaza waited until all of them could see what he wanted to do and ordered the first of the men to come to him. He saw this technique work only once when he was a young pirate and under the orders of another. The first man came to him shaking with fear, Kaza leaned forward and silently whispered in the man's ear, "Will you work for me?"

He whispered because he didn't want the men to know the question and therefore could not just give him the answer he wanted.

"Yes," the man whispered back and was thrown aside and into the custody of one of the pirates.

"Kill him!" Kaza ordered.

Another man was pushed in front of him, just like before Kaza leaned forward and whispered "Will you work for me?"

"Yes," the man said and this time Kaza threw him to his other side and shouted, "Keep him!"

Another man now came to him, "Will you work for me?" he whispered.

"No," the man said and Kaza grabbed him and threw him behind him off the side of the ship where the man screamed and disappeared in a second. Kaza continued this process each time killing all those who said no and splitting all those who said yes into two parties, this made the pimp's men scared, not knowing what Kaza was asking them and not knowing the right answer to keep their lives and so this made the men all honest when they answered.

After the last man was thrown aside Kaza turned back to address them all, "You in both parties both said you would work for me. I split you up in two groups so you would think that there was more than just a yes or no answer, the truth is you will not be killed. The two groups were actually only one, the ones who would work for me. Now you have said yes you must now prove it. I want your first jobs to be to pick up your dead companions and throw them overboard. My men will watch you carefully. If any of you get and clever ideas of trying to strike back, we will kill you and the man next to you, after this you will each individuality come and speak to me so I can decide whether or not you will make worthy pirates.

"Also to my men, you know the drill. We may have just been fighting but as far as I'm concerned these men are now part of my crew and part of yours, so whatever one of them just did to you I want you to forget about it, understood?"

"Yes Captain!" the pirates shouted back.

"Captain we have one here!" shouted Dillon, the pirates' pilot and holding onto the pimp's pilot.

"No wait, I'm a pilot, I can work for you, I can work for you!" the pilot screamed and Kaza only grabbed him and pulled him close, shouting in his face, "I already have a pilot!" and threw him overboard.

"Let that be a lesson to all of you!" Kaza shouted to all his men, "If I don't want you then I *will* throw you overboard my ship! I don't like crew members that are useless to me. Now get to work, all of you!"

Kaza now entered the cockpit of his ship and found Val there with Dude and Zoudiva as well as one of his pilots.

"So how do you like our bargain?" Val asked him.

"I like it Dead Man, as far as I'm concerned me and you are friends. You will get no trouble from me nor any of my men, and like I promised, whenever you are on-board the Scarlet Arise I will take you where you need to go. Now what did you say your name was again?" Kaza said holding out his hand. Val shook it realising he now had a useful ally.

"Val."

"So where is our first destination Val?" Kaza finally corrected.

"To Hiro Captain Kaza!"

"Please, you have no need to call me Captain Val. You are not one of my men, just call me Kaza. Dillon, Smythy!" he called to his two pilots. "Set a course for Hiro!"

"Aye Aye Captain!" they shouted back.

"So Val now we have time, maybe you would tell me what your story is then?"

"I will shortly Kaza. I will let you be a captain and do your duties first," Val said and as the Scarlet Arise was finally under his control he thought to himself, *here I come Raiden. I finally have a skyship, and we can finally make our way to the temple.*

33

Out on top of the Skycrawler was a large and luxurious wooden decking that overlooked the country below it. The ship sailed gracefully in the sky despite its massive size. It was like a cruise ship of the sky, no weapons were fitted on this ship, just like the Scarlet Arise. This kind of ship was only used by the army to transport men or heavy machinery, meaning it was huge in size and capable of flying whilst carrying more heavy materials but slow and steady unlike the fast, swift but small Scarlet Arise which was only built as a prototype scout ship for the Anglish Armada. Hours passed and Acarlie stood out on the decking thinking she could now drop all her formalities now she wasn't in the presence of elders, presidents or commanders of the Anglish. Acarlie felt a small relief as she stood close to the edge of the ship and peered over Calmaron at the plains of green grass and woodland, wild lizziers were running free beneath the ship and she remembered the talk she had with the president. She couldn't help but wonder if the choice she made was the right one and episodes began in her mind with different scenarios of the outcome of the other choice she could have made; giving up her pilgrimage and becoming a full-time elementalist of Mecroyles, possible fame and fortune for saving Hiro but being hated by her own people down in Eloma, and without her help her lost friend Val never found as she was unable to continue her quest to find him. She heard the heavy and familiar footsteps of a tigian behind her and said without turning, "Hello Sheeria."

"Are you ok Acarlie? You look troubled."

"I'm fine Sheeria."

Sheeria had heard this answer many times before and stepped closer to Acarlie, "What did the president say to you?"

"He wanted me to be High Elementalist representing Calmaron. Without me now they are a country which cannot compete in the league. He wanted me to help in return for Calmaron marching to Racoves to assist Hiro in its attack."

Sheeria stayed silent, she knew the size of this decision Acarlie had just made and looked over at Acarlie who now was leaning up against a banister with her hands covering her face.

"I just feel like I have made the wrong choice. What if Hiro is destroyed and I had the chance to save it? But asking me to leave my pilgrimage and mission to find Val..."

She couldn't finish her sentence as Sheeria now had her in her arms comfortingly and stood there stroking her hair.

"Don't worry about that Acarlie this is not your fault. He was wrong to put that kind of decision on to you. He just didn't understand that's all."

"I know but what was I supposed to do?" Acarlie said whilst embraced in Sheeria's arms.

"You did the right thing Acarlie, this mess isn't yours to clean up. I've been trying to tell you this all along. Don't feel bad for turning down an opportunity to save people. You did what you were meant to do and stayed on course of your destiny. You now have three elements out of seven and word is slowly spreading of your current success Acarlie, you must stay on track of the pilgrimage to become the Elemental Lord."

Acarlie remained silent then knowing Sheeria was right and just stayed safe in her arms secretly thanking the fact that she was there with her. More hours passed still, day turned to night, night turned to day and still the Skycrawler was passing over the ocean on its way to Hiro. Acarlie had just finished reporting to Commander Chez about the Feydon army and what they had done to Mecroyles out on the deck. The sun was now bright and even though high in the air, a warm wind swept past the outer decking of the skyship. Chez listened to every word of what happened to all of them in the group, knowing that he would have to soon report this news back to his superiors back in Angland. His concentration was broken when one of his men came running out onto the deck shouting for him in a panic.

"Commander, we have a situation sir!"

"What is it?" he quickly asked back.

"It's better if I show you sir, it's important."

Seeing the fear in his eyes Chez followed his crewman, Acarlie and her companions followed behind him. They were led down into the cockpit of the ship and his crew member passed him a pair of binoculars and pointed to a small dot floating in the sky beyond.

"What is it?" Acarlie asked squinting her eyes so she could make out what it was.

Chez didn't answer straight away but stared at the dot before finally realising what it was, "It's a skyship," he finally reported.

"That's not just a skyship sir, look closer at it. Look at its shape and model," his pilot informed him.

Chez did as his pilot said and soon realised and said dumbstruck, "The Scarlet Arise!"

"What's the Scarlet Arise?" Acarlie asked again now seeing that it was a ship up there in the sky.

"It's a ship that belongs to the Anglish army, a prototype that was stolen from us. It has been lost in the sky until now. Mister Flanskin, set a course for the Scarlet."

"I don't know if we should do that sir," the pilot reported back to him.

"Why is that?"

"Look closely; look at the people on board."

Chez looked again, this time longer trying to make out the passengers on board.

"Pirates!" he said.

"Pirates? You can't be serious about this decision Commander Chez! What about taking us back to Hiro?" Acarlie asked again.

"The ship looks like it's heading for Hiro Acarlie, we're not going out of our way. We have been searching for this ship for a long time, it's very important that we recapture it."

"If it's so important, how could you lose it in the first place?" Raiden asked breaking his silence and putting an awkward question to Chez.

"That's not important Leo and if you still want this lift to wherever you want to go then I would like to add that this is still my ship and I decide where I go with it. Set course for the Scarlet Arise Mister Flanskin, gather the crew and get ready to board the ship. We're going to cut all those filthy, stinking pirate thieves from the sky." He went to walk out of the cockpit but was blocked by Raiden.

"If you're serious about doing this then you're going to need my help. I am stronger than anyone on board and you'll have the ship cleared quicker if I was on your side."

"Very well then Leo, go with the crew and fetch your armour. We'll board the ship and kill all who's aboard."

"Raiden, how can you do this?" Acarlie asked him.

"Look, we need this done as quickly as possible so we can get to Hiro, right? Just stay here and keep safe. Once we're there I will have the job done quicker."

Acarlie stayed quiet then knowing she could not stop Raiden if he wanted to go.

"Be safe then and come back in one piece," Sheeria added. Raiden nodded and left the cockpit followed by Chez. Acarlie looked back through the wind shield of the ship and onto the approaching small skyship in front of them.

Val was sitting inside the cargo room with Zoudiva on the Scarlet Arise. Some boxes from when the pimp was loading up were still on-board as Captain Kaza did not want to lose the cargo. Otherwise the room was pretty empty apart from a few crew walking up and down. Zoudiva was lying on his stomach with his head resting on his paws when he felt Val stroking the top of his head.

"Zoudiva, tell me about your race. The kingnines, what are they?"

"You mean you really don't know? Who are you Master? I have never known a man who knows as little of the world as you do?"

"It's ok Zou', just call me Val."

"No, you are my Master and that is what I shall always know you as until I die or you give me to another human to serve."

This reply shocked Val a little, "You were born into servitude?"

The kingnine just looked up at his master and answered him quietly in his husky, echoing voice, "Born into servitude? We kingnines were bred for servitude. Every single kingnine that has ever walked the sphere has served a human master. We are the protectors; genetically engineered by human cross-breeding the strongest and loyal of ancient creatures called wolves and leos."

"Leos? So you are related to the leos then?"

"The same way you are related to the mute aeomon, our ancestors were of the same blood. Our species has handed the legend down from father to son, mother to daughter that when the leos were in servitude to the elders the humans tried to accomplish the same idea but the only other animal which were loyal to them were the wolves, dogs and k-nines. But as loyal as they were, their strength and intellect was nothing compared to the newly evolved lions, what we now call leos, so the humans mixed the species together."

"But why? What was the point of this? Were the humans just jealous of the loyalty the leos gave to the elders?"

Zoudiva looked up again in disbelief but answered his master bluntly, "The Leo Divide Master? The one separating the leos from the humans."

Val remembered Raiden speaking of this when back in Walton, "Yes, wasn't that the divide where the leos controlled the world and enslaved or killed the humans?" he asked him.

"No Master, the divide you are talking about was the one before the one I am talking about. *The Leo Divide*, also known as the 'Last Divide', the one where the humans began to strike back at the leos and take the planet back. We kingnines were engineered then to help our masters in battle with the leos; mixing the two together, K-nine, Feline... Kingnine. But it was always told to me in my upbringing that we were a mistake. Originally the humans wanted a creature that could walk and talk and fight like a leo but stay loyal to the humans like the K-nines did but instead they got us. We cannot walk like the leos but talk like them and because of our primitive four legged bodies we are better fighters and that makes us the only creature on the planet that can kill a leo in a one on one combat. But it gives us a disadvantage not walking on two feet like our masters and so we serve, ever protecting them from the monstrous leos we may be genetically linked to but have always waged war upon."

Val knew what this meant and asked Zoudiva anyway, "So what would you do then if a leo happened to approach me?"

"Then I would rip the beast's head off and offer it to you as a symbol of my loyalty to you. You freed me from my last master and saved me by getting me on this ship. It may have been nothing to you Master but it was a big deal for me back then."

"Well you asked for a better master in our bargain and you got one Zou'."

"Let's just be thankful that there are no more leos around Master."

The ship suddenly rocked violently and the voice of the captain came from little speakers in the corner of the room.

"This is Captain Kaza, I want all men on deck immediately. There is a large ship heading towards us and they don't look friendly. Everyone grab your weapons and get out on deck! The Anglish want their ship back and I'm not prepared to give it up easily!"

Many pirates started running past them with their swords unsheathed and heading for the deck above them. Zoudiva quickly leaped to his feet and dashed off following them and Val slowly stood up, called his staff and ran to the cockpit to find Kaza.

The two ships almost collided if not for the piloting of Dillon and Smythy, gently manoeuvring the ship around the large thrusters of the Anglish ship. The pirates all stood out on the top deck of the Scarlet Arise. They held up their weapons, shouting and screaming when the two ships now drew level and they could see the Anglish, well dressed army standing on their deck next to them. They stood there in the safety of their own crew members taunting the crew on the other ship, separated by a large gap which went down for miles before meeting the water below them as the two ships now flew side by side, like two battleships of the ocean. The pirates chanted and taunted like football hooligans and thugs whilst the Anglish stood strong and repeatedly struck the bottom of their weapons on the ground in successful timing making a loud drumming sound.

Kaza stood in front of his men and looked over to the army, their leader in the grey uniform was holding up his sword and pointing it at him. Kaza jumped up on the side of his ship and held on to a banister supporting himself and holding up one of his bladed tonfas with his other hand.

"If you want this ship!" he called over the chanting and drumming of both groups. "Come here and take her from me!"

His shout was followed by a roar of excitement of his men, now hyped up for the fight and ready to battle.

"Sir, what's the order?" one of the Anglish asked Commander Chez. Chez looked over the ship at the enemy pirate standing on the banister, now climbing back down, "Kill them all," he said bluntly and watched as his men quickly pulled out a sliding bridge with two banisters with strong hooks on the other side which hooked into the side of the Scarlet Arise giving the soldiers a safe access to the ship.

"Let them come boys! We can take them once they're aboard, let them walk across the bridge and either fall to their deaths or fall onto our steel!" Kaza shouted to his men, while clenching his jaw and gritting his teeth. He smiled and gripped onto his weapons waiting for the first soldier to cross the small bridges. Like a wave the soldiers leaped across the bridge. They only had a couple of steps to take before they had jumped onto the deck of the Scarlet and into the crowd of pirates and their blades. Some soldiers swung from ropes onto the ship and within only a few minutes the whole of the deck was filled with both Anglish and pirates alike. Like rival gangs they rumbled on top of the small scout ship, screams were heard from both parties as they were thrown overboard or stabbed continuously until they stopped moving. Blood was spilled and soaked into the decking making the floor slippery for the fighters and caused more casualties. Swords and knives clanked as they connected with each other, voices screamed every now and again from fatal wounds and the continuing sound of fists, feet and weapons filled the air. Finally, to the pirates' horror, a leo leaped from one ship to another, picking up the first pirate he could grab and throwing him overboard, then another and slammed him into the ground cracking his skull.

Raiden peered through the fighting soldiers and pirates, slashing at the pirates in his way and trying to find the leader. He knew he could take the ship if the crew lost its captain. He ran to the centre of the deck in a rage and became the main focus for all the pirates on board who tried to attack the beast but were slain by the soldiers defending him. Beyond a few more pirates in his way he found what he was looking for. One single pirate holding two long bladed tonfas. This pirate had just finished off one of the soldiers by flipping him over and slashing his arm across so that his weapon sliced his throat open and blocked another attack from a neighbouring soldier. He kicked him in the groin and stabbing him in the heart swiftly and cleanly. Next to him was another fighter dressed differently. This fighter was battling two soldiers himself with a staff. Raiden did not take any notice of this other man until he saw that this man fought differently than everyone else. His stance was lower, his movements were stronger, his roar was loud and threatening. Raiden watched this man drop his staff and jump for the man and start repeatedly punching the soldier, rolling to one side quickly dodging another attack and slashing like a leo would. He couldn't believe his cat-like eyes. There was Val not only standing there large as life but also fighting like a leo as he taught him, "Val!" he called out amongst the crowd of fighting pirates and started charging towards him barging everything that was in his way. He was about to reach Val when a frightening deep voice barked and snapped at him with razor sharp teeth that even the leo felt fear towards.

"Stay back from my master you dirty monstrous bastard!" yelled the creature standing in front of Raiden, blocking his path.

Raiden immediately saw red and a fiery rage swelled and exploded when he saw this creature before him. A kingnine, the creatures used to exterminate all of his kind and natural enemy, now standing there defending his human brother, like *he* was the enemy.

With a wild roar that took everyone's attention Raiden charged and slammed into his quadruped nemesis, picked him up and threw him again. Zoudiva only pounced back up and sprang up at the beast he was born to murder, teeth barred and together they started bundling into each other like a man fighting a dog, viciously striking one another and biting each other's fur.

Val heard the screams of his kingnine and looked up to see Zoudiva battling, his opponent, none other than his brother and mentor.

"Raiden!" Val called out and leaped into the two fighters and tried separating them apart.

"Stay back from it Master, the beast will kill you!" Zoudiva called out.

"Val keep back from that dirty cur! That's the creature that killed all of my kind!" Raiden barked and ordered.

Zoudiva growled but quickly noticed and looked up to Val, "Wait Master, you know this monster?" Zoudiva asked.

Raiden seemed to rediscover an ancient, youthful anger and malice then, screaming back, "You're the monsters! You genetically engineered abominations! You exist only to serve bastard humans and wipe out the strong and honourable!" He pointed a bloody claw angrily down at Zoudiva.

Val still held them apart and shouted over the commotion, "Stop this both of you! Raiden, this Kingnine is mine. I saved him; and Zoudiva, this is my brother and mentor Raiden. You must not attack him."

Raiden was the first to step back; he cared deeply for Val and knew that the kingnine would not hurt him, when reality struck him. He looked at the violence around him and turned back to Val.

"Val these people are fighting their allies!"

"What!?"

"Tell the leader of the pirates to stop fighting. Trust me Val, do it! I will do the same!" Raiden insisted then disappeared back to find the commander.

Val looked back at Zoudiva who stood there bewildered and looked back up to find Kaza. He sprinted to Kaza, grabbing onto him shouting, "Stop the fighting Kaza, call off your men!"

"Why should I?" he asked punching a solider and popping his nose.

"Because my friend is with the soldiers, he will call them off as well. Trust me Kaza, do it! Call off your men!"

Kaza stared at Val then and into his eyes seeing the honesty and desperation. He knew he wasn't lying and even though he didn't want to stop, he trusted Val and held up his hand and started calling out, "Stop fighting!" pulling his men away from killing more soldiers and repeating his words. Val copied him and soon the rest of the pirates followed. At first the soldiers started believing that the pirates were forfeiting and carried on slashing away but another call from the other side of the ship started calling off the soldiers until there was only Kaza and Chez left pulling their men back and silencing the crowd.

Everyone stood panting and watching the two party leaders now facing each other.

"Now tell me why I have called off my men Leo," Chez asked Raiden behind him still staring at the pirate before him.

Val stepped forward and spoke to the commander, "Sir, if you are a friend of Raiden then you are a friend of mine and I will ensure that none of your men are further attacked, isn't that right Kaza?"

Kaza said nothing but stood there strong and stared at the commander in the eye, his arms crossed like Raiden always does and let Val continue.

"If it's the ship you were after then I'm afraid you're too late to reclaim it. The man who stole it from you traded the ship with me for his life. I then traded it with Captain Kaza here for a lift wherever I needed to go. So I'm sorry but this may have been a stolen ship but it now legally belongs to the pirates behind me."

"You lying little..." the commander started but Raiden broke in.

"Chez, Val is not a liar. He is one of us. He is the one Acarlie is looking for?"

A sudden and secret excitement quickly filled Val when he heard her name, *Acarlie! She is on this ship and looking for me, so she is safe?*

Chez believed Raiden as he knew he was with Acarlie and knew Acarlie would vouch for him as well. He knew he could not ever get the ship back legally now. He had no choice but to believe Val about the trade.

"Where is the man responsible for stealing the Anglish ship then? I would like to punish him myself?"

"He's dead. Thrown overboard, you can search for his body if you like, it might be a little damaged though since it would have spread itself all across the Anglish desert," Kaza put in and Chez quickly replied back to Val.

"If that is so then you did not keep your side of the bargain."

"Actually he was trying to steal the ship back after I already had traded it with Kaza here. We caught him trying to steal it and reclaimed it back swiftly."

Val slightly changed the story here but he knew the commander wouldn't know and therefore could not do anything about it.

Chez's face reddened with anger then. It was checkmate and he knew it. The ship was stolen from him but now it belonged to these pirates. He knew that the ship wasn't a legal trade to begin with since it wasn't the pimp's legal property to trade in the first place but he knew the laws about trade, and right now the pirates had legal ownership here and there was absolutely nothing he could do about it. He turned back to his men and signalled for them to pick up the wounded and carry them back aboard the Skycrawler.

"We're both flying for Hiro so we'll fly together. You, Pirate; I know the ship is yours and I will not try to take it from you," Chez said to Kaza. Kaza did not cheekily smile here nor make a witty remark but stood there in the mutual agreement and waited.

"But right now I need you aboard my ship to discuss what is going to happen to Hiro. If you are with this boy and this boy is with the Elementalist then we are on the same side, you too boy. We need to talk to you."

Too many questions came then all at once.

"What's going to happen to Hiro?" Val asked.

"You're with an elementalist?" Zoudiva asked.

"Everything will be explained inside. Call back your men and fly beside the ship," Commander Chez suggested and walked across the plank followed by Kaza who quickly informed his men what was happening.

"Before we go in Raiden this has to be done," Val said pulling him aside.

"What's that then?" Raiden asked but then was stood before the kingnine again.

"Zoudiva, I want you to listen to me very carefully. This is Raiden, my brother, mentor and best friend. As long as you are under my service then you will protect Raiden as you would protect me understand? I know your two species have history but Raiden is very special to me and you will not harm Raiden in any way at all," he ordered his kingnine.

Zoudiva was hesitant at first but bowed his head, "This is very untraditional Master. But if you wish." He growled like a feral wolf towards Raiden.

"Good and Raiden, this kingnine's name is Zoudiva. He

saved my life and in return I freed him from his old master, Captain Kaza and now gave him a master who would treat him as an equal, me; so as long as he's with–"

"I get what your saying Val." Raiden shrugged off Val's grip and warned them both, "Just keep your new *pet* away from me."

Zoudiva bowed his head again in agreement and they both gave themselves the same silent look each saying to each other, *if only Val wasn't here.*

"Just know that if that *thing* so much as looks at me while you're not around I'm going to skin it and wear it's hide!" Zoudiva again barked and snapped while Val held him back. Raiden spat down on the deck and turned his back on both of them and boarded the other ship.

"How can you know that evil monster Master?" Zoudiva asked once Raiden was gone.

"I'll explain it all later Zoudiva. Just stay out of his way."

"With pleasure," he growled and finally turned. "I suppose you'll need the Quite One to accompany us. I'll go find him Master."

34

At first glance of the giant juggernaut of a skyship Kaza didn't like the look of the Skycrawler. It was too big for his liking. The ceiling was unnecessarily too high for him and all he thought about when he walked down the corridors with Val, Dude, Raiden and Zoudiva was how bad this ship would be if he controlled it. Being too big it would make it really slow, good for carrying and smuggling spice and other things but easy to spot in the sky. Glowglobes hung from the ceiling giving a light in the darker corridors at night, another thing Kaza didn't like but after he saw the cockpit and crew for the first time he had to credit the ship for being handled so professionally and skilfully in keeping this heavy bird in the sky as well as they did. The cockpit in the Skycrawler ran like an office, only a small murmuring was heard from the cabin crew as they steered and kept the ship afloat with computers and controls, unlike the Scarlet Arise which could be piloted by just one person if needed, but ran more efficiently with two. Dillon was the pilot and Smythy was his co-pilot, Kaza first hand picked them for his crew a few years ago after his last one crashed his seaship in a long venture that ended up with him forming his current crew. Val waited in the cockpit patiently while Raiden went to fetch Acarlie and the others. Dude who was now wearing dark goggles he found in the Scarlet's infirmary tightly over his eyes looked strange because he looked like a swimmer now but refused to take the goggles off or change them for glasses. Val thought maybe Dude wanted to keep them because they were harder to lose since they were tightly wrapped around his head with a strong elastic strap, but really Dude wanted to keep them because he simply liked them. Not often did Dude have something new for himself that wasn't handed down or given away so now he had a brand new pair of dark goggles all for himself and this allowed him to see out into the world at daytime without burning his eyes and turning him blind. He knew he looked weird now, a tailless aeomon wearing a pair of swimming goggles with blacked out plastic lenses so no one could see his eyes but at least he could come outside now. He still hurt from his beating as did Val who still had a black eye and many bruises, but at least they were still breathing. The doors opened again and out of the door running with excitement was Acarlie. She looked around briefly looking for him and as soon as she saw Val standing there with these strangers she ignored them and ran straight for him. Heart racing with joy and excitement Val held out his arms and waited for only a split second before Acarlie jumped into his arms, together they shared the moment like they were the only two people on the ship, hugging each other tightly and smiling uncontrollably in each other's embrace. Val put her back down and ran his fingers through her hair, putting it back behind her ears and seeing the smile he never thought he would see again. Acarlie only needed to glance at Val before her smile disappeared and she suddenly looked concerned at the state of him, reaching out and gently touching his bruised, cut face.

"Oh Val, what happened to you? What did they do?"

"I'm ok Acarlie, I just had a bit of trouble getting the skyship, but it's all ok now."

"I was worried for you Val. When Raiden first told me that you were taken hostage I thought I would never see you again. What happened to you? We were on our way to search for you Val."

"Really, but why? What about the mission and your pilgrimage?"

"We decided to put the mission and pilgrimage on standby until we had you back with us. We didn't want to carry on without you Val. I once left you behind back in Lachine, I promised I wouldn't do it again."

"Why was Raiden with you then? Last I spoke to him he only cared for the mission. Why did he accompany you as well?"

"You're wrong Val. The mission wasn't the only thing Raiden cared about. He also cared about you. He was hesitant at first but soon came around to the idea of coming with Sheeria and me to find you before we carry on with your mission and my pilgrimage."

Val didn't say a word then but smiled embarrassingly still holding onto Acarlie who rubbed his beaten face again, "Oh what happened to you Val?"

"Remember when I said back in Hiro that I had made a deal with someone for a skyship?"

"Yes, I do. What happened?"

"I was taken to another country with this aeomon here, his name is Dude. He is mute so can't speak but he was there with me watching your last Elemental Battle in True Hiro and has been helping me all the while. Dude this is Acarlie, the elementalist I have been travelling with."

Dude and Acarlie both smiled and shook each other's hand.

"Why with the goggles Dude?" Acarlie asked.

Dude looked over to Val and Val got the message and answered for him.

"Dude was raised in True Hiro so he has been in the darkness for so long that his eyes can't take the brightness of the sun. These goggles are to help him see and stop him from going blind."

"Oh, I see. I'm sorry Mister Dude," she quickly apologised, but Dude just smiled and lifted his hand with a, "*That's ok,*" gesture.

"We were sent to steal an ancient relic in exchange for use of the ship but we were tricked and after we escaped the country we were left to die in a desert. We managed to break free but were lost in the desert and almost died if it wasn't for this kingnine," he told her whilst patting Zoudiva's head.

"This is Zoudiva my kingnine, I am his master. Zou' this is the elementalist Acarlie, all the while you are with me I want you to protect this girl from any harm, ok?" he told Zoudiva who had already stepped forward and bowed his head to her.

"It would be my honour Master to serve an elementalist, Miss Acarlie..." he went to finish off his sentence but stopped after he saw a look of shock and confusion in her eyes. Acarlie knew what a king-nine was but had never seen one in real life and also never heard one speak before. She had been in her small town for all her life so this was a new experience for her just like Val when he first met him.

"I never knew the kingnines could talk?" she confessed.

"That's normal Miss Acarlie, a lot of people have never even heard of our species and therefore never knew we had the gift of speech. It's because none of my species are wild and so people have only seen us when met with our masters," Zoudiva looked up to see her smile at him explaining this in his deep voice and found him fascinating to listen to.

"My great, great grandfather was a guide to an elementalist long ago. It honours me to carry on in his footsteps and protect someone who learns in the ancient, sacred teachings. I would gladly lay down my life if it meant ensuring the safety of you Miss Acarlie."

Acarlie knelt down and stroked the top of his head, "Thank you Zoudiva, I would be happy to have you by my side but you're not a guardian yet so save the formalities and vows until later, ok? To become a guide you must go through procedures with an elder present."

"Yes Miss Acarlie."

"Zou' here took us to his master. I made a bargain with him to have the skyship and take us back to Hiro and I was going to pick you guys up then head for the monastery. This is Captain Kaza Caines, leader of the pirates and commander of the ship next to us, the Scarlet Arise."

Kaza stood forward and quickly shook her hand, "Actually I have seen you before Acarlie. I saw a recording of the last E.B you did back at Hiro. That was a good fight and even won me a bit of money, thanks."

"Umm...You're welcome, nice to meet you Captain Kaza."

"What happened to you then? I was told about something about Hiro, is it ok?" Val asked and listened as Acarlie started telling them all what happened to them since the last time she saw him. The news of the broken town Mecroyles was a shock to all of them apart from Val who didn't know what it was and the news of the Feydon army marching toward Hiro for an attack was unsettling to all of them especially for the kingnine and the quiet aeomon who stood there mouth opened wide in fear of what may already have happened to his home.

Shortly after Acarlie explained their mission of finding Val and carrying on with her pilgrimage having Raiden and Zahied accompany her, Sheeria and Zahied both walked into the control room and each shared their joy as they saw Val safe with them on the skyship.

Val only had enough time to tell his story again and introduce the new members of the group to each other when Commander Chez walked in and interrupted the formal introductions. Totally ignoring the others he walked past them and stood in front of the ship's wind shield so the others including his pilot crew could see and hear him. After he got the attention of everybody he stood up straight and said to them.

"Now everybody is here I can begin the assessment of the situation. Please correct me where I go wrong and don't be afraid to give me any useful information that may be valuable." Chez spoke clearly and loudly like any good leader should and even had the pirate captain standing in silence to hear what he had to say.

"Now Acarlie, you asked the King of Hiro to send us to come and pick you up from Mecroyles and bring you back to Hiro, right?"

"That's right?" she answered him.

"And you wanted us to come back to Hiro so you could find your friend, the man standing before you, yes?"

"Yes."

"And Raiden, you tell me that apart from the Elementalist's pilgrimage you have been travelling with, you need access to the monastery in Aragorth, right? Because what the king asked us to do was not to take you as far away as that and we have our own business to attend so we can't waste our time or fuel taking you around the world like a taxi."

"I thought you were to take me wherever I wanted to go?" Acarlie interrupted loudly trying to correct him.

"I only said I would go where you needed to go to find your friend Val; since Val is here then my contract with you is completed."

"Then how are we supposed to reach Aragorth in time?" Raiden burst out.

Calmly and coolly Kaza answered him, "I still have a bargain with Val Raiden, as long as Val is aboard my ship..." he silently and secretly smirked then as he saw the commander wince in the corner of his eye when he said 'my ship,' "...then I'm obliged to go wherever he chooses to go. If that means taking you guys across the drink to some old monastery then so be it."

Raiden smiled and nodded at Kaza then silently thanked him with a slight nod and an agreement with the eyes. Zahied was the one to interrupt now, asking what the others wanted to know.

"Wait, what about Hiro? Isn't Hiro still in danger? We should go there right now and warn the king."

"Yes, thank you Zahied, that brings me to the other situation. As we all know now, the city Hiro, capital of Racoves is about to come under attack by the Feydon army that has marched from the city of Alpha for reasons unknown."

"This can't be true; my people have no reason to attack Hiro. There must be some mistake here?" Zoudiva broke in.

"Wait, you're from Feydon Zou'?" Val asked him.

"All kingnines are from Feydon, that is where we are born and raised. This helmet on my head is not something that Captain Kaza gave me Master. It is part of the Feydon armour, the red lights in the eyes are for all us in the army to see in infrared, to help us fight in the dark. When I first heard of the Feydon army invading Mecroyles I didn't quite believe it; and now you say that my people are about to invade Hiro?"

"You better believe it cur," Raiden sneered at him. "Mecroyles was totally destroyed, only a handful of the town's people were left, tell us what you really know!"

"Raiden stop it!" Val said in Zoudiva's defence.

"It's ok Master. I know what everyone here is thinking here, and yes I am from Alpha; a Feydon kingnine born, raised and trained in the arts just like every other one of my kind to come off the assembly line. Sold to one human as a guardian then sold to another and to another and so on. It is normal for my species. But I have been away from home for so long now being with Captain Kaza that I have grown apart from my home, my army and even my own species apart from others who have had the same fate as me. If we fail the test to fight in the barracks then we are either put down or sold, never set free. So Raiden I say to you now that I know nothing of what Feydon has been doing! I barely even know my own kind anymore, so back off!"

Raiden growled followed with Zoudiva matching his growl with one of his own and were separated by Zahied again.

"This still doesn't answer my question, what are we going to do about Hiro?" he directed his question back to Chez.

"Well like I said, my contract is over with you now so what I do is my own business."

"You won't even help a city when it needs you?" Zahied said again.

"I never said that Zahied. As from now my service to Elementalist Acarlie is over. I am flying my ship to Hiro to warn the king of the threat approaching it. If you fly with me then so be it but after the warning I am flying back to Angland."

Acarlie felt a little offended by his words but knew he was right. He had helped her just like he said and knew that Hiro wasn't his business so warning the king would be all he could do. She turned to the pirate still standing there coolly with his arms crossed leaning back against the wall.

"What about you Captain Kaza? What are you going to do?"

He lifted an eyebrow and thought for a second. He looked around and saw that everyone was waiting for him to answer especially the mute aeomon.

"Well, my answer depends on Val's answer really. Wherever he wants to go then I'll take him there, it's the least I can do."

Val looked over to Acarlie. He knew the decision wasn't really his, "I guess I'll go wherever the Elementalist wants to go. Acarlie, you were willing to stop the pilgrimage just to find me so I know I'm not your guardian but as long as we get to Aragorth, I'll go wherever you go."

"Does this mean I'm taking you to Hiro first?" Kaza asked her.

"Yes, if you're ok with doing that for us?"

The pirate sighed, "Well I'm not keen on going one way then another direction entirely; the price of the petrol will be a little much."

"Don't worry about the petrol in your ship's tank. I shall speak to the King of Hiro about supplying you with plenty of fuel to take us there."

"Then we have a deal Acarlie, if you're going to Hiro and Val is accompanying you then I will be the one to take you there."

"Then that settles it. My men will take the bridge away soon and the two ships will fly side by side until we both get to Hiro, so if anybody wants to fly with the pirates now is the time to go." Chez told them.

"I think it will be easier if we all go with the Scarlet. If we are to fly with them later then we should want to know the ship and crew since we would be on there for a few days," Sheeria suggested before everybody agreed. Acarlie said her goodbyes to the commander as well as the others except Kaza who silently led the team out of the Skycrawler and back onto the Scarlet Arise where he felt at home.

Once on the ship the bridge was pulled back onto the Skycrawler and the two ships broke apart from one another and flew side by side towards Hiro. The Scarlet being only just a little in front of the Skycrawler being naturally faster but having to cruise the sky rather than speed across it so it wouldn't leave it behind. Kaza felt so much more comfortable now he was back on his own ship and back in the cockpit where his two pilots Dillon and Smythy, his quartermaster Oran and his female navigation officer Midia were waiting for him.

"Welcome aboard Capt'n, what's the situation with the Anglish then?" Oran asked him.

Kaza sneered and jokingly replied, "They are sore since they can't have the ship but are heading in the same direction as us and have promised they won't try and take it from us."

"Do you believe that Capt'n?" his pilot Dillon asked him whilst steering the ship through the sky.

"As long as Val and his friends are on the ship I don't think they will but I want the crew to be on guard whilst they are around. They may be an army but that won't stop them from stealing it back from under our noses so tell everyone to stay sharp ok," he said to Oran.

"What's our next destination then Capt'n?" The ship's dark, long haired beauty Midia asked him coolly. Kaza turned and headed for the door again, "Our destination stays on course as before. We head for Hiro but for another reason. It seems that Feydon has gathered and army from Alpha and has Hiro as a target, the Elementalist Acarlie wants us to go there so she can warn the king."

"Wait, Elementalist? An elementalist is on the ship, a real one?" Midia asked again.

"Yes, and not just any but the one that broke the dome at Hiro. You remember don't you? We all watched it together before the boy arrived. And that's another thing; we have more women aboard now so I want the crew on their best behaviour. We have near royalty on board so I don't want them acting like a bunch of crazy, horny bastards, you hear me? Assemble the crew and inform them what is happening. I'm going to my quarters where Val and the others are. I want to acquaint myself with them properly since we will be taking them across the drink for a while."

"Yes Capt'n," Oran said and headed for the door and to a receiver that he spoke through to speakers in each room of the ship and told the pirates to assemble on the upper deck of the ship for orders.

"Dillon, Smythy, that's some good flying you did back there. Now keep the pace steady since we can't leave the soldier boys behind. Don't worry about the fuel, our tanks will be filled for us once we reach Hiro."

"Yes Capt'n, thank you Capt'n."

Hours passed and the crew, now back to work let the elementalist and her friends rest. Zahied saw to Val and Dude's wounds and used some old caster tricks to help them recover while Val filled everyone in on the stories both Dude and himself witnessed. Raiden stood at the back in silence and watched in relief as Val spoke to his friends again. Acarlie hanging onto his every word and telling him about their venture to Mecroyles. Eventually Sheeria noticed his silence and lead him back out onto the upper deck. Now empty of pirates and crew members, the upper deck was a lot more peaceful than it was when Raiden first stepped aboard. Some blood stains still stained the floor but the majority had been cleaned away now. The wind was blowing smoothly and the Scarlet slowly glided across the sky with the Skycrawler still trailing behind it. Raiden stood there out in the wind and watched Sheeria step to the side of the ship and peer yonder at the water below them. The sun set a warm glow around them and the silent wind gently waved all the small hairs of her fur to stand on end. Raiden watched, calculating her body language and finally asking, "So what's the matter then Sheeria?"

"I saw you watching Val. The last time you spoke was in a heated argument. You want to apologise but I think you should let him rest a little first. " She turned around to see that Raiden was standing before her with his proud straight stance and crossed arms.

"Come now Sheeria, I know you didn't want to bring me here just to keep me from speaking to Val so soon. Something is on your mind Sheeria," he raised an eyebrow and said in a matter of fact tone. When he said this she looked at him straight in the eye and knew he had realised what she was trying to do. She knew well that something was wrong and wanted to talk but didn't know if Raiden would have spoken to her about it. She knew she could not back down now but turned away from him so he wouldn't see her face when she said.

"I worry Raiden. I worry for our missions. If either of us fails then both my and Acarlie's lives will be over. It's fine having one thing but two sometimes feels like it's too much."

Raiden knew then where she was going with this; she feared being an alanode just like many guides before her. The thought that after all she and Acarlie had been through, Sheeria would have to eventually bury Acarlie and carry on a life without her, banished from her home and left to drift the Sphere alone if she did not take her own life herself. He stepped forward and stood beside her glancing at her face riddled with a secret doubt that she had been keeping since the start of her journey.

"What would you do if you were to become an alanode Sheeria? Where would you go?"

"I won't Raiden, Acarlie is a strong elementalist and I have total faith in her," she said but Raiden noticed her eyes flicker and look down and he could almost see and hear the thoughts in her head as they played out a scenario of what would happen if she would fail.

"It must be hard sometimes, being a guide," he finally said softly.

"You have no idea Raiden. You see, no one thinks of the guide when they see the elementalist in battle. No one remembers the guide if the elementalist becomes great, but it is us who have the constant job of not only protecting them outside the arena but making sure that they train, rest and eat properly. To ensure that they're never too hot nor too cold to continue and always vowing to die if it meant keeping the elementalist from harm at the price of absolute shame. Acarlie will always be in the light and in the public's eye while I shall always be standing behind her if she falls. But lately she has constantly made my job harder by turning away from her pilgrimage and towards a dangerous path."

"That is the problem she shares with Val, a human with a big heart will always use it. She is not doing it to hurt you."

"But she also doesn't know that she is Raiden."

"Then why don't you tell her."

Sheeria didn't bother answering him then. He understood why because they both knew the answer. They knew that Acarlie wouldn't listen to Sheeria if she asked her not to go to Hiro, she would carry on doing what she felt was the right thing to do.

"I guess that you just have to persevere with this Sheeria. Just like you said before, Acarlie will probably do something like this again you know that," he told her whilst turning back around.

"It's not just that Raiden; I also wanted you out here so I could know for sure. I have been thinking recently and I think I know why you are out here, risking not only your life but a complete race for the sake of the planet."

Raiden stopped then realising what she meant, *we've been through this once already Sheeria, let it go*, he thought and waited for her to continue.

She turned around to see the back of the leo standing there, waiting and she continued, "You're still ashamed about what your race did to the world once long ago. You think that by saving it then your race would be forgiven. Why else would you do this Raiden? Don't you understand that right now you are so special to the whole of the planet? Thousands of years of memories, names and faces lie solely in your DNA. That you would risk them all just so the leos would be remembered is foolish."

Raiden sharply turned around now. He wanted to sharply shout at Sheeria for poking her nose in again but swallowed and took a breath.

"You really want to know why I am here?"

"Yes I do."

He tensed his jaw and finally told her why, "Yes, I am the Last Leo. After I die then my whole race will be extinguished from the Sphere and soon we will be forgotten but I don't go on this journey to keep my ancestors' memories alive, but I go because fate has brought me to this mission. The planet is in danger and it knows it, so out of every soul in the world it could have chosen to go it took me. The last of the leos, to wander the Sphere with a young stranger to find information that could save it. I go because I know the planet has called out to me and I'm answering its call. A once proud and strong race now gone and only one remains, the planet calls for this strength because it knows no other will do it. I am to the planet what you are to Acarlie Sheeria. I know I can save it and I know it needs me for what I am. If I die then my race and the planet itself dies along with me. So I won't die! I will answer the planet's call even if it means sacrificing my race's legacy along with it."

Sheeria stood stunned by what he said and believed him. She thought about it and he was right, out of every living soul, human, elder or tigian to stumble on this mission it came to not only a leo but the last one left on the planet, surely that meant something.

"But luck has been on my side too for Zahied, Val and I because out of all the people to cross paths with we cross them with an elementalist and her guide, or maybe that is the planet that has brought us together."

"What do you mean?"

"Well fate has brought Val back to us, hasn't it? Along with a ship and a crew to fly it. You have a lot of doubt in your mind Sheeria but have more faith in us, in Sphere and in Acarlie."

He turned again and this time walked back to the side of the ship and left her there to think about what he just said. She turned and faced the open sea once more and closed her eyes and let the salty wind sweep past her and wonder what else the planet had in store for them.

35

The once crowded busy streets of Hiro were now empty and desolate as the rich folk on the upper part were moved away from their homes and hidden in either the massive pyramid-like building of the king or down in the slums where they were given safe hostels and flats away from the slum folk. The city had never been as quiet now as only the king's small army protecting the city marched across its empty streets. The king himself was stationed back at his home with his personal security and advisers around him. He wore his armour and had his sword by his side, waiting for the strike to come from the army that was slowly marching towards them. He was first advised by some of his army that routinely scouted around the city when they saw this army appear from over the horizon and immediately reported to the king giving him and his council enough time to get the people to safety and assemble his troops. He waited on a large open balcony from one of his many rooms so he could see clearly over his city. The sun shone down over his kingdom and far out into a everlasting horizon of plains and forests. The light from the magnificent sun reflected back up from the windows of the many buildings. The city never felt so tense he thought. It was like a calm before a storm, quiet but with an impending energy of a dark day in its history. One of his personal security guards moved into the room quickly with almost a run in his step, "Your Majesty! Two ships docked and the crew from them wishes an immediate word with you."

"Now isn't really the time Pete," Kerry told him, still gazing over his soon-to-be battlefield. Even the birds were now flying away as if they too felt the imminent danger.

"But Your Majesty, one of the people is the Elementalist Acarlie. She says it is urgent that you speak to her."

His ears twitched when he heard the name and changed his tone, "Send her in then."

"At once Your Majesty," the young guard said then quickly turned and ran out the door.

Only moments later the doors opened again and Acarlie and a few others appeared with her including the Commander of the Anglish skyship that the king had sent to find Acarlie.

"Good, now that you are here maybe you have some information on what is happening here Miss Acarlie?" the King asked.

"Your Majesty, your city is on the verge of being attacked!" she quickly burst out.

"Yes, I am aware of that Acarlie but what I want to know is why and by whom?"

Commander Chez stepped forward to tell the king now since he knew that Acarlie was rushing her words in a panic and wouldn't be much help until she calmed down a little.

"It is Feydon, who intends to invade you King Kerry, but their reasons for doing this are still unclear. They have already torn down Mecroyles, I have seen it with my own eyes."

The king turned from them briefly and glancing back out of his balcony wondering to himself, "So it's Feydon is it? I wonder why they would attack us? We have never upset them. Queen Angel and I have had a mutual understanding for years now. It confuses me why she would go back on this now for no reason."

"We believe that the army marches for a single purpose Your Majesty," Chez began. "When they were in Mecroyles they only stayed for one night, destroyed the city then were seen marching towards your city. We all have been flying back here so we could warn you."

"I think it's a little late for warnings Commander. What I need now are reinforcements, the army draws closer every minute and I don't have the whole of my army to defend my city and not enough time to assemble them."

"What do you intend to do Your Majesty?" Raiden asked.

Being that he was trained as a leo like Val was, the king was not one for backing down in a fight. He turned back around to face the small crowd behind him and told them straight.

"I intend to protect my city with whatever it takes. I thank you for your concern and warning us but I don't need a warning, I need help."

"You have all of my men and crew left aboard the Skycrawler to help at your disposal Your Majesty. I will send them where you need them to go," Chez informed him.

"You have my crew too King. We may be pirates but we're good fighters and would help you if you need us," Kaza told him.

"How many are in your crew then?" Kerry asked them.

"My crew numbers two hundred, that includes engineers, cooks and medics but they can all fight."

"My crew is of thirty. We have employed more since and have also lost some through injuries so I can't tell you the exact amount."

"That's good enough, your help would be appreciated. Commander, assemble your men. You will be led to an armoury and each given a weapon and a shield. Assist my men out on the front line and..." he turned to face Kaza, "...I take it you are the captain of the pirates?"

"That's right King. My name is Captain Kaza Caines."

"Ok then, please assemble all of your men and head down to True Hiro; I have no men down there to protect my people since they are all above to fight. I will send for an escort to meet you to take you around the lower parts of the city."

Dude suddenly lifted his hand and waved it around getting the pirate's attention. Kaza turned and saw Dude pointing to himself.

"What's he trying to say?" the king asked.

"I think he wants to be the escort. He lives down in the slums so it would make sense to send us there with him. He will know the streets more than anyone else," Kaza said.

"Ok then, please go you three and take a receiver from one of my guards each and an electric shield. I will be transmitting to all of my troops from up here giving out orders. Kaza, I will need you to report to me what is happening down there since you will be the only eyes and ears I have down there, ok?"

"No problem, come on Dude let's go," but before he left he turned to Val. "Val, whatever happens meet back here, if you don't show up after all this then I'm not going to wait for you, ok?"

He didn't wait for an answer but exited the door with Chez and Dude, each taking a receiver and only Dude took the electric shield since Kaza didn't want one and Chez said he didn't need one. Acarlie wondered then why Chez would send his men to the front line when before he said he would only warn the king but the realisation came to her quickly; if Chez's men pulled it off and successfully helped the king then relations between Hiro and Angland would be stronger giving more trade and jobs to both countries and she could only guess that the pirates would want something in return for helping the king.

Val was stumped now. They only came to warn the king but now were stuck here again without a skyship to take them to Aragorth. Raiden realised the same revelation and asked the king, "Where will you need me Your Majesty?" He could feel Sheeria's stare at him as he said this but ignored her.

"No Raiden, it is too dangerous for you to go," the king said.

"Don't give me that King, I have the right training to help you fight off these soldiers and since we cannot ride out of here in a skyship then I can at least help you fight them off."

The king looked stumped for a minute. He knew the important position Raiden was in for his race but couldn't turn down the help of a leo. He rubbed the scar running down his face and accepted his proposal, "Ok then Raiden, if you want to fight then take a receiver and a shield and go down to the troops, they will need your help."

"Raiden, no! You can't go down there, what about your mission?" Acarlie broke in.

"Like I said Acarlie, we can't go anywhere now since the Anglish and the pirates decided to help out our king, so I might as well make myself useful. These soldiers will need the help of a leo anyway."

"If you're going then I'm going too Raiden," Val finally said, summoning his staff. "I'm not waiting here for you to come back here."

"I go where my master goes, if it's battle he wishes then I will follow him to the heart of the fight," Zoudiva growled quietly. "My help would be needed anyway since I have been trained as an Feydon solider, so I would know how they fight."

The room became quiet then, the king and his men smiling and nodding but Acarlie and Sheeria were disgusted with worry.

"What about you, will you help us?" the king asked Zahied.

"I don't know if I'll be any help to you on the battlefield Your Majesty. I am only a caster, the only help I would be able to give you would be as an adviser."

"In that case I want you to go with the elementalist and her guide to Logan and the other elementalists of this city; they are not far from this room. You are to make sure that nothing happens to the elementalists and their guardians. Keep them safe."

"Yes Your Majesty."

"Then that settles it, Raiden, Val and his kingnine will go down to the battlefield and Zahied will go to protect the elementalists and the guardians." He turned to one of his guards, "Make sure that Val and Raiden are equipped for battle."

They left the room and started walking back down the hallways of the king's palace when the guards stood forward with two receivers and what looked like two long sleeved, black, fingerless gloves. Raiden turned them down and now the receiver and the black glove was given to Val. He put it on his left hand and looked at it. He was told to take his cloak off since it would get in the way. The long, black glove went from his palm to his elbow covering his forearm completely and a small button was fitted inside the woven material of the glove in the palm which when pressed revealed a large, blue, oval electric shield that Val could hold like a normal shield. He understood now that he had to take his cloak off when he wore it so it wouldn't get in the way.

"Wait Val please," Acarlie pleaded as she ran out of the room and up to him, "Please don't do this; you know this is a stupid thing to do."

"I'm not going to leave Raiden down there on his own Acarlie, it's going to be ok. I will be right back."

She was hugging him tight now when he said this and let go of him, raw concern and worry in her eyes, "No, it's not going to be ok Val, this isn't like what you have done before, this could mean war. They're going to try and kill you!"

"She's right; you can't keep trying to throw your lives away," Sheeria said from behind her directing the conversation over to Raiden as well.

"I'm only helping my king in an hour of need," Raiden said. "Isn't it you that wanted to come here and help in the first place?"

"You know that this is not what I wanted. I only wanted to come here to warn the king then be back on the path," Acarlie told him.

"Well now we don't have a choice, we have got to help out a city in need. Val I'll be waiting for you on the ground floor."

"Val," Acarlie said again this time holding his hands, "please don't do this."

"I'll be right back."

"That's what you said before."

"Yeah, and I came back didn't I?"

"No, it was a miracle that we found you on board the ship when we did, if you go down there you're going to die."

Val could see that she only worried for him and tried comforting her with a kiss on her cheek then pulling away.

"I will be fine Acarlie, don't worry about me. I will be right back, I promise."

He turned back and ran to catch up with Raiden. Zoudiva by his side stopped, turned around and addressed Acarlie himself.

"If you worry for Val and the Leo I want you to know they will be safe. Feydon and especially the soldiers from Alpha will not be expecting a fellow kingnine to be fighting them. I assure their safety."

Acarlie stepped forward and knelt down and stroked Zou-diva's large, armoured head, "Watch him closely Zou'. I don't want him doing anything stupid."

"You have my word Acarlie," he bowed to her then turned and followed his master.

She stood up and watched Val running down the hall, Sheeria behind her putting her paw on Acarlie's shoulder.

"They will be fine Acarlie."

Acarlie thinking out loud said what she thought seeing him run after Raiden, "Stupid bastard."

Outside the city the army approached on foot, on lizzier back and even in some armoured vehicles. The largest armoured vehicle slowly trailed across the ground looked similar to a tank but much larger. This vehicle was used for the commanders and leaders of the army and ensured their safety wherever they went. Through double reinforced glass windows the busy command centre with many workers inside just like the cockpit of the Skycrawler, each pressing buttons, communicating to the soldiers marching outside and with one lone tigian standing in the centre. The shaded spots of the vehicle covered his person and there he stood in the darkness staring out onto the city Hiro. His shoulders were squared by strong shoulder pads with a large dark overcoat resting over his shoulders and hanging down like a cape. The tigian stood straight, poised with his arms crossed glaring out of the command centre as it slowly edged forward towards the city. One of the working men from the command post behind him stood up and approached him from behind, kneeling down before him and casting his eyes to the floor so he wouldn't see the shadowy figure standing there in front of him.

"The men are all ready my Lord, what is the order?" he said still bowing.

The tigian did not turn but stood still, arms crossed and in a strong, icy voice said, "Tell the troops to move forward."

"Yes, my Lord," the young man said then stood up and went back to his post.

The large shadowy tigian watched as his men started to move forward again now almost reaching the city entrance of Hiro. He squinted his sharp, tigian eyes towards his goal and said in a low voice under his breath to himself, "Well then King Kerry, let's see what your great city can do against me..."

36

Outside at the edge of the city Val stood beside Raiden and Zoudiva. The wind blew dust in his throat and blew around the hundreds of ready soldiers of the city's defence around him, each eager for protecting their home and families. Val had now rolled up his left sleeve of his cloak so he could wear it whilst fighting and still use his shield. He looked around to see the entire city's army geared up and waiting for battle. He saw commander Chez was on the other side of where they were stationed waiting just like Val was. The air around them was cold but the voices of soldiers sung in the air until they suddenly started cheering, clapping and pointing to the sky. Val squinted and shielded his eyes as he looked up to see the huge electric shield of the city began to rise up from its circular line. Val and everyone else watched in wonder as this large shield rose up from the ground in front of them and way up into the sky where it eventually curved and met itself high above the city turning into a dome of electric shield protecting it. Now all Val could see when he looked around was the inside of the massive dome, just like the walls of the prison back in Lachine.

"Is there any way of breaking through this shield?" he asked.

"With enough force, yes I think they can," Raiden said as he checked the straps of his shiny, blue leo armour.

"I doubt it will happen though, Feydon doesn't have enough force to break open the shield," Zoudiva informed them.

"My Lord, they have activated the city's electric shield, your prediction was correct," the young Feydon officer said bowing down again before his commander.

"Good. Issue the order, bring out the forbidden weapons. We will break open their line of defence with it. Send in the troops," the dark, shadowy tigian ordered.

"Yes my Lord and what about—"

"Yes...Send him in too. I'm sure he would appreciate the chance to prove himself to me."

"Yes my Lord, it will be done."

Dude was finally back down in the slums where he was at home. He could now safely take his goggles off and stick them on his head so he could see clearly now. Kaza and his crew were behind him.

"So then Dude, we are to keep the people safe right? Well then, it's your job to show us where would be a good spot to protect them from."

Dude nodded and looked around his homey, dirty concrete jungle of complete darkness and artificial rain. The streets were not so empty as the slum people either didn't know of what was happening up there or simply did not care. Some shops were still open giving light to the dark, wet streets. He tried to think of somewhere where he could take them but all his life the only places he knew more than anyone else were the rooftops. Being a thief all he knew was how to escape from danger and now he had the chance to prevent it. He signalled for the pirates to follow him with Oran, the broad shouldered quartermaster and Kaza, leading them around the back into the alleyways showing them the ways of climbing up the buildings until they were all sat on top of one of the buildings, giving themselves a clear but dark look down onto the streets.

"Good job Aeomon. This place is perfect, if anyone comes down here then we're going to be the first to know about it. Just one question, how would we get back down?"

Dude just thumbed his hand and hit his chest like he was saying, *"You let me worry about that."*

A faint rumbling sound came from way above them and the pirates all looked up into the darkness and saw nothing but all knew where it came from.

"Something's happening up there, I think it's started."

With several loud booms and cracks, the city's shield wall began to take severe damage from the Feydon army's weapons. Several cannons were fired from the Feydon lines into the electric shield, each time bouncing off it but weakening the wall. The thundering sound echoing off it as each one struck it like a giant's fist.

"Your Majesty, Feydon uses cannons on us! Soon they will breach the wall!"

When he heard the news the king sprang back to his balcony and screamed out in his fury, "They use forbidden weapons on us! This is not right, we are staying to the universal laws and they break them on us now! We have no chance if they just use cannons! What are swords and shields to the likes of what they use against us? Curse you Queen Angel! If I survive this I will see to it that you will never command again!"

His face turned red from both terror and anger as he could only watch as his shield took one cannon shot of solid metal or shrapnel after another. His men all at the bottom on the floor started to move around uncomfortably constantly looking up in the sky.

"What is the order Your Majesty?"

As he looked out he could see the shield start to flicker, short circuiting and cutting out.

"Lower the shield; it's finished. Tell the men to attack!"

Zahied was watching out from another balcony in the same room as Acarlie, Sheeria and all the other elementalists of Hiro including Logan. Acarlie now having three different elements was now the strongest in the room and refused to speak to anyone else and instead sat down on one of the large sofas with her head in her hands with Sheeria sitting beside her. Some of the elementalists were only children and trying to make conversation with her saying how great she was beating Logan. Logan himself, was looking after the children. Logan saw the flicker of the shield and went over to Zahied at the balcony.

"What's happening out there?" he asked.

"They are using forbidden weapons on us. They're using cannons to fire projectiles at us to weaken the shield," Zahied told them.

When she heard the news Acarlie stood up and ran to the balcony.

"How can they do this? The weapons that are forbidden are supposed to be safe, protected by elders. If they and other united nations find out about this it will mean war, even another divide! Feydon has gone too far!"

"The weapons may have been hidden away and protected but the information to create more will not have been destroyed and the scientists in Alpha are the best in the world," Zahied told her.

"But what about the treaty after the Last Divide? The one that made weapons like this forbidden in the first place?"

"Obviously Feydon doesn't care for any promises and treaties anymore. This will end in war between Racoves and Feydon. Maybe even Calmaron and Angland will help in the war too."

"Oh no, this is terrible; Val and Raiden are down there!" Acarlie cried out as the electric shield now fully disappeared and the roaring sound of the two armies started charging towards each other.

"Val!" she cried out again.

Val, Raiden and Zoudiva stood amongst the crowd of soldiers inside the city's dome. The shield now was being pelted with large pieces of metal and shrapnel fired from the cannons, and every thump the shield took shook the floor and scared the army.

"They use forbidden weapons on us!" the soldiers called out in fear.

"We are lost! Feydon has forgotten the treaty and are using weapons far more advanced than our own!"

Raiden now remembered the remains of Mecroyles and realised what he never did before. The reason Mecroyles was in such a bad state was because of the cannons, the army had obviously used these canons on the city to destroy the buildings.

"What are these weapons they're talking about Zou'?" Val asked him.

"Forbidden weapons Master. All of the nations including Feydon signed a treaty to never use nor manufacture such weapons ever again since..." he didn't finish his sentence since he was standing next to Raiden and overheard. Zoudiva felt shamed and lowered his head and waited for Raiden to finish his sentence.

"Since the Last Divide. These were among some of the weapons used along with the kingnines to wipe out my species. Now Feydon, the very country that first made the forbidden weapons and genetically engineered the kingnines now uses them on their own species. This is why the treaty was made in the first place. Mark my words Val; this will lead to another divide of the likes that Sphere has never seen before. Even the elders will take sides on this one for this truly is an act of pure evil."

Another thump struck the shield and now the shield started to flicker and short circuit. The crowd now activated the electric shields on their arms and now every soldier's left arm was covered by a blue, oval, translucent shield.

"Remember your training Val, don't lose focus. Fight like a Walton Warrior rather than a Leo do you hear me? You have more training that way and stay close to me. If we get split up, then meet back here," he said turning to Zoudiva as well, "All of us."

"You needn't worry about me Leo; I will keep close to both of you," Zoudiva growled, not to Raiden but to the wall that flickered again.

The troops now held up their weapons and psyched themselves up by shouting and calling out. "For Hiro!" one shouted.

"For Racoves!" shouted another and one by one they screamed to each other.

The shield flickered one last time and Val could see the army on the other side of them, waving their weapons in the air, their armour he couldn't make out but looked alien and strange.

"For Hiro!" the men called out again.

Zoudiva took a deep breath and exhaled and tensed his muscles as the shield finally disappeared and the sound of screaming men charging towards each other mixed in with the cannons firing and crashing into the city's buildings and crumbling them. He heard fellow kingnines roaring on the other side of the battlefield along with tigians, screams of the battle aeomon and only one almighty roar of a leo he stood beside sung the chorus of war.

37

The sound of charging men echoed all through the empty city, the king's palace and even down to the dark streets of True Hiro below them. The two armies charged towards one another, weapons held high and shields activated. It was devastating for any of the rich folk hidden away in the king's palace as they could only stand and watch their husbands or sons charge into a wall of men and weapons. Acarlie was standing on her balcony with Zahied and Logan; each not daring to blink as they stared out and saw the two armies draw closer and closer together. The wind whistled and fear swept through the essence of the day for all except the soldiers, with adrenaline flowing through their blood forgot about the fear of death and only thought about the safety of their families. The two armies of humans, tigians, aeomon, kingnines and as single leo sprinted for one another. This battle called for no rumble between species like in the old days of Sphere but now a mix of the species on both sides of the field charged for the death for one another. The two waves of men and weapons met each other with an almighty clash. The sound of screaming men was now muffled by the sound of metal against metal, swords now swung from side to side clanging as they met each other and the sound of their war cry was now only the sound of pain, screams of terror and death as their opponent's weapons met the insides of their bodies. The battle raged for a further twenty minutes and the tired soldiers began to be the first to fall. Val stood there in the middle of the field having just flipped a soldier over his hip and stabbed his heart with the soldier's own knife. The Feydon army's armour seemed strange to Val at first. It was made from a thin and loose metal. Their helmet looked more like a gas mask with a nozzle hanging from their faces amplifying their shouts with a digital echo. Their eyes were red just like Zoudiva's. Val remembered what he told him about the red eyes put on the helmets so they could see in infra-red and felt lucky that they were not fighting in the dark. Their weapons consisted of either knives and a different kind of electric shield to the one he was using, one that covered their left side in the shape of a rectangle rather than a small oval. They used the same staff that Val used (but without the gift of summoning it whenever they needed it). Bodies now scattered the floor and the smell of blood, sweat and death clogged his nose but still he fought on, having a Feydon soldier swing for his stomach, take out his feet from under him and slice at his legs Val now walked with a limp. Blood stained his already messy, short, light brown hair and blood soaked his purple cloak. He didn't know if it was his blood or his enemies'; the pain racking his body suggested it was his though. Val had a quick check of all his vital organs with his hands and continued fighting.

Where has Raiden and Zou' gone? Damn! Why did I have to lose them now? If only I could have stayed by them maybe I would have a better chance... He tried to think of something he could do to find his companions when another strike from a rectangular shield struck his head. He fell to the floor looking up to see a large, heavily armoured soldier standing before him, his arms held over his head and a large, blood stained battle axe that gleamed in the sunlight. Rolling to a side narrowly avoiding this axe Val tried getting to his feet but found himself lying on the floor again with a pain in his back where a foot had struck him. Now he lay amongst dead bodies, scattered across the floor. Puddles of blood soaked his front where he lay and above him, many feet of the armies not caring for his misfortune carried on rushing around fighting amongst themselves. He flipped over onto his back and saw the same large Feydon soldier raising the large axe over his head. Feeling the button on the palm of his hand Val quickly held his left hand out and activated the shield as the heavy axe came down, strik-ing the shield and sliding off the side. The soldier lost his bal-ance with this and toppled over, landing on the shield again. Val screamed in agony as the weight of this man pressed his shield into his body, squeezing him into the floor. Val tried to move this man but found himself completely stuck, paralysed. All he could do was to wait for the soldier to get back on his feet. Instead of doing this the soldier sat on Val's waist and repeatedly punched the shield into Val. Every strike was more painful than the last and the fear of death was now more than a consideration in his mind. This giant man would take his life if he did not take his first. Val reached out amongst the dead corpses for something sharp he could use. His fingers slithered across blood, flesh and cloth before they finally reached something solid and had the cold feel of metal and was sharp, a knife; if only but a small one. The knife, still grasped in the dead man's hand Val struggled to free, hoping that the muscles in the corpse wouldn't have seized up. He felt the shield now weaken and the large man finally shoved his left arm aside and had a clear shot to punch Val hard in the face, and again with his other hand. The knife was now in Val's hand and one more punch came to his face. He felt his nose pop and blood came gushing from it as the soldier now leaned aside for his axe. While he leant to one side Val now took his time to strike, screaming as he did with a loud war cry and stuck the knife into the soldier's neck, pushing with all the strength he could gather to penetrate the thin armour and do enough damage to stop his attacker. The solider made a gurgling sound as the knife went through the centre of his throat and filled his lungs with his own blood, the sound was amplified as it went though his mask. Val still lay under this soldier and he started to convulse as his lungs filled up and he couldn't breathe. Val took off the mask to see the eyes of the man; many battle scars on his face. The man looked like he was once a strong and fearless fighter, even a leader of his troops but now was looking into the eyes of the small man who had just defeated him. There was no anger in his eyes but fear; like he had realised that he was about to meet the same fate as the people he killed before, the lonely road of death stood before him and now he would never see nor feel his family ever again, killed by a young boy about the same age as his son.

His eyes never left Val and Val who was still stuck under him could not look away, the shaking stopped and the life from the man's eyes faded and froze, staring at him. Now one more corpse lay around Val. He slowly pushed the deceased off him and rolled back over to catch his breath. When he looked back over to the body he pulled the knife from he recognised the body as commander Chez of the Anglish army, now lifeless with his dead eyes staring out into the sky. The knife Val held in his hand was Anglish and its owner was the very one that brought Raiden and Acarlie back to him with a wound in his side, the pain was too much for him to bear and the commander died out there on the battlefield, but even in death was able to save Val. Val silently thanked the commander and shut his eyes for him. He got back up on his feet looking at the knife he had received from the dead solider. The knife looked strong with the steel of the blade curving at the end giving the point more of a tip and right back at the bottom of the blade it curved back into itself, looking like you could open a bottle with it and the handle was ivory with a woven elastic around it for a better grip.

Whilst still looking at the knife another soldier came charging towards him, like an instinct and natural reaction Val activated his shield again by tensing his fist, pressing the button on his palm and stepping aside, quickly pushing the soldier with his shield and before Val knew it the knife he held found its way past the soldier's defence and into his chin, killing him immediately. Val pushed the man off his knife and looked at it again and back at Chez.

"Thanks again Chez, hope you don't mind if I keep this knife," he said knowing the commander wouldn't answer him back and knelt down to find the case for the knife on the dead commander, after he found it he took it off the corpse and tied it to himself.

"I bet you wish you took the electric shield now, don't ya?" he said again and stood back up. His face and front now covered in red like a boy just been playing football in the mud, his electric shield activated again and a new weapon in his hand. He felt like he was ready to fight again when he looked the wrong way and didn't see the fist flying at him from the other side, striking him hard under the chin and knocking him to the floor again.

Kaza and his fellow crew of pirates stayed sitting on the roofs of the buildings in True Hiro with the sound of battle way above their heads as just a faint sound in the black abyss above them. The artificial rain had subsided now and left a gleam of water to soak the streets reflecting what little light they had down there so they could see clearly down below. The water here would soon be drained away down pipes and recycled and used again, this was so the city below never flooded. Dude, the mute aeomon sat perched on the edge of one of the concrete buildings and peered down onto the streets below. Streets lamps and shop signs and lights from passing M.Vs were all he needed to see down here. After being in the natural sunlight for so long he realised how much he preferred the darkness now, this was where he was comfortable and this gave him the advantage over the pirates who could not see so well in such damp darkness. In a world so dark and covered by all that was natural the wind still managed to pass down here, whistling through like a giant draft that slipped down from a crack in the giant ceiling that held an entire city. The people walked the streets like they usually did and Dude watched as a person in a long, dark overcoat walked down an alleyway past two men standing beside one another. The two men were looking at one another and nodding, following the man down the dark alley. This man would either be some sort of illegal drug dealer or simply a man getting mugged by these two men Dude thought but overlooked it; he had seen things like this down here many times before. To Dude this really was a city of sin but also his home and now when he heard that it was in danger he wanted to do his part to ensure its survival. The first of the pirates began whispering and pointing to the ceiling grabbing their captain's attention. One of the large circular elevators was beginning to descend down to them. Dude looked up and only he could see a small platoon of Feydon soldiers stood on the elevator, weapons at the ready.

"What do you see Aeomon, is it Feydon?" Kaza whispered then signalled for all his men to hide in the shadows of the buildings' rooftops. The elevator was a little far away for the soldiers to see them outright but Kaza didn't take any chances. If even one of the crew saw that there were reinforcements in True Hiro then their element of surprise would be taken from them. Dude nodded at the captain's question and slid across the shadows to the other side of the building and watched as the elevator now touched the ground below them and the platoon of soldiers got off the elevator and started to march across the streets. They marched right past the buildings the pirates were hiding above, way too high to jump down and take them by surprise and way too high for the soldiers to see them all peering over the edges and watching them march along. Many drunk bums and crack heads tried approaching them in a drunken manner and were either silently killed outright in the middle of the streets or simply knocked to one side.

"They're heading for something in particular Capt'n," the quartermaster Oran said.

"What do you mean?" Kaza whispered back.

"Well look, they're not ransacking the shops nor are they pillaging or torching the place. They're simply marching. They gotta be looking for something in particular."

"What would the slums down here have that the army wants? It doesn't make sense, Dude get over here..."

Dude slid over beside them and Kaza pointed over to the marching soldiers.

"Where are they going?"

Dude peered over at the city below and saw nothing important that the soldiers would want, offices, shops, flats and some small factories and warehouses, nothing useful to the army. Dude shrugged his shoulders.

"Come on, there must be something out there that they would want, what it is?"

Dude looked again, scanning the city for every building seeing nothing until he saw the old museum in the ancient and forgotten elemental school. Long ago when True Hiro was the only Hiro this school would have been the school the elementalists trained at. When the upper city was built a new school was built and the old school was forgotten just like the rest of the city. It became a museum for the school children to learn about the old elementalists who used to train there as well as the battles that were fought there. It was the only thing that made sense in Dude's mind but why the army wanted it still puzzled him.

Dude began pointing at it hoping the pirates would understand him.

"What is it? Do you know where they are going?" Kaza asked and Dude nodded and started pointing at the building.

"Ok why? What's over there?"

Dude thought for a second about how he could tell Kaza and started pointing at the small puddles of water next to them on the roofs, splashing it and pointing to the water but Kaza simply didn't get it.

"Look, just take us there alright? You should know these streets like the back of your hands; they're your home. Show us the shortcuts and we can get there before them and outflank them." Kaza said wanting Dude to take him the quicker way.

Dude led them across the buildings, jumping from one to another having the pirates silently follow him in single file. Dude was home again, once again he felt the freedom of the climb. To run the same routes he had all his life. He knew all the jumps, every pipe that needed climbing and every break-fall. He was surprised also how well the pirates managed to keep up. A long and exhilarating free-run later and Dude was standing, panting on the corner of one last buildings and gesturing with his hand that they had arrived to the captain who jumped one last gap and rolled when he hit the floor. He picked himself up slowly and walked over to him.

"Nice work Dude, where are we off to now then?" Kaza asked him.

Dude pointed at the broken old museum in front of them, it looked desolate when it was closed for the night, almost abandoned after hours but still in one piece.

"Is that where they're headed then?" Kaza asked and Dude nodded and pointed again.

"Then that's where we'll wait for them. Boys, draw your weapons and get down there, they have no choice but to fight us and we outnumber them as well. Just don't let your guard down; they're still soldiers so let's make sure we make it simple. Get down there, kick their teeth in and get back up before it's dark, ok? I want no prisoners, no cowards."

"Aye aye Capt'n," his crew all whispered back.

38

Acarlie still stood in the king's palace on a balcony of the room she shared with Sheeria, Zahied, Logan and the young elementalists. The clothes she wore were her travelling clothes, dark in colour but light in weight so she could get around easier. The cloak she wore was resting up against the door behind her as she stood, leaning over the balcony trying to see as far as she could so she might be able to see Val or Raiden. She was still upset with why Val disappeared in the first place, all that worrying she did before and hated him for just walking straight into the first battle that came his way. His lame excuse of only going down there to fight just because Raiden did enraged her even more. Sheeria stayed quiet in the background, tending to the children elementalists, asking them about themselves and what they had learned. She knew this was a very dangerous time and if the Feydon army managed to break through the last line of defence then they would come straight for the palace, the children would have to be kept calm and she played her part well by connecting with them and telling them all the story of what had happened to her and Acarlie so far. She couldn't help but let her mind drift every once in a while, thinking about what Raiden had told her on the Scarlet Arise previously. She found herself worrying for him, a feeling she put aside and knew she must pay attention to Acarlie, not Raiden.

"You should stop trying to lean over the balcony so much Acarlie. You won't see anyone from there," Zahied was saying to Acarlie as she leaned over the balcony again.

"If you fall then it's a long way down."

"I'm not going to fall Zahied and I can just about see the fight happening over there," Acarlie argued with him shortly but was silenced as the thundering sound of a cannon booming and a building close to the palace smashed and crumbled loudly. Large pieces of the building now fell from their foundations and to the floor. The sound jolted the balcony that Acarlie was leaning over again and tilted her forwards. Zahied sprang forward and caught her briefly before she fell and pulled her back on the ground. Her hair blew over her face and covered her shame, fear and anger, "Damn them!" she blurted out. "How are the soldiers supposed to fight against weapons like this? I'm going back to the king. He has to stop this," she snapped again hastily and stormed out of the room. Zahied followed her, quickly nodding to Sheeria letting her know he will be with her. Acarlie now forgot all her formal manners and even that she was addressing the king and did not knock on the door but slammed it open, seeing the king and his advisers all still standing there, receivers at their shoulders and speaking into them to the army outside giving them orders.

"What do you think you're doing?" the king snapped as he saw her storm in his room.

"Your Majesty, how can you keep your men out there when the city is just being bombed by cannon shells from a distance? Why won't you just talk to them and give them what they want and end the bloodshed? Can't you see that–?" She was silenced as another cannon shell shot out into another building, bouncing off the side of it and falling into the side of the king's palace, taking out a small room below them and shaking the whole building. Screams were heard from down below them as the rich folk hidden in the palace also felt the tremble of the building. Being that he was trained as a leo, the king was a very proud ruler and did not answer Acarlie but turned around to his advisers and told them to keep attacking the Feydon army until there were none left. Acarlie, being offended by the king ignoring her shouted again but this time the king turned around and shouted back to her.

"If you don't mind Acarlie, I would like to get back to my work of protecting my people from an attack! You have been given a safe room to stay in. Go there and wait for the battle to finish."

Zahied came into the room as the king finished his sentence, saw that both Acarlie and the king were now glaring angrily at each other. He quickly got behind Acarlie and held her back and pulled her out of the room.

"What do you think you're doing Acarlie? Do you want to get us arrested?"

"The king is being a fool Zahied! He's sending his men into death. They have far more advanced weapons than us and he is telling them to carry on fighting!"

"Acarlie, he's a king! *Your* king! So just keep quiet and do as he says, ok? He knows what he's doing otherwise we would already be dead. Elementalist or not you can't just storm into the king's quarters while he is directing his men into battle and lecture him on how to do his job!"

Acarlie fell silent then, looking to one side still angry and frustrated but knew he was right. She may have been an elementalist but not Hiro's elementalist. She looked back up at Zahied and stared at him for a minute before finally calming down a little and whispering, "Alright then."

She thought to herself why she would burst out with something like that as she walked back. Maybe she was tired from all the training and journeying she had just done and that this was a normal thing for a tired elementalist to do or maybe because she was simply still upset with Val, worrying over him and how she had only just found him and had to deal with the idea that he might be killed all over again. She considered it was a mix of the two and decided that rest would be the best option for her. They re-entered the room with the elementalists and was met by Logan, "Sheeria? She is not with you?"

A new wave of worry now overwhelmed the already tired Acarlie when she noticed that Sheeria was nowhere to be seen.

"I thought she was in here with you?" Zahied said.

"No, she went out about ten minutes ago in a hurry. I thought she came to find you guys."

Acarlie knew immediately where Sheeria would go, down to the battle to find the others. She tried to sprint for the door but was held back again by Zahied.

"Let me go! I have to find Sheeria!" she screamed and squirmed in her anger trying to free herself from Zahied's grip.

"No Acarlie, I can't let you go out there looking for her, it's too dangerous."

"But I know where she has gone! She's gone down the battlefield! I have to go and find her!"

"You don't know that Acarlie! What if she is not there? You would have run into the battlefield for no reason."

She squirmed again and tried sharply whipping her head back to hit Zahied and shouting, "Let go of me! She is my Guardian, if anything happens to her!"

"For the sake of this argument I am your Guardian Acarlie, and I have to keep you safe, now calm down and wait for her to get back."

She squirmed and struggled until she got a hand free and pulled herself away from him and turned around.

"If you're my Guardian then you have to go wherever I go! And if I want to go and look for my *real* Guardian then you *have* to come with me!"

Zahied stood stunned for a minute calculating from her tone then that she wasn't lying, "Is that true?" he asked Logan.

"I'm afraid it is. If a journeying elementalist loses his or her guide then they can use up to one other person to accompany them and to protect them until they are reunited with their guide."

"And if I don't go?" he asked again.

"If you don't go then I'll just go on my own!" Acarlie snapped.

Zahied was in check mate now. He had to go with her because if anything happened to her then not only would he never forgive himself but Sheeria would likely rip his arms off.

He sighed angrily, "Go on then, let's go find Sheeria. Once we find her we're coming right back you hear? She is going to be pissed off with me as much as it is."

"She knows the laws and rules Zahied. She knows I wouldn't want to leave her behind, that's why she went without telling me."

"This is a mistake, you know that right?"

"There's no mistake about trying to help my guardian and friend."

Zahied sighed again, "Ok then, lead the way, I'm right behind you."

Val was back on floor on the battlefield. A soldier had knocked him to the floor and ready to pounce on Val. He jumped onto Val's chest, knocking the wind out of him but was not quick enough to stop Val quickly stabbing him with his Anglish knife, pushing with all his strength to push the soldier off him and stabbing him further more until he was satisfied that he wouldn't be a problem to him. Val staggered back to his feet and tried to catch his breath. *I'm really bad at this*, he thought to himself as he felt his cut and bruised leg and summoned his staff so he could use it as something to lean himself up against while he caught his breath back. More bodies now covered the floor as fewer people were left standing but still fighting, killing and moving onto the next person, leaving the dead or dying to lay there and slowly bleed out. As he looked around he noticed that the Feydon army still outnumbered the Hiro troops and they didn't use the cannons on the battlefield, only on the buildings around them. This was maybe because they didn't want to kill their own troops or that they only wanted to use the forbidden weapons to scare the city into surrendering. If that was so then it wasn't working because the Hiro troops were fighting valiantly, more so every time they saw a comrade fall to the ground. It was now and only for a few seconds that Val noticed that this scene was familiar to him. The scene of men fighting people stuck in his mind like a forgotten memory, like the strongest case of déjà vu anyone would have again. He quickly wondered if this meant anything about his mysterious past, considering he was trained somewhere just like Theydon and Raiden found out. This was possibly another clue to his identity and what a horrific place to have this revelation for the first time. The soldiers' screams of pain still continued on and the sound of metal weapons still filled the air as they constantly connected with each other.

Val had no time to understand the strange phenomenon as another soldier rushed to him and tried to knock him back to the floor. Val quickly side stepped and activated his shield and looked back at the soldier. The soldier's eyes beamed red and stared at him through his helmet and he stood in a low stance, gripping onto his weapons, ready to go one on one with Val. Val quickly folded his staff in half and holding it like a baton in his hand, shield in the other and waited patiently for the attack to come. This soldier was much bigger than him and his weapon was a mighty axe that Val only guessed would have torn into his skull easily. The soldier held up his axe and stepped forward ready to pounce at Val but to Val's shock stopped suddenly. A quick and swift, sharp sound cut through the air and the soldiers winced when the almost silent sound quickly stopped, then another, and another. Every time the soldier winced even more until he stood momentarily before Val in pain. Val was still clueless now of what was going on here and watched as the soldier fell to his knees, then onto his face revealing three arrows in his back. Val looked and saw in the distance a large, black bearded man holding up the bow from which the arrows came. Many other archers all stood beside this man, each firing many arrows with precise aim and cutting into the Feydon soldiers, evening the numbers.

Val didn't even need to look twice to recognise the man who just saved him and ran over to him, "Zack!" he shouted.

The people from Plainess, having just returned in the skyships the king had sent to rescue them now all stood behind the battle lines and acted as archers for the city's army. Zack welcomed him with a quick embrace, "I'm so glad you came when you did Zack!"

"I'm glad we got here in time too, any later and it looks like we wouldn't have anywhere to go." Zack said while letting him go and patting his shoulder firmly.

"What happened to you?" Val asked, shouting over the still screaming voices of the two armies.

"Well, we flew back which took a couple days, rounded up all the survivors and equipment and headed back. When we got here we saw that the city was being attacked so we all grabbed our weapons and here we are," he answered while holding his bow up and releasing another arrow to fly straight and true into another soldier.

The king, now over the moons, cheered with excitement as his advisers told him help had just arrived and he leaned over his balcony and watched as the new platoon of the town's people he had rescued now were returning the favour for him. Their sky-ships now docked and were empty, all but women and children were out there in the battlefield doing their part of protecting Hiro with their mastery of archery, having had to use this skill just to keep themselves alive for ten years now they could use their skill and help wipe out the invading army.

"This will surely draw the army back!" the king shouted as he punched the air. "If this works I will personally make sure that every one of these people has a new home here with my people."

"The tactic seems to be working so far Your Majesty, Fey-don's numbers are dropping, soon they will have to retreat," his advisers told him.

"Excellent news, tell the men to keep up the fight! We can do this!"

Back at the mobile command centre the shadowy tigian stood still glaring out onto the battlefield. One of his communicators came behind him and knelt down to report to him what he could already see.

"My Lord, the city Hiro has found back-up in the form of archers. Our numbers weaken as long as they stand."

The shadowy tigian growled in disappointment with his arms still crossed and thought for a second before replying in his deep, croaky voice, "Hmm, Hiro has got some back-up now have they? Tell the men that the mission carries on as planned..." he then paused thinking and added, "Turn the cannons to attack at the archers. We only leave after the mission is complete."

"Can I suggest that we send *him* in now?" the small man said again, still knelt down.

"Yes, now is the time...Send him in and tell him to target the archers. I want to see them all ripped to pieces. Hopefully now I can finally see him in action."

"At once my Lord."

39

Raiden stood out in the crowd of battling soldiers more than anybody else because of his size. Even the largest of tigians didn't stand out as much and that made it difficult for Raiden to ever catch his breath. Every time he killed or injured an attacker another would take his place almost instantly attacking him more so. Eventually he began to wear down from exhaustion so when the attack from the archers came he felt relieved and took the time to quickly catch his breath. Only a few cuts and bruises scarred his body but compared to the injuries he had given to his attackers were nothing to worry about. His armour now stained in blood and his bottom jaw too was stained from someone else's blood. He had just bitten and ripped a hole in the man's flesh. He breathed heavily and stood out of the way for a few minutes, bending his back and with his hands on his knees. He smiled and remembered his heritage. Here he was in battle against humans, slaughtering those who attacked him with his leo claws. The silvery-blue metallic leoium alloy armour once again tasted the blood of the humans. His father and brother would be proud he thought. He was lending his leo strength to protect a city, in the armour of his brother and protecting his brother's old apprentice's people. He felt nothing could stop him, when a fierce growl changed his mind.

"Well, what do we have here brother?" said the growling voice. Raiden looked up to see two almost identical kingnines standing before him glaring at him with their evil looking red eyes. Their voice croaked like a younger Zoudiva's and echoed with a youthful fire.

"I can't say brother but it looks to me like a legendary Leo standing before us," the other one answered.

"That it is brother, perhaps even the last leo to ever walk the sphere. You know brother; I have never tasted the flesh of Leo like our fathers and grandfathers before us."

"So you could say that this might be the last chance we will ever get brother. We could even be the kingnines that finally put an end to the whole of the Leo race," they bantered and mocked Raiden. His pride suddenly turned to an old anger and even fear then. He barred his blood stained teeth and tensed his arms; but again was stopped by another voice.

"You would have to go through me first," Zoudiva pointed out as he appeared from behind Raiden, standing between him and the other kingnines.

"What are you doing Zoudiva? Go away, I can handle this on my own," Raiden growled under his throat.

"Shut up, I'm trying to help you," he whispered back.

The two kingnines were now even more shocked as another kingnine on the other side of the battle appeared and growled back at him.

"This is even more shocking. What is your name brother?" they asked him and Zoudiva stood forward, straightened his back and almost roared back at them to show his strength, "I am Zoudiva! Kingnine and protector of Hiro!"

The two kingnines sneered back at him then looked to one another, "Looks like we made a wealthy find brother. The last ever leo and a traitorous brother in the same place at the same time. Killing these two would make us heroes among our race brother, fortune and glory awaits us when we arrive back home."

Zoudiva now began to pace back and forth in front of Raiden, gritting his teeth and growling deeply. Raiden having now got his breath back lowered his stance and waited for the attack to come.

"Tell me brother Zoudiva, what made you become a traitor as you are now? Why do you insist on defending the very dirty creatures you have been created to destroy? You forget your family's bloodline and insult the whole of your race."

Zoudiva did not answer but stayed focused and paced up and down as they taunted him more, "You; the abomination of your race would rather remain quiet and protect the leo than reveal to your brothers why you are doing this? When we arrive back home we shall spread the word among our kind that Zoudiva, the abomination of kingnines abandoned his kin and forever will be known as the coward and traitor who took the side of the Final Leo."

"Enough talk!" Zoudiva snapped and pounced on top of the taunting kingnine. The four way fight between three king-nines and a leo began with Zoudiva scratching at the taunting kingnine and being thrown off, rolling to one side. The other pounced at Raiden and immediately tried biting at his face. Holding it back Raiden pivoted and threw the creature into the ground and jumped on it trying to straighten out its neck so he had a clear shot at biting his neck. The other kingnine tried to jump on top of him now but was pulled back by Zoudiva, pulling him back by its fur and shaking his head viciously trying to tear the flesh. The fight went on with Raiden and Zoudiva trying to separate the two kingnines from fighting together but these two were trained better than Zoudiva ever was. Because he was sold to become a servant and protector he never finished his training with Alpha and so had the disadvantage in the fight. Raiden who naturally had the disadvantage since the kingnines were born and bred to fight and conquer the leos was weakening as well and soon they were on the losing side of the fight. Raiden was on the floor with a kingnine on top of him scratching and mauling him when another feline roar came from somewhere close in the battlefield and out of nowhere Sheeria sprang over him taking out the kingnine. Raiden rolled over to his side and saw the tigian kneel on top of it and swipe a mighty scratch at its face, catching its jaw. As it yelped in pain and waited for it to try and squirm free from her, Raiden quickly jumped up and onto the bottom of the kingnine knowing that if it started attacking Sheeria then it would overcome her quicker since she would be the weakest of the three species. With Raiden putting his weight on the beast Sheeria took the time to strongly and violently snap its neck by twisting it. The other kingnine looked back to see his brother now killed by the tigian and backed up when he now saw he was outnumbered. Zoudiva, who now was bleeding from teeth wounds took the chance to bite down on his attacker's legs and waited for Sheeria to pounce on it. Raiden too pounced on the creature and it looked like they all bundled on top of and started pummelling it until Raiden struck the final blow and punching it in the throat. When it started to panic and choke he gripped onto his head and with all his strength, twisted until he was sure the neck bones had separated inside the neck and left it there limp and lifeless.

"What do you think you're doing here Sheeria!? Shouldn't you be looking after Acarlie?" Raiden asked her as they stood up.

"It looks to me like I was saving your hide Raiden. A thank you would be nice," she answered sarcastically.

"Thank you," said Zoudiva while he paced around weakened by his pain. Sheeria quickly knelt down and tended to the wounded fighter, Raiden all the while just standing there still frowning at him.

"Sphere's divide Raiden! Do you have to be so cold all the time? This kingnine nearly died fighting trying to protect you and all you do is stand there?"

"I never asked him to," Raiden countered stubbornly.

"Go and find him a medic!" she screamed at him.

Raiden growled but turned in defeat and did as instructed.

"You did well then Zoudiva; you're going to be ok."

"Those two were right; I am an abomination and a traitor of my race. I have forgotten my birth right and began to protect the very creature I was born to kill," he said in his pain.

"Don't say that Zoudiva. You are not a traitor nor abomination, you were protecting your king and your people. Did you know both Kerry and Val are trained as leos? To not protect them would be going against your master and isn't that what really makes a kingnine a traitor? You did remarkably well then Zoudiva, forget what they said, you are a strong and faithful kingnine and never let anyone else tell you otherwise."

Zoudiva felt slightly better after she told him and felt a moment of shock when he heard that Val was trained as a leo but soon put it aside and quickly said as he realised his master was missing.

"Master! Where is my master?"

"Whoa, slow down a second. We'll find Val in a minute, we have to quickly bandage you up first," she said as Raiden returned with the army's medic and started treating Zoudiva and his wounds.

Sheeria stood up and addressed Raiden, "Don't you have something to say Raiden?" she gestured to the injured kingnine on the floor.

Raiden growled, "Where's Val?" he quickly changed the conversation.

"We'll all find him in a moment then I'm bringing you all back do you hear me?"

Raiden nodded and waited for Zoudiva to have his bandages tightened around him then when they were ready all three different species began running around the battlefield looking for Val.

Val was standing side by side with the newly arrived archers who had to come to Hiro. He stood and tended to his cuts and wounds as they protected him with a wall of arrows no soldier would dare try and come up against. Mack, the leader of the archers was ordering them to keep firing. Since he had one missing eye, he had no depth perception and therefore made him a poor archer. But with his good eye he could still see the army attacking and directed his archers in the right positions for combat. Every now and again the cannons would fire more solid metal cannon balls into the city and impacted the building around it but the archers ignored this loud noise and concentrated on their aim. Zack was standing in front of Val now, pulling back his bow and releasing an arrow to fly onto the battlefield.

"So how is Acarlie Val? I never got to see her Elemental Battle, did she make it?" he asked him quickly whilst still looking out onto the battlefield.

"Yes, she defeated the elementalist here and acquired the element and I hear she even went to a place called Mecroyles as well and obtained another element."

"That's great! I can't wait to see her again."

Zack was going to add more to the conversation but was silenced as a cannon ball cracked and exploded on the floor around the archers, splitting them up immediately. Mack screamed for organisation of his troops but again another cannon ball split them up until he had to scatter them around the outside of the battleground. Amid all the confusion Val and Zack found themselves apart from the other archers again and into the front line of the assault. Zack immediately drew his sword and knife and began fighting the soldiers around him without his bow whilst Val helped him all he could. Soon the archers began to draw the fight to their side again by taking the numbers of the Feydon army down but this didn't mean much for Zack and Val as they were now in the centre again trying to fight off their attackers. Val had quickly taken down a soldier when a Hiro troop was thrown into him knocking him aside. Quickly rolling to one side to get to his feet Val saw Zack fighting like a true warrior of his clan. He had been fighting demons and other creatures for so long that these soldiers seemed like a walk in the park for him. That was only until Val watched in horror as a sword appeared from Zack's chest, piercing him from behind. Howling in pain Zack closed his eyes and fell to the floor, his life instantly taken from him and his attacker pulling his sword from out his chest. Val watched as this sword sharpened itself with a gel that ran from the hilt of the blade to the tip of the metal and when he looked up he noticed he recognised the man. A man he knew only as Miles...

40

Miles wore different armour than the other Feydon troops. His armour looked heavier and without a helmet so it made it easy for Val to recognise him. He stood broad and strong amongst the Feydon troops and with his new armour stood in a whole new light from when Val last saw him with some scars still on his face from when Raiden threw him out of the window back in Lachine. His sword Razor still at his side and now tainted with the blood of his old companion whom he literally stabbed in the back.

"You...You bastard!" Val screamed at him when he wiped Zack's blood off his sword.

Miles chuckled at Val's anger and stepped forwards toward him, waved his arm to his fellow soldiers to back off so they wouldn't bother them and said, "Did you really think that fall in Lachine would stop me? I was back on my feet only hours after medical treatment."

"But why Miles? Why join Feydon?" Val asked interested of why he would do it. "Feydon couldn't possibly offer you much money and that was the reason why you last betrayed us."

Miles chuckled again and answered him blankly, "Feydon has the strongest army on the planet. This was the best way for me to finish my training and fulfil my lifelong mission of revenge but that's something you know nothing about. It wasn't hard for me. My last deal with the president of Isolies was not for money but travel to Alpha so I could offer myself to the queen. It wasn't hard, I only had to kill a few soldiers for her to see the potential in me and put me in one of her groups of special solders. My first mission was to lead the attack on the unknowing city of Mecroyles."

The more he pointlessly explained himself the more Val felt enraged. This traitor was responsible for Mecroyles being attacked and now is here to attack Hiro, to kill everyone, even Zack who had helped save him in the past. Miles finished his sentence with an evil sneer and lifted Razor up to point at Val, "I believe we have some unfinished business to attend to Val. We were interrupted back in Lachine wouldn't you say?"

"You talk too much you know that?" Val said summoning his staff, something Miles was now familiar with and activated his electric shield.

"It's funny, I never actually thought I would encounter you again Val, and especially here out of all places to be found, in the heart of battle. I misjudged you Val. You're no different from me."

"Let's just get this over with," Val said, now gritting his teeth and remembering his training.

"Very well then Val, if it's death you want then I will be the one to deliver it to you," Miles finally said before the two fighters plunged into one another in combat. This time they were both better equipped than they were last time and their training had improved. Immediately though Val began to weaken in the fight. His muscles tired from all the fighting he had been doing and Miles had only just walked into the battlefield with not a drop of sweat on his brow. His heavy armour also made the fight difficult for Val since he could not trip him over and Miles's razor sharp sword made it hard to get close for him to stab him with his knife. Soon Val had to turn to a defensive tactic since he could not strike Miles and found that his shield was his best weapon. Miles's sword may have been able to slice through flesh like butter but to an electric shield it was like any other blade. Since Miles did not have a shield Val tried to swing Miles around and strike him with his staff but soon his failed attacks became predicable and Miles could easily know his next move. After Miles had worn him down enough he let off a strong offensive line of attack and repeatedly struck his shield hoping that it would have the power down and leave Val defenceless.

The weather over Hiro was now covered in a dark grey sky, like the whole city was covered by one giant cloud and tiny spits of rain began to fall on the tired soldiers. Tiny pieces of dust kicked up from the battlefield and floated aimlessly around as the screams of the dying soldiers became fewer since there were less men now standing. Val lay back down on the floor after a vicious assault from Miles left him battered and beaten. He lay there defeated clutching a large wound in his side from where his shield powered down and couldn't prevent an attack from Razor that cut into his right side. Silently praying this didn't puncture his liver or any other important organs Val moaned in pain. His hands now stained with his own blood from holding his right side. His injury prevented him from using any of his weapons and the pain of it weakened him to the point that he could not do anything but lay there in agony and look up at the man who defeated him. Miles made sure that Val could not try any sneaky attacks and kicked him repeatedly until he was sure Val was unable to move. With pain all over his body now, Val tried to keep his consciousness by looking up into the grey sky but all he could see was Miles's evil grin beaming down at him. His vision began to blur and he heard the voices of the soldiers all around him and one that stood out was a deep, charging voice shouting, "Master! Master!"

With one giant leap Zoudiva snapped at Miles and caught his hand and bit down hard and pulled him away from his master. With his hand still in the kingnine's mouth Miles shouted in pain briefly before swinging a punch to Zoudiva trying to catch his soft nose but Zoudiva pulled down hard and dragged Miles away, shaking his arm like a doll trying to break through the armoured wrist protectors Miles was wearing. Sheeria and Raiden appeared in front of Val and knelt down to tend to him, "Are you ok Val? Speak to me!" Sheeria cried as she took him in her arms. Val blinked and shook his head and tried to focus on Sheeria in front on him. He found that he kept feeling like he was nodding off like he was tired and every time he tried focusing he only saw the tigian there holding him in her arms and shaking him awake.

"Look at me Val! Look at me, stay focused for me. I'm gonna get you back to the palace, ok?"

He could see that the state of him had distressed her as she looked down to his wound and every time he went to look down she held his head back up repeating, "Look at me Val!"

"Who has done this to you Val?" Raiden said as he knelt down beside them and gripped onto his hand. Val slowly held up his hand and pointed to one of the deceased bodies on the floor, Sheeria and Raiden both recognised it as Zack. Sheeria especially felt the sting as she remembered Zack sneaking up and saving her from the demons and night feeders back in Plainess. She followed his blood stained finger as it went from the dead Zack to the heavily armoured soldier fighting Zoudiva, grabbing his sword and now swiping for him, catching Zoudiva's leg and injuring him. With a yelp Zoudiva fell to the floor, his body already injured from the previous fight with the other two kingnines and whimpered as he could not stand and could only lay there like Val. When Sheeria recognised who this was a whole new blur of rage overwhelmed her as she placed Val back on the floor and roared in pure aggression to kill the traitor who sold them out to the Lachine President. Raiden at her side now began to bring the assault to Miles, the two felines alike fighting the heavily armoured human man who had now killed an ally and nearly killed another two.

Ducking and diving out of the way of her first attack Miles quickly stood back on his feet and glanced back at the leo and tigian. Noticing them immediately he laughed and shouted over to her.

"So where is Acarlie Sheeria? She can't be far, right?"

He got no answer but another aggressive snarl and evaded the swipes she tried for him and kicked her back. Not even the leo's scare tactic worked on Miles as Raiden found out. He tried to scare him into stepping back but instead the fearless human only stepped forward and swung his razor sharp blade for Raiden's face, glaring at him after and adding, "I won't be subjected to you surprising me from behind this time Leo. This time it's me and you!"

Raiden watched as Sheeria leaped for Miles again in her rage and watched Miles almost toy with her, ducking and evading her heavy but slow attacks. His wrist protectors he used as shields that blocked her claws and his taunting only angered her more.

She's getting too angry to take control of the fight, Miles knows this and is using it for his advantage, Raiden thought and knew if he was to be brought down he would have to do it himself.

Miles was still taunting Sheeria, blocking her attacks and wearing her down, calling out what he would do when he found Acarlie and soon Sheeria became not the tigian she was but so infused with rage that she became like a wild animal and this was what Miles was waiting for. He knew that if he could anger her enough then soon she would make a mistake and he could make his final blow. He kept his wits sharp though as he saw the leo charge him from the corner of his eye and ducked out of the way. Now showing his true skill in the battlefield Miles now solely fought the leo and tigian by himself. He was quick and could jump away from Raiden's attacks and could block Sheeria's, punching and kicking them whenever he had the chance. Sheeria began to tire out soon and this gave him the edge of the fight, now only concentrating on Raiden. He swung Razor from side to side trying to catch Raiden's legs or arms, jumping back when he needed to and staying away from a close up fight. He knew this leo's strength better than anyone and knew not to get too close.

Raiden began to pick up his game now. He realised Miles's skill now and couldn't help but kind of admire this human. His training was now at the peak of his fitness and even Raiden had trouble getting close to him. He knew very well that the sword he carried was especially sharp and would easily cut through his golden fur. He looked for holes in his fighting style, if something repeated or was predicable that he could use in his advantage but found none. Miles was a true Sphere warrior and the best fighter on the battlefield. His style was different from anything that he had ever seen before and could only detect the training of Alpha martial arts in his style mixed in the other one he knew. After ducking an attack, kicking down at Raiden's knee bringing him down to his level and swinging his body around, bringing his elbow up to connect with Raiden's chin Miles stepped back, "You know, has anyone ever told you how much you looked like your brother Valadad?" Miles said to him.

So this is his angle? He wants to anger me does he? Raiden thought while he wiped blood from his lip with the back of his wrist. Miles sneered again and continued, "You know I was there when he fell? Killed in action by the very soldiers that stand before you. He died like a fool, sending his platoon away and taking on the army by himself, it didn't take long for someone to stick him."

Raiden instantly thought of his old deceased brother Valadad, but he stayed focused and didn't let his mood drift onto the road of anger. He knew his boundaries and he knew bringing up his dead brother was something his younger self would have never let pass but he was patient and leaped to one side again swiping for Miles. He took his time and waited for Miles to swing back at him, believing his angering tactic to work was Miles's only mistake as he swung for Raiden, Raiden catching his arm and bringing him close to him. With his arm twisted Miles could not move as Raiden took his sword away from him and threw it aside, pressing him down to the floor. He knew his arm would not take long to break since it was now in the hands of a leo and so Miles had to think fast. He felt on the floor a brick from the rubble and took it up and swung back around, knocking Raiden on the chin with it. When Raiden let go in pain and recoil Miles quickly stood back up and smashed the brick again into the dazed leo's head. Not even the leos; the strongest of all the smart creatures on Sphere with their thick skulls could stand the force of a brick to the head. Raiden fell to the floor. His head still in one piece and his brain undamaged but his consciousness gone, lying there like any of the other dead bodies. Miles did not take the time to celebrate like a fool, like any other human would have done, taking out this large creature but instead turned to Sheeria, now being held back by his troops. He slowly walked forward and picked up another brick and stood before her smirking, "I want this one alive. I want her to see what my plans are for the elementalist after our mission is complete."

Sheeria screamed out, "No!"

"Don't feel bad Sheeria, look at it this way, at least you won't have the trauma and shame of being her alanode."

He laughed one more time then just like he did with the leo, smashed the brick around poor Sheeria's head and watched her go limp in the soldiers' arms, head bleeding but the body still breathing. Miles, triumphant over all the fighters now walked back to his sword and picked it up, walked straight past the still injured Zoudiva and back over to Val.

Val who now still in extreme pain looked up from the spot where he lay. The warm puddle of blood he lay in now began to feel cold and his eyes began to drift again looking up at the sky.

Miles stood over him again, putting the tip of his sword on Val's chest, "Well Val, any more surprises? It looks to me like none of your friends could protect you this time, not even the leo, isn't that a shame?"

Val felt the sharp tip of Miles's sword sticking into his chest and could only look up in defeat as the better man stood over him, waiting for his death to come.

41

Down in True Hiro the pirates had found a way into the old elemental school turned museum via a back door they had to silently break into. No alarms were installed in this place because not only did people rarely ever come here but nothing of value ever lived there that could be stolen. It was the stadium itself that was worth anything and it was the people of True Hiro who rallied together and kept it as a landmark. The museum would be open throughout the day and closed at night, tramps or drug dealers used to use this place as a shelter but soon like every other squatting place around the city they moved on to another place leaving the old stadium in peace. It stood tall and large like a warehouse. A metal roof covered it with many lights hanging from the ceiling in rows giving plenty of light to fill the whole building even in the darkness that shrouded it outside. Fans and pipes directing the artificial rain away from the building ran across the roof of it and down the large metal girders holding it up. In the centre of the museum now with rope around it was a very large pool with the stadium seats only on one side of it as they knocked down the other side to make room for a wall of paintings of the previous elementalists that used to train there all those years ago.

The pool had served different purposes in the past. When Dude was young he learned to swim in there whilst it was a communal swimming pool. But it was soon turned into the museum since the pool was so incredibly deep that children and weak swimmers drowned in there because the lifeguards simply could not swim deep enough to save them and still to this day the bodies haven't been found. With all his men inside Kaza looked around at the old stadium and turned back to Dude, "What would the army want from this place? It's a dump."

Dude just shrugged his shoulders and walked across to the wall he had seen a thousand times before to look at the old portraits, still kept in a decent condition all these pictures were cleaned a special way to protect the paint from smudging. Every picture had a different elementalist standing there, wrinkled with age standing next to the pool, some were very young and never lived to have the old age picture done and some were only children, all with names under the portrait and some with the title *Elemental Lord* under them. The pirates stayed with their captain and soon they all heard the sound of the army outside the front door, slamming into it, piercing the silence with force to break open the huge metal shutters. Kaza ordered his men to quickly hide behind the stadium seats and to watch what these soldiers were here for. A brief moment of silence came between every loud knock, Kaza waiting patiently with his men, gripping onto his weapon and watching the shutter doors, denting every time.

What is it they could possibly want from this place? He sat thinking while the doors slammed again. *If it's something to do with the elementalists then why don't they go to the official one above us? They must know it is there, there is nothing here that is worth anything, but still they invade the city as only a decoy as they send in their special group to come to this old dump.*

The doors slammed again one final time before the large, metal shutter doors fell from their hinges with a screaming clatter that echoed through the city. The soldiers that walked in didn't notice why the lights were already switched on and didn't bother to ask. The leader of the soldiers wearing the same heavy armour as Miles was the first to step in, looking around briefly and seeing nothing and signalling for his men to follow him until they reached the pool in the middle.

"Sir, where should I set the charges?" said a soldier carrying a large, heavy, wooden box.

Charges? So this is why they are here, they plan to blow up the stadium just like they did with Mecroyles! This puzzle seems to get more complicated each time we find something out. That's it! I'm going to find out some answers, Kaza finally thought as he was about to stand up.

The leader of the soldiers lifted off his helmet revealing a young, manly face, short black hair combed over to one side neatly and the look of inexperience of battle in his eyes. He turned to his companion and pointed to the far end of the pool, "Set the charges over there."

"Umm sir, we have company."

The soldier looked around to see Kaza being the first to stand up followed by his men, walking down from the old stadium seats and calling down to them.

"Sorry boys, the museum is closed for the night, if you want a tour you'll have to come back later in the week!"

It only took one look at Kaza for the inexperienced but heavily armoured soldier to burst out into laughter.

"And there I was worried that there would be a problem here. Pirates! All of what Hiro's council could have sent down here to protect the old city and they send pirates!?"

The other soldiers all laughed with him as Kaza and his men now all stood before them.

"You know I don't like your tone, makes my boys feel a little unappreciated that does. What say you give them all an apology and make your way back up to the city above?" Kaza sneered sarcastically.

The soldier let out another laugh at the threat of the pirate, "Please pirate, do you know who I am?"

"Are you going to back away now or are we going to have a problem?" Kaza threatened again avoiding any further conversation. He had seen something like this done once before by the old captain he used to work under. He learned from him that if you want something you have to show you are willing to take it; he wanted information and so needed to show these soldiers that he was not to be messed with. The soldier ignored the threat again and turned around to address his men with a cocky attitude, "Now watch and learn boys, this is how you take care of a pirate that acts too big for the boots he walks in."

The soldier spun back around ready to go through a textbook example of grappling an enemy but quickly found that this pirate was not too big for his boots and received a hard punch in his face, a kick under his knee joint and in only a second, found that he was on his knees in front of his men. The pirate before him had his arm reached out in front of him and holding a long bladed weapon in the style of a night stick, pressing it up against his throat.

Kaza knew he had this man where he wanted him now, "Wow, you really need to keep practising ay? It looks good when you do it in a class in front of your instructors but it's a little different when you need to use it on the field, right? Now tell me, why are you guys here? Why blow up an abandoned school when you have the official one above us?" Kaza asked pressing his blade up against the soldier's throat.

The soldier changed his cocky tone and spat down at Kaza's boots, "Screw you pirate, I bet you don't even have the courage to slit my throat do you? Yeah, you can punch a guy but deep down all you are is just a dirty smuggler."

"Don't test me boy?" Kaza warned.

"Ha! And you call yourself a pirate? If you were a real pirate you would finish the job!" the soldier called out.

This boy really has something to prove, I like that. Pity though...

Kaza held his arm out for a few more seconds. His pirates behind him all knew what was coming and silently waited for it while the soldiers all stood in an uncomfortable tenseness since they did not know what this one pirate in front of them was capable of. The young soldier leaned further into the blade without any fear at all but the cocky grin he held suddenly disappeared as Kaza whipped his arm to one side, his weapon now dripping in blood and the soldier, now with his throat cut held his neck with both hands and gargled briefly as he tried to breathe. With his other hand Kaza pushed him to one side to spasm and convulse before dying violently and loudly in front of all his men.

"Now who is the next in the chain of command?" Kaza asked the shaken up men. Now he really did have these men where he wanted them, just like how a leo could strike fear into humans Kaza had achieved a similar fear, these men now had lost their commanding officer to a pirate in cold blood. His men behind him set an uncomfortable tension to the soldiers. But not all of the soldiers were affected, one masked guy stood forward, "I am next in command Pirate and if you try anything like that on me my men will kill all you."

"Take off your mask. I can't hear you through that speaker coming out of your helmet."

"No, boys, battle positions!" the soldier ordered and he and all his men stood firm and activated their electric shields.

"Set the charges! We'll take care of the pirates!" he called out to the soldier carrying the heavy box that slipped away behind them. Kaza quickly whistled through his teeth at Dude, clicked and pointed at the soldier making his way to the other end of the pool and like a dog ordered to kill the aeomon was away, chasing the man down. The soldier knew he was being followed and safely placed down the box of explosives close to the edge of the pool, careful not to trigger anything that would explode and tried to draw his sword to fight but Dude was already close enough to attack him with Fireshaver. Before the soldier could move or duck out of the way the fiery blade was stuck into him, skewering him into the floor. A large echoing sound came from outside the old stadium and the sound grew until it was so loud it was unmistakable to know what the sound was. The soldier now in command turned round to see that a giant mob, hearing the sounds of them breaking into the museum had gathered together and grabbed any weapon they could, police and criminals alike stood shoulder to shoulder holding up torches and weapons. Kaza didn't need the guy to take his mask off to know he had gone completely pale at the sight of these town's people, who now heavily outnumbered him and his men, all angry that they had slipped into their city, marched their way through and busted their way into the only landmark they had.

"I guess your plan of using the army above us to decoy the soldiers away from the real mission here failed on one principle? You forgot that the people of True Hiro don't care for strangers and much as the posh upper floor folk, ay?" Kaza laughed at the soldier who turned to him then back at the upcoming crowd thinking what he could do, they were now trapped and had no means of escape.

"Shit," were the famous last words of the soldier as he dropped his weapon in defeat and the crowd who now had reached him and his men bundled on top of him and his men, beating them down to a pulp. There were no survivors.

42

Acarlie approached the battlefield cautiously after sprinting down there with Zahied by her side. The sound of screams and roars from tigians was disorienting for her as she hoped every time she heard one it would be Sheeria or Raiden. The archers from Plainess noticed her searching around and the word got out that the Elementalist was on the field. Mack ordered the archers to back her up and keep her from harm while she was searching, even going as far as sending two escorts with her. But she was adamant about finding Sheeria and refused again to leave. Whenever a guardian left the company of their elementalist, neither of them would be allowed to go further on the sacred pilgrimage. It was one of the strict rules that were never broken, a 'guide' (or later known as 'guardians') would always be with the elementalist every step of the way, ensuring the right training and protecting them from anything outside of the arena. They were always supposed to go side by side on every step, acting as two parts of the same contender of the League of Elementalists. To be without the guide was to be without the other half of their person. So it came custom for elementalists to be turned away from school doors if they did not have their guide present just like if the guide showed up without the elementalist. It was because of this that the high elders soon added a rule that the elementalist could choose a temporary guide to help them find their permanent ones and if the guide should die on the journey then the elementalist would have to stop the journey until they have found another guide. One that they are satisfied would uphold the rules and fulfil the sacred oaths until the journey is complete and they have become the Elemental Lord. In this case Acarlie took Zahied as her temporary guide but as soon as she came to find Sheeria on the floor his job was complete. She screamed for Sheeria who was still unconscious on the floor and ran over to her noticing Raiden was also unconscious on the ground. Zahied quickly ran to Zoudiva who was whimpering in pain and was grateful for the help from Zahied, searching his body for any more possible wounds that needed treating and began work on helping him back up. Acarlie did not even reach Sheeria when in the corner of her eye she saw Val lying down on the floor with a soldier standing over him, his weapon pressing down onto his chest. She froze briefly in fear and she felt stunned as her blood rushed cold and her stomach jumped into her throat when she saw the state of Val bleeding out on the floor looking back up to the man standing over him.

"Val!" she cried and caught his attention and nearly fell back in terror when she saw the man over him turn around and saw the cocky, evil grin of the man who betrayed her. As soon as she saw him she knew he was responsible for Val, Sheeria and even Raiden injured on the floor. Thoughts of Miles slaying her companions and guide rushed through her head and stuck in her mind like a needle that she couldn't get out. Miles, who once she thought she had loved now stood over the very man who saved her life. His weapon stained in the blood of her friends and now turned his attention from Val and on to her.

"There you are Acarlie! I was wondering when I would next see you, it's good to see you!" he called over to her in his sarcastic tone and stepped away from Val now and left him there. The two archers playing her escort stepped forward to protect her but she quickly put her hand up, signalling them back. This was her problem and she would have to deal with it herself. Over and over in her mind she remembered that night she shared with Miles back in Lachine. It was her first time she physically loved anyone and the fact he immediately betrayed her sent waves of fury in her mind and sent adrenaline through the veins in her body. Now he stood before her, having beaten her friends and nearly killed her guardian and this would have sent ripples down her pilgrimage that could possibly end her chances of winning.

"Miles..." she said softly trying to control her anger. "Why are you here? I thought you were against Feydon? Didn't you fight against them in the Battle of Osiris?"

"I'm here in this outfit to let my training as a warrior grow. I am near completion of being one of the greatest fighters on the planet now Acarlie! With my tribe's training mixed with the training I am learning from Alpha I will finally be able to use this to get revenge on the people responsible for wiping out my tribe."

"But you don't even know who did it Miles! How can you seek revenge if you don't even know who had done it to you?" she called out.

"That's true I don't know just yet but I'm getting closer Acarlie, and if I don't find out then I will just have to kill everyone. I'll start with this one."

He turned his back on Acarlie and back to Val lying on the floor. She knew what he was about to do and had to stop it. All the emotions and feelings she felt for Miles now only drove her to a higher point of anger. This man had to be stopped and that meant by any means necessary. She couldn't let this man live and she knew that. He could have killed Sheeria and now was going to kill her dear Val right in front of her without a second thought.

Miles stood over Val again and lifted up his blade but instantly it felt like it was taken away from him from behind. He knew no one was there and turned to see his blade now floating in front of Acarlie. Her hands out, not holding the blade but using her element; her power of magnetism, drawing the sword away from him and wherever she wanted it to go. He chuckled evilly when he saw that she was resisting him and stepped back in her direction, content on beating her as well as the tigian and leo.

The shadowy tigian back at the mobile command centre stood to one side now, facing a wall with a projection of the battle closer up. His ears pricked up when he noticed the elementalist in the middle of the field and using the touch screen projection scanned in closer to get a better view of her.

He crossed his arms and watched her closely thinking to himself. *She is no caster, she is an elementalist. Why would an elementalist be here in the middle of the battle? She must know she is not allowed to use her gift on the battlefield. Using the elements in the field is forbidden. Maybe this is the king's counter strike for me using the forbidden weapons?*

"My Lord, the discovery crew from down in True Hiro have not checked in," his adviser reported from behind him.

"Carry on as planned for the meanwhile. The decoy army is fine. Report to me if they don't call in again."

"Yes My Lord."

"And one more thing..." he paused so he had his adviser's attention, "Direct the cannons to the elementalist in the middle of the field. I want everything we got fired at her."

"At once My Lord."

Now let's see what this elementalist can do...

"You really think you can beat me Acarlie? There is no water here and the wind is too open for you to use it against me, you will kill everyone around us."

Acarlie ignored everything he was saying and focused on only beating him. She knew he was tougher and stronger than her but she had a major advantage and knew it. She glared into his eyes and he stared back grinning. They both pictured their night together as lovers in each other's arms. Miles, now smiling devilishly tried to provoke Acarlie.

"It's a pity you couldn't stay with me Acarlie. Quit your pilgrimage and allow me to kill these people you call friends. Become my concubine and watch me become the greatest fighter on the planet. With you by my side not even the Elemental Lord has a chance."

She could only picture him when she first met him, all innocent and handsome, helping her travel and saving her from demons. Now he stood before her like a demon himself. Val, Sheeria, Raiden, Zoudiva and even Zack all lay before him. Anger built inside her and her fingers began to twitch, ready to fight him. Miles only saw her silence as an uncomfortable rejection to his proposal, "If you will not come by your own will then I will have to take you for myself!" he called to her.

Her mind flickered. She knew she wasn't allowed to use her powers in a sided battle but she thought about Sheeria on the floor and a brief picture of herself tied up and dressed how Miles wanted her dressed, a slave to him, a sex slave to a walking human monster and finally Val lying down on the floor. He needed her now more than ever, the man who saved her twice now dying before her unless she did something about it. All these emotions and pictures swam around her head, speeding up as she tried to control them in her fury, all these faces in her mind flickered of her companions and only one remained, Miles. She held out her hand and let out her fury as she used her power to grip onto Miles's armour. She screamed in anger as she picked him up like a child picking up a doll and smashed him down on the floor. She heard him scream as his ribs cracked from the impact and threw him into a crowd of Feydon soldiers who froze in fear as they realised Hiro now had an elementalist on their side. Miles rolled over and stayed there, gasping for breath on the floor and Acarlie slowly held her hand down.

Screams from the Hiro troops began as they all began to point upwards and pointed to a wave of falling cannon balls just recently fired from the cannons with a large crack. Acarlie saw the fired projectiles now speeding through the air towards her, smashing down on the floor or the soldiers beside her, bouncing or crashing into the floor. The sound of them smashing down into the floor all around her was terrifying. A single blow would instantly kill whoever got in their way and she instantly became just like any of the other soldiers on the field, fighting for her life to avoid these raining death balls now all around her. She had enough time to dive out of the way as the sky now opened up and rained down with the large metal cannon balls from one side and arrows from the Plainess archers on the other. Every ball that landed came closer to her until she was on her back, crawling backwards and trying to spin around and pick herself back up off the floor, cowering in fear and turning away and holding her face when one of the cannon balls landed right next to her head and bounced away. The floor shook and small pieces of concrete smashed on impact and sent flying debris everywhere, falling over her. The sound of the metal balls exploding on the floor around her frightened her and muffled her screams as she scrunched into a ball on the floor and tensed her body in terror. Another ball fell close to her again leaving her to tighten herself in the ball even more and in only a split second of thought she turned and held up her hand to the sky. A large repeating, cracking sound rang around the battlefield like several thunderbolts all at once and every ball now in the air was stopped. Several large blue circles of magnetic energy appeared in the air and blocked their path to the floor. These blue circles spread all across the sky one by one, blocking out the sun and one by one the cannon balls struck each circle with another almighty crack. These were actually electromagnets Acarlie directed upwards so the metal balls would fall into these and once they disappeared, there was no more force in the speed they were flying at anymore and had no choice but to fall harmlessly to the floor now, without injuring anyone.

"My Lord, are you aware that Hiro has now the advantage over the decoy battle?" the adviser asked the shadowy tigian.

"Yes, I am aware of that," he answered growling in disappointment. "Has the discovery crew reported in yet?"

"No my Lord, they remain unaccounted for."

The shadowy tigian growled in his contemplation before adding, "Bring the soldiers back in."

"My Lord?"

"You heard me!" he barked back at his adviser. "Bring them back in, the mission failed."

"Yes my Lord it will be done. Where is our next destination?"

"Take the men back to a safe part of this country and set up camp. We need to rethink our strategy, they will not attack us since they will be busy rebuilding. Ensure my personal ship is at the ready too. It looks like I'll have to go back to where this all started," he said glaring at the monitor screen, staring at Acarlie who had foiled his attack in one swift move and now was kneeling down with the wounded man with the purple cloak in her arms. Her head buried in his chest, weeping for him.

This elementalist may prove to be a problem...

43

The battle ended with a retreat order from the mobile command centre outside Hiro. The Feydon troops gathered all their wounded and retreated back leaving only the dead. A mighty cheer of success came from Hiro and all the Plainess archers and all who survived the onslaught. Weapons were held high in the air and provoking curses, sticks and stones were thrown at the retreating army as they gathered their wounded and left. Acarlie, who still was kneeling down, clutching onto Val and weeping into his chest. She now felt like she truly had lost everything. She once again had broken sacred rules made by the elders and the familiar wave of extreme depression swept over her. With Sheeria on the floor too she felt like this was the end of her pilgrimage. All she wanted to do now was to pick up the knife from Val's side and jam it into her heart. A moment's pain would ultimately end her shameful pilgrimage that dishonoured not only her school and country but the whole League of Elementalists. She would now never be shown gratitude like the elementalists she admired as a child. Instead she will be known as a traitor, a black sheep and a deserter of the teachings. She picked up Val's knife and slowly ran her fingers down the blade, tears now running down her face. Her throat sore and mouth trembling. All she wanted to do was quickly end the pain, give in to the desire she felt overwhelming her to kill herself. But as she held the knife out her eyes caught Val still lying in front of her. His eyes were now closed but his chest was still moving steadily, still breathing. She remembered the promise she made with him and when he asked her not to ever try and harm herself when she felt like she had to. All the while he was still breathing she could not bring herself to strike the knife into her heart. The promise she made with Val outweighed the desire put on her by her teachings. All she could think of now was Val and how she could not let him down. She made a promise to him and even though it hurt her every second to carry on breathing she remembered him standing before her telling her to remember the moment she promised. Pain still swept through her as she felt herself fight the urge to drive the knife into her heart knowing what she had now become. She took a breath and threw the knife aside, lifted Val's dying body back up and cradled him in her arms. "I'll keep my promise Val, I will..." she said amongst her tears. "Just keep your side of the bargain! Stay with me Val, just stay with me!"

A great feeling of an uncomfortable stillness came over her then. Uncomfortable though it was it felt like a great wave of relief passed through Acarlie's blood. She felt like this should have been the happiest moment of her life but because of the circumstances she wept more. She never knew why but deep down in her subconscious she felt happy and relieved, like a heavy weight was lifted from her shoulders she never knew was there and even though she felt this way, this strange, free feeling troubled her but she was too traumatised to think about what it could be. Now even with her guardian lying unconscious and wounded nearby and the whole pilgrimage at stake, for the first time in her life she didn't care. All that mattered was the man she held in her arms now. His safety meant more to her now than her life itself. His blood now stained her skin she began to cry out and call for help.

Zahied was the first to retrieve her and while medics began to lift him from the floor in stretchers, Acarlie picked up the knife from the floor, took one last look at it and safely putting it back into its sheath on Val's side. Sheeria, Raiden, Zoudiva and all of the other wounded soldiers and archers became the priority of the army now as they were helped in ambulances and all rushed into the city's hospital. Acarlie clung onto Zahied's arm, wiping her sore eyes and watching the ambulances drive down the city.

"Is he going to be ok?" she asked him.

Zahied sighed and nodded to her, "Yes, I'm sure they all will be ok. Zoudiva will be fine I can tell you that now, Raiden and Sheeria are strong and Val..."

She looked up to him as he finished his sentence "...Val has a mission to do. He won't leave us so easily."

The next couple days were the quietest Hiro had in decades, everyone from above and below the border separating Hiro from True Hiro mourned the deaths of their family members and neighbours. The king took this time to be with his people, visiting them and making formal broadcasts to speak to them. He told them that the people from Plainess, the archers that saved them in the battle and all their families would now stay with them. He welcomed them into his country and city and honoured all those that fell for him and his people. Also he celebrated the heroic Anglish soldiers with his people who helped them all even though they were simply passing by. All the surviving Anglish were sent home and returned to Angland as heroes, the commander Chez would now become a local legend for his people and the stories of his courageous act of saving a city from Feydon at the cost of his life would be changed and changed again and eventually turned into a child's bedtime story of myth and legend. From that day relations between the two countries had never been so close, the king had spoken to the President of Angland and thanked him for all his help, this made even more trade between the two countries and Angland also sent in builders, doctors and soldiers into the city to help with its recovery. People from all over Racoves began to gather in Hiro to pay their respects. The king announced that this was an act of war between Feydon and Racoves, the President of Angland announced that he would stand beside the king in his decision and also the recovering Calmaron would also stand beside them. The king said that they would wait to lick their wounds first and pick themselves back up off the floor before charging in but assured that the Queen of Feydon would have some heavy explaining to do and the proper punishment would be dealt out.

All the while this happened the intensive ward in the hospital had never been so busy. Doctors and nurses ran all round the building tending to injured soldiers that had fallen in battle. The local casters from all around the country (including the help of Zahied) also helped the recovery of the people and soon even the country's elders were welcomed into the city to help with the sick and injured.

When Sheeria opened her eyes she found herself lying down on a large bed in an extension to the hospital. A giant tent covered her and many other soldiers lying in their beds, the doctors gathered round them and seeing to them. A nurse walked up to her as she woke and read the clipboard on the end of her bed, "Ah, Sheeria Katsan, Guardian to Elementalist Acarlie, it's good to have you back with us."

Sheeria moaned and rubbed her head. Her wound had now closed up but her headache was mind splitting.

"How long have I been asleep?" she asked the nurse.

"You have been in a coma for five days now. Try not to move too much since your muscles will be weak. We will get you some paracetamol if you still have a headache and something else to eat."

Instead of doing what the nurse said Sheeria turned and sat up, silencing the nurse's advice of staying put and saying "I'm fine, I'm fine, where is Acarlie my Elementalist?"

"The Elementalist has been waiting in the visitors' waiting room for your recovery ever since she got here. I don't think she has left the building yet."

"Please, you must take me there at once. I must see her as soon as possible."

The nurse hesitated at first but said, "Ok then. Follow me."

Sheeria was lead out of the extension of the hospital and through the hospital itself. She walked slowly but managed to keep herself on her feet even after being in a vegetative state for five days. She tried looking as she walked through the halls into the hospital rooms to find her comrades but didn't see any of them, believing that this meant that she was the last to wake. The nurse finally made a stop at the visitors' lounge. Chairs and vending machines scattered around the room. This room looked more depressing than the hospital's rooms themselves. People sitting round falling asleep in each other's arms, wrapped up in blankets they had been given and sprawled out between two or three chairs trying to get some sleep. Sheeria saw that Acarlie was one of the people lying down half awake and when she noticed Sheeria finally standing there after days of waiting she jumped up and ran over to her.

At first Acarlie ran up to her and hugged her tight, "Sheeria!" she called out squeezing in Sheeria's chest but then pulling away and striking her in her chest in a fit of anger and bursting out into tears again.

"Never do that to me again Sheeria! What do you think you were doing? You may have been killed then our pilgrimage would be finished. If I hadn't have followed you would all be dead Sheeria!" she cried out hitting her chest again, "Never do that again Sheeria, do you understand me? Never!"

Sheeria just held Acarlie close to her, burying Acarlie's head in her shoulder as she continued to cry.

"I was so worried for you. I thought you were never going to wake up," Acarlie sobbed.

"I'm sorry to worry you Acarlie but I had to go. I couldn't let Raiden, Val and Zou' go out there on their own." She paused and asked, "...Where are the others?"

Acarlie pulled back and wiped her face and took a breath before answering Sheeria, "Zoudiva and Zahied are fine, they are waiting back at the king's palace for us. Kaza and his crew also wait there. I managed to persuade him to wait for the injured to wake up. He's using the time to gather more crew down in True Hiro, and Dude being one of them has joined his crew and wants to continue on with us. Val is in intensive care still. His wounds are being healed and are having loads of stitches and medication to help him. No one can see him yet."

"What about Raiden?"

Acarlie now paused as she wanted to break the news softly to Sheeria, "Raiden... has become the main priority for all the city's elders and high doctors. Because he is the last of his kind they are doing everything they can for him...but it's not looking good at the moment. He's still in a deep coma, worse than yours. He was hit very hard in his head and suffered a massive internal injury that only his thick skull meant he managed to barely survive."

Sheeria felt an incredible sting when she first heard the news. After the fight with Miles, Raiden sustained such a bad head injury that he now lay in one large room in the hospital away from all the other injured soldiers. Doctors, nurses and even the elders who have travelled through the country have gathered by his bedside to heal him. The people all knew he was the last of his kind and this was now a difficult time for him and his injury now endangered an entire race, so they truly were doing everything they could to help him back on his feet.

"What happened to the battle?" Sheeria asked Acarlie again.

"The Feydon troops retreated after I had to intervene with the battle. It's reported that they are still in the country but are afraid to attack again knowing that Hiro would have doubled its numbers by gathering its country together. Right now the king is talking to the President of Angland to sort out Hiro's defence and safety but has told his people to expect war."

Once again Sheeria felt an uncomfortable sensation when Acarlie mentioned that one word but Acarlie carried on. "It's also been said that the Senate in Chippenham now know of the humans manufacturing forbidden weapons. This now could not only be war between nations but a new Divide..."

"Miss Acarlie!" called a nurse as she rushed into the patient's waiting room interrupting their conversation, "Val has woken up. He's asking for you."

Raiden opened his eyes to the sight of smiling elders and doctors around him, almost cheering for the success of his recovery, shaking hands and hugging one another. His head felt dizzy from the lack of food from the last few days and he felt overwhelmingly confused.

"What happened?" he asked everyone around him and the doctors answered him smiling happily.

"Welcome back Raiden. You have been under for the last seventeen days now. It's thanks to the elders that you're even back with us now. Please don't stand, your muscles will have to get used to the movement once again or you could do yourself much more harm. Everybody in the city has heard of your heroic act and has been waiting for you to wake, especially your friends who have been at your side since the fall you took."

Raiden took all the information in well and didn't move much but the only thing that stood out was how long he was under for, "I was under for seventeen days? Where is everybody else?"

The doctor filled him in on all the information of what happened after Miles knocked him out. How Acarlie had stepped in and took Miles out and saved Val. He told him Val was seriously injured but had been making a miraculous recovery like nothing he has ever seen. He still had the bruises and cuts and stitches but every day seemed to become stronger. His inner defence system seemed to work almost twice as quick as a normal person's. He also told him about the pirates all waiting for him to wake so he could begin back on his mission and told him about Sheeria's slow but steady recovery from her head wound also given to her by Miles.

Damn that Miles! Raiden thought after the doctor finished telling him. *How could one man be so strong, after all my training since birth? Everything I have been brought up to believe about leos being stronger than humans and this one man alone takes out Val ,Sheeria, Zoudiva, Zack and myself all in one go?* The thought of what happened puzzled Raiden and he couldn't get his head around how he done it. He remembered the strange martial art Raiden had never seen before and how Miles had fused it with the fighting skills of the Feydon soldiers.

The next couple of days Raiden still could not leave the hospital as much as he wanted to, but had to use the time to exercise his legs and body back into shape before being let back out to see his new friends waiting for him back at the king's palace where they had been staying. He was greeted by them with applause from everyone in the room, including all the pirates under the command of Captain Kaza. He felt overwhelmed by this and waved a thank you to all of them. Acarlie was the first to approach him and wrapped her arms around his shoulders, followed by Sheeria then Val who stepped up still with a limp and smiled at him and patted him on the back. Even Zoudiva stepped up and bowed his head towards him, "Welcome back Master Raiden, I'm glad to see you back on your feet."

After all Raiden and Zoudiva had just been through and the history between the two races Raiden finally opened up a little to him then and knelt down, "Thank you Zoudiva...You did well then back in the fight against the other two kingnines. I never got the chance to tell you, I'm sorry for misjudging you before."

Zoudiva bowed his head, "I'm guilty of the same sin Raiden. I hope we can now fight side by side as companions."

They both nodded in their mutual agreement as Raiden stood up to address the captain of the ship waiting for him.

"Now I am back Kaza we should make our way to Aragorth so we can finally reach the temple." He now had everyone's attention in the room and spoke clearly for them as a true leader, "this mission has been going on for far too long now, with one thing after another standing in front of it, blocking our path to finally reach our goal. So now that we have a skyship, a captain and crew willing to carry us there and nothing now in the way I want to start going there before we get sidetracked again."

The captain now stood forward and also spoke to the crowd and crew of the Scarlet Arise.

"We will at once Raiden. But first, now everybody is here I should use the time to report what happened down in True Hiro. The information has already been told to the king and now I was waiting for you to tell the others..."

Acarlie and everybody else all looked interested now, "What do you mean?" Zahied asked.

"You say that the soldiers destroyed Mecroyles, yes? The elemental school was torn down and nothing was left standing. Well, the attack from above that you all witnessed was only a diversion, a decoy to pull the city's soldiers to one part of the city while a special squad was sent down below."

"Why would they be sent there?" Acarlie asked.

"Well, they made their way with an explosive down the streets and into an old elemental school that used to be the one Hiro would use before it became two levels."

Sheeria now stood forwards, leaning onto a sofa close to her and asked, "Are you sure they wanted the elemental school? If they had explosives then they might have been going for the giant pillars holding up the whole city. If the pillars were destroyed then the whole city would collapse on itself and destroy everybody above and below."

Kaza nodded, "That's what I thought at first, but why would they kill everyone? Even their own army? No, that makes no sense. They were looking for something, something so important they sacrificed their men to get their hands on it."

Acarlie broke in now remembering the elders of Mecroyles, "The elders from Mecroyles said the same thing, they said they were looking for something."

"Precisely my point!" Kaza said pointing at Acarlie. "If they are looking for something it would have to be of some value right?" Kaza said again and Raiden finished his sentence for him, "And where better to find something than the ancient schools of the elements? They have been around for thousands of years now."

Kaza pointed and nodded to him agreeing, "Which is why they went to the old school under the city rather than the official one on top. There must be something hidden under every elemental school in Sphere, and whatever it is the Queen of Feydon knows about it and is willing to risk everything to reach it."

Everything Kaza said seemed to make sense for Acarlie then but then the realisation suddenly hit her like a ton a bricks. "If there is something under every school, then Feydon would surely invade every school on the planet until there are none left!"

Sheeria knew then what she was getting at. Their home town Eloma would not have a chance to defend themselves against the forces of Feydon. They would be all wiped out, her school torn down, her friends killed, her elders and her home.

"When this breaks out of all proportion, there could be chaos, even the elders will take sides on this one. Whatever Feydon wants they're ensuring another divide for it. This must be so important that they must not have it," Zahied stated.

"But we don't even know what it is they are after yet, it might just be for money," Raiden said.

"No, money is not what they are after, Alpha is the richest city in the world, it simply does not need it. They are after something else, something so important that it has had to be hidden so well that for over a thousand years no one has known about it. It makes sense really, if we had something no one wanted the world to have, we would give it to the elders. They have no concept of value and could hide something easily in the schools. They're like temples and the teaching would forbid it to go around the depths of the schools looking for something," Sheeria said again.

"Then if the elders know about it then the only place we could learn about it is in Aragorth, the monastery there has details of everything important that has ever been recorded there dating back even before the First Divide, millions of years ago when the original sun died out," Zahied stated, stepping forward into the conversation.

"Wait a second," Val pointed out as he realised what the others didn't. "If you're saying there is something important under each school then Feydon must already have one thing right? Because they would have already gone through their own school back in Alpha."

"That's right, and Delta. Feydon has two elemental schools so they would have already found two things and three if they found something in Mecroyles!" Acarlie said.

"That's only if there *is* something under every school, there might just be one thing under one of the schools and Feydon is simply looking for it," Kaza pointed out.

"So what is going to happen about all this? Because I don't think Feydon will hand anything over even if they *do* possess something, nor will they give up the arms they used against us today," Val asked but Zahied interrupted asking another question.

"What are the world leaders doing about this? Blowing up elemental schools, using the forbidden weapons against the cities when they should be within the treaty? Right now they dishonour all the fallen leos and humans who lost their lives in the Last Divide and risk another."

"The king only told me that action would be taken all in good time," Acarlie replied. "I don't know what this means but I think that the United Nations would rise up against Queen Angel and Feydon, perhaps this means Septura, the entire continent itself would be the war zone for years to come."

Raiden, growing tired of this conversation decided to end it sharply, "Whatever is going to happen we have no choice but to go to Aragorth and find the information about it. Let's not forget there is a giant black hole floating around in space waiting to destroy the planet itself! Acarlie still has her pilgrimage as well so we must stay focused and continue on with the mission. We will find out what we need to know from there."

"Actually my plan was to drop you guys off at the monastery and make my way back here to try and see what it is Feydon is hiding for myself. I hate the way the government takes ages to try and get something done," Kaza pointed out and Raiden snapped back.

"But we shall need you further along our travels! The Elementalist will need passage to her next city."

Kaza didn't like being told what to do and knew the bargain he made with Val and stuck with it.

"Hey, let's not forget who owns the ship you will need to ride! The ship goes where I choose and I say we should split up!

Everyone who needs to go to the monastery will go with Raiden, everyone else including my crew will backtrack to the Feydon army base camp and try to find out what we can from them. If all fails we can always make a quick getaway." His strong leader-like sentence silenced the leo and everyone else in the room, "Now, who is with the monastery crew?"

Raiden did not need to answer for it was established he was already going. Val was the first to step up, "It was also brought on to me this mission. I have many questions for the elders anyway. I'm going."

Zoudiva now stepped in knowing his master had just spoken, "I will go wherever my master goes, if the ancient monastery is his destination..." he did not even need to finish his sentence.

"I will go with Val and Raiden. From there I will travel to Toshiro in Anavrin for my next Elemental Battle," Acarlie stated speaking for both her and Sheeria.

Zahied thought for a second and stood forward, "Val, Raiden, I have been on your journey from the start and would love to learn from the ancient scrolls but if Kaza intends to infiltrate Feydon's base camp then he will need help from a caster and since I am the only one here who qualifies then I should go with them after we reach Aragorth."

Dude who couldn't speak did not even move now, for he was now a crew member of Kaza's men and was counted for when Kaza spoke.

"Then it's settled, Raiden will go to the monastery with Acarlie, Sheeria, Val and Zoudiva to find out what they need to know and will carry on their way to Anavrin, to the city Toshiro where Acarlie will gain her next element. Everyone else will stay on board the ship and make our way to the base camp and try to find out what we can about the enemy. We will all rendezvous at Toshiro after we have found out what we all know and decide what we can do about this situation then. Are we all agreed?" Kaza finally said and every voice (apart from the mute aeoman) agreed and watched as Captain Kaza lead the way to the door,

"Good then, let's get aboard the Scarlet Arise and begin the journey..." He turned and added, "Every once in a lifetime a single group of people has the power to make history. The world may not like it but now it depends on us, a crew of pirates, a stranger, the Last Leo and an elementalist, against an army using forbidden weapons, an upcoming new divide and a black hole resting in space. Sphere's divide! This is so much more fun than smuggling..."

44

The Scarlet Arise glided steadily over the large oceans silently. The night sky now was fully open and the stars beamed down onto the peaceful and undisturbed ocean as the ship sailed the sky above it. The ship had now been in the air for the past three days. The injured had used this time to recover from their wounds and use a series of exercises to strengthen the muscles they had lost previously while Acarlie used the time to study her elements and practised her elemental katas. The past few days Acarlie had been quiet with Val since she was still a little upset by his act back in Hiro but also had a lot on her mind, as did Val.

She finally came out to look for him on this night. The air was warm but the movement of the ship gave it a slight chill. The sun would not be up for another few hours and only the silvery glow of the moonlight lit up the oceans below them, reflecting the stars and stretching darkness as far as the eye could see. She found him at the edge of the ship, on the decking above. All the pirates and crew members were either working inside the ship or were resting for the night. Only Val stood there, leaning up against a banister on the edge of the ship and staring out into the perfect sky.

To Val it was a truly magnificent sky that night, like he had taken a magic knife and split the sky open from its skin and could see all the wonders of the universe in all its true glory. One of the moons had now settled in the west while the other still sat high in the sky and the stars now gleamed around it like millions of micro diamonds in a velvet sky. The harder he looked the more stars he could see, hiding between others so small he could only just see them.

Acarlie stepped up from behind him and stood beside him and gazed up at the beautiful, black sky above them.

"It's a nice night," she said, fumbling with her words deciding what she should say to him.

"Beautiful isn't it?" he then looked over to her and saw her head facing the ground. "What's on your mind Acarlie? You have been quiet since we boarded this ship."

She looked up from the ground and told him, "Val," she paused again. She really didn't know how she could tell him but managed to force herself, "I want to ask you something."

Val noticed her fidget uncomfortably, "What is it?"

She fumbled with her words again and finally looked up at him and said, "I want to make you my Guide."

Val now felt a little shocked, "What!? Me? Really!"

She knew she had started now and so again forced herself to tell him the rest, "Yes. You, Raiden and Zoudiva."

"But why? I thought Sheeria was your Guide?"

"She is Val, I don't know why but I just feel like I'm safe with you that's all." She took a step forward and leaned on the bannister beside him and looked down at the shimmering ocean below them, mirroring the stars above. "It's like deep down I know that I will make it far with you at my side." She could hear the words leaving her mouth and knew how bad they were sounding but had to carry on to relieve the weight she was carrying on her shoulders. "I've felt this way ever since what happened at Hiro. I just feel like it's the right thing to do. I know Raiden and Zoudiva will travel wherever you go and so I want them to be my guides too."

"But I don't know any of the teachings or sacred rules of being a guide," he confessed.

"That's not important. All that matters is that the guide is willing to give everything up for the elementalist, I know I'm making the right choice here."

"What about Sheeria? Won't she be your guide anymore?" he asked.

"Yes of course she will, I'm allowed as many guardians as I like. It's just I have to make sure that they will always be one hundred percent behind me and my choices. So Sheeria will agree with me here and if she don't then she will at least not try to stop me. Also since we are visiting the elders from Aragorth they will be able to authorise it."

Val stood back and thought for a second. He wondered if this would be a blessing or a burden on his mission and wondered if Raiden would agree with it. He leaned back against the banister again and looked back over to Acarlie. The wind blowing to an angle taking her long, dark hair to one side. Her brown eyes now reflected all the beauty of the stars above them and he saw how they were calling out for him. He remembered the promise he made to himself before and answered, "Ok then, when we are done at the monastery I shall become your Guide. I will be travelling with you anyway so it makes sense really."

When he said it he saw there was still something troubling in her eyes, "There is one more thing I have to ask you," she said.

"What's that?"

She now did not pause to consider the words to say but instead took his hand and spoke what was in her mind, staring up at him she said, "You have to promise me you will never do anything stupid like you did back in Hiro. If you're going to be my Guide then I will need you with me at all times." She thought again of how she could tell him, "You see, a while ago Sheeria told me I was too generous with my emotions...I gave all of them to Miles too quickly and he hurt me. I just don't want the same thing to happen with you Val so you can't go running out nearly getting yourself killed for no reason. I was so worried for you then, back at Hiro when you were injured that I..." she did not finish her sentence but decided to keep it a secret and instead followed on. "Just promise me you won't do anything like that again."

Val never knew what happened on the battlefield after he passed out. He heard that Acarlie took Miles out but he never knew the whole story so he felt a little confused by this but still understood what he done, "Ok then, I'm sorry Acarlie, I won't do anything like that again, if I'm your Guide then I will do my job properly."

Now she did smile even though she still felt worried and wrapped her arms around him, hugging him tight, "Thank you Val, you won't regret this."

Val began to think to himself, *maybe this is the chance I need to find out about her conditioning and try to help her. I don't want her to die and now I have the chance to really help her.*

She kept her head resting up against his shoulder and looked over her shoulder at the ocean and the stars above them, "What was you doing out here anyway?"

Val let go of her now gently and looked back over the dark horizon, "I was just thinking about what I would learn about myself from the elders when we get there, wondering what my parents are like, or my friends and home, or if I even have any at all."

"What will you do once you find out? I mean what would happen if you found out you are a spy for Feydon or something? Would you go back there?" she asked him carefully.

He thought about it for a second. The wind around them gently breezed past and out into the darkness beyond. He still didn't know who he was. He could have been anyone, a traitor, a royal, a husband. The only thing he knew about himself was that he was Val. And only Acarlie and the others made him Val. If he was not there with her and her pilgrimage, or with Raiden and the mission then he had nothing, no identity, no purpose; no Val.

"No," he gently confessed and looked back at her, waiting eagerly for his answer. "No, I wouldn't. I would stay with you and finish the mission, our mission. It's just the thought of finally finding out about myself seems so exciting I don't know how I am going to take it. Whatever happens though I will still stay with you, I will keep my promise."

She smiled again and he returned her smile. She stood close to him again and rested her head against his shoulder and together they both stared up into the open sky and stared at the bright and beautiful stars above them still decorating their night. They kept their thoughts to themselves and took the time to enjoy each other's company in silence. To them they were all alone now, a peaceful and blissful silence came over them as the Scarlet Arise carried on its journey and Val and Acarlie stood as the only people on the deck, apart from the silent kingnine who sat at the door with his head resting on his paws, watching over the two humans as they enjoyed the rest of the night.

45

A nother day passed and they finally reached the shores of Aragorth. It stood as a large island off the coast of the continent Remaynies. The ship landed gracefully onto a large green field at the bottom of a hill that lead up to the monasteries that stood on the top of the hill. A cliff side close to where the monasteries overlooking the ocean gave it a very peaceful look and gave a different view of how the elders lived for Val.

Kaza and his men including Dude and Zahied all stood briefly at the Scarlet's cargo doors for Acarlie and her companions (including the four lizziers that were with them from the start of the journey) to say their goodbyes to the crew.

Raiden first spoke to Zahied, "Thank you for all your help Zahied, we will meet again."

"Of course we will Raiden, this is only a temporary mission. We shall all meet you at Toshiro soon."

Val went to Dude who nodded to him and patted his shoulder, "You keep yourself alive Dude do you hear me? I feel bad we have to go our separate ways for a short time but I guess this has to be done, good luck."

Dude nodded again and shook hands and gestured with a small knock on Val's shoulder like he was saying, "*Look after yourself.*"

Acarlie went to address Kaza last but Kaza felt like a busy man and kept it short, "Right then Acarlie, hurry up and get the information from the monastery and make your way to Toshiro. If we're not there then wait for us. We're not going to abandon you."

"Ok Captain, thank you for the passage on your ship."

Kaza laughed, "Hey, no need to be so formal with me Acarlie. Sphere's divide! I'm a pirate not a cruise ship captain, and you're always welcome aboard my ship. This ain't about pirating no more. This is about the planet so get off my ship and meet us at Toshiro, you got me? There's a storm coming anyway and I want to beat it before it catches us over the ocean."

"Yes Captain," she smiled and walked off the ship with Sheeria at her side.

As they watched the cargo doors close from outside the ship they heard the captain shout to his crew, "Ok then boys, ready the ship! Get the thrusters on and get ready for the quick flying procedures!"

The silent aeomon stood at the door and they all watched as he was the last person they saw, waving to them with his sword on his back before the doors closed and the ship lifted off the ground, turned around and sped off into the distance using its thrusters to travel at thrice the speed it was when they were on board.

Raiden turned to his Lizzier Bluey and jumped on his back, "Ok then we're finally here, let's go!"

The monasteries were massive when Val first saw them, all close to one another like they were one building. The land around them was almost desolate, just fields lay around them. No paths, no spaces for M.V's nor skyships to land, just forest space and plenty of uncut grass spaces all around. The cliff on the other side of the monasteries were high up from the ground. Being up on high ground was good for the monasteries since they had to stand for thousands and thousands of years. Because of this the monasteries were extremely old but still stood strong, built out of marble, rock and stone they stood the test of time whether that be under the influence of the elders or not. Raiden was the first to dismount when they reached the doors. Rain now began to spit down as the sky had grown dark again and stormy rain clouds drew over them. The giant, old, wooden doors opened before them and the elders on the other side greeted them.

Once again as soon as Raiden saw the faces of the elders he bowed down to the floor, Acarlie also bowed as did Sheeria, Val was a little reluctant as before but he bowed all the same and only after he did, Zoudiva bowed too.

"Greetings travellers, what brings you all the way over the waters to our quiet, peaceful island," one of the elders said.

"Elders of Aragorth. I am Leo Raiden I was sent here by Elder Amber from Walton. I have travelled from the far side of the world to see you elders. We seek only information from you."

The elders smiled, "Very well, first let's get you all inside in the warm and dry, your lizziers too look hungry from the journey, come in please."

They were led inside and into a long and wide corridor, with marble pillars on either side of them, spaced apart from one another and reaching up to support the ceiling above them, with small artificial, electronic lights beaming down on them from the top of where the pillars met each other in their pairs. Rain started to pour down outside and tap repeatedly on the tall coloured windows high above them and many doors either side of them led out into more rooms and hallways similar to this one.

"Who travels with you then Raiden from Walton and what brings you here?" the elders asked him.

"The human male is Val. He has been on the journey from the beginning. He wishes to know more about who he is and we think you are the only hope, with the ancient knowledge of the planet's scrolls that can help us. The kingnine with him is Zoudiva, a great warrior of his clan and protector to Val. Acarlie is the human female with us, she is an elementalist from Eloma on her pilgrimage. Sheeria the Tigian is her Guardian, they have decided to join us here to accompany us while we find out what we need to know."

"Ah, an elementalist is in our presence, we do not often get visitors here, especially elementalists. Tell me Acarlie, whom is your elder back in Eloma?"

Acarlie bowed again and addressed the elder in her formal tone, "Elder Argo is the master and High Elder of my school. We have travelled far since my pilgrimage started and I have gained only two of the seven elements so far on my journey."

"Seven? There are eight elements my child."

"No Elder, there are only seven. On our journey we found out that Lachine made their own element by stealing the traits of the Element of Wind in Eloma. The Element of Metal is now no more. We are going to travel to Toshiro once we have found out what we need to know from here."

"And what is it you need to know?"

"Before I begin I should tell you Elder Amber's vision," Raiden began, "She saw that out in the midst of space lies what is known as a black hole. A giant mass of gravity so powerful not even light itself can pass through nor escape it. It threatens to destroy Sphere. Val and I have been sent from Walton to find out information on what could be done to stop this from happening. Please elders, you now are our only hope."

The elders gave a worried stare to one another then turned into a small huddle to speak amongst themselves. They turned back round saying, "Such a universal force of destruction truly cannot simply be destroyed, but perhaps there is something that can help it from destroying the planet."

Raiden almost jumped when he heard the news, "What is it?"

"This would be better if we showed you rather than just tell," the elder then nodded to another and continued, "please walk this way."

The elder lead them out of the huge hall and into what looked like a giant library, bookcases several stories high filled every corner of this large room with every gap closed off with a book or scroll. Ladders that connected to the top of the shelves rolled across the floor and reached high up to reach even the highest of books.

"Is this where the planet's scrolls are kept?" Val asked in wonder.

The elder chuckled, "No no Val, these are simply pieces of literature we keep to read over the years, some are thousands of years old; some are even older. All the real scrolls are stored in a special place in these monasteries, to ensure that they are safe from not only thieves but from the planet itself."

"What do you mean by the planet itself, does it want to destroy them?"

The elder chuckled again, "No, no, not at all. You see age will eventually change everything, even rocks and cliff sides will erode due to age and wear away. These monasteries were built by not only the elders but the humans of their time as well. These are built to withstand time itself. The humans knowing that one day other humans would want the power of knowledge, gave the monasteries to us elders to stay here ever since, passing down the responsibility from father to son for over a million years now."

"Wow these monasteries are *that* old, detailing every piece of information here? Surely there isn't enough room even in this giant library to store every piece of information about the world's history?" Val said as they were led into the middle of the library, into a large circle on the floor. A small panel from the floor opened and up and out came a metal arm with a square control panel on it next to the elder. He pressed a series of buttons and slowly a small glass frame appeared from the circled line below them, like it was trapping all of them inside it.

"No, not in here," the elder said to Val as the glass frame had now gone all the way up and everyone got a small shock as the circle they stood in now lowered an inch, then another, then began to descend into the ground below them. The library now above them was getting smaller and smaller until it was only a speck of light in the distance.

Total darkness now consumed them all but the elder spoke to them all comfortingly, "Please don't be alarmed. I am taking you to the real monastery now, the one where we truly keep all the records of the planet's history. This is only a human made elevator to hide it from everyone else, the monasteries you saw are only a cover to keep outsiders from ever finding this place, only the human world leaders and the highest of elders in the council know about this place. To everyone else this place is only a myth and that is how we like to keep it."

"Is this how you meant to protect the scrolls from ageing, a place where no salty wind can damage the paper?" Raiden now asked.

The elder did not answer but only said, "Look down now my friends. Now you can see it."

They all looked down to see the ground below them was now like a giant cave, spreading miles down into the distance. They could see no edge of the cave, only darkness from where a strange blue glowing light could not reach. Down on the floor was now a large rectangle building with many more extensions spreading down them all made with metal, rock or dry mud but the mud here glowed blue. It filled the floor and every building. It was like a country itself, buried miles below the planet's crust, safe and secure from anything that may have threatened it, shining like a miracle down there in the total darkness.

To Acarlie and everyone else it was a truly amazing sight to see for the first time, "How does it glow that colour?"

"We have always been told that the ancient elders used these special crystals to mix in with the mud which would always glow in total darkness. These crystals were apparently forged by the elders from flowers that shone in the darkness."

Acarlie remembered the flowers she saw when she first started her journey and nodded and agreed, "So it means you will always have light down here."

"Precisely that. Many people would think it magic when first seen, but really like everything else on Sphere it is just something that is explained a little differently than how the humans explain things. Now please walk this way."

They were led away from the elevator and through the glowing blueness of the land under the planet. The buildings looked like laboratories from the outside. Val took his finger to the glowing blue mud on the floor and saw the tiny crystals in the mud, staining his skin like all mud and even on his cloak as he wiped his finger on it. It was an amazing sensation for seeing such a lit up and wonderful cave so far down in the planet but brought up countless questions in the beholder's mind of how long it must have taken to build such a cave. Inside the monastery down below, it was a lot more like a laboratory. It had working lights down there which also glowed blue. The walls, floor and ceiling were all made from metal. The elders finally led them into a room with a shallow pool in the centre, small chairs for the elders to sit on around the outside. They directed them to stand in the pool in a circle. Zoudiva being only a kingnine could not stand on his hind legs and so had to sit aside and watch from outside.

Sheeria was the first to step in, shuddering when she did and spoke of the coldness, followed by Acarlie, Raiden and lastly Val.

They all stood in a circle in the dimly lit room as the elders all sat in their chairs and concentrated. One of them said, "This room was made to show the humans what information they seek. For you see, there are no real scrolls to be kept. All the information is stored within us elders. We are the scroll keepers and pass down our memories from our ancestors' memories to our children and they become the keepers. This is what we have brought you here to see."

Val was about to ask how he could see the information then but suddenly the light in the room became darker and the pool lighter. It glowed blue, the same colour as the mud outside and soon they could all look down and see small, shining white particles swimming around their feet. The light particles lifted up out of the water's surface and floated in the centre of the circle they had made. Like billions of pieces of glowing dust the particles all floated together and formed a sphere, resembling the planet then slowly turned majestically like it was in space.

"What we are going to show you is what really happened to the planet all those years ago," the elders began and they all sat and watched as the particles all changed from one shape to another as they told the story. "In the beginning there were elders and humans. Elders so wise of the planet and humans so intelligent of the universe itself all lived in harmony between them. This stayed this way for a very long time. Until they had to deal with a problem that threatened every life on the planet. For you see, the sun, mother of all life was dying out. The humans knew that she would expand, using up the rest of her energy and in this movement, the planet would be destroyed. The humans and elders got together and decided to save the planet by sending up a satellite that would orbit the sun. This satellite was as big as a city itself and manned by a skeleton crew at first. This satellite works the same way as a giant teleporter of energy. It uses the energy from a neighbouring star and teleports it to our sun, refuelling it."

"Yes yes yes, we all know the legend. What has this got to do with the black hole though?" Raiden began to say getting frustrated as they all stood and watched the light particles form a small satellite and float around in front of them.

"This satellite is the answer you're looking for Raiden. We believe that if anything can save the planet it is this. If it can teleport even a far away star's energy into the sun then it will be able to deflect the black hole's energy somewhere else. If you turn it into itself it would implode on itself, destroying it completely."

"How do you know that will work?" Sheeria asked.

"That is what the planet is telling us."

"But how are we going to get up there into outer space? The last time someone went up there was millions of years ago." Val asked now.

"Good question, there were three rockets made. One took the satellite up; one took the crew up and the other was hidden somewhere on the planet," the elders then paused. "That's strange?"

"What is?" Raiden asked.

The elder closed his eyes like he was searching the files documented in his mind, "There are no records of what happened to the last rocket. It's like the file has been deleted from our memory banks."

The realisation hit Val suddenly, "Do you think this has something to do with what Feydon is looking for?"

"Yes good point Val. Elders, what is buried under the elemental schools of the planet? Feydon has been searching for something under every one and we believe that this might be connected with them," Raiden shouted over to them.

The elders searched again and repeated, "The file has not been found, but it's not like it was never there, it was like it has been removed."

"Ha! There you all are. I thought I would find you all down here!" shouted a mysterious voice from the door behind them. They all swung around to the deep growling voice to see a tigian now standing in the shadows of the doorway.

The shadowy tigian now stepped out into the light to reveal himself as a large built tigian with strong shoulders and a cloak over his square frame. Acarlie, Sheeria and Raiden instantly knelt down when they first saw him, bowing toward him like he were an elder, but Val who was unaware of who he was stood his ground.

"Who are you?" he called out.

"Val, mind your manners! That's the Elemental Lord!" Acarlie told him.

One of the elders now stood up and walked over to him, "Ah, it is good to see you again Elemental Lord. My friend, Zane..."

46

They all stood before the shadowy tigian that had appeared from the door from which they came, having used the elevator only minutes after they used it he managed to catch up with them before they left the room. As all the others bowed down to the Elemental Lord Val did not and neither did Zoudiva, only following his master. Val knew of this tigian and had heard about him from before. The Elemental Lord, the strongest elementalist in the world, who had gone on his pilgrimage and defeated every school and got to the top. He also knew Acarlie must have felt very tense now since she would one day have to face this tigian and have to kill him to take his title, but from what he had heard before, from Catch the Aeomon on the ship they were granted passage on telling him that Zane was not only the Elemental Lord but the single greatest elementalist that ever walked. His reign has gone on for years now and he had never been defeated.

There was something unsettling about Zane for Val that made him weary about his presence, "Why are you here?" he asked but Zane did not answer. He simply looked over to Acarlie bowing down at him and said, "Rise Elementalist." He spoke with an almost enchanting dominance in his voice, like he could order the world itself with a whisper.

She did as instructed as did Raiden and Sheeria after her. As he was the Elemental Lord he was like the king of kings, having access to every country and place. The world belonged to him and everybody in it, especially the other elementalists would answer to him.

"How do you know I train in the elements my Lord?" she asked formally still bowing slightly.

"I recognise you from the battle in Hiro. It was you who stopped my attack—"

"So you're the one behind the attacks on Hiro and Mecroyles. Why Zane? What is it that you know? Are you trying to stop this black hole as well?" Val asked.

When he said this, a light clicked in Raiden's mind as he understood. Zane was the one behind the attacks, the Elemental Lord himself.

Zane laughed at Val's question and smiled back at him, "Stopping the black hole is the last thing I want to do. I original-ly found out about the black hole when I received a message from Walton, from an Elder Amber who thought it best to inform me. But what she didn't know is that this is the exact thing I have been looking for over a thousand years for now."

Everybody in the room including the wise elders now stood still, hanging on Zane's every word. His presence there was intimidating for Val and soon everybody else, and it was Val who asked what everyone else was thinking, "What do you mean over a *thousand* years, you can't be that old?"

Zane laughed again, "Boy, I am *a lot* older than I look. I watched the clever water show the elders used to explain how the satellite was put into space but they didn't finish the rest of the story."

"The rest is only a legend my Lord," Raiden said. "That after the sun was refuelled it gave off a different radiation that harmed the planet and was killing off all life forms. This is the story of the First Divide. The humans and elders split apart from one another blaming each other and wars broke out between the two species. The humans used a shelter to protect themselves from the radiation while the elders discovered a cure but did not share it with the humans."

"You have been doing your homework Leo. Well done, but it's the next piece of the story that is relevant."

Val kind of remembered Raiden telling him this story as did everyone else in the room but still listened as Raiden continued, "The divide was ended when a human outcast formed with the elders, being trained by them and becoming the first record-ed elementalist. He used this power and training to overthrow the human government and ended the divide with peace. The humans and elders then put their minds together and formed a way to save the planet. Using special satellites on the ground, the humans deflected the radiation in one part of the planet while the elders used their powers to heal the planet from its core, that's all I know."

"But you don't know the most important piece of this story," Zane began and explained it to them. "When the Sphere was being healed it called out to the elders healing it. It called out asking for a life form to merge with. It said to heal properly it needed a life form that was as strong as it was courageous. Only the life form of a true hero would do and the elders then used the only thing they had," he paused and smiled like he remembered it all yesterday. "A human, the very human that saved the humans and elders from the First Divide. His name was—"

"Zane." Raiden finished.

Zane laughed loudly and clapped when he heard the name and started almost shouting, directing a finger at Raiden who only stood there in the water and stared up at him.

"That's right you clever little thing! Being a true hero Zane accepted his responsibility and merged with the planet, but when he did something happened to him. You see every time a life form dies on Sphere its energy and spirit returns to the planet and becomes another life form. But having given a part of himself to the planet, Zane's spirit could never be recycled and used again. Instead when Zane died, merging with the planet he was instantly reborn with the same mental capabilities. His body was only a baby. He could not speak nor move for his muscles were weak but he grew in a different body without anybody ever knowing. Again and again Zane lived until old then died, over and over again for death did not want him."

"What are you trying to say here? That you're the very same Zane that saved the planet millions of years ago now?" Val asked.

"You are an inquisitive little bastard aren't you boy? Who gave you all your smart genes then?" he said loud and sarcastically, almost spitting in aggression, "Yes boy, me! I have lived long and have seen the planet change and change again. I've seen whole species evolve from amoebas and die out and become extinct."

The elders now began to exchange worried looks to each other while Acarlie and the others all stood shocked in disbelief of what they were hearing.

"Please everyone, evacuate the monastery and continue this conversation outside," the elders said and they started moving everyone out of the room which they stood in. This made sense for everyone for the more they heard, the more they knew Zane would be trouble for them but even Zane being old and respecting the monastery followed them into the elevator, standing at the other side to them and staring at them.

"So are you trying to tell us that you're immortal or something? Also, if you were once a human why are you a tigian now?" Val asked.

With his arms crossed and staring at Acarlie he answered, "No, I am not immortal. I can die just as easily as everyone else but the only difference is that where you would all find that dark place and eternal sleep I would carry on, born again in a different body, whether that be human, tigian, aeomon," he looked to Raiden, "or leo. I truly am a god amongst you people. I have waited for so many years and have been many different species. This time I was lucky and have been born a tigian with elemental blood. So I became an elementalist and with my knowledge from the past, learned the elements easier than others, since then have never been defeated..." he looked over to Acarlie again, almost like he was warning her. She understood the threat and sunk her head to the floor.

Val still wasn't satisfied with what Zane was saying and every time he said something it brought up another question in his mind.

"So if you were once the saviour of the whole planet, the true hero that sacrificed himself for the life of the sphere, why are you trying to destroy it now?"

This was a good question and everyone on the elevator looked over to Zane for his answer.

Zane now changed his tone and growled over at Val in a deep threatening voice.

"Boy, do you have any idea what it is like to be as old as I am?" he scowled at him. "To know that everyone you have ever and will ever love turn to dust and will be forgotten before you will? To know that a woman you love may even be a descendant of yourself? I can tell you that the most of the millions of years that I have lived have been forgotten, simply because the brain cannot take in that much information. Only the very important faces and memories remain, all else is gone. I can remember only up to three life forms ago, still dating hundreds of years ago but all else is blurry, only small things remain. I have been the immortal hero of the planet, grown tired then become the child that would commit suicide over and over again, then facing the facts and trying simply to live normally; then been the tired old man wishing for death to come but it never did. Over and over again, year after year, body after body until I couldn't take no more and that was still a million years ago now. So now I have heard of a black hole that is threatening to destroy the planet all together and now is my only chance for sleep, even if it means destroying the planet itself. I have given my life for the good of the planet and this is how it has repaid me. I will ensure that this rocket never makes it to space and crush everyone who tries to stop me."

"Then it's true, what you are looking for under the elemental schools are connected to the satellite in space." Val said again as the elevator now reached back up in the library and the glass containers now slid back down in the floor sealing the underground monastery.

There was something odd about Zane's actions here that Raiden had noticed. He was the Elemental Lord and knew they were in his way of ensuring the destruction of the planet but he did not attack them. He had the power to wipe them all out there and then and carry on with his mission but he didn't. He took a few steps back still staring at Acarlie, like he knew something about her that she didn't know herself, like he was almost afraid of her.

"So what is it that you have? Where is the rocket?" Val demanded and Zane only snapped back at him.

"What kind of idiot do you take me for boy? Tell me your name Human."

"Val."

"Well Val, like I said, I am not a moron. What I am looking for I am not going to tell you. Keep asking me stupid questions Val and I will see to it you never speak again."

Acarlie had heard enough now. She had remained silent all this time knowing he was the Elemental Lord and therefore like an emperor to her but now he stood before her telling her he is going to try and destroy the planet altogether. She knew she had to step forward. All this time it had been about saving the planet and becoming the Elemental Lord and now both missions ended with the same person. He is the enemy, her enemy, the planet's enemy; life's enemy.

"If you will not tell us what you know then we will find out for ourselves. We already know all we need. We know the schools hold something explaining the whereabouts of the rocket and we know where your men are stationed. I am still on my pilgrimage and will visit the other schools before you get a chance. I will learn all the elements and destroy you in Alpha. As Elemental Lord you have to accept my offer in your country and city. I will come to Alpha and defeat you on your own ground."

"If that is so then it's in my best interests that you never leave this island then, isn't it?" Zane scowled.

The elders began to stir and call out, "Please, no violence, take this outside! Don't fight inside these sacred walls."

Val remembered all what Raiden and Acarlie had told him about the Elemental Lord. He was from Alpha and the city's element there was fire, the strongest of all and this was his home element so where he knew all the elements including the wind element Acarlie knew, fire was his strongest point. But Acarlie would be stronger with only her wind element, also known as the weakest of all the elements. He also knew that neither of them could legally touch each other unless they were in the arena so this put them in a stalemate position. Zane could easily wipe out Val, Raiden, Sheeria and Zoudiva but Acarlie wouldn't stand for this. Zane knew that if he attacked them she would protect them even if she is not supposed to. He knew this and even though he was stronger, the thought of this still was uneasy for him knowing that she was different from every other elementalist he has ever seen before.

"Please!" called out the elders again, "Don't bring violence to the monastery! Any differences can be settled by–" the elders were silenced suddenly as a small ball of fire appeared in the palm of Zane's hand. It doubled in its size until it became a large fireball Zane fired out into the elders, knocking them back into the bookshelves. Small spits of fire caught on the books and the ancient dry old paper instantly caught light. Seeing the elders knocked back instantly filled Raiden with rage. His natural masters being attacked by what is supposed to be their greatest ever work. Raiden leaped forward growling and snarling towards Zane, Sheeria by his side and Zoudiva ran to one side to help the elders. The fire now spread quickly, the room was large and soon would be engulfed by raging flames. Sheeria held a hand back to stop Val from stepping in beside them. She knew she was the better fighter and would have a better chance of fending off the Elemental Lord, "Run Val! Get Acarlie safe!"

Val knew this was his only chance and quickly turned. His heart racing from both fear and adrenaline. The flames from the fire now burning the side of his face as he grabbed Acarlie by her arm and pulled her back, tripping as he did and jumping back to his feet. Acarlie began to call out for Sheeria and Raiden but Val again pulled her to her feet, sprinting to the door. Another fireball shot across the library, narrowly missing Raiden who ducked out of the way and sped through the air over Val and Acarlie's head, smashing into one of the bookshelves in front of them and setting the books ablaze. Val charged through the door, stumbling again when he was out and back into the huge hallway. He heard Acarlie scream for him and he turned to see her back on the floor, reaching out for him. He picked her up again and together they sprinted for the exit of the now burning building. They heard the sound of the large cats fighting, roaring and snarling at one another before hearing the deafening sound of the leo roaring in agony and despair.

Another five fireballs sounded and shot through the air, smashing through the walls of the library and into the hallway and exploded into the pillars above them. The whole room shook then as they impacted the pillars, exploding spits of fire to fall around Val and Acarlie and damaging and tearing away at the pillars until they began to break away. The impact of the explosions shook the floor and sent Val and Acarlie flying into a far wall, hitting their heads against the floor. Feeling his head bleeding again and his old wounds that were not fully healed ache all over again, he shook his head and looked up to see one of the pillars crumble and fall to the ground, smashing against the ground and sending rubble and debris flying across the room. He knew their only chance of surviving this would be to escape the building. He climbed to his feet again. He heard the sound of another pillar creaking and leaning to one side about to fall. This one was a lot closer to their position and he instantly turned to pick Acarlie up again. Death was imminent, fire and falling concrete were all around them with their companions fighting for their lives behind them but still they ran, even though their muscles ordered them to stop and their heart wanting to turn back and help the others. They ran amongst the sound of more fireballs charging through the air and exploding into the walls above them. Plaster and concrete fell all around them and the air was now thin from the smoke, rubble and dust now filling up. Together they ran until they reached the giant wooden doors, charging through them and slamming them open in desperation and outside into the pouring rain, thunder and dark night sky.

"Acarlie, quickly come this way!" Val called as he tugged on Acarlie's arm and made their way to the cliff edge.

"What are you doing!?" she called out amidst the sound of heavy rain soaking them and the heavy blowing wind of the storm. Val looked over the cliff to see the ocean twisting and turning, fighting the storm as well.

"Out here you have the water behind you and the wind all around you! You have a better chance of fighting him with the elements closer to you. His fire won't work if you have water to cancel it!" he shouted to her.

"Val, why is this happening!?" she called out again.

Val looked behind her to the monastery now fully ablaze, broken and falling apart. Down at the door entrance was the towering figure of a shadowy tigian. The flames from the burning building now behind him he slowly marched towards them. His strides seemed powerful and every step closer to them sent more fear into them. Raiden and Sheeria were nowhere to be seen. His hands now glowed like he held a blue fire and walked towards them, holding his head up in the pouring rain of the black night sky, looming towards them like death itself.

Val took off his cloak and remembered his electric shield he still kept from Hiro and activated it, "Get behind me," he told Acarlie as he summoned his staff, and holding his hand back to stop her from running.

Zane now stood before the two of them. Val standing firm, protecting Acarlie with the wind and heavy rain pummelling against his back. His racing heart pumping hot blood through him was the only thing keeping him warm in the freezing cold downpour.

"Step aside Val. I will make this quick for both of you!" Zane called out as he stood towering over in front of them.

"No, Zane! Leave us alone!" he called back defiantly.

Zane now leaped forward, roaring and straightening his back like Raiden did before.

"I'm not going to tell you again boy! This is your last chance!" he called out louder than before.

Val felt the fear inside him. Zane was making his insides tremble. But he remembered Raiden's training as a leo. He felt too afraid now, more than he ever had done before. Zane could easily kill him and he knew it, the cliff face behind him meant only one attack from Zane would knock him back to fall to his death and that was only if Zane didn't rip his skin off with his tigian claws.

I must not fear him, fear is what he wants me to feel, and to fear is too lose the battle so I must show him I am not afraid if I want to survive, he thought to himself, reciting it over and over in his mind, clenching onto his staff, *I must not fear, I must not fear.*

"No, Zane!" he called out again stepping forward into his stance ready to fight. His stomach dropped and his legs began to tremble, *I must not fear.*

Zane then growled again and leaped at Val, swinging for him trying to catch his head. His claws and teeth called out for Val's skin but Val did not answer, blocking with his shield and ducking out of the way, countering whenever he had the chance. Right now his life did not matter to him, only Acarlie's life mattered. Now he knew how Sheeria had felt when she had fought for her. He felt now he truly was her guardian, and she was his elementalist.

Val kept fighting Zane as best as he could. His electric shield was taking a pounding and soon his arm ached but it was saving his life and once Zane made a mistake Val struck Zane across his head, knocking him to the floor to roll aside. Together the fighters fought on top of the hill. The sky was now black. Only the bolts of lightning lit up the scene and showed the two fighters briefly before condemning them back to the violent storm and darkness. The fire of the monastery in the background was setting a small orange glow to the cliff side. All this time Acarlie was standing poised to the spot. She could not bring herself to use her elements for Zane was the Elemental Lord and Val was too close to him. She looked over her shoulder to the cliff behind her, nowhere to run and nowhere to hide. She could only rely on Val now. Val took the time to catch his breath as Zane got to his feet. He knew he had upset Zane now as he only stood up tall and stretched his back and neck and put his chin to the sky.

"You remind me of myself a long time ago Val, it's a pity...!" he called over to him then pulled his hand back, a blue fireball began to burn in his hands ready to fire it to Val.

Val knew the only thing he could do here was to charge at Zane, close off the distance between them and maybe Zane would not able to use his fireball against him. Val screamed as he ran, holding up his shield. The rain still pouring down on him and his elementalist behind him. He slowly ran into the tigian standing there with his hand back to one side brewing the fireball ready to fire it at Val who step by step was drawing closer to him until he was practically touching him. Val could only think of Acarlie now as he charged for Zane, this was his final move at trying to protect the elementalist from death. Zane let out a mighty roar as he shoved his hands forward firing the ball of flame when Val was only inches from impact, the ball exploding instantly as it impacted the electric shield and sent Val screaming through the air backwards in a blaze of fire, rolling when he hit the floor. The heavy rain putting out the fire on his clothes. Now only Acarlie stood. Her last line of defence was lying on the floor in agony but Val was right before. With the ocean behind her she could use her water element to attack Zane and the wind of the storm still raged on, this was her only hope. But everything she had learned, Zane had already learned before. He could also control the water and he could control the wind. He wore neither metal armour nor metallic clothing so she knew she couldn't attack him like she did with Miles. But there was one thing she could do that Zane couldn't and maybe she could use this to scare him, even slightly. If she could strike fear in him then she could possibly take control of the fight.

Zane still stood before her, breathing deeply and catching his breath. Not only could he use the fire from the blazing building behind him but he could control lightning and since the storm thundered above them he could use this as well. Acarlie knew this was now her last hope, fail this and suffer an eternity as a failed elementalist in the valley of the dead. She knew the consequences of facing him, another sacred rule that clearly states that battles and fights will only be held in elemental battles, which are held in the arenas will be broken. But now she knew the rules didn't matter. She knew she would be shunned by her people but there was a chance she already was. This would be the third rule she has broken but now it was for a real purpose. This tigian in front of her, even though he is like a god in the body of an emperor, will always be unstoppable but now must be stopped. The people will never believe her because of the love and credit he receives from every person on the planet and now he secretly wants to destroy the whole thing. Even if she is eternally shunned, she must do what she can to save the people. She concentrated on the ground she stood on and pointed her hands to the floor and used her elemental power to lower the gravity, until her feet left the ground and it looked like she was using her hands to levitate off the floor.

She glared at Zane and she saw not fear but an unsettling, uncomfortable feeling coming from him. She knew he did not fear her but something about her caused him to be a little cautious.

Zane straightened his back and called over to her, "Elementalist Acarlie of Eloma! I am your Lord! Elementalist Zane of Alpha! I order you to stand down!"

She heard his demands and just like her wish to stab her heart or to jump from the building before she wanted to obey him, like her teachings were fighting against her instincts.

Zane called again, "Stand down Elementalist Acarlie! Turn around and jump from the cliff! This is an order from you Elemental Lord!"

Again she fought the urge to obey him. She lowered to the floor before strengthening her resolve. His voice seemed to echo within her mind. She tried to fight the urge to resist. She wanted to release her control of the gravity, turn around and jump from the cliff. She wanted to obey. But she didn't, she couldn't. Val still lay before her, steaming from the subdued fires by the pouring rain, and now his defeated body reminded her of her own defeat. She already was a failed elementalist and should be destroyed. But as much as she wanted to give in and obey the orders of her Lord, the realisation of what her weakness would mean to the world stopped her. If she obeyed, then the world would pay, destroyed by this evil, highly evolved tiger with complete planetary control and a mastery of all the elements. She couldn't let him win. She had to fight for the planet, for Sheeria and Raiden; she had to fight for Val.

Her head twitched again and a sharp pain thumped her temple as the battle within her mind continued. To fight for life itself, or to give in, and surrender to death.

She looked up and shouted in defiance, "No!"

Zane still let out a small smile and nodded. She now was doing what he thought she would, facing him rather than falling to her knees and begging for instructions from him. It was the fact that she was rebelling that was unsettling for him. He knew she would be a big problem for him if he did not kill her quickly now. But before any of them could bring themselves to fight each other a cry came from behind them causing Zane to turn around.

Down at the blazing monastery; the elders, now back on their feet were now standing close to one another. Their hands all close to another and summoning a huge fireball to fire back at Zane. Instantly Zane knew they were now the biggest threat to him, for he was only a tigian and their power would always be stronger than his, even one would easily defeat him in a challenge of the elements but now three stood together, combining their powers together and looking back up at him.

Zane now forgot about Acarlie and sprinted back towards the elders. One by one the elders fired the balls of flame and lightning towards him, causing him to duck and dive out of the way. Zane leaped from one side to another but could never get close enough to them. Finally Zane knew he could not try and fight them and turned and ran away. He may have been immortal but if he died he would lose his tigian body and Elemental Lord status and he needed that to fulfil his mission. Instead he decided to live to fight for another day and disappeared into the darkness of the storm where he would board his small skyship and return back to his camp where he could plan a different approach of how to defeat the elementalist who stood in his way of sleep eternal.

Acarlie now floated back down to the ground after he left and dropped down to where Val was still lying on the ground.

"It's over Val, it's over, he's gone," she said kneeling down to him but noticed the very still Val lying there, she paused staring down at him.

"...Val?" She shook him once but his body was still.

"Val?" She shook him again now. His still body now scared her as she tried again this time almost violently shaking his body in her arms and calling for him, "Val!" But still no answer.

Instantly she panicked. Her emotions burst out and she held onto him tight in desperation. "Val!?" She called as she shook him again with him in her arms, but his body was unresponsive. "No, no. Not again, Val! Wake up! Wake up Val!" She began to shout at him shaking him over and over again, the elders rushed up to her and knelt down beside her.

The fear of losing him again brought back a familiar sensation of despair and depression as well as anger for Acarlie. She began to cry out more angrily and shake him violently now but his body still refused to move.

"Step aside we can help him," they suggested.

"Get away from him!" she screamed out at them in her despair and put her ear to his mouth. "...He's still breathing," she said and pulled him back into her arms, holding his head close to her breast and looking down upon it. Her tears were now lost within the rain as it continued to pour down her face. She began tapping his cheek, "Come on Val, wake up, please wake up."

She rolled his head from one side to another and slowly his eyes began to open again. A great wave of relief flooded over Acarlie and she let out a cry of, "Yes!" when she first saw him react.

The first thing Val saw when he opened his eyes was Acarlie's face beaming down at him in tears. His first reactions was to jump to his feet and fend off Zane again but was stopped by Acarlie when he tried to move.

"Take it easy Val, it's over. Zane is gone, for now anyway, we're safe."

"What about the others?" he asked and the elders answered for him.

"We were all saved by the kingnine. Raiden and Sheeria held Zane back long enough and when he came looking for you the kingnine carried us out one by one."

Val looked over from the spot where he lay in Acarlie's arms still and over to the monastery. There was Zoudiva walking out of the burning monastery into the pouring rain with Sheeria slumped over his shoulders, Raiden behind them carrying one of the other elders.

"What about your monastery?" he asked again.

The elders all looked at each other and nodded, "Yes, it's time we put the fire out, isn't it? We've lost many books tonight but none of which are important, and it will only give us something to do about fixing the damage."

Acarlie helped Val to his feet and embraced him. He called out in pain as his body was still sore but he held her tight too. Zane was gone. He had done it. She was still safe thanks to him, now he really could be her guardian.

47

A day had passed and now the storm had subsided and one of the monasteries remained a health risk and became out of bounds. Acarlie and the others were still given the time and space to rest with the elders in one of the other monasteries. They were promised a ship would come to the island in a couple of days to bring trade and bring news to the elders so they could gain passage over the waters when it arrived. For now though they used the time to finally rest. The weather was calm and the ocean was peaceful now if with a little rain now and again. Val was walking down the corridors with the oldest of the elders. He wished to know information and thought the oldest would be the best to tell him. Down candlelit corridors they walked, Val in his traveller's cloak, now washed and clean and the elder in his old tattered monk-like cloak to his left.

"What is it you would like to know Master Val?"

Val looked behind him to see no one there but empty clay walls and decided to finally ask the first of his two questions. He stopped and looked out a small window to see Acarlie outside on the grass, spending time with Zoudiva and told the elder, "Before I learned that the elementalists have very strict rules and when they break these rules either by accident or on purpose, would fall into a fit of depression and take their own lives. I have seen Acarlie attempt this back when I first met her. It's like she wasn't herself then. I know you elders have something to do with this and even though no one else can see it, I can. What have you done to Acarlie?"

The old, wise elder sighed and looked out to Acarlie too, "I see. Val, from what you witnessed yesterday about the history of Sphere what did you learn about the first elementalist?"

"That Zane was the first."

"That's right. Learning what we did yesterday we now know that Zane is responsible for all elementalists that ever lived. He was the beginning of the elemental bloodline."

"What do you mean by the elemental bloodline?"

"It's hard to explain this to a human Val, but I think you can handle it..." the elder sighed again and told him. "Elementalists are the result of evolution. Humans and all creatures mixing with the elders, slowly becoming better than all of them. You see, elders and humans have as much in common as they are totally opposite. Elders fear the greater power just like humans and we ensure that the greater power does not ever get the chance to overpower us. We have always known that one day a strong elementalist like Zane or even Acarlie would rise up against us and side with their born species, for an elementalist is a species of their own but you can understand how Acarlie will see herself as human more than an aeomon elementalist ever will. So we decided instead of killing them to teach them to control their power, all the sacred teachings are actually like mental barriers that will keep them from harm against themselves. They are dangerous creatures and must be watched at all times. If ever an elementalist would go against the rules it would be difficult for the humans, elders or any of the other species to gain control of them again."

"I'm not quite sure I understand. So the elementalists are like mutants or something?"

"No Val, not at all." The elder sighed again and thought of how he could explain it better to him.

"Val, do you know what a pholcidae is?"

"Umm no," Val confessed rubbing the back of his head.

"It's a spider that has a thin body and long legs, most people call them *Daddy Long Legs*."

"Oh, ok yeah I know what they are."

"Good, the pholcidae has deadly venom in its glands that some people would even call super venom. Luckily for us though the long legged spider's fangs are too small to penetrate our skin. But let's suppose that this venom started showing up in the common wasp, a creature that could constantly sting someone even if un-provoked. This new wasp would be a threat to every living creature right?"

"I understand what you mean now. You're saying Acarlie is the wasp."

"And her elemental gift is the venom."

"I see. So instead of killing them you condition them to kill themselves, let them believe in lies that they will face a greater punishment than death if they carry on living, drilling it into their minds until they would give their lives believing it," Val finished.

"We are not proud of it Val, but yes. There is no other way and not just the elementalist but the whole race together. Humans are smart but easily turned aside by different beliefs. That is why they do not live long, the human born elementalists. They live only to amuse the people watching them but they are so powerful that even their short lives can fill over a million people's lives with happiness and joy, wherever they go they are worshipped. It's their programming and conditioning that keeps them from realising their power and becoming monsters like Zane. But Acarlie is different and Zane knows this too if he is as he claims he is."

"What do you mean?"

"Well, like the rest of the world, word gets around. We heard about Acarlie breaking her barriers and still she stands outside with the kingnine like nothing has happened, all other elementalists would have killed themselves long ago but she continues to breathe. Zane fears this. I know he does because he has never seen it happen before. I know because it has never been recorded before. An elementalist has broken her programming and threatens the Elemental Lord himself. Never in over a million years has this been done, not even Zane himself has done what she has done. Acarlie now is the deadly wasp we have all feared but she doesn't know it yet. She must never know about this Val and if you are to be her guardian like she wishes then it is your responsibility to keep her safe from the truth, no one else would understand Val but because you are not from around here–"

"That brings me to my other question Elder, the one that has been with me my whole journey so far. Who or what am I and why I am here?"

The elder smiled, "I knew this moment would come. When I was last speaking with the planet it told me you would ask and I have the answer for you. Val your identity is nothing. You are no one and you are everyone."

"Please don't answer this with more questions than I originally intended," Val sighed.

"Val, the planet knew it was in danger. It knew about the black hole and it sent a weapon to defend itself. You are that weapon Val. Just like the planet sent for Zane all those years ago, your physical body is of a deceased person who died and your spirit was injected into it. The planet used up its energy and spirit to reanimate the dead tissue and brought a whole new life form to life, that life form was and always will be you."

Val stood stunned like he didn't know how to take this news or even to believe it.

"So who are my parents, my family?"

"You have no parents Val, the sphere itself is your life giver. What you see physically is only an outer shell of a fallen human, returned back to the planet to be reborn again."

"So after all this time and all this way. I've travelled across the entire planet to find out I'm just a ghost, a parent-less demon placed in a dead body?"

"I knew you wouldn't like the news at first Val but trust me, soon you will come to terms with it. The planet has created you for one special reason, that's a whole lot more than anybody else can say. You are here to end the planet's misery and save it from total destruction."

Val took a breath and stepped back placing his head against the wall, it explained his memory loss when he woke next to the crashed skyship and it explained why he had no injuries then. He was not unconscious. He had just been born. There were no memories forgotten because there were none in the first place.

"What about the lions!" he remembered.

"What's that?"

"I can remember old things like lions, and martial arts have been conditioned in my fighting style, Raiden told me when I first met him."

"That could be either your spiritual energy once lived on the planet long ago when lions existed, saved for such an occasion, or maybe they are memories left in the brain of the person who died. We will never know Val and my best advice is to leave it at that. You now know who you are. You are the chosen one to save the planet, now shouldn't we get moving along? You have a special ceremony to attend to, don't you?"

"I guess you're right. I still don't agree with it though," Val nodded and smiled.

"One day you will Val. Come now, Acarlie waits."

Val waited as the elder began to walk away and thought to himself everything he had just told him, *I am only a weapon for the planet. Elder Amber must have known about this. This explains why she sent me on the mission in the first place,* he couldn't stop thinking about it. All this time thinking about what his history will be; who his parents were and this was his answer? But now he had to put this aside for he had to think for Acarlie. She needed him now to be her guardian. Only he and the elders knew the truth about her now and he had to keep it from her. She now had the potential of becoming the greatest elementalist that has ever lived, even greater in fact than Zane himself since she has done what no one in over a million years has ever done before. Somehow she has broken her conditioning and the programming of the elders and now has the potential of becoming the greatest threat to the planet apart from Zane himself. Val knew she must never know about this and had to keep a promise to himself never to tell her. Soon he would be her guardian as well as Raiden and Zoudiva and together they would rest here until a ship arrives but right now he had to stay close to Acarlie.

The night was calm, the sky was clear and the stars were out again, gleaming down on the monastery. The air was still moist from the night before and felt fresh. The ground still soft and wet with tiny water droplets sitting still on the grass blades, shining from the light from the two moons.

Zoudiva was silently walking outside the monastery. He had just finished an important ceremony with Val and Raiden. It turned out that Acarlie wanted all of them to be guides for her and since they were in the company of the old and wise elders they used the opportunity to make it official. As he walked around on the grass outside, his paws getting wet from the damp grass he remembered the ceremony. Val and Raiden knelt down while he only sat for the shape of his four legged body, all with their heads bowed and recited the oath as the elders recited it for them with Acarlie and Sheeria standing in front of them. He remembered the look on Acarlie's face when they all stood up again knowing she now and always would have four guides now. The night now came quickly and they all used the time to relax for the first time on their journey. A ship would not come for them for the next few days and so they could only wait. Their mission was now clear on what they had to do but for now all they could do was to sit and heal, gather their strength back. Zoudiva looked out down into the wooded areas beyond him, Sheeria and Raiden had gone together into the woods about an hour ago and still haven't returned. Zoudiva could only guess that they were hunting together or maybe Sheeria was using the time to explain in more detail what the responsibilities of being a guide would be. In any case he was not worried for the two large cats and left it at that. He walked round the building further more until he reached the room his master was staying in. He walked up to the window and peered inside to see Val sitting there, on a large sofa with many large pillows. In his kingnine vision he could only see through the open window since he could not see through glass. Acarlie was by his side and he sat with his arm around her. She was smiling at him and together they shared their time in happiness, chatting away like school children, not taking their eyes off one another. Zoudiva smiled and nodded as he crept away from the window and to the door of the monastery and sat down on a concrete slab by the doorway and looked up at the stars. He always admired the stars, for a creature who could only see in heat, looking up at an almost black, cold sky and still seeing small balls of flame light years away amazed him. He remembered the promise he made with Val, Val promising him a better master, the master turning out to be him, *my new master is young and full of spirit. Yes, I am going to like my new master,* were his final thoughts on the matter.

He also remembered his grandfather before him. He was now also a guide to an elementalist and knew he would be making his family proud. Yes, this truly was a peaceful night he thought, the cats were out together doing what they love to do and his master and elementalist were safe and sound, happy in each other's company. Even the elders were happy, enjoying the company they rarely have.

Somewhere out there their companions Kaza and his men, Dude the silent aeomon and Zahied the Caster will be travelling above the water, heading towards the Feydon camp site to infiltrate and find out what they can. Raiden had sent a message to Walton through the elders' way of communicating with the planet, so Elder Amber would receive it and pass it on to Theydon and the others on the Walton council; that they knew what must be done and would not stop until the black hole is destroyed. Their mission was still far from complete. The rocket was still to be found to destroy the black hole and Acarlie still had four elements to learn but for now they all rested in the blissful night of calm wind and pleasant cool air. Zoudiva sighed and looked back up at the stars, yawning in his comfort and stretching out his front paws and rested his head, closed his eyes and fell asleep.

FIN.

THANK YOU FOR READING.

J.C.Norman

Now read
The exciting and thrilling second chapter of
the 'Sphere's Divide' saga:

SPHERE'S DIVIDE

Part II

Composer of Wrath